#1

ARIFURETA ZERO:
FROM COMMONPLACE TO WORLD'S STRONGEST

ryo shirakome   takayaki

MILEDI REISEN

"O-O-KUN, DON'T LOOK!"

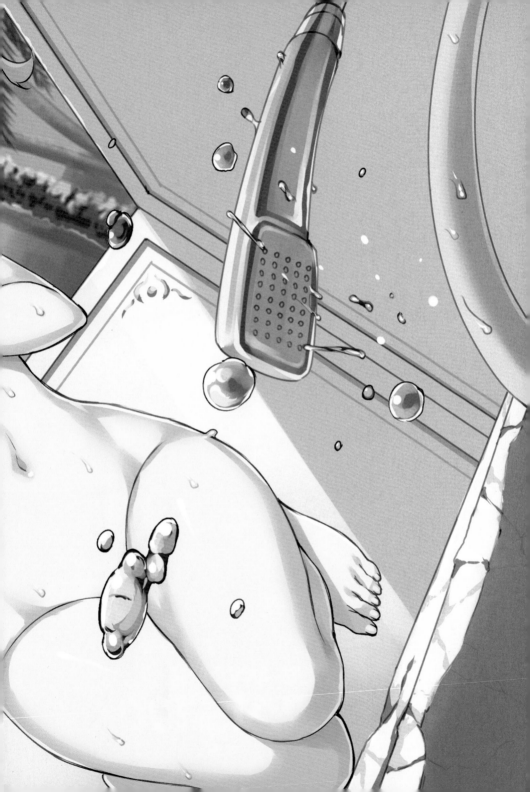

OSCAR ORCUS

"I'M JUST YOUR AVERAGE SYNERGIST."

ARIFURETA:

ARIFURETA SHOKUGYOU DE SEKAISAIKYOU

FROM COMMONPLACE
TO WORLD'S STRONGEST Zero

ARIFURETA: FROM COMMONPLACE TO
WORLD'S STRONGEST ZERO, VOLUME 1

Copyright © 2017 by Ryo Shirakome
Illustrations by Takaya-ki

First published in Japan in 2017 by
OVERLAP Inc., Ltd., Tokyo.
English translation rights arranged with
OVERLAP Inc., Ltd., Tokyo.

Follow Seven Seas Entertainment online at
sevenseasentertainment.com.
Experience J-Novel Club books online at j-novel.club.

TRANSLATION: Ningen
J-NOVEL EDITOR: DxS
COPY EDITOR: Cae Hawksmoor
PROOFREADER: Christina Lynn
LIGHT NOVEL EDITOR: Nibedita Sen
PRODUCTION DESIGNER: KC Fabellon
MANAGING EDITOR: Julie Davis
EDITOR-IN-CHIEF: Adam Arnold
PUBLISHER: Jason DeAngelis

ISBN: 978-1-64505-173-2
Printed in Canada
First Printing: September 2019
10 9 8 7 6 5 4 3 2 1

ARIFURETA:
ARIFURETA SHOKUGYOU DE SEKAISAIKYOU
FROM COMMONPLACE TO WORLD'S STRONGEST *Zero*

#1

Presented by
RYO SHIRAKOME

Illustrated by
TAKAYAKI

CONTENTS

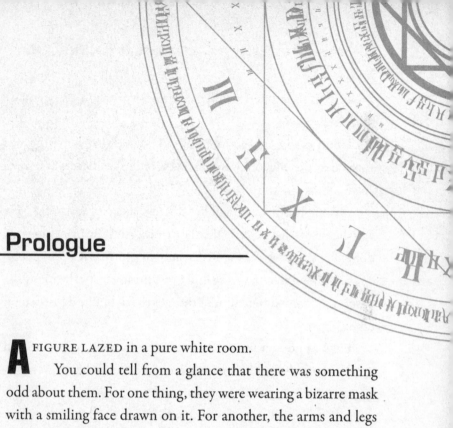

Prologue

A FIGURE LAZED in a pure white room.

You could tell from a glance that there was something odd about them. For one thing, they were wearing a bizarre mask with a smiling face drawn on it. For another, the arms and legs poking out of their milky-white robe, while artfully crafted, were clearly made out of metal.

A golem was lying there.

"Ugh, I finally managed to finish my repairs. Damn that little boy. How dare he leave explosives behind!"

The voice was both youthful and feminine. Its owner, the golem lying in the center of the room, was Miledi Reisen. She was the creator of the Reisen Gorge, one of the Seven Great Labyrinths, and a Liberator.

She stared up at the sky and screamed.

"The next time I see him, I'll teach that brat a lesson!"

She looked like a child throwing a tantrum, thrashing on the floor.

Her robe flapped wildly, and the expression of her mask morphed.

Upon closer inspection, you could see that her robe was charred at the edges, covered in soot, and that there was a small crack in her mask.

Hajime was the cause of her distress, and her sorry state. He was the first to have cleared her labyrinth. And the first thing he'd done after defeating her was to demand she give him her possessions.

She'd planned on giving him everything except the items she absolutely needed to maintain the labyrinth, but he'd insisted on taking even those.

He was no conqueror, just a thief. No good person would ever demand that a labyrinth master hand over all her possessions. That was the act of a common brigand.

Naturally, Miledi refused. Half in jest, she'd tested out her toilet shortcut, and flushed them from her labyrinth. However, just before they'd washed away, the boy threw some grenades as a final parting gift.

They'd not just blown up the deepest chamber in the labyrinth, but a good portion of her private quarters as well. In tears, Miledi set about the task of repairing her precious labyrinth. She'd only just finished.

She cursed at Hajime for a while longer, complaining about the unfair retribution she'd received for the harmless prank she'd played on him. Objectively speaking, it was pretty hard to feel sympathetic toward someone who'd flushed people out of her home.

Once she was done, complete silence returned to the room.

Miledi was this labyrinth's only resident. It sat deep underground, at the bottom of a gorge everyone avoided. A dark place where the light of the sun never reached.

Without Miledi's cursing, there was no noise at all. As she was a golem, there wasn't even the sound of her heartbeat or breathing.

Miledi raised her hand up to the ceiling.

Had there been any light, her metallic hand would have gleamed. The golem had been made by someone very precious to her. The crystallization of all their hard work. This inorganic hand was very unlike the actual hand she'd had when she was alive.

"To think...someone who could really clear our trials..." She balled her outstretched hand into a fist. The reality of it was finally hitting her. She glanced over at a corner.

She was in her bedroom, and her personal possessions were all stored here.

There was a bookshelf in the corner, a number of picture frames lining the shelves. Long ago, an exceptionally skilled Synergist invented a device that could perfectly record all the details of a scene and copy them. The pictures he'd taken with it were his gift to Miledi, and her greatest treasure.

Miledi walked up to the pictures and examined each one in turn, starting from the end. She'd done so hundreds—no—thousands of times, but a different emotion welled up within her this time.

"How long has it been since that day...the day that we were defeated. The day we swore to carry on, to create a light of hope for those who would come after. It's...definitely been more than a few centuries. A thousand years? Two thousand? Aha ha, I don't even remember..."

Most of the pictures were of a young girl. There was one of her standing in the middle of a city, another of her surrounded by nature, and yet another with her in the rugged wilderness. In all of them she was smiling, the people in the background all smiling alongside her.

The person who'd taken the photos knew how to capture her radiance better than anyone.

Miledi's gaze stopped on one of them. It was a picture of seven people standing atop a hill, the sunrise at their backs.

One of them was a blonde girl. She was pulling a bespecta-cled, flustered man closer to her. Next to her stood a stoic, but gentle-looking, man; a seductively smiling dryad woman; a stern, balding old man; a Dagon woman who was smiling triumphantly; and lastly, a demon man who was staring at the blonde girl with a look of mild disapproval.

"Guys...it's finally happening. Time's moving forward again. It's not a dream. The path we chose...it really did pave the way for those who came after us."

Had Miledi retained her human form, she would have been crying. Her voice trembled and broke.

Her fingers brushed the image of the bespectacled boy.

"O-kun. Can you believe it? Those kids cleared your labyrinth first. It was supposed to be the hardest, the last. And you know what else? Their leader is a Synergist, just like you. What an amazing coincidence." Miledi chuckled.

"His personality's the complete opposite of you, though. Still, he's amazing. Those artifacts of his are crazy. He must have made them using the techniques you left behind." She talked until she ran out of words. Overcome with emotion, she brought a hand to her chest.

She turned her gaze to the final picture. This one was special. It combined Oscar's wondrous invention with the regeneration powers of another of her comrades. Together, they created a picture of the past. A smiling young woman with red hair. She was wearing a maid uniform. Beside her was the same blonde girl from the other pictures, except she looked younger. There was a look of confusion on her face.

"It all started with you. The journey I inherited from you is finally coming to a close."

Miledi didn't have much strength left. She probably had enough power stored for one last fight, but that was more than enough. She'd been prepared for this for millennia.

Miledi looked back up at the ceiling. She was thinking of the young boy who'd conquered her labyrinth. *Finally*.

Quietly, she prayed.

"May the people finally be free..."

It was a lone, silent wish.

CHAPTER I
The Meeting
That Started It All

V ELNIKA, in the Kingdom of Velka.

Velka was in the southwest of the Northern Continent. A vast network of tunnels ran directly beneath its capital.

These tunnels were filled with abundant green glowstone, which earned them the name "the Greenway."

Monsters and cutthroats prowled their depths, so it was by no means a safe way to travel. However, because of the rare ore that could be mined there, the tunnels were still popular.

Velka itself could trace its origins back to the Greenway. The kingdom started out as a mining town that sprouted up to harvest the ore. Merchants and craftsmen flocked there, and eventually it grew into a flourishing city. That city then grew into a small country, until it eventually became a mighty kingdom.

The country manufactured all of its own weapons, its tools, and even magical artifacts. Velka was known to the rest of the world as a kingdom of inventors and craftsmen. The other nations were more than a little jealous of its wealth of natural resources and talented citizens.

The engineers and craftsmen of the kingdom were always competing, and there were a few exceptionally talented and famous guilds.

One of those was the Orcus Workshop. It admitted only the most talented Synergists. Its fame was so great that even nobles considered it an honor to apprentice there. Their primary focus was weaponsmithing. And, thanks to the current political climate, they were in rather high demand.

The Orcus Workshop's headquarters dwarfed the surrounding buildings. Today, too, the workshop was filled with the sounds of Synergists chanting and master craftsmen chastising their apprentices.

As with all Orcus buildings, the headquarters was partitioned into sections, each housing a different specialty. You could usually guess each section's specialty by looking at their tools and materials.

Most craftsmen were surrounded by weapons, armor, and the materials needed to make them. Others were buried in piles of everyday goods.

As the workshop's main business was weapons, it made sense for most sections to be dedicated to that. Your standing there was determined by the quality of goods you could produce.

However, there was one craftsman who was surrounded by something else. His section was radically different.

The young man working there had gentle, feminine features and a long, slender build.

He wore black-rimmed spectacles and had his shoulder-length black hair tied up in a ponytail.

He wore an apron over his simple blue shirt and off-white trousers. Gadgets of dubious function stuck out of the numerous pockets in his apron.

He stared earnestly at a magic circle and the materials contained within it. Then, he clapped his hands together. The circle in front of him began to glow. His mana was a warm yellowish-white. It was reminiscent of sunlight, the kind you might see on a warm spring day.

His materials coalesced. The young man's creation had a perfect curve, impeccable balance, and a well-crafted handle that showed consideration for its wielder.

He stared at what he'd made, seemingly satisfied.

"Perfect. That's a great pot."

He seemed proud of his work. Tenderly, he picked up the dull gray pot, and carefully placed it in a box. It was already full of pots, frying pans, plates, and other cooking utensils.

Scattered around him were other mundane goods—lanterns, fancy desks, building tools, scissors, stationery, and other everyday things.

There was not a single weapon in sight.

There were technically some sharp implements, but only cooking knives. Knives for chopping vegetables, knives for cutting meat, even knives for cutting bread. And they were all of exceptional quality.

However, they were still cooking utensils. While all the other craftsmen were trying their hardest to create exemplary weapons, this young man was making mundane items. He stood out, and not in a good way.

Everyone hated him, especially because the Orcus Workshop treated him favorably, despite his obvious shortcomings.

"Tch..."

"Hmph."

People scoffed.

The young man turned around to see two elderly masters staring at his work with disapproving glares.

He smiled awkwardly and returned to his own work, trying to ignore them.

While most hated him, they didn't do much to get in his way. They were too busy focusing on their own work.

But in every group, there was always a small minority that refused to conform. The same was true here. While most people were content to leave the young man alone, some felt compelled to make his life miserable.

The young man scattered wood chips around the pots, cushioning his creations. It was then that someone walked up, looking for trouble.

"Hey, loser. How long are you going to keep making junk like this? What happened to the stuff I asked you to make?"

This new voice was derisive and unpleasant.

The newcomer was short and fat, and flanked by two lackeys. One was tall and lanky, while the other had eyes that looked like they were bulging out of their sockets. All three of them were smiling wickedly.

"Hello there, Waress-san. I've already finished what you asked for."

Ping Waress was the third son of the noble Waress family. The young man turned to the duke and bowed his head respectfully, despite Waress' condescending attitude.

The "stuff Waress had asked him to make" was actually Ping's work quota for today. He'd just been too lazy to do it himself. The young man picked up a nearby box and held it out.

"What, already? Hey, you better not have half-assed this! Earl Holden requested me specifically for this job. I asked for your help so you'd have a chance to polish your skills. You'd better not repay that goodwill by spitting in my face!"

The earl hadn't made any such request. He'd brought some armor to be repaired, but he'd asked the workshop as a whole.

In fact, most of the repairs were handed to more senior craftsmen. Ping was only in charge of fixing the straps.

In other words, he'd just happened to have been assigned that task.

The young man knew that as well, but he disliked conflict. So, instead of arguing, he just furrowed his brows. He'd had a lot of practice placating people.

But before he could even say, "Take a look for yourself," one of Ping's lackeys spoke up.

"Come on, Ping-san. Don't you think 'loser' is a bit much, even for him? The least you could do is call him a former prodigy."

Torpa Parson, the man who'd spoken, was the second son of Baron Parson.

The bug-eyed man was Raul Streya, fourth son of Baron Streya. He backed up Torpa, gesticulating like a buffoon.

"Now, now, Torpa-kun. We should drop the 'former' bit, too. After all, he is an orphan the Master scouted out personally. Sure, he can't make a weapon to save his life and spends all his time crafting junk, but he's still a genius. After all, he gets paid for all that junk he makes! We should applaud him. Come on, don't you think you should show us those skills that impressed the master so much? Don't tell me age made you rusty; you're still young. You've still got it, right, Oscar-kun?"

Nearby onlookers sniggered at that.

The other craftsmen didn't have any personal issue with Oscar, but they were annoyed that an orphan was given special treatment. Especially as they'd never seen his supposed genius.

Oscar just smiled and bowed his head. He quietly held out the box that Ping had asked for.

"Why won't you say anything, huh?" Ping opened the box and frowned. Despite the fact that Oscar had done as he'd asked, he seemed displeased.

"It's as you say. I'm still an inexperienced craftsman, taking advantage of the Master's generosity."

"If you know that, then you should just get the hell out of here. You're a disgrace to the Orcus name! The fact that you bear it is an insult!"

Even an apology wasn't enough to pacify Ping. In fact, it only seemed to make him more irate. His angry screams turned him into the center of attention.

Not only was Ping short and fat, but he was also petty—the kind of person to insult others behind their backs and bully anyone weaker than himself.

Still, he rarely lost his temper, at least not enough to shout.

Looks like the worm's even angrier than usual today... Did he mess up something else earlier? Still smiling outwardly, Oscar desperately thought of a way to calm Ping down. However, before he could, Ping continued.

"Seriously, I can't believe the Master called *you* a genius. I guess he can make mistakes sometimes too."

Ping was so worked up that he didn't notice insulting the Master made everyone's attitudes shift. The other craftsmen's scorn was now directed at him. Even his two cronies grimaced and whispered to each other.

Oscar had to defuse the situation before someone lynched Ping. The current head of the Orcus Workshop was well-respected;, they wouldn't stand to see him slandered.

However, before he could do anything—

"Oh, you think I'm going senile, do you? Do you mean to tell me that I, Orcus, have made a mistake, Ping? Someone seems awfully full of themselves."

"Hiii?!" Ping squealed like a stuck pig.

Orcus' voice wasn't particularly angry, but Ping shrunk back anyway. His face was pale with fear. Torpa and Raul looked even worse.

Orcus was a hulking bear of a man. Not only was he massive, but his entire body was covered in thick hair. His thighs were large enough to crush a man's skull.

In fact, he was often mistaken for a bearman from the Haltina Commonwealth, although he was human through and through.

Ping smiled guiltily and tried to smooth over his mistake.

"M-Master... Wh-what are you doing here?"

"It's my workshop. What's wrong with me being here?"

"U-umm, nothing! It's just, I heard you had business at the palace today."

Topp Karg D. Orcus, the current head of the Orcus Workshop, harrumphed and peered into Oscar's box. He didn't bother to answer Ping's question.

He plucked something from the box and examined it carefully.

The silence that followed was so oppressive that the other craftsmen stopped working and waited.

Once he finished looking, Orcus glanced back at Ping.

"This was supposed to be your job, Ping... Why is Oscar the one who made it?"

"Th-this is a misunderstanding, Chief. He was spending all his time making junk, so I thought if he was free, he could help me a little. I'm still the one who made it." Ping prostrated himself before Karg.

However, Karg didn't even bother listening. He turned back to Oscar, who was wearing the same awkward smile as always.

Karg sighed.

"I see," he told Ping. "I suppose that means I can expect this level of quality from your next work as well?"

"Huh? What?"

Karg smirked and showed Ping the object in his hand.

"This clasp is exceptionally well done. It's pliable in all the right places, so it absorbs impact well. Also, it's been crafted in such a way that a Synergist could easily repair it if it broke in battle."

"I-I see..."

The other craftsmen all turned in surprise. Their expressions were difficult to read.

Only Ping failed to grasp the implication. He couldn't understand why everyone was looking at Oscar.

Seeing his confusion, Karg put it more plainly.

"Rather than trying to show off your own skill, you crafted this clasp to perfectly suit the needs of its wielder. It may look plain, but it's clearly a first-rate clasp. So I'm asking you, Ping, can I expect this kind of high-quality work from you in the future? Well?"

"......"

Cold sweat poured down Ping's back. Karg was asking for more than he could deliver. He didn't possess the skill.

"I-I'm honored by your praise, Chief. However, even I'm surprised by how well this turned out. To be honest, uh, I can't say with confidence that I can do it again. Besides, putting so much effort into every one of my projects would slow me down too much..."

"I see. In that case, do your own jobs. Work hard until you're good enough to make these kinds of goods, instead of wasting your time chatting."

Karg's glare was intense enough to wither a dragon.

"Hiii?! Y-yes sir! I'm sorry, sir!" Ping accepted the box and nearly tripped over himself in his haste to escape. Torpa and Raul hurriedly followed. The other craftsmen lost interest in the commotion and returned to their work.

"Umm... Chief? Thanks for helpin—"

"Come to my office."

Karg turned on his heel and stalked off.

Sighing, Oscar chased after Karg, an awkward smile still on his face.

"What the hell do you think you're doing, Oscar?" The moment they got into Karg's office, he started yelling.

Karg flopped onto the ancient sofa in his room. The springs creaked under his bulk.

"I'm not sure what exactly you mean, sir..."

"We're the only ones in here, so spare me the niceties. And wipe that moronic smile off your face. It disgusts me."

"That's pretty mean, old man." Oscar dropped his nice guy act, but he didn't stop smiling. He'd gotten so used to using it to get out of unpleasant situations.

"I remember you saying that you'd only cause trouble if you stayed. I also distinctly remember telling you to stay anyway. I didn't keep you here so you could spend your time doing that viscount's idiot son's work for him."

"I know. Still, I can finish something like that in between breaks. If that's all it takes to keep Waress-san quiet, then I don't mind."

"Fool. Guys like him won't ever be satisfied. If you give in to them once, they'll just keep coming back for more. If he's causing you that much of a problem, then I can have him expelled."

Ping, Torpa, and Raul had all gotten into the Orcus Workshop through Ping's family connections. Although they were Synergists, they weren't qualified to be a part of the esteemed Orcus Workshop. Karg initially let them join because he didn't want to insult a bunch of petty nobles, but—

"I'll say it as many times as I have to. Oscar, you're going to be the next generation's Orcus, so—"

"Gramps." Oscar's voice was quiet but firm.

Karg sighed, realizing Oscar still hadn't changed his mind. Inheriting the name of Orcus meant becoming the leader of the workshop.

It was tradition that the current Orcus would pass down his or her title once they found someone who surpassed them in ability.

"You're already a better craftsman than me. Hell, you left me in the dust years ago. Your skills are on a completely different level."

"……"

Oscar wasn't sure how to reply to that. After all, everything Karg had said was true.

"When I first met you at the Moorin Orphanage, I knew you were special. The toys you made for the other kids were better than my workshop's best work… To be honest, I couldn't believe it at first."

Oscar was dumped in front of the Moorin Orphanage when he was a baby. Although there were no large-scale wars in the past few decades, small border skirmishes happened on almost a daily basis. The political instability exacerbated the problem. The constant fighting left the land full of orphans, and many new orphanages had popped up to care for them.

It reached the point where the country wasn't able to fund them. Karg had already become the head of the Orcus Workshop then. He'd been a friend of Moorin's, so he decided to help fund it.

The day he'd met Oscar had been like any other. He'd gone to drop off some money at the orphanage and see how Moorin and her kids were doing.

When he looked around, he noticed there were a lot more toys.

He'd asked Moorin if she'd gotten another sponsor, and got an answer that he wasn't expecting.

Oscar, who'd just turned ten, had made all those toys.

Karg was shocked to learn that the toys had been transmuted by a young boy. They were of masterwork quality.

The building blocks fitted together seamlessly. The dolls were so accuratelycrafted that Karg almost mistook them for real children. The toy swords were perfectly balanced. Even the fake dishes Oscar had made for the girls to play house were good enough to cook with.

All of those works of art were created by a ten-year-old boy. Karg couldn't believe it. He brought Oscar over and asked him to demonstrate. When Oscar crafted one of those toys right in front of him, Karg had had no choice but to accept reality. At ten years old, he was already as skilled as the country's finest Synergists.

When Karg had asked where Oscar had learned his skills, all he said was:

"When I saw you fix that pot the last time you came, I thought I might be able to do it, too, so I just tried."

Karg remembered that incident. He had indeed come by a month prior to fix a broken pot. Thinking back on it, Oscar had watched with keen interest.

Karg froze. He felt a sudden chill, as if someone had slipped an ice cube down his back.

After watching just once, he'd mastered it? In just one month, he'd reached the level of a master craftsman through trial and error? If that was true, then how much better could he get, given proper instruction? Karg was both excited and terrified at the prospect.

He decided then and there that he would make Oscar the next Orcus.

After tutoring him personally for three years, Karg admitted him into the workshop.

"It's been a long time since you first joined. By all rights, you should have inherited the name of Orcus years ago. But you know, Oscar, I don't want to force you. I stopped you last time when you said you wanted to quit, but if you still think this isn't for you, you're welcome to leave. Believe it or not, I don't want to make you suffer."

"I'm...really grateful to you, Gramps. I know the other crafts-men don't like me, but there's nothing I can do about that. I've already accepted it. Working here isn't that bad, really."

"But still..."

Karg grimaced, but Oscar kept going.

"I like being a Synergist. I get to help everyone in the city with my work, and I can send money back to the orphanage, too... What more could I ask for?"

"Why, Oscar? Why do you hide how talented you really are? If they knew, they'd agree that the title of Orcus doesn't even do your abilities justice. Is it that you don't like making weapons? Or that you don't think you're fit to be a leader? It's probably both. Still, you know, don't underestimate me. I can tell there's another reason you don't want to take the title. Did you think I wouldn't notice?"

"......"

Oscar just smiled his usual smile. The smile that said, "I'm not going to argue, so just say what you want."

"I know this might be a bit presumptuous, but...I think of you as my own son. I just want you to come into your own and show people what you truly are. But I guess that's not what you want, is it?"

Oscar had known Karg for a long time, so he understood Karg's feelings.

Oscar would never admit it, but he'd started calling Karg "Gramps" instead of "Karg-san" because he thought of Karg as his father.

Honestly, Oscar was happy that Karg had such high expectations.

It pained him that he couldn't tell Karg the real reason he hid his talents.

But even so—

"Gramps...you said my skills were on a completely different level, but that's not true."

"There's no need to act humble with me. I know how good you really—"

"They're not on a different level... They're completely abnormal."

"......"

Karg fell silent. Oscar's choice of words gave him an inkling of the real reason.

He'd never seen Oscar look like this before. He had a dark expression on his face and was looking off into the distance. It was as if he was gazing into the future.

Karg knew it wouldn't be as wonderful as he'd described. He didn't know what he should say, but he knew he had to do something. But before he could, Oscar continued.

"Anyway, I enjoy the work I'm doing now. Don't pretend like you don't know. All of the tools and furniture I've made have been well-received by the townspeople. In a way, I'm still helping increase the Orcus Workshop's fame." Oscar spoke cheerfully, trying to dispel the gloom that had settled into the room.

Karg realized this was as far as he'd get and nodded with a sigh.

"Haaah... You're right. Neither the Limster Workshop nor the Vagone Workshop even bother making things for the average citizen. Even though it's their hard work that lets us focus solely on our craft. They're the ones who provide us with the ore we use and the food we eat."

The workshops Karg had named were also in Velnika. Both of them only took orders from nobles, royalty, and rich merchants.

That was what they'd chosen to specialize in, and no one could blame them too much. Still, that didn't mean the townspeople liked it. In fact, most of them were quite angry. While everyone else helped each other out, they only looked to make a profit.

On the other hand, the Orcus Workshop had no restrictions on who could place an order. As a matter of principle, they were forced to prioritize the nobles' requests, but if there were craftsmen free, they were put on orders from regular citizens. Furthermore, the current Orcus had begun donating the workshop's excess funds to various orphanages.

Most importantly, the workshop now had a craftsman whose sole task was to handle the citizens' requests. Because of that, the Orcus Workshop was well-respected.

Oscar was known for being fast, skilled, and able to adapt to the needs of any request. Thanks to that, the townspeople often helped out during crunch times. They'd bring the craftsmen food, sell them raw materials at discounted rates, give them priority for wholesale deals when supplies were low, and even bring spare uniforms and blankets.

Although Oscar's work didn't stand out, he was doing a lot to help. In fact, it was precisely because it didn't stand out that so few people appreciated it.

"Gramps, I still need to deliver my orders."

"Alright, alright. My lecture's over. Go deliver your stuff... actually, wait. There is one thing."

"Huh?"

"You've heard the reports of people going missing from the less prosperous parts of town in the past few months, right?"

"Yeah, I have."

"Try and keep an eye on the kids at the orphanage. Most of the people who've gone missing were very young. They were all from the slums, so people are saying they likely went off and tried to strike it rich somewhere, only to end up dead in a ditch."

Karg had a feeling it was much worse than that. His serious warning reflected that foreboding.

"You can take the rest of the day off. Go see how everyone is at the orphanage."

"That's what I was planning on. I'll be careful. Alright, see you later, Gramps."

Oscar bowed to Karg and left the room. He felt bad for always making Karg worry about him.

"If you have to keep up that fake smile all the time, you should go off and do something you actually like. Dumb kid..." Karg muttered to himself, quietly enough that Oscar couldn't hear.

⁕⁕ ⁕⁕ ⁕⁕ ⁕⁕ ⁕⁕ ⁕⁕ ⁕⁕ ⁕⁕ ⁕⁕ ⁕⁕ ⁕⁕ ⁕⁕ ⁕⁕

Once he finished delivering the day's orders, Oscar headed back to the orphanage. It was located on the outskirts of the capital, so it was a long walk from the workshop.

Oscar was already independent, and had his own place closer to the center of the city. For him, a trip to the orphanage took quite a bit of time. However, he still considered the orphanage his home. Oscar was just as worried as Karg about the recent disappearances, and he'd been coming back to the orphanage more often these past few months.

The outskirts weren't very safe to begin with. Many of the buildings were dilapidated and abandoned. In a word, his orphanage was in the slums.

It housed a lot of children, so it was bigger than all the surrounding houses. Still, it wasn't in much better shape. A run-down wooden house like this wouldn't even be allowed to exist in the center.

Fortunately, it was much sturdier than it looked. By the time Oscar arrived, it was already evening. The setting sun cast deep shadows among the alleyways.

He stood in front of the building for a few minutes, then circled around to the back.

"Looks like the alarm's working."

Oscar placed his hand on the ground. After a few seconds he took it off. He walked around to every corner of the building and did the same thing. Finally, he closed his eyes and placed his hand on the building itself.

"The strengthening's...holding up pretty well. The barrier and mana accumulator are working just fine, too." Oscar breathed a sigh of relief.

Although his actions seemed random, whatever he had discovered appeared to relieve him.

Pleased that his security measures were working, he walked back to the entrance and knocked.

Moorin told him that the orphanage would always be his home, and that he didn't need to be so formal. But since he'd moved out, he felt it was better to knock.

"Hmm...?" Normally, one of the kids would have answered, but nobody came.

Maybe I knocked too lightly? Oscar tried again.

Still no response. He couldn't even hear the sound of the kids playing.

"Ah?!"

Oscar had a very bad feeling about this. Something must have happened.

"Mom! Guys!"

Some small, rational part of his mind told him to calm down and assess the situation. However, his body moved on its own. Every second mattered.

He wrenched open the front door and rushed into the living room.

"Dylan! Corrin! Ruth! Katy! Mom! Anyone!"

He yelled the kids' names as he barreled toward the dining room. It was around their usual time for dinner.

His heart lurched when he heard no reply, and he practically ripped the dining room door off its hinges. Inside, he found—

"Welcome back, dear. Would you like dinner, a bath, or...me, Miledi-tan?"

A girl he didn't recognize. She was wearing a frilly apron and looked to be around maybe fourteen or fifteen years old.

Her long blonde hair was tied back in a ponytail, and it almost seemed to defy gravity as it swished back and forth. She had slender legs that were covered by knee-length socks. One leg was bent back at a cute angle, and she was standing on one foot. Underneath the apron she wore a sleeveless shirt, and in one hand she carried a cooking ladle. She made a peace sign with her free hand and winked at him.

He could have sworn a star flew off from that wink.

The pose was so perfect that it annoyed him. Faced with this unexpected sight, Oscar reacted the only way he could.

"Sorry, looks like I've got the wrong house."

He closed the dining room door and backed away.

I must actually have gotten the wrong house. Ha ha, maybe I'm tired from working so much.

However, this mysterious and oddly cheerful girl had no intention of letting Oscar escape.

"Wait, don't just leave! I can't believe you closed the door on me! An extremely beautiful girl just offered herself to you, so you should be moved to tears! I know you want to gaze upon these perfect legs! There's just the right amount of skin showing between my skirt and my socks. I know you can't resist them. We both know you're a huge pervert, O-kun!"

Oh, just shut up. Quit acting like we're best friends when I don't even know you. Besides, you're obviously crazy.

In a second, Oscar had already made his judgment about her.

He adjusted his glasses and spoke as calmly as he could.

"You said your name was Miledi, right? It seems you've wandered into the wrong house. It's getting late. Surely you should be getting back to your own home. On the off chance you came here on purpose, that would mean you're trespassing. In Velka, trespassing is a serious crime. If you don't leave within the next three seconds, I'll have to arrest you."

Oscar grinned as he shot Miledi a thinlyveiled threat.

"That's not a thinlyveiled threat at all! You obviously want me gone! How mean! I'll have you know it was my destiny to meet you, O-kun—"

"Alright, your three seconds are up. Put your hands in the air."

Oscar pulled a small object out of his pocket. It was a transceiver. Its range was limited to the capital, but it was still a valuable piece of equipment. Usually, only nobles could afford them. Naturally, he'd made this one himself.

The girl recognized it as well, and began to panic. Just then, a bunch of kids jumped to her defense.

"Waaaaaaaaah! Onii-san, wait!"

"She's not a suspiciou—okay, she's pretty suspicious, but she's our guest!"

"Onii-chan, please forgive her. I'll apologize, too! I'm sorry she's so annoying."

"I'm innocent, Onii! It's all that noisy lady's fault!"

Children crawled out of various hiding places in the dining room. Oscar had only been able to handle Miledi so calmly was because he'd spotted them peeking out when she opened the door.

"H-hearing them insult me so nonchalantly kind of hurts..." Miledi muttered and sunk to the floor. Oscar sighed and turned to an older lady who had just walked into the dining room.

•ı• •ı• •ı• •ı• •ı• •ı• •ı• •ı• •ı• •ı• •ı• •ı• •ı• •ı•

"I can't believe even you were in on this, Mom..."

"I'm sorry. But Miledi-san seemed so excited about playing this prank. And I've never seen you surprised by anything, so I thought it'd be fun."

"Fun, huh…? Well, it wasn't very fun for me. I was really worried about you guys." Oscar sighed again.

Moorin, the orphanage manager and everyone's surrogate mother, smiled at him. She was nearing her seventies, but when she smiled she barely looked a day over thirty.

Once everyone had settled down, Oscar sat down with the kids for dinner. The girl, who'd said her name was Miledi, joined them. It appeared she'd come here with business for Oscar. He had asked, but apparently it was a long story. At Moorin's suggestion, they had dinner first.

The refined way in which she ate suggested that Miledi was of noble upbringing. The two seven-year-old girls sitting next to her, Corrin and Katy, began whispering to each other.

They blushed, glanced at Oscar, then squealed at each other. He doubted they were saying anything nice. He glared suspiciously at Miledi, but she only smiled.

Gods, she's annoying. Oscar desperately wanted to say that to her face. But he didn't. He didn't want to set a bad example for his cute little sisters.

Corrin had tied her red hair back into a ponytail in the same style as Oscar's. Out of all of the children in the orphanage, she was the shyest. Her puppy dog look could make instant slaves out of anyone who wasn't family. They were already used to it.

Katy, on the other hand, kept her chestnut brown hair in pigtails and was the most distrustful of all of them. She didn't trust anyone outside the orphanage.

The fact that those two girls were willing to relax around

Miledi meant that, while she might have been annoying and perhaps a little touched in the head, she wasn't a bad person.

Oscar didn't think it would be right to insult her.

"I see, I see. So O-kun's a kind and reliable big brother."

"Y-yep! Onii-chan can do anything!" Corrin smiled and proudly puffed out her chest. Oscar smiled in return.

Miledi grinned. Oscar frowned in return.

The children forgot about their food and began explaining just how amazing Oscar was.

"That's right, Miledi-san. All the toys and stuff in the house were made by Onii-san. And he made them all when he was my age!"

The oldest kid in the orphanage, Dylan, boasted about Oscar's accomplishments. He was the mediator between all of the other kids. Like Corrin, he had his brown hair up in the same kind of ponytail as Oscar.

"Did you know? Onii works at the Orcus Workshop! The chief guy said he wanted him! Isn't that amazing?!" Katy's eyes sparkled as she spoke.

"Onii-chan gave us all something to show that we're related." Corrin held out the small coin dangling from her neck. The other children all pulled out their coins as well. They didn't look valuable, so no one would even bother stealing them.

Still, Miledi didn't make fun of them for it.

"Wow, you guys are all really close, huh?!"

She seemed honestly impressed. The kids all smiled proudly and continued regaling Miledi with tales of Oscar's awesomeness.

"G-guys. Come on, give it a re—"

Embarrassed, Oscar tried to get them to stop, but Miledi cut in.

"Tell me more, Onii-chan! I want to hear about how wonderful you are! I knew I was right to pick you, Onii-chan! Don't you think so, too? Hey, Onii-ch—"

"Call me Onii-chan one more time and I will end you."

Although he was smiling, there was murder in Oscar's eyes. He'd tried to act civil, to set a good example, but he couldn't take it any longer.

"Oh my, you've got a surprisingly wild side to you, O-kun..." For some reason, Miledi was blushing.

"Please don't call me O-kun, either." He managed to reign in his emotions and sound calm. He didn't want to act rude in front of his family. Although internally, he thought, *Call me O-kun one more time and I'll strangle you.*

Miledi stared at him for a moment.

"Don't wanna!" she exclaimed, a smile on her face all the while.

There was a loud crack as Oscar snapped the fork he was holding.

Dylan and the others turned to look at Oscar's hand. By the time they did, the fork looked as good as new.

He'd repaired it with his transmutation. The children tilted their heads in confusion.

"Wow, that was amazing! I've never seen anything like it!"

Oscar had even gone so far as to hide the glow of his mana to repair it in secret, but Miledi had to blow his cover.

"Aren't you just a loser right now?" said a cold voice, sounding more irritated than Oscar felt.

Dylan and the others turned around in surprise.

The person who'd spoken was Ruth. He was looking down at his plate. Ruth had spiky black hair, and had recently turned eleven.

"Hey, Ruth!" Dylan yelled.

However, Ruth looked up from his plate and glared.

"It's the truth! Even though he works at the Orcus Workshop, he doesn't make any weapons. He's just a loser who only takes requests from regular citizens! Everyone knows it!" Ruth pointedly avoided looking at Oscar.

Like Oscar, Ruth was a Synergist.

Among the orphans, he was the one who had looked up to Oscar the most. When Oscar still lived at the orphanage, Ruth followed him everywhere. They had the same striking black hair, and people often thought they were siblings.

"Ruth, apologize to Oscar. That was uncalled for."

Moorin had been smiling the whole time, but Ruth's words made her frown. Her tone was soft but firm.

Ruth hesitated, then stubbornly repeated himself.

"But it's true! If he's not a loser, then he should show it to everyone! If he showed them how strong he really was, then all those dumb people would shut up, but he doesn't do anything! And you know what, it's because he can't! He just grins like an idiot all the time and doesn't say anything! He's just a weakling who doesn't want to fight back!"

It was like a dam had burst inside him. Once the words started flowing out, he couldn't stop.

It felt like a betrayal, seeing the man he idolized so much end up like this.

Oscar understood that, so he didn't say anything. He just smiled his usual smile. If he really was that great, he should show it. If he wasn't, then it'd just hurt Ruth even more.

Ruth wanted Oscar to argue back, to say it wasn't true. Instead, Oscar's smile only annoyed him further. Ruth stood up, unable to bear it.

"That's not true!" A cheery voice stopped him. "You think O-kun's amazing, too, don't you, Ruth-kun? I can tell."

"I-I do not!"

"Yes you do~! My special Miledi eyes can see through everything! I know exaaactly how you feel~! You actually think O-kun's amazing, I know!" Miledi said smugly.

Everyone stared at Miledi in surprise, even Oscar. Her tone was as cheerful as always, but her words had a strange weight to them.

"This is why I wanted to see O-kun. I've spent so long searching for someone like you."

She turned to face Oscar, her gaze piercing through him.

"I've finally found you," she went on, her voice barely a whisper.

She closed her eyes and smiled. She looked sincerely happy to meet him.

Oscar felt his heart skip a beat. *What on earth does she know about me?*

Yes, surely his heart must have skipped a beat, because he was worried how she knew so much. Definitely not for any other reason. At least, that was what Oscar told himself. He adjusted his glasses to hide his expression.

Unfortunately for him, Miledi's eyes really could see everything.

"Oh my, doth mine eyes deceive me? O-kun, did your heart just skip a beat? Was my smile that captivating? Well, was it? Come on, say it~!"

"Shut up, you're annoying."

At that moment at least, that was how he felt.

Miledi and Oscar's exchange dispelled the strained mood that had fallen over the dining table, and everyone returned to their dinner.

Even Ruth sat back down and returned to staring sullenly at his plate.

However, Miledi's words still swirled around in the back of Oscar's mind.

He didn't know why she'd come to him, but he could tell it was extremely important.

Her declaration almost sounded like a profession of love. Corrin and Katy certainly seemed to think so. They kept on looking back and forth between Miledi and Oscar.

"Ahem... Miledi-san, now that everyone's eaten, I think it's time you tell us why you've come."

"Come on, don't be so formal. We're friends, right, O-kun? You don't have to act so distant!"

"What do you mean, 'friends'? I just met you today. More importantly, why—"

"Not telling! Not unless you call me Miledi-tan. And put some feeling behind it, okay?"

"H-ha ha... You're an interesting one. Anyway, enough with the jokes—"

Oscar's patience was running out. Sadly, Miledi didn't seem to care.

"Wait, don't tell me the reason you're being so cold is because... you already have someone you promised your heart to?!"

"What?!"

"I see... I understand now. My superior intelligence has deduced the truth. I should have expected O-kun would want to make Corrin-chan and Katy-chan his wives!"

"If you don't shut up, I'll sew your big mouth shut for you."

Unable to contain himself anymore, Oscar lashed out at Miledi. Corrin and Katy gasped.

He turned and saw Corrin blushing furiously. Katy, on the other hand, wouldn't meet his gaze.

"Onii-chan, do you really want to marry me?"

"W-well, I don't want to marry him! B-but if Onii insisted, then maybe..."

They'd taken Miledi's words seriously. Meanwhile, his brothers looked at him in disgust.

"Onii-san, I respect you, but this is a little too much..."

"Tch... I should have known the loser was a pervert, too."

They'd taken Miledi's words seriously as well. Dylan and Ruth edged away from him.

Then, Miledi delivered the finishing blow.

"Oh, O-kun... You're such a pedo!"

Oscar adjusted his glasses again, losing his temper.

"That's it. You're coming with me, you fucking bitch!"

Oscar grabbed Miledi by the collar and dragged her outside.

⁕ ⁕ ⁕ ⁕ ⁕ ⁕ ⁕ ⁕ ⁕ ⁕ ⁕ ⁕ ⁕

The moon's pale light shone through the gaps in the clouds. Oscar and Miledi stared at each other in the orphanage's back-yard, underneath the beautiful half-moon that would surely become a crucial part of the memory of their first meeting...

Although Oscar had tossed her out of the door, she'd seemingly ignored gravity and lightly landed on her feet.

"O-kun, you monster! I can't believe you'd throw someone out of your house like that! You're not human!"

"Says the girl who just ignored gravity."

Oscar sighed. He knew that if he let himself be led along, their conversation would never get anywhere. He glared sharply at Miledi with a grim expression.

"So what do you really want? I played along with your dumb game. It's about time you came clean."

Throughout the meal, Oscar worried she might try to take the kids hostage.

Moorin and the kids had taken a liking to her, which meant she probably wasn't evil. However, she knew things she shouldn't. She claimed she'd come to meet Oscar, but instead of going to his house, she'd headed straight for the orphanage.

Intentionally or not, she'd basically said, "I can get to your family any time I want to."

That's why he'd changed tactics.

If the kids were wrong about her and she *did* mean them harm, he'd eliminate her without a second thought.

"Don't glare at me like that~! Didn't anyone ever teach you to treat girls nicely?"

"……"

Oscar glared harder. He didn't look anything like the loser everyone thought he was.

"Aha ha, I guess I should probably get serious, huh? Anyway, sorry about that. I didn't mean to cause a misunderstanding. Look, I promise I don't want to hurt your family. I mean it. I don't lie."

Oscar had a hard time believing that, but he nodded anyway.

"The reason I came to meet your family first was because I wanted to learn more about you, O-kun. I went around asking the townspeople about you, too."

"So it's not like you knew about this place beforehand?"

"I came here on a wild goose chase, really. I'd been told that there was a genius orphan somewhere. I visited so many different countries, checking all the orphanages I could find. I was searching for a genius. Though now that I think about it, there was no guarantee the genius orphan had to be a kid."

Oscar nodded in understanding.

Even when she'd been joking around, Miledi's gestures were refined. He guessed that she'd grown up in a noble family, or as the servant of one. Her story cemented that assumption. It was something of a fad among nobles to seek out highly talented individuals and bring them into their household.

Miledi turned around and looked up at the moon. After a few seconds, she glanced back at Oscar.

"It was only after I talked to those kids that I learned about your abilities."

Oscar narrowed his eyes. There was a dangerous glint in them.

"My abilities? I'm just a failure of a Synergist who can only make household goods."

"Aha ha, you're such a jester, O-kun. No failure could make those magic items of yours. In fact, it's so good that you might as well call them artifacts."

Oscar's eyes opened wide in surprise. He'd expected Miledi to have heard the rumors about how he'd been a prodigy, or that he was secretly hiding his talents.

To think she'd figured out the alarms I set around this house... Oscar eyed her warily.

"Seriously, quit glaring at me like that! I'm standing here even knowing what you can do, so can't you trust me a little?"

"Well..."

The traps Oscar had set around the orphanage were lethal. With one word, he could engulf his target in a hail of lightning, wind, ice, and fire.

Furthermore, once it expelled the intruders, it would deploy a five-layer barrier and start ringing an alarm.

If the intruders somehow managed to get past his barrier, his trap would re-summon it. On top of that, all entrances to the building were reinforced with the hardest material Oscar could find.

It looked run-down at first glance, but Oscar had transformed the house into a fortress. Any attempt to break the walls would result in a lightning counterattack. Oscar had transformed them all into reactive armor.

That was the real extent of Oscar's skills. He wasn't just a genius; he could imbue magic into ore. Create artifacts.

He could use magic. The magic that, according to legend, the gods used when they still walked the earth. The only people who could use it now were Atavists, who had inherited the gods' blood.

There was a reason he'd told Karg his abilities were abnormal. On top of everything else, he could freely control his own mana, and didn't need magic circles or chants. The things master craftsmen took years to accomplish were mere child's play to Oscar.

"Honestly, this orphanage is better defended than even the royal palace. No simple Synergist could have made an artifact-class defense mechanism."

Miledi saw through it all somehow. Oscar really couldn't let his guard down. There was more to her than her frivolous attitude.

"If you think I can't be trusted, why not activate your fortress and kick me out? But unless you do, I won't leave until you hear me out."

Ah, now I get it.

Miledi really didn't seem to have any shady ulterior motives. She'd found this place by coincidence. However, she'd been amazed at its defenses, so she'd asked about who lived there. From that she'd learned about Oscar, and decided to wait until he showed up.

Here, where Oscar had access to his most powerful weapons.

She'd let him haul her to the backyard, but she hadn't left, which proved she was at his mercy.

"Why don't you try and act serious, then? That stupid attitude of yours makes you hard to trust."

Oscar relaxed slightly. He let the tension drop from his shoulders and stopped glaring.

"I have no idea what you're talking about~! I'm just your ordinary, cheerful, happy, beautiful girl~!"

She winked at him again, making the same clichéd pose as last time. It annoyed the hell out of Oscar.

It was a wonder anyone could combine frivolity and earnestness the way she did. It seemed he'd caught the eye of a very odd woman. He had a headache just from dealing with her.

"Okay, so what is it you wanted? Let me guess, you want me to make an artifact for you."

"Nope, you're totally off~! It's up to you if you want to make anything for me. Wait, don't tell me you get off from being ordered around by women? Sorry, I'm not really into that kind of thing..."

"Thunder Snake."

"Abababababababababa?!"

Miledi spasmed as Oscar hit her with one of the orphanage's anti-intruder countermeasures. The one he'd activated summoned snake-like electrified wires from underground that wrapped themselves around Miledi.

As the electricity faded, Miledi slumped to the ground.

Oscar adjusted his glasses, then looked down at her.

"I'm not a pervert!" he yelled at her.

"F-first you attack me, now you're yelling at me... Even I didn't expect that..."

Trembling, Miledi rose to her feet. Plumes of smoke were rising from her clothes.

"Can you say two sentences without having to stick a joke in between?"

"It's one of the best things about me; I can't just stop. Won't you please accept me for who I am, O-kun?"

Oscar glared. After a few seconds of sulking, she straightened up and adopted a serious attitude. Oscar's heart skipped a beat again, and he inwardly cursed at himself.

"I have only one goal. Oscar-kun, I want you."

"You...want me? What do you mean?"

It can't possibly mean what I think it does, can it?

Miledi looked back up at the moon.

"Have you ever thought...there was something wrong with this world?"

"Ah..." Oscar fell silent. He couldn't formulate a reply.

"Well, O-kun? You're a Synergist, and clearly on a different level from all the others. If you showed the world your skills, you'd probably become the most famous person alive. In fact, you'd probably be remembered by history as a hero. Yet you stubbornly hide your abilities. What is it you're so scared of?"

Isn't it obvious? If I did that, all the important people in the world would seek me out.

Sure, he might receive fame and glory. Hell, he might even leave his name in history. But he'd no longer be free. And more than anything—

"Is it the Elbard Theocracy that you're afraid of?"

"I should have known you'd figure it out. You know what my abilities are, after all." Oscar smiled wryly.

Yes, Oscar was afraid of losing his freedom. But even more than that, he was afraid of the church.

The Holy Church of Ehit... They followed a doctrine that humans were above all other species, and preached that humans should reign supreme. Almost all the humans on the continent were followers.

Those who could use magic from the age of the gods, or special magic that only monsters could use, were considered to be the gods' descendants and taken under the church's protection.

By force, if necessary. Oscar would suffer the same fate if he revealed his talents.

The Holy Church was as powerful as an entire kingdom. In fact, the leader of the Elbard Theocracy was the Holy Church's pope. Alone, Oscar would never be able to escape their grasp. Even if he could, there was no telling what they would do to his family.

Miledi gave Oscar a knowing smile.

"Escaping from the Holy Church wouldn't be easy. No matter where you go, they're around. In every kingdom, in every village, their taint can be seen."

She practically spat out those last few words.

"Of course you're scared. I mean, think about it. They're supposed to be in control of just one country. But, wherever you go, there are temples. Every country takes them in, and they even let them dictate national policy."

"H-hey, you can't just say that out—"

Oscar nervously looked around.

Insulting the Holy Church was tantamount to suicide. If anyone had heard Miledi say that, she would be executed.

But Miledi didn't stop.

"Even when countries are at war, if the Holy Church says something, they stop right away. And when there's peace, a word from them can start a war. We're too worried about being branded heretics to do what's right, or even what's legal. We're taught that Ehit's will is supreme, and things like love and justice are secondary. In fact, they may as well not matter at all."

"M-Miledi...kun..."

Miledi turned back to Oscar, her bright blue eyes looking directly at him. There was a clarity in them, mirroring her own unwavering resolve. Oscar inadvertently gulped.

She gazed at him for a few seconds, then smiled.

"O-kun. You must have realized how twisted this world is. More so than the kings of this world, you fear the so-called righteous Holy Church. That's why you hid yourself. So that they wouldn't hurt your family in an attempt to get to you."

Normally when someone insulted the Holy Church, they were instantly decried as a heretic. If you didn't, you too would be considered a heretic. Unless you were particularly close to the blasphemer, you had every reason to turn them in.

But Oscar didn't call her out. Shaken as he was, he didn't want to stop Miledi. Because she'd said the things Oscar had always thought, but never had the courage to say.

Miledi was overjoyed to finally have met someone who wasn't a blind believer. Emboldened by Oscar's silence, she continued.

"I belong to a certain organization."

"Organization?"

"Yes. A world where people live by the law, and by their own morals. A world of order and justice. A world where everyone is free to speak out against injustice. Where people come together to discuss what's right. Where different opinions and ideas are valued instead of suppressed. A world where people can be free. That's our organization's goal."

"Are you planning on starting a new religion or something?"

Oscar only just managed to keep a look of incredulity off his face. He congratulated himself for keeping enough composure to retort with a joke.

Still, her words shook him to the core. The ideals Miledi's organization espoused meant that they were basically rebels. A gathering of heretics.

This was no joke. She was inviting him to an organization that had effectively made humanity its enemy.

"Do you think we're a gathering of crackpot terrorists or something...? Aha ha, well, I guess you're not entirely wrong."

"Please leave." Oscar responded to Miledi's lighthearted comment with a flat refusal. "Sorry, but my answer is no. I promise I won't tell anyone about this, so please don't ever come close to me or my family again."

He spoke quietly, but his expression was dead serious.

Miledi stared at Oscar for a few seconds before quietly replying.

"I see..."

She turned on her heel and walked away. Her retreating figure seemed exceptionally small to Oscar.

It was hard to imagine a little girl like her was fighting against the world. *What on earth drove her to make such a suicidal choice? Maybe she's just crazy...*

It would be easier for Oscar if that were the case.

That way, he could convince himself her words hadn't moved him.

"Oh yeah, could you tell everyone the food was delicious?"

"I will."

Miledi glanced back and smiled. Then, without another word, she vanished into the darkness.

It was as if she was nothing more than a spirit.

Oscar clenched his teeth, only just keeping himself from saying something.

They'd never see each other again. *And that's for the best,* he kept telling himself.

◦◦ ◦◦ ◦◦ ◦◦ ◦◦ ◦◦ ◦◦ ◦◦ ◦◦ ◦◦ ◦◦ ◦◦ ◦◦

The next day...Miledi showed up at Oscar's workplace.

"Hello, good citizens of the Orcus Workshop! I'm the world renowned idol, Miledi! Where's my cute little O-kun?"

A number of hard-faced craftsmen stared in confusion at the girl who'd just shown up at the back entrance. It seemed she'd forgotten her manners in the womb. Miledi brazenly strode past the confused craftsmen without so much as an "excuse me."

"Wow, I should have expected one of Velka's big three workshops to be amazing. The country is known for its technology after all. There are master craftsmen everywhere~!" Miledi exclaimed in wonder as she looked around.

At the back, Oscar was struck dumb. He'd expected never to see Miledi again. Wanting to avoid being seen, he quickly hid himself. He was glad there'd been enough orders that he could hide behind his pile of finished work.

Wh-wh-what on earth is she doing here?! He adjusted his glasses.

The craftsmen looked at each other, wondering who this girl was.

Although she was grinning like a fool, her expensive clothes marked her as a noble, or at least someone rich. Normally, anyone who barged into the workshop like this would be thrown out, but Miledi was so blatant about it that the craftsmen hesitated.

If she was some noble's daughter, then they couldn't afford to be rude.

Just as someone ran off to get the chief, a young man stepped forward. Although he was a noble himself, he wrung his hands like a groveling merchant. Ping was never one to let slip an opportunity to make important connections. He smiled as flatteringly as he could.

"Miss, what is it you need? Perhaps I could be of assistance. Ah, excuse me for not introducing myself sooner. I'm Ping Waress, son of Viscount Waress."

"Hi...! I'm Miledi."

Miledi observed Ping carefully for a few seconds, then broke out into a smile.

The onlookers could easily tell that this smile was fake.

"Miledi, was it? A beautiful name to suit a beautiful person such as yourself. Pardon me for asking, but which family do you hail—"

"Does that really matter?"

Miledi was still smiling, but her eyes were cold. Even an idiot noble like Ping got the message.

Ping hurriedly tried to smooth things over.

If she could take that kind of attitude with Ping, a viscount's son, then she must have been a very important noble. Or at least, that was what Ping thought.

"Oh no, not at all. My apologies. Truly, forgive me. Regardless, what is it you needed? I guarantee you that I, heir to the Waress family, can fulfill any order you care to place!"

Even then, he still tried to sell his family name. Torpa and Raul hurried over to Miledi as well, hoping to get into her good graces.

However, before they could reach her, Miledi dropped a bomb.

"Is O-kun—I mean, Oscar-kun here? I came here to see him..."

"Huh? O-Oscar?" Ping's eyes widened. Torpa and Raul stopped in their tracks. Even the craftsmen stopped working.

Oscar groaned to himself. *You idiot! My position in this workshop's already bad enough, and now you've made it ten times worse!* The other craftsmen couldn't believe a noble lady would be asking after the least-skilled member of the workshop. Even more surprisingly, she'd called him by a nickname.

Everyone turned to look at Oscar's cubicle.

"Pardon me again for my forwardness, but what business do you have with Oscar? You may not know this, but his skills are, well, lacking... There are many other more skilled craftsmen who would be happy to fulfill your order."

"Hm? I just wanted to see how O-kun works. I don't really need anything. Oh, is that where he works? Thanks, Pinwa-san~!"

"Umm, my name is Ping War—"

Before he could correct her, Miledi dashed off to Oscar's workplace. She'd followed the other craftsmen's gazes to figure out where it was.

Ping just stood there, dumbfounded.

A high-ranking noble lady had come to the Orcus Workshop just to see Oscar work.

She soon spotted Oscar hiding behind his pile of boxes and bounded over to him.

"Ah, there you are, O-kun! It's me, Miledi-chan! I haven't seen you since last night!"

Oh great, this is going to cause even more misunderstandings. Oscar's expression stiffened.

The other craftsmen started muttering to each other about how Oscar had slept with a noble girl.

Ping glared at Oscar, his eyes burning with jealousy and hatred. He rushed over to Miledi and Oscar, trying to act polite as he warned her away.

"Miss Miledi. Though he may be a member of the Orcus Workshop, as I said earlier, he's just a third-rate Synergist. He's only allowed to work here because the chief took pity on him. Moreover, he's an orphan. He has no manners and no education. Don't you think someone as distinguished as yourself should be more careful about choosing the company she keeps? At the very least, I don't think he is deserving of—"

"Oh, you're still here, Piress-san? I'm good now, so you can go back to work...or is it that you don't have any work to be doing?"

"Pfft...!"

A few of the craftsmen couldn't hold back their laughter. Miledi was spot-on.

Regardless of whether she'd intended to insult him, she'd hit Ping where it hurt. He blushed in embarrassment, and his fake smile cracked.

"My apologies, but—"

"Umm, Miledi-san! I finished the thing you ordered from me last night. In fact, I was just about to go deliver it right now! Why don't you join me? And thank you so much for your patronage! I hope you come back to the Orcus Workshop if you need anything else!" Oscar hurriedly cut Ping off.

He wanted to stop this before it turned into a fight. He also emphasized that she'd come for work, to dispel any potential misunderstandings.

Unfortunately, it seemed Miledi didn't get the hint.

"Huh? Ordered? But O-kun, I didn't—"

"Come, let's go!"

Oscar loaded his cart with inhuman speed and glared pointedly at Miledi. He was grinning, but the smile didn't reach his eyes.

Miledi broke out into a cold sweat.

"Crap, I may have gone too far..." she muttered to herself as she followed.

Naturally, his crappy acting did nothing to dispel people's suspicions.

The craftsmen turned to gossip with one another. No one noticed Ping, who glared venomously at Oscar.

⁂ ⁂ ⁂ ⁂ ⁂ ⁂ ⁂ ⁂ ⁂ ⁂ ⁂ ⁂ ⁂

"Hey, hey, O-kun. O-kuuun. Stop ignoring me~! Hey, listen to me~!"

"......"

Oscar silently trotted down the street, pulling his cart.

Miledi followed, occasionally waving a hand in front of his face to try and get his attention.

As Oscar was the only craftsman who took orders from ordinary citizens, he was pretty well known in the area. People recognized his cart, and would often stop and chat when he passed by.

However, no one greeted him this time around. Despite the fact that he was drawing more attention than usual.

There were two reasons. The first was the strange girl bouncing around him. The second was the grim expression on Oscar's face.

It was doubly frightening because none of them had ever seen Oscar without his customary smile, yet the girl following him wasn't perturbed.

"You mad? Like, really mad? Did you really not want me to come see you at the workshop? Hey, hey, O-kun. All the guys think you're going out with me now! Things are gonna be pretty rough for you working there! But don't worry, I'm a responsible young woman! I'll head back with you and tell everyone what's really going on! I'll let them know all I'm actually after is you!"

"Are you trying to ruin my reputation?!"

Oscar suddenly came to a halt, then smacked Miledi on the head when she poked out from behind him.

For some reason, that made her happy. Her ponytail swung happily from side to side, mirroring her emotions.

"Yay! You finally responded, O-kun."

"Because I realized ignoring you only makes you more annoying. Sheesh, you're like a walking disaster, you know that?"

"Ehe he, you're making me blush."

"That wasn't a compliment. Seriously, would it kill you to act like a normal person for even five seconds?"

Oscar tiredly rubbed his temples.

Miledi was right—going back to the workshop now wouldn't be pleasant. He wondered if his half-assed acting had done anything to stop the rumors. Probably not.

He knew he'd have to keep this walking incarnation of chaos away from there, if he didn't want them getting any worse.

"O-kun, what's wrong? You look like someone who just got fired."

"And whose fault do you think that is? I'm begging you, at least realize what it is you're doing. Anyway, you broke your promise. I thought you were a more sincere person than that, but I guess I misjudged you."

Oscar started walking again.

"Excuse me! I *always* keep my promises!"

"Not this one. You said last night that you wouldn't ever come near me or my fami—"

Oscar cut his words short, realizing something. When he'd asked her that...

"All I said was, 'I see...' I didn't say anything else. You just assumed~!"

In other words, she'd just acknowledged that's what Oscar wanted. She hadn't actually promised to do anything.

"I-I can't believe you."

Oscar ground his teeth in frustration. He knew it was his own fault for not squeezing an actual promise out of Miledi, but that didn't make him less mad. Especially because now she was rubbing it in. Still, if he let his emotions get the better of him, it'd be over. Oscar adjusted his glasses and did his best to wrest his emotions under control.

"Then I'll ask you once more. Please don't ever come near me or my family again. As things are right now, your ideals are too dangerous. Please. Don't get me, or the people I love, involved."

Miledi ran up in front of Oscar. She turned to face him and continued walking backward, hands behind her back.

"My ideals aren't the real danger here. It's this world. Please,

O-kun, don't avert your eyes from the truth. You already know how twisted and unfair this world is, don't you?"

"Yeah, but that's no reason to bring its wrath crashing down on my head. At the very least, we're living in peace right now. As long as I live quietly and don't stand out, there won't be any problems."

"You really are a loser, O-kun."

"No I'm not. I'm just realistic. Anyway, will you please—"

"Absolutely not!"

"Want me to turn you over to the inquisitors?" Oscar's eyebrow twitched dangerously, but Miledi just smiled.

"Nooo! Don't abandon me, O-kun! I'll do anything for you!"

"Damn you, Miledi! You purposely screamed that in a street full of people!"

Oscar finally lost his calm as Miledi clung to him.

Many of the passing housewives shook their heads.

"Oh my, I can't believe Oscar-kun would make a girl cry. What a brute," one of them said.

The other pedestrians, too, hung on to every word.

The street's attention was focused on Oscar and Miledi. At this rate, the inquisitors would come for him first.

"Fuck," Oscar muttered as he dragged Miledi away.

⁎ ⁎ ⁎ ⁎ ⁎ ⁎ ⁎ ⁎ ⁎ ⁎ ⁎ ⁎ ⁎

"How long are you planning on following me?"

"Until you agree to join me, I guess?"

"Then you'll be following me for the rest of your life... Anyway,

I need to deliver these orders to my customers. Can you at least promise you won't say anything misleading? If not, I really will turn you over to the inquisitors."

"Okaaaaaay! He he..."

Despite Oscar's cold attitude, Miledi seemed happy. He glared at her suspiciously.

"Is it really that fun watching my reactions?"

"Not really? I was just thinking that even though you keep saying I'm dangerous, and you don't want to be seen near me, you're not actually reporting me."

"Don't mistake it for goodwill. I just don't want to have to deal with the trouble. I still wish you'd go away."

"Hmm..."

Miledi smiled; it was clear she didn't believe him. Oscar shook his head and tried his best to ignore her.

That lasted all of a second.

"Hey, O-kun. Last night, when I was leaving, were you thinking of saying something?"

"Wh-what?"

Oscar was taken aback. He hadn't expected her to see through that. But even though this was a perfect opportunity for her to tease him, her expression was serious.

Because of her usual frivolity, the moments she was serious stood out even more. Oscar found himself being drawn into her piercing, bottomless gaze.

"I won't leave until you tell me what it was you were going to say."

"There wasn't anything. Maybe I might have said 'Hurry up and get out of my sight' or something, but that's all."

He pulled himself away with some difficulty.

"I see," was all she said in return. After that, she returned to her usual cheerful persona. "Hey, hey, O-kun. What are you delivering?"

"We're almost to my first customer. The owner of that restaurant over there ordered dishes."

Miledi nodded and peeked curiously into the boxes in Oscar's cart. He once again reminded Miledi not to say anything misleading, and knocked on the restaurant's backdoor.

A well-built woman answered.

"Oh my, if it isn't Oscar. Welcome! If you're knocking at the back entrance, then it must mean you have a delivery."

"Yep. Here you go, Daisy-san. I brought the butcher's knives and frying pan you asked for. Are the goods to your satisfaction?"

Oscar handed over the box filled with cookware. She looked inside and nodded in approval.

"As always, you work fast. I asked for these the day before yesterday and you're already finished. Thank you so...hm? Who's this?"

Daisy looked at Miledi, who was poking out from behind Oscar curiously.

Oscar cursed inwardly. He put on his best fake smile and quickly came up with a good cover story. Before he could say anything, though, Miledi opened her mouth.

"Hello! I'm O-kun's friend, Miledi! I'm here today to see what his work's like."

Oscar let out a sigh of relief when he heard Miledi give a proper introduction. He tried to signal Miledi to leave, but Daisy's interest was piqued.

"Oh my, I never knew Oscar had such cute friends. How long have you two known each other?"

"Since yesterday! When I first met O-kun I felt, like, a spark. You know what I mean, miss?"

"Oh, but of course! When I first met my husband, I felt like I'd been struck by lightning! I see now, so that's how it is. Good for you, Oscar. We were all worried about you. You're handsome and great at your job, but you've never even flirted with a girl before. Me and the other housewives were starting to think I should try and set you up with my daughter!"

Oscar knew girls got friendly with each other easily, but he hadn't expected Daisy and Miledi to hit it off so well. They kept on talking, mostly saying embarrassing things about Oscar.

It got more and more awkward for him. He wished he could crawl in a hole somewhere and die.

The housewives' rumor mill was something to be feared. But he didn't have time to spare thinking about their secret meetings where they discussed finding him a wife. He had to do something about Miledi's not-so-subtle hints that she was trying to marry him herself.

The only saving grace was that Daisy was unlikely to guess the truth. Namely that Miledi had meant, "I thought this guy would be perfect for my anarchist society" when she'd said she'd felt a spark.

"Daisy-san! Sorry for interrupting, but can I explain what my goods do?"

"Huh? Oh, yes. Sorry, Oscar. I got a little carried away there. She's a really nice girl, though. You treat her well, you hear?"

Oscar replied with his usual smile. He could see Miledi grinning out of the corner of his eye, but he ignored her.

"Umm, so these butcher's knives have serrated edges. That'll help keep them from getting stuck when you're cutting through particularly tough meat. Though I haven't really tested them too much myself, so could you tell me how they're holding up after a month or so?"

Both Daisy and Miledi examined the knives appreciatively.

Oscar continued, explaining how things wouldn't stick to the frying pan even if Daisy didn't use oil. One of the main reasons Oscar was so popular among the common folk was because he put extra touches like that on his goods.

"You always pay attention to the little details like this. Alright, I'll let my husband know, too. And whenever I get a chance, I'll drop by to let you know how it feels to use. By the way, did you carve some weird name on this one?"

Daisy examined the knives and the frying pan suspiciously.

Miledi tilted her head in confusion as Oscar sighed.

"No, as you requested, I didn't mark these with my brand. Why don't you like it, anyway?"

Daisy replied with another question.

"Out of curiosity, what exactly did you name these knives and this frying pan?"

Oscar puffed his chest out proudly.

"Glad you asked. The knives are called Meat Shredder Mk. III, while the frying pan's named Slide Master Alpha. What do you think? Cool, right? If you want, I can still engrave the names—"

"No thanks." Daisy shot him down before he could finish.

"Why...?" Oscar muttered quietly.

"O-kun...you've got a terrible naming sense."

"What do you mean, 'terrible'?! Shouldn't you have my back here?!" Oscar cried out.

Daisy nodded in agreement with Miledi's statement, leaving him with no one to turn to.

Although Oscar was beloved by the citizens, they all unanimously thought the names he engraved into his goods were terrible.

Although it pained him to do it, he'd begun complying with his customers' requests to stop engraving them. He was careful to keep them plain in the workshop's ledger as well. All craftsmen of the Orcus Workshop were required to record their transactions.

That way, he didn't have to listen to people say his naming sense was terrible.

Oscar took his money from Daisy, then quickly moved on to the next customer. He was still a little sulky about the names.

The rest of his deliveries went by smoothly enough, but each conversation left him a little more mentally drained. At every delivery, Miledi would hit it off with the customers and cause some sort of misunderstanding that Oscar would desperately try and rectify.

By the time they finished the last one, Oscar was exhausted.

"O-kun, O-kun. You look realllllly tired."

"And whose fault is that?"

"Wow, it's already past noon. What's a good place to eat around here? I'm starving."

"Listen, when people are talking to—oh, I give up! I need some food myself or I'll collapse."

Grumbling to himself, Oscar led Miledi to a nearby restaurant. It was run by an acquaintance of his.

Since it was still lunchtime, there were quite a few people inside. Although it was in a seedier part of the city, the restaurant itself was impeccable. There were pictures of its menu stationed outside, too.

Fortunately, there was still one empty table left in the corner, so Oscar claimed it. Miledi sat down next to him.

"Hm? Is it just me, or are people staring at us?" Miledi looked around the room.

Oscar looked around and saw some residents, a few adventurers, and even a table full of local girls sitting at the nearby tables. The restaurant attracted all manner of customers, so that wasn't too unusual. What was unusual was that each and every one of them was staring at him.

Oscar knew Miledi was probably the reason, so he ignored them and called for a waiter.

"Hello~! Ah, Oscar-san, wel...come?"

A bright teenage girl came over to take their order. The clean white apron she was wearing suited her nicely.

"Good afternoon, Aisha-san. Could we get two of the daily special?"

Oscar ordered for Miledi as well. He didn't want to ask her what she wanted, since that would've given her an excuse to say something.

However, the way he so casually ordered for Miledi seemed to crush Aisha. She glanced from Oscar to Miledi before suddenly bursting into tears.

Oscar was completely taken aback. Miledi smiled wryly, realizing what was going on. The diners watched on with interest, wondering how Oscar had made her cry.

"O-Oscar-san. I-I-I-I didn't realize you had a lover..."

"Huh? Oh, no, I don't. This girl's just—"

"This girl?! You're always so polite to everyone, but you're so close to her that you refer to her so casually... I-I can't believe it."

Aisha stumbled back, one hand over her mouth. Miledi didn't chime in with her usual teasing this time. Even she didn't want to crush a pure little girl's heart.

"Umm, I think you're misunderstanding something here. O-kun and I—"

"O-kun?! You call him O-kun?! Even I've never used such a casual nickname with him!"

"Err, well, umm..."

Before Miledi could say anything else, Aisha turned and ran.

"Waaaaaaaaah, I thought I had a chaaaaaance! Daaaaaaaaad, two daily specials!"

She disappeared into the kitchen. An elderly man's voice rang out through from the back.

"Two dailies, coming right up! Thanks for coming!"

Even when her heart was broken, Aisha still did her job. And it said something about her dad's dedication to his own job that he took the order without batting an eyelid. Like father like daughter.

Wails of lamentation could be heard in another corner.

Oscar turned and saw a group of local girls slumped over at their table. The cause of their despair was evident.

"You're pretty popular, O-kun."

"No comment."

Objectively speaking, it made sense. Oscar was well-respected, came from a distinguished workshop, was rather handsome, and even had an amiable personality to boot. And because everyone knew he was a bachelor, the girls all thought they had a chance.

Oscar adjusted his glasses to cover his expression.

Two of the adventurers stood up and walked over to him. They were grinning.

"Yo, Oscar. Looks like you've finally found yourself a girl."

"Nice going, kid. You always turned us down when we offered to introduce you to someone. We were so scared you might be into men that we stopped putting in orders for a while. Thank Ehit we don't have to worry about that."

The two adventurers patted Oscar on the back. They hadn't ordered weapons and armor from Oscar before, only miscellaneous traveling equipment. Things like lanterns, cookware, tents, and other things that every adventurer needed. Oscar's items were always sturdier and easier to use, so he was popular. Most of the adventurers who made this city their base carried around items made by Oscar.

"Umm, guys. She's not actually—"

"Hey missy, how'd you get this stubborn fool to fall for you?"

Oscar tried to fix the misunderstanding, but before he could, they turned to Miledi.

It dawned on Miledi that basically all of the diners here knew Oscar, and they all loved him.

She thought back to poor Aisha and the girls despairing a few tables over, then decided to answer honestly.

"The truth is, I haven't yet. I'm still trying to make him mine."

The girls jolted upright. They stared at Oscar, a fierce determination burning in their eyes. Aisha, too, came running out of the kitchen. She hid behind a pillar and stared at Oscar.

"Miledi...why do you keep adding fuel to the fire? First you had to go and make my workplace hell, and now you're destroying all the places I visit... How much do you have to ruin before you're satisfied?"

Oscar massaged his temples.

Seeing his reaction, the two adventurers realized what kind of relationship Oscar and Miledi had. They smiled sadly and patted Oscar on the back.

Although they looked scary, the two of them were actually quite soft-hearted.

They cast about for a different topic, hoping to distract everyone from the girls now staring at him like he was a choice cut of meat.

"Oh yeah, speaking of your workplace. You know that shitty noble brat that's always getting in your way?"

"Err, you mean Ping-san?"

"Yeah, that fool. I've seen him and his cronies skulking around here recently. It's always at night, too."

"Ping-san comes here at night?"

Ping was basically a walking bundle of pride. He held as much contempt for the residential areas of the city as he did for Oscar.

He wouldn't ever come down here for fun, nor would he willingly associate with any of the people living here. Like he'd said to Miledi, he only associated with nobles.

"Yeah. Weird, right? I dunno what that little brat's up to, but be careful. You're the only reason I can think of for them to come down here."

"Yeah, exactly. And the streets have been dangerous lately..."

"You're referring to the missing people?"

"Mhm...that too. But the templar knights have been poking around the mine shafts. There's no way those elite soldiers are there just to chat with the miners. Word among the adventurers is that there's an insanely strong monster hiding somewhere down below. None of us are willing to go too deep, just in case."

"I see..."

Fortunately, the serious topic managed to calm the horde of hormone-crazed girls.

Just then, Oscar and Miledi's food arrived. The adventurers said their goodbyes and returned to their table.

Oscar eagerly dug in. After a few bites, he finally noticed Miledi wasn't touching her food, even though she'd said she was starving. He looked up.

"Miledi?"

"Hm? Oh! This looks great! Time to eat!" Miledi stuffed her face full of food.

Oscar felt a sense of foreboding. He hadn't liked that thoughtful expression on her face.

Once they'd finished, Oscar was on guard again. *She isn't really going to follow me back to the workshop, is she?*

"Thanks so much for hanging out with me today! Can I come back again tomorrow?"

Well, I didn't see that one coming.

He wanted to refuse, but instead he found himself saying something else.

"Even if I say no, you'll come anyway, won't you?"

That was basically the same as giving her permission.

"Ehe he. See you tomorrow, then!"

He realized too late what he'd done. Before he could call out to her, Miledi slipped into the crowds.

Oscar scratched his head and walked back to the workshop. He still needed to figure out what kind of excuse he was going to give his coworkers.

◦◦◦ ◦◦◦ ◦◦◦ ◦◦◦ ◦◦◦ ◦◦◦ ◦◦◦ ◦◦◦ ◦◦◦ ◦◦◦ ◦◦◦ ◦◦◦ ◦◦◦

A week had passed since then.

Although she came and went as she pleased, Miledi spent

most of her time hanging around Oscar. At this point, all of the common citizens knew her.

Oscar spent most of their time complaining, but the others just took this as a sign of their closeness. After all, he was reserved and polite to everyone else.

And in fact, the two of them had talked quite a bit over the past week.

Most of it was Miledi going on about something, but as time passed, Oscar found himself replying more and more. Although the conversations were never serious, Oscar still found himself learning more about Miledi. At the same time, he opened up to her as well. Slowly, he gave up on getting her to leave.

Oscar walked down the twilit street, heading toward the orphanage. He made sure to check up on everyone at least once a week.

The pale orange sunlight cast long shadows on the ground, and the cries of crows echoed in the distance. For some reason, the sight made Oscar feel empty.

This was his first time coming back to the orphanage since meeting Miledi. He was still a little wary. Although he may have opened up to Miledi, she was still a heretic. If the Holy Church found her, they'd kill her, and anyone she'd been in contact with.

Still, if he'd really wanted Miledi gone, Oscar could have used his artifacts to chase her away. At that point, he didn't fully understand why he hadn't.

She's no ordinary person, that's for sure. There's no guarantee I can beat her, even with my artifacts, so it's better not to poke the hornet's nest. That's right, I'm just being careful here. I'm just being cautious, that's all. Oscar tried to convince himself that was the reason he hadn't done anything more than yell at her.

However, things couldn't continue for much longer. Miledi was already rather well-known among the citizens. If she got herself arrested, Oscar's involvement would almost certainly come to light. He needed to put an end to their relationship.

"Sheesh, she's such a handful..."

Oscar surprised himself by muttering that. He hadn't said it in his usual annoyed tone. No, in fact, he'd sounded almost happy.

No matter what he said or did, Miledi was always smiling. Although he'd said a few truly hurtful things, for some reason, she never lost any of her cheerfulness. It was infectious. Even Oscar couldn't help but loosen up.

"What the hell's wrong with me?"

Oscar smiled and shook his head.

Tomorrow, I'll cut my ties with her for good.

If he had to, he'd use his artifacts to force her out. Although she was pushy, and always fooling around, if Oscar really put his foot down, she'd listen. He hoped.

With that, his strange days with this odd girl would finally be over. He'd go back to living simply, hiding his true strength and making basic necessities for the people. He'd be made fun of and insulted again. However, that was a price he was willing to pay. Or at least, he thought it was. Regardless, he knew there wouldn't be any problems.

"Hey there, O-kun! It's me, Miledi-chan-in-the-evening!"

"Why do you have to go and ruin the mood every single time? What the heck does 'Miledi-in-the-evening' even mean?!"

Miledi popped out of nowhere as always, making Oscar retort. The tension drained from Oscar's body as he watched Miledi laugh. He'd psyched himself up to finally chase her away.

Miledi looked at Oscar's soot-stained face and smiled.

"I figured since you were heading this way after work, you'd be seeing your family today!"

"Yeah..."

"Hey, hey, O-kun. I want to eat Moorin's food again. It was delicious."

Miledi casually invited herself over for dinner. Normally, Oscar would have adjusted his glasses and told her to get out.

That's what Miledi was expecting.

However, contrary to expectations, Oscar just looked at Miledi with a serious expression on his face.

He'd steeled his resolve once more.

Miledi could sense it, too. The time had come for them to part.

"O-kun, can we talk for a bit?"

Miledi's smile faded as she spoke.

Oscar deliberated for a few seconds, then nodded.

The two of them silently walked over to a nearby bench and sat down.

The sun sparkled in the evening sky, as if determined not to set. Miledi's profile was dyed bright orange by the light. Her blue eyes looked off into the distance.

Finally, she began to talk.

"My name is Reisen. Miledi Reisen. Daughter of Earl Reisen, and the last living member of the Reisen family. I come from a long line of executioners. We manage the Reisen Gorge Execution Grounds for the Grandort Empire."

Oscar whistled in surprise. The Reisen name was so famous that even people in other countries had heard of it. *The whole family supposedly died a few years ago...but I guess one of them survived.* Miledi smiled sadly at Oscar and continued her story.

Her tone was serious throughout the entire tale, which she started from the very beginning.

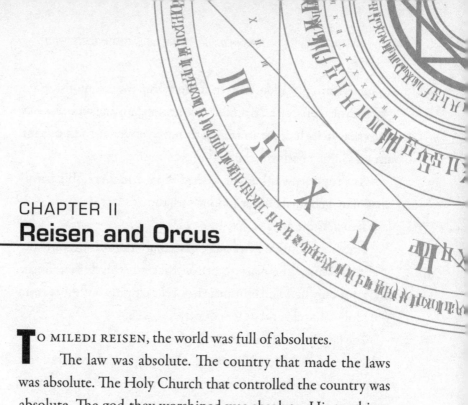

CHAPTER II
Reisen and Orcus

To MILEDI REISEN, the world was full of absolutes.

The law was absolute. The country that made the laws was absolute. The Holy Church that controlled the country was absolute. The god they worshiped was absolute. His teachings and doctrines were absolute. The conventions of her house were absolute. Everything from when she got up in the morning, what her tutors told her, what her father asked of her, and her role in the family, was absolute.

The Grandort Empire's influence was vast. It stretched from the central part of the continent all the way to the east. The Reisen Gorge was within it. It was well-known for its magical prowess, and although most of its mages weren't as strong as the demons, they were still the strongest the humans had.

As magic was the forte of most citizens, they all considered the Reisen Gorge, which dispersed mana inside of it, an execution ground. Without the aid of their spells, no Grandortian could hope to survive in a place like that, teeming with powerful monsters.

Political prisoners, criminals, witnesses...anyone who was sent into that hellish crack in the earth never returned. "Execution ground" was a fitting term.

As the gorge was known around the world, the noble family that managed the lands around it was, too.

That was the Reisen family.

They were known as a family of executioners. The family ran and maintained the massive prison that was the Reisen Gorge. They not only handled criminals from the empire, but those from the Holy Church, and other countries as well.

The family dated back so many generations that some scholars believed they'd existed since before the founding of the Grandort Empire. No one was sure if the gorge got its name from the family, or the other way around.

Regardless, the family was known for being utterly ruthless. They were called a family of executioners not only because of the job they handled, but because of the fear their name struck in the hearts of others.

And Miledi was the daughter of that ruthless and terrifying earl.

Because she could use gravity magic, and control her mana directly without any need for a circle, she was hailed as a genius Atavist.

Normally, she would have been taken under the Holy Church's protection and raised as one of Ehit's descendants, but because of the influence the Reisen family held, she was allowed to remain home. According to history, the very first Reisen was able to use ancient magic as well. Records claimed that he'd used it to turn the gorge into a magic-sealing execution ground. Because of that legend, Miledi was allowed to remain.

The only people Miledi ever saw were her grandfather, her parents, her uncle, her cousin, the doll-like servants, her tutors, her father's soldiers, and the criminals that came to be executed.

She was completely isolated from the outside world, and spent her days learning how to be an upstanding member of the Reisen family.

That was all that was expected of her, and all that was granted to her. Nothing more, nothing less.

To the outside world, Miledi's family would have seemed cold and inhuman. Whether for good or ill, however, Miledi didn't see it that way. She had nothing to compare her situation to.

Once she turned eight, she began helping out with the family business.

Every time she sat down with a criminal, she was met with cursing, begging, and despair. Still, they were criminals. Someone had to take on the job of executing them. The law was absolute, and the law said that they were to be cast into the gorge.

And so, Miledi did her job. She read out the charges to the condemned, and watched as they were flung into the gorge.

Those that tried to flee died at her hands.

Those that tried to climb their way up were shoved back down.

Over the course of a year, Miledi lost all emotion. Their despair, grudges, and lamentations no longer moved her. After all, what did it matter? They were here because they tried to go against an absolute. It was absolute that they would face retribution for it. Their fates were decided.

It was all pointless, and Miledi found it easier not to feel anything at all.

By the age of ten, Miledi had become the perfect Reisen daughter. She was taciturn, expressionless, and emotionless.

One day her father, Colt, summoned her to his office.

"Father, it's Miledi."

"Enter."

The same inorganic voice greeted her when she knocked on the door. But she didn't seem to mind, and entered the room.

"This is the next person to be condemned."

"Understood."

Miledi took the documents her father handed her.

Inwardly, she was a little confused. Although each criminal was given a chance to plead their defense or repent their sins, it was only to seem fair. In truth, all who passed through the estate's gates were doomed, so why was her father bothering to give her the details?

"Their punishment is death. The execution will proceed at the appointed time. But before it happens, I want you to ask them something."

"What would that be?"

Miledi looked down at the documents.

"The condemned is a heretic, but there is a strong possibility they weren't working alone. There may be an organization that they belong to."

" 'May'?"

"The Holy Church captured them. They tried to interrogate the heretic, but learned nothing. One of Ehit's descendants oversaw the interrogation, so there's no reason to believe they were deceived. That's why they are still unsure."

"......"

Miledi's lips twitched at the mention of the word "interrogation." She knew what the Holy Church did was torture. She wondered what kind of state the criminal would be in. Colt was in charge of this particular criminal, so Miledi hadn't met him. Chances were he'd be on death's door already.

"How do you want me to phrase the question?"

She didn't ask why Colt wanted her to do it. An order from her father was absolute. Questioning it wasn't allowed. She only needed to fulfill her duty.

"As if you were a child."

Her father's words were so surprising that Miledi almost laughed. She knew what the servants said about her. She was probably the most adult-like ten-year-old in existence.

All thanks to the Reisen upbringing. *Though acting like a child would be...I suppose I do still look like one. There is certainly a possibility they may be more willing to open up to a child.*

"I am not asking you to pull off a perfect act. Simply do what you can."

"Yes, sir."

Miledi bowed her head. Manners were also part of her upbringing.

As she left, she put the condemned man out of her mind and began thinking about how to act like a child.

That evening, Miledi stood before a man dressed in rags. He was flanked by two guards, and standing on the execution platform that overlooked the gorge.

One push, and his fate would be sealed. Without magic, survival was nigh impossible. Even the man's remains would be eaten by the monsters. In practice, execution was simple.

The criminal was lying in a heap on the stand, not even twitching. He was already at death's door. In fact, he was likely to die before Miledi got the chance to push him.

However, work was work. The rules were absolute. Whether the condemned was deceased or not, she would push him into the ravine.

"Davy Consman. You have been charged with heresy. Your crimes include denouncing Ehit's doctrine and attacking a priest. You have rebelled against our lord, and thus will be executed."

Miledi spoke emotionlessly, reading from the document.

There was no response. Normally, this was when they started hurling curses.

She waited for a while, but when it was obvious he wasn't going to say anything, she signaled to the two guards.

"You two are dismissed. I'll handle the rest."

"Miledi-sama?"

"What's this about?"

The two guards followed the script to the letter. Miledi curtly replied with, "That's an order," and watched them shuffle away.

Then, after a moment of feigned hesitation, Miledi leaned closer to the man.

"Umm, can I ask you something?"

She did her best to sound like a child.

There still wasn't much emotion in her voice, but it was a far cry from the inorganic way she'd read the charges.

Davy stirred. Miledi could see empty eyes staring at her from behind his dirty bangs.

"What?" he answered, to her surprise.

"Why did you attack that priest? You should have known what would happen."

What she really wanted to know was what organization he'd been a part of. However, she figured asking that right away would look suspicious, so she started with something innocuous.

Davy stared at Miledi. His empty eyes began to glow with a fiery determination.

"How horrible."

"Hm? You definitely did something horrible. But if you knew that, then why—"

"I can't believe you're like this already, at such a young age."

"What?"

This time, Miledi's surprise wasn't feigned.

Davy smiled. He struggled to his knees, coughing up blood.

"Why? It's simple. Because you're making a face like that, little girl."

Miledi had no idea what he was talking about. He'd done it because of her expression? That didn't make any sense.

Was he messing with her? Or had the torture addled his wits?

Either way, it didn't seem he was going to open up to her.

In that case, she'd just end it. Like she always did.

Her father had only told her to try, after all. She'd fulfilled that order.

"What worth is there in a world where children can't smile?"

"Ah..."

He spoke again before Miledi could condemn him.

She didn't have an answer. For once, she was dumbfounded. It felt as though she'd been stabbed through the chest. By the time she returned to her senses, Davy had stood up at the edge of the platform.

How can he stand with wounds that bad?

"Sorry, but I can't answer what you really want to know."

He tottered unsteadily. One more step and he'd fall. Yet his eyes burned with life.

"But I believe. One day, the world will be free."

"Free?"

She spoke it hesitantly, like she'd never heard it before. Davy's words didn't make sense.

Davy coughed up another mouthful of blood. He was practically dead. And yet...he smiled.

"Hey, little girl. Don't you want to live your life smiling?"

"Ah—"

Davy leaned backward and fell into the gorge.

He put an end to his own life, denying Miledi's right to execute him.

The wind blew across the empty platform. For a while, Miledi just stood there.

✤ ✤ ✤ ✤ ✤ ✤ ✤ ✤ ✤ ✤ ✤ ✤ ✤

From then on, Miledi often sunk deep into thought. She continued fulfilling her duty, but she would spend just a little more time talking to the condemned, asking questions her job didn't require. She came to learn what kind of people these criminals were.

Even she wasn't sure why she did it. But, as she continued, something built up inside of her.

One of the criminals was a man who'd lived by the northern lake. He had loved that lake, and prayed to the creature living inside it every day. That was a sin.

Another criminal was a merchant. He had given medicine to a wounded demon. The demon was grateful, and the two had formed a lasting friendship. That was a sin.

Yet another was a mother. She begged the Holy Church not to take her gifted child, at least not until they'd grown into an adult. That was a sin.

Yet another was a beastman youth. That was a sin.

Were they really sins, though? Some of the condemned were certainly criminals, and many of them deserved to be punished. But were their crimes truly deserving of death? Miledi couldn't allow herself to ask such questions. You did not question absolutes. Especially not if you were a Reisen.

Although Miledi kept telling herself that, the doubt had been planted. And it continued to grow.

One day, a maid walked up to Miledi.

"From today onward, I will be your personal attendant. My name is Belle. It is a pleasure to serve you, Milady."

The maid's curtsy was perfect. Her red hair was tied neatly behind her back with a ribbon. She was, without a doubt, beautiful.

When Miledi asked why she had been given a maid, Colt answered. According to him, by the age of ten she had acquired most of the knowledge necessary to be considered a full-fledged member of the family.

In a few years, he would no longer act as an intermediary for her duties. She would be expected to deal with the emperor and the Holy Church on her own.

Belle was the daughter of a nobleman's mistress, but she had been brought up with a proper noble's education. She would act as both Miledi's maid and her tutor, filling in the last few remaining gaps in Miledi's knowledge.

Miledi knew this day would come. She had no right to refuse, nor did she have any reason to. However, she wasn't the same girl she had been. With all the thinking she'd been doing, she found her new lessons distracting.

Still, after spending one month with Belle, Miledi had to admit she was an efficient teacher. No matter the situation, Belle never let her facade of elegance fade. Although it made her appear a bit stiff, it was still impressive.

In time, Miledi learned to conduct herself in the same manner.

She was grateful that although Belle was with her at all times, she only spoke when necessary.

However, she could always feel Belle's eyes on her...although maybe that was because she wanted to do her job properly. *After all, it is a teacher's duty to watch her pupils closely.*

At times it felt like Belle's gaze had some other meaning. Miledi shook off those thoughts, deciding not to get in the way of Belle's job. She had no interest in getting close to her, so there was no reason to think too deeply about it.

The day after Miledi came to that decision, something happened. For once, Belle wasn't following her around. After she finished work, Miledi returned to her room. She casually opened the door to her bedroom and found—

"Oh, welcome back, Miledi-tan~! You sure work hard for someone so small~!" Belle was waiting for her.

And she'd greeted Miledi in a ridiculously cutesy way. Belle was sitting on Miledi's table eating some cake.

Did she just call me Miledi...tan?

"......"

"Oh? Oh my, what's wrong, Miledi-tan? It looks like you're wondering why your prim and proper tutor is acting like this."

"......"

Belle grinned at Miledi. This was the first time she had seen her tutor smile. Belle looked satisfied, as if she'd pulled off the biggest prank.

Once the shock had worn off, Miledi found herself...

"Hello? Earth to Miledi-tan? Squishy-cheeked Miledi-tan~! If you're in there, then say something~! You're going to make me cry~!"

Disgusted. She found herself disgusted.

Belle wrapped an arm around Miledi's shoulder and pinched her cheeks.

Miledi had never been treated like this before. Although she was irritated, she was at a loss for how to react.

Belle was being exceedingly rude. She was the illegitimate daughter of a noble, while Miledi was a member of the powerful Reisen family.

Someone of Belle's station could be executed for acting so casually.

"Do you want to die?"

It seemed Miledi was even angrier than she'd realized. Normally, she would never have retaliated like that.

The threat had a different level of weight when it was muttered by an executioner. However, Belle didn't seem to mind.

"Come on, don't be so glum. Are you this cranky because your boobs are small?"

"Shut up!"

This was the first time Miledi had ever yelled at anyone, and it was over a stupid jab at her chest size.

That said, Belle's breasts were certainly something to envy. They were two mountains of enormous proportions.

Miledi was still a child, so naturally hers hadn't developed yet, but that didn't make the insult sting less. She was honestly surprised she cared that much about being feminine.

Belle shrank back and stared joyfully at Miledi.

"She got mad... Our Miledi-tan actually got mad!"

Miledi took a deep breath to calm herself.

"Is this what you're really like?"

"Yep!"

Belle grinned mischievously. Miledi did her best to hold in her mounting anger.

"I have no idea what you hoped to achieve by doing this, but do you really think such rudeness will go unpunished?"

"I do!"

Miledi activated her gravity magic, and Belle sunk to the floor. Unfortunately, the floor in this instance was a very luxurious carpet. It probably felt good.

"What were you thinking?"

Exasperated, Miledi canceled her magic. Belle continued rolling contentedly on the floor, heedless of Miledi's glare.

"I wanted to be your friend, Miledi-tan."

"......"

Miledi blinked in confusion.

"I've been watching you this past month, and I've decided I like you quite a bit, so I figured we might as well be friends. What's so weird about that?"

Am I supposed to laugh at that? I wasn't taught how to deal with this situation. The teachings of the Reisen family had no wisdom to offer. Without them to fall back on, she found herself confused.

"Hey, Miledi-tan, say something. Come here. Come on, it feels good."

Belle spread herself out on the carpet and patted it invitingly.

Do you realize how unbecoming it would be for someone of my station to do something so ridiculous? Miledi knew she should report Belle for acting improperly and have her dismissed.

"He he he. Welcome, Miledi-tan."

"Stop calling me that."

But before she knew it, she'd walked up to Belle. She spread herself over the carpet, her instincts ignoring the voice of reason that was screaming at her to stop.

It was quite fluffy. This was the first time she'd ever lain on it. Sleeping on the floor was something a noble lady should never do, after all. However—

"Well? Comfy, right?"

Miledi ignored Belle, who had ruined the moment. She could see Belle grinning again out of the corner of her eye. A strange, indescribable feeling welled up within Miledi.

She pouted and turned away from Belle.

Still, she couldn't deny what she'd discovered.

Being on the floor like this was exhilarating.

Despite Belle's rudeness, Miledi couldn't bring herself to punish her. In fact, she couldn't even bring herself to report her, or get her fired. From then on, Miledi's odd relationship with Belle continued.

Around her, Miledi couldn't keep her composure. The emotions she'd locked away for so long escaped when Belle was around.

However, they only acted like that around each other. In the presence of anyone else, Belle was the perfect maid, while Miledi was the dutiful, obedient daughter.

Even then, hints of their true personalities shone through.

One time, Colt was distracted by something when he gave Miledi her instructions for the day. Miledi took that opportunity to blow a silent raspberry. Belle gave her a thumbs-up for that. Miledi found herself addicted to the thrill of breaking rules, and began to incorporate gravity magic into her pranks.

Another time, Belle brought sweets to Miledi's room, and they stuffed themselves silly. Belle claimed she'd bought them from somewhere, but they tasted distinctly like the desserts the Reisen chef made. Miledi strung up Belle for lying while continuing to wolf down the stolen sweets. The despair on Belle's face as Miledi ate through them made her week.

As payback, Belle gave Miledi a very special book. She told Miledi it was a popular romance novel. She kept pestering Miledi to read it until finally she caved in and opened it up...only to discover it was erotic fiction. Very explicit erotic fiction.

Belle teased Miledi for days afterward about how red she got.

"Miledi-tan, what did you think of the book? How'd it make you feel? Hey, Miledi-tan, say something. It looked like you were really into it! So, what was it like? Come on, tell me!"

In the end, Miledi snapped and hung Belle from the ceiling for a day.

As those days continued, Miledi realized she was beginning to change. She couldn't express it very well, but she felt herself growing looser. Or perhaps 'softer' was a more accurate term. She could feel it.

She became certain of her transformation one day around two months after learning of Belle's true nature.

Belle was fixing her hair, and Miledi caught sight of her face in the mirror.

She had a relaxed expression on her face. That surprised her.

That's me? Since when did I start looking so lax? Miledi looked up and found Belle smiling at her.

Miledi blushed and looked away, but it was nice, having someone smile at her.

That feeling would end up changing Miledi's fate, though she didn't know it at the time.

⁕ ⁕ ⁕ ⁕ ⁕ ⁕ ⁕ ⁕ ⁕ ⁕ ⁕ ⁕ ⁕

Miledi had been ordered by Colt to interview a criminal.

The condemned was a young man charged with falling in love with a beastman, which made him a heretic.

"You went against the teachings of Ehit. A crime deserving of death. Do you admit to your crime?"

Miledi read out the charges and asked the usual question.

Regardless of his answer, his fate was sealed. As always, he didn't see the error of his ways.

"What do you mean a crime deserving of death? I did nothing wrong!"

"However, you did fall in love with—"

"Is love a sin?!"

"It..."

Miledi stopped short. A few months ago, she would have said,

"It is" without hesitation. But now, after all she'd come to learn, she couldn't get the words out.

"If you deny you ever loved that woman, even if that's just a lie, it may prove your devotion to Ehit. Your life may yet be spared."

"Huh?"

Even the young man wasn't expecting that reply. He'd yelled at Miledi precisely because knew there was no saving him.

However, the girl standing before him had a troubled expression on her face. He stared at her in amazement.

"I can put in a request for a retrial, but don't expect too much. If it goes through, lie like your life depends on it. For her sake."

"Huh? Ah, w-wait!"

Miledi walked away without responding. This was the first time she'd broken an absolute.

In the end, Colt denied her request for a retrial before it made it to the Holy Church. She was expecting that, of course.

The execution was moved up, and the man was dropped into the gorge the same day.

But things weren't the same anymore.

Miledi had done something uncharacteristic.

She was so efficient at her job that her father was planning to make her the next head, yet she had covered for a criminal. That wasn't something Colt could ignore.

Who is it? Who is it that corrupted the future head of the Reisen family? Who put these ideas into her head? Colt poured all of his family's resources into finding the culprit.

As a result—

❖ ❖ ❖ ❖ ❖ ❖ ❖ ❖ ❖ ❖ ❖ ❖ ❖ ❖

"Belle!"

"Miledi-sama..."

Miledi watched as Colt's soldiers rushed into her room and arrested Belle.

Miledi rounded on Colt, who followed in after his soldiers.

"Father, what is the meaning of this? She is my—"

"Your what, exactly?"

Miledi flinched. His voice was colder than ice. Colt threw a sheaf of documents at her. As she read them, Miledi's eyes went wide.

"That woman is a member of an anti-church organization. We are conducting an investigation into the noble who vouched for her identity. She's someone to be feared if she truly did manipulate a noble family... Take her away."

At Colt's command, the soldiers roughly marched Belle away.

"B-Belle!"

"It's all true, Miledi-tan."

Despite the situation, Belle smiled. Colt and the others assumed her words were a confession. They thought that since her secret was revealed, she'd decided to admit her deception. However, Miledi knew. She knew what those words really meant.

Belle meant those days they'd spent together and the smiles they'd shared had all been real. They were no lie.

Miledi tried to chase after Belle, but Colt stopped her with a few harsh words.

"Letting yourself be fooled by a heretic was a serious blunder. Compose yourself, Miledi Reisen. This is your last chance. A Reisen who cannot perform their duty is of no value."

Miledi stopped in her tracks.

Colt harrumphed, and with one last disappointed look, left the room.

An oppressive silence followed. Miledi simply stood there, staring at the door.

That night, she slipped past the guards and headed to the prison. She was going to meet Belle.

"......"

When she reached Belle's cell, she was speechless. Belle had clearly been tortured. Deep, fresh cuts covered her from head to toe. She was handcuffed to the wall, and hung from it limply.

"Oh? Miledi...tan? You...came?"

She spoke slowly, pausing between words. The pain in her voice was evident. Still, Belle lifted her face and grinned.

Tears formed in Miledi's eyes. On her way here, she'd agonized about what to say, what to ask. She hadn't been able to figure it out. But now, with Belle in front of her, the words spilled out.

"Belle...I'll help you somehow, so tell me everything. I'll beg the Holy Church. I'll save your life, I promise!"

Miledi figured she might be able to convince the Holy Church to use Belle's knowledge to topple the rest of her organization.

She knew it was a long shot. It was a terrible plan, but it was the best she had. The absolutes and her lack of knowledge about the outside world weighed her down. As she was, this was all she could do.

However, when Belle saw Miledi crying and clinging to the bars, she smiled. The happiness in that smile was genuine.

"No thanks~!"

"Huh?"

Miledi looked up in surprise. She couldn't believe it.

"Ba ha ha... What's with that look? You're ruining your good looks with that expression. Well, I guess you always were a hopeless beauty. He he hee..."

"B-Belle!"

This wasn't any time for jokes. Miledi was angry.

Still, Belle just smiled kindly back. But since Miledi asked, she would tell her everything.

"Miledi, let me tell you my real name."

"Belle's not your real name?"

"Yep. My name is Belta Lievre. I was originally a member of the Lievre family. My family's been archbishops of the Holy Church for generations. And I was the divine priestess who'd received Ehit's blessing."

"A divine priestess..."

Miledi didn't know what to say.

A divine priestess had received a revelation directly from Ehit. They were among the highest-ranked members of the Holy Church. They held no direct political power, but their influence was great.

"When I was around your age, I also spent my time fulfilling my appointed duty. I'm an Atavist, too, so I can use special magic... Mine's divination. It lets me see the possible paths of a person's future."

"The paths of a person's future..."

Miledi absently repeated Belta's words. For some reason, they left a deep impression.

"Every day, I saw people who wanted to change their fate. There should have been ways for all of them to achieve happiness, but their fates were distorted by the values, the doctrines, and the principles of the Holy Church. Whether it ended up good or bad for us, everything bent to *His* will."

"His" will. Miledi could guess who Belta meant. Their lord and creator, Ehit.

"But I still believed. I thought Ehit's design would surely lead most of us to happiness. Even as I dealt with the grief and rage of the people, the bishops still told me, 'You did well leading the people today,' every time."

It must have felt awful.

Belta smiled bitterly at Miledi.

Ah, I understand now.

"Pretty similar to your own situation, wouldn't you say?"

"Yes..."

"Thought so," Belta said as Miledi nodded.

"Though to be honest, I didn't expect the heir of the ruthless Reisen household to be so kind-hearted."

I didn't expect it, either, Miledi thought with a smile.

"Just like you, I needed to see something shocking before I realized."

Before she'd realized how twisted this world truly was.

"One day I saw a certain someone's fate. No, that's not quite right. Rather, I couldn't see it. There was a girl whose future I couldn't read. All I saw ahead of her was darkness. It was as if she was alive, and yet not. She was...she wasn't human!"

Belta practically screamed those last words. Miledi realized she was shivering, as if she was terrified of the past.

"Belle... Belta!"

"Ah."

Belta took a few deep breaths to calm herself. Her eyes were focused on the present again, and she looked at Miledi. *What could have terrified a cheerful girl like her so badly?*

"That...that *thing* wearing the Holy Church's robes was unbelievably beautiful, but it was also not of this world. I was so scared that I prayed."

It was then that she received Ehit's words.

"You see too much."

When she'd returned to her senses, there was a shortsword sticking out of her chest.

Still confused, she'd slumped to the ground. It felt like the very source of her life was flowing out. She was going to die.

Before she lost consciousness, she asked something in a hoarse voice.

"Lord Ehit, why?"

The reply he'd given was beyond her expectations.

"We're free to do what we want with our toys, no?"

"I definitely died that day. Yet for some reason, I awoke in one of Elbard's back alleys, even though I should have been dead. All I was wearing was rags."

"So then..."

"I didn't know who brought me back or why, but I knew it hadn't been Ehit's mercy. He's not that kind of god. When I awoke, I heard a kind man's voice telling me to run."

From then on, Belta lived as an orphan. Her only possessions were her life, and the knowledge of what Ehit truly was. Her brush with death divested her of her special magic, and took most of her regular magic as well. Still, Belta tried to gather comrades to fight against this unfair world and its hateful gods. Eventually, she found enough people to form a proper organization.

"So when you came here..."

"In order to save my comrades, and any prisoners who might join hands with us, I infiltrated the mansion."

Although, Belta hadn't expected to meet a girl who reminded her of her old self... She smiled at the thought.

"Miledi... I decided to fight back of my own free will. That's something I'm never going to give up, even if it means my death."

Miledi understood that Belta would never give in. Miledi's words couldn't dissuade her.

"I-I can definitely save you."

Miledi sounded like a spoiled child. She couldn't even meet Belta's eyes.

"Miledi-tan...smile."

How can I smile?

Miledi just mumbled, "I know I can save you," one last time

and walked away. She told herself over and over that there had to be a way. However, no solutions came to mind.

⁕ ⁕ ⁕ ⁕ ⁕ ⁕ ⁕ ⁕ ⁕ ⁕ ⁕ ⁕ ⁕

She sat on her bed and thought. The question of what to do swirled in her mind, but nothing she came up with seemed likely to work.

She didn't know how long she sat there. Eventually, with no other ideas available, Miledi decided to beg Colt. She tried not to think of her previous failure as she headed to his room.

My only purpose is to fulfill the duties of the Reisen family. I'm just a cog in the execution machine. That's all. And that's absolute, a cold, unfeeling part of her mind whispered. She stopped in her tracks.

She didn't want to give up on the person who'd shown her how to feel. She started walking again and, before she knew it, she was in front of her father's office. Miledi took a deep breath, her palms slick with nervous sweat.

She steeled her resolve and knocked on the door.

"Huh?"

But there was no reply. Normally, her father would still be in his office.

"What's wrong, Milady?" a passing servant called out to her.

"Where is my father?"

"Were you not informed? He left for the execution grounds just recently."

Miledi's veins turned to ice.

"Now?"

"Indeed, Milady. He claimed the heretic was dangerous and needed to be dealt with immediately. Not only did she serve as your maid for months, but she was apparently the head of an anti-church organization..."

Miledi dashed off without listening. The servant yelled after her, but Miledi was long gone.

Cold sweat poured down her back. Sheer desperation lent strength to her legs.

This was too soon. Far too soon. Her father's interrogation of Belta shouldn't have finished yet. *So why is he doing this already...*

She finally arrived at the execution platform.

A crescent moon hung in the night sky.

Colt was standing before the platform, together with his soldiers.

Belta was nowhere to be seen. The execution platform was empty.

"Haaah... Haaah... Father. Wh-what happened to Belta?"

Please let me be in time—

"The execution has been completed."

Miledi's world went silent. Everything grew blurry.

Colt continued talking. Something about how Belta had confessed everything, which was why he'd executed her. He hadn't wanted to give her a chance to negatively influence the Reisen family any further. Miledi ran.

"Miledi! What do you think you're doing?!"

She jumped off the execution platform.

The wind whistled past. Casting oneself into this gorge that silenced all magic would normally be suicide, but Miledi could cast spells dense enough that the gorge couldn't disperse them.

"Obsidian Vortex."

This was the most basic of gravity spells. It allowed the caster to create a localized gravitational field and thus adjust their weight.

Miledi decelerated rapidly and landed lightly at the bottom of the ravine.

The moon's light barely reached the depths. Countless sinners had met their end down here. Miledi found it disconcerting.

She made a ball of light with magic and examined her surroundings.

"She's not here..."

Miledi had prepared herself to see Belta's broken body lying at the bottom, but there was nothing. *Don't tell me monsters already ate her...* Just then, she heard a roar a short distance away.

"It can't be."

Miledi dashed off toward the sound.

Rounding a corner, Miledi saw her.

A girl slumped with her back to the wall. It seemed she'd somehow managed to survive the fall and had tried to escape, but now she was surrounded by a few dozen wolf-like monsters. She must have been chased from the moment she fell.

"Bel!"

"Hm? Mi...ledi...tan?"

Her voice was weak. Miledi sent the ball of light ahead of

her, illuminating the area. It was then that she noticed...Belta was sitting in a pool of her own blood. Miledi could tell with a single glance. She'd lost too much.

"Graaaaaah!"

The wolves were overjoyed to have more meat. Their claws and fangs were dripping blood. Belta's blood.

Miledi felt something inside her snap.

"Die."

She said that single word in a voice colder than ice.

A second later, the wolves were crushed flat. The ground underneath them sank. They hadn't even had time to scream.

"Aha ha ha. You're...amazing, Miledi-tan."

"Bel! Bel, keep it together!"

Miledi rushed over to her.

When Miledi saw her up close, she grew certain. Belta's wounds were fatal. Still, she cast healing magic on her anyway. She picked the strongest spell she could cast instantly and used it. However, her magic was greatly weakened by the gorge.

"Shit, shit, shit!"

That was the first time in her life she had ever cursed.

Tears in her eyes, Miledi poured even more mana into her healing. She'd burn through it all if she had to. Belta raised a blood-soaked hand and raised it to Miledi's cheek.

"Hey, Miledi. Is working together...a sin?"

"Huh?"

"What about...opening your heart? Or...laughing together? Or...telling the person you love... that you love...them?"

"It's not a sin."

Miledi took Belta's hand into her own.

"Exactly. These aren't...things you can make fun of...and trample over. We are... humans are...not their...toys."

Miledi watched as the light slowly dwindled in Belta's eyes.

No matter how much she cried, no matter how much she screamed, she couldn't change fate.

Miledi saw her own tear-stained face reflected in Belta's jade eyes.

"You were like...a little sister to me."

"I thought of you like my big sister, too."

Belta smiled.

"I pray...the time comes...that humans can live...freely. I pray for a world where you can...smile..."

Belta's hand went limp.

A young girl's cries echoed throughout the gorge.

❖ ❖ ❖ ❖ ❖ ❖ ❖ ❖ ❖ ❖ ❖ ❖ ❖

Miledi took Belta's body into her arms and used gravity magic to fly back to the execution stand.

Colt was waiting for her. Not just him, either. Her mother, her grandfather, her uncle, and her cousin were there, too, along with a contingent of soldiers. Behind them was a row of people shackled together.

Colt stared at her icily. He never really treated Miledi like his daughter, but he had never looked at her like she was trash before, either.

"Do you realize what you're doing?"

Miledi ignored him and looked over the row of prisoners.

They were disheveled and watching Miledi in awe. No one had ever come out of the gorge. However, what surprised them even more was that the daughter of Earl Reisen had leaped into the gorge to save someone.

When she didn't reply, Colt threw up his hands and gave Miledi her final warning.

"Dispose of that trash."

Miledi turned back to her father.

"Trash?" she muttered.

Colt didn't hear her, and continued.

"This is my final warning. Fulfill your duty as a Reisen. Pass judgment on that heretic's comrades with your own hands."

To him, that was the only value her life had. Miledi hung her head.

She looked down at Belta's face, and came to a decision.

"I'm sick of this."

"Excuse me?"

Colt's eyes twitched, and he pointed at her. The Reisen soldiers unsheathed their weapons. They were planning to fight, but Miledi wasn't fazed at all. She looked up at Colt.

"I am Miledi Reisen. I am my own person. I am the only one who decides my life's purpose."

Those were words of rebellion. Miledi had declared she would no longer follow the family's orders. After all, to live as an individual meant discarding their ideals.

Colt sighed. His soldiers began chanting.

"It's a shame to lose the power of your ancient magic, but a rotten branch must be cut off lest it infect the whole tree. Eliminate her."

Up until the very end, Colt never treated Miledi like his daughter.

Miledi hugged Belta's corpse and steeled her resolve. Remembering how her friend always smiled, she grinned.

It was a forced, misshapen grin, but Colt and the others had never seen her smile before, and they hesitated.

Miledi looked down and spoke in a tone laden with emotion. "Eliminate me? I'd like to see you try."

There was no turning back.

⁕ ⁕ ⁕ ⁕ ⁕ ⁕ ⁕ ⁕ ⁕ ⁕ ⁕ ⁕ ⁕ ⁕

The sun had long since set, and night blanketed the sky.

After she finished her tale, Miledi fell silent.

"After that, I destroyed the Reisen family and freed Bel's comrades, the Liberators. They're the same organization I belong to. A lot happened, honestly. I had a run-in with a silver-haired nun while trying to find out if the gods really were evil. I barely escaped with my life. Then, I spent a long time training so I could get my revenge on her, saved a lot of other Liberators, protected people who came to us, scouted others with the same ideals... until at some point I became the leader."

Miledi laughed, and Oscar gave her a sidelong glance. Although she was always acting cheerful, he could tell her resolve was unbreakable. She wouldn't falter, even if she had to fight Ehit himself. The events that had built up her resolve were so heavy that Oscar didn't know what to say.

She looked at him, her eyes clear as a mountain spring.

"Bel was telling the truth, so I've been searching all this time for comrades who will help me fight against the world. Comrades strong enough to fight on even terms."

She repeated the same words she'd said when she first met him.

"And now I've finally found you."

Silence. Miledi had laid everything out for him. All that was left was to wait for Oscar's reply.

Oscar pushed up his glasses, hiding his expression.

"Miledi."

"That's me."

Oscar refused to meet her gaze, as if doing so would weaken his resolve.

He paused for a second.

"I...can't go with you."

"Ah..."

He noticed Miledi tightly grip her hands.

"Just like that girl was important to you, my family is important to me. Even if what you say is true, I can't afford to get them wrapped up in this."

Oscar stood up. Miledi gasped.

"I don't want to be seen with you anymore. Please, try and understand."

Oscar turned his back on her and walked away. A clear rejection.

"Th-then, can I come see you when there isn't anyone around tomorrow?"

Oscar stopped. He struggled to rein in his emotions.

"Please don't come near me ever again."

He resumed walking.

He didn't hear footsteps chasing after him, which he'd grown rather used to.

Oscar was silent for the remainder of the trip. His footsteps were heavy, and he took a long detour on his way to the orphanage.

Honestly, he just wanted to be alone. He told himself over and over that he'd made the right decision, that keeping his family safe was what mattered most. However, he couldn't banish the voice in his head that kept telling him, "You actually wanted to help her, didn't you?"

Don't you actually want to use your powers to the fullest? Don't you really want to help the people who need you? Why were you born with this power? So you could live your life hiding? Can you really bring yourself to abandon her?

"Shut up!" Oscar yelled.

He agonized over his decision, and before he knew it, he was on the same street as his orphanage. He knew he must've looked suspicious, mumbling to himself in the dark.

"This was for the best."

Even if the gods were evil, even if humans were just pawns in their twisted game, it was better to live out his life as an average person than to become a terrorist.

If his family was put in harm's way because of him, he knew he'd regret it forever.

That was why he'd made this choice.

He repeated that to himself over and over, trying to calm himself.

Starting tomorrow, he'd be back to his usual life.

He walked up to the orphanage, his stride confident, without knowing that the unfairness of this world had already caught up to him.

Oscar found himself in front of the orphanage. Something was off, though. It was long past dinnertime, but there was someone standing in front of the building. It was Moorin. She was looking around uneasily.

The moment she spotted him, she dashed over.

"Oscar!"

"H-hey, Mom. I'm back."

Oscar felt a rising sense of dread as he watched Moorin run over.

"Mom, what's wrong? Why do you look so panicked?"

He suddenly had a very bad premonition.

Moorin glanced about to make sure no one was listening.

"Oscar, you wouldn't happen to know where Dylan is, would you? He and a few of the other kids haven't come back."

"Dylan? No, I haven't seen him..."

It seemed that Dylan, Ruth, Corrin, and Katy hadn't returned.

Once they were old enough, the orphans started taking on odd jobs at nearby restaurants and workshops. That way, they could support the orphanage and make money for themselves.

Dylan and the others worked relatively close to the orphanage, and usually returned home together.

As such, they were normally back long before the sun set. If they were going to be late, at least one of them would come back to tell Moorin.

However, none of them had returned. Something suspicious was going on.

Oscar's heart pounded in his chest. He pushed his glasses up and tried to remain calm.

"Have you told the town guard yet?"

"Of course. But they didn't care. They told me they don't have the soldiers to spare to look for a few mangy orphans..."

Moorin bit her lip. Her frustration was evident.

"But, Oscar. They were acting even stranger than normal when I went to them."

"What do you mean?"

"I mean...it was almost as if they knew what was going on, and didn't want to get involved. Like this is part of something way bigger than just a few missing orphans. It was obvious they were turning a blind eye."

Moorin was exceptionally perceptive when it came to people. Oscar was inclined to believe her assessment. There was something bigger going on here.

He thought back to the disappearances that had been plaguing the city. The guard must have heard about them as well. And yet they chose not to get involved? *This isn't good... Does that mean someone with enough authority to silence the guards is involved?* Panic gripped his chest.

This wasn't the time to worry about keeping secrets. He pulled a metal sheet out of his pocket.

It was silver, and about the size of his palm. At a glance it seemed no different from a regular Status Plate, but its function was completely different.

"Activate protocol one. Trace targets Dylan, Ruth, Corrin, and Katy."

Oscar's activation chant sounded extremely mechanical, completely unlike most spells.

The plate glowed with a faint light. The light coalesced into four distinct points.

This was one of his artifacts, the Silver Slate. It was linked to the coins he'd given all the kids.

Those coins had been crafted with ore he'd enchanted with the light magic "Tracking." He'd then linked those beacons to his Silver Slate, so he could always know where they were.

Tracking was good for tailing targets, or keeping track of one's allies when visibility was poor. However, in both cases, it required the user to mark their targets beforehand.

Furthermore, if the caster's mana ran out, the spell faded. In other words, the caster was forced to continually maintain their concentration to keep the spell up. Despite its convenience, the spell was difficult to use.

Ore already enchanted with the spell didn't exist beyond what Oscar had created. Although its effects seemed plain, it was a high-class artifact and worth a fortune.

"The four of them are all together...and judging from the distance and the direction, they're...in the mine shafts?"

"Oscar?"

Oscar turned toward Moorin. She gasped, surprised by how serious his gaze was.

"Mom, I'll bring Dylan and the others back. Do you remember how to activate the orphanage's defenses?"

"Y-yes. I'll be fine."

Oscar nodded and continued.

"Don't set foot out of the orphanage tonight. I don't care who comes, don't answer the door unless it's someone you absolutely trust. Even if it's soldiers, chase them away with the defense system. Take care of the other kids for me, too."

"Okay, I will. But, Oscar...you be careful out there, you hear? I know you'd do anything to protect your family, but take care of yourself, too..."

"Don't worry. I'll be fine, Mom." Oscar smiled reassuringly, but it had no effect. She smiled sadly. *I guess I should have expected that.* Moorin knew her children better than they knew themselves. She even knew Oscar hid his abnormal talents to protect his family.

Long ago he'd been much more cheerful, always smiling when the things he'd created made other people happy. But as time went on, he got so accustomed to keeping that false smile plastered on his face that it had become the norm. Moorin watched as the eldest of her children dashed off into the night. He'd grown into a fine young man, but she worried he was sacrificing too much of himself.

❖ ❖ ❖ ❖ ❖ ❖ ❖ ❖ ❖ ❖ ❖ ❖ ❖

After leaving the orphanage, Oscar made a quick stop at his house. He wanted to stock up on equipment.

Once he'd grabbed everything, he dressed himself all in black. Black pants, black shirt, black boots, black coat. And, for some reason, a black umbrella. His hair was black as well, so it really looked like every inch of him was covered in darkness.

He blended perfectly into the night. Although, with his stylish glasses and umbrella, he looked more like a gentleman out for a stroll than an assassin.

"They're not moving..."

Oscar kneeled down. A second later, he leaped a dozen meters into the air and landed atop the roof of a nearby building. After that superhuman jump, he ran across the rooftops with unbelievable speed.

This was another one of his artifacts, Onyx Boots. They increased his leg strength exponentially, and were enchanted with wind magic to aid jumping. He could also create mini-barriers beneath his soles, allowing him to leap off of the air.

Oscar dashed over Velnika's rooftops with the speed of a gale. Before long, he'd reached the entrance to the Greenway.

The Greenway was the backbone of Velnika's economy, and many merchants, craftsmen, and adventurers made their livelihood from it. Because of that, there were restrictions on who could enter, and when.

But there weren't many people this late at night.

No one took any notice of Oscar as he passed through the gates.

He sped through the mine shafts, following his Silver Slate. He'd been in here before, but tonight, the light of the green glow-stone felt eerier.

He reached the end of the first floor. His beacon was nearly overlapping with Dylan and the others.

"Shit. I should have designed it to detect elevation as well."

At this distance he should have been able to see the kids, but the only thing in front of him was the tunnel wall, which of course meant that Dylan and the others were further below.

The problem was, he didn't know how far below.

"Wait, now that I think about it..."

Oscar recalled something an adventurer once told him. Apparently a lot of templar knights had been spotted in the middle floors of the Greenway, between fifty and seventy levels down.

Do they have something to do with the kids' disappearance?

"Guess I'll head there first... There's no time to waste, so we'll do things the fast way. Nothing matters more than their safety. Even if someone spots me, it's worth the risk."

Oscar concentrated.

A second later, he was surrounded by a swirling halo of mana. It was so bright that it lit the floor up like a sun.

※ ※ ※ ※ ※ ※ ※ ※ ※ ※ ※ ※ ※

Around the same time, children's sobs echoed throughout the sixty-fifth floor.

Inside the complex network of passages was a prison. The jail cells were carved directly out of the bedrock, with iron bars to cover the front. The children crying inside had been given only a single flimsy blanket to ward off the cold. They huddled together, hugging their knees.

Among them, only one boy wasn't crying. Tears welled in his eyes, but he stubbornly refused to let them fall. It was Ruth.

As Oscar had feared, Ruth and the others had been kidnapped on their way home. They'd all been given some kind of magical inspection, and Ruth alone was separated from the others.

What did they do to everyone else? Why'd they take only me? What's going to happen? Those worries swirled around inside Ruth's head, paralyzing him with fear. However...

Ruth looked at all the children crying around him. They were all around the same age. When he saw them, he was reminded of his own siblings.

"It's the eldest's job to protect his younger siblings."

The words of the guy he'd used to look up to, the guy who'd betrayed him.

"I'm nothing like that smiling idiot!"

Ruth used his anger to beat back the fear. He made up his mind and walked up to the bars.

He made sure there weren't any guards posted outside. After he was sure, he bent down and picked up a stone. He started scratching the ground.

He was drawing a simple magic circle. The guy he no longer respected had taught him that, long ago.

"You're just like me, Ruth."

Like Oscar, Ruth was a Synergist. Oscar's voice echoed in Ruth's mind. He was the one to teach Ruth the basics of transmutation.

Back then, Ruth truly respected him. Oscar was kind, talented, and always worked hard. He could make anything a reality, and had been scouted by the head of one the city's best workshops. It wouldn't be an exaggeration to say Ruth worshiped him.

He'd been prouder than anyone.

His dream had always been to be as good as Oscar, and have his name known across the world.

"I'm not gonna give up! I'm not a loser like you! I'm gonna be the greatest Synergist ever, just you watch! Transmute!"

Blood dripping from his fingers, Ruth placed his hands on the ground and breathed life into the circle. Bright orange mana illuminated his corner of the cell.

The other kids watched in astonishment. Ruth was trying to escape. They watched with glimmers of hope in their eyes. However...

"No...how come?"

Ruth's magic activated, but neither the bars nor the ground changed. Ruth chanted the spell again. He kept going until he was nearly out of mana. Sweat beaded down his forehead, and he shivered.

Unfortunately, reality didn't care how much effort he put in.

"Why?!"

Ruth's mana dissipated. He slumped to his knees and banged his head against the bars.

Despite squeezing out enough courage to fight back, he was unable to do anything.

"Are we ever going home?" one of the girls whispered.

The children's despair multiplied on watching their last glimmer of hope snuffed out. They resigned themselves to their fate.

"Don't worry, I'm here for you."

If it had been the old Oscar, Ruth might have even believed those words. If it had been the Oscar who hadn't laughed insults off with that creepy smile, he might have believed it. He would have continued to hope, and maybe share that hope with the others.

As it was, he couldn't. All that came to mind was the boy who'd accepted being called a loser. And so, he didn't say anything. He was about to give in to despair.

Just then—

"Hey. What was that?"

A suspicious voice called out. It didn't sound angry, but the children shrank back in fear.

One of the guards had noticed the light from Ruth's transmutation and came to investigate. The guard was actually a knight. He wore gleaming plate armor, and bore an insignia on his chest. He seemed conspicuously out of place in the Greenway.

The children didn't recognize the insignia, but most adults in the city would have. It was the emblem of the templar knights, the elite soldiers sworn to the Holy Church.

The knight didn't have his helmet on, but he still cut quite the imposing figure in full plate. Little wonder the children were scared of him. His intimidating presence left them all speechless.

Ruth scrambled away from the bars, tripped, and fell on his back.

The knight's gaze fell on him, then on what was in front of him...the transmutation circle.

"You brat... Were you trying to escape?"

"Hiii..."

A dangerous edge crept into the knight's voice. Ruth trembled, unable to do anything but scream.

"I guess I should have expected as much from one of the Incompatible. You don't even realize what an honor it is to be chosen... I was told to keep you lot alive, but no one said I couldn't rough you up a bit. Bad kids need to be punished, after all."

The knight raised his hand. The magic circle engraved on his gauntlet glowed.

Those well-versed in magic would have recognized it as the circle for the Fireball spell.

The knight looked down at Ruth's legs, his thoughts written all over his face.

There was nothing Ruth could do. He couldn't even move. And so, he squeezed his eyes shut.

The other children shrieked and backed away.

"I'll burn the greatness of Ehit into your flesh!"

◦╎◦ ◦╎◦ ◦╎◦ ◦╎◦ ◦╎◦ ◦╎◦ ◦╎◦ ◦╎◦ ◦╎◦ ◦╎◦ ◦╎◦ ◦╎◦ ◦╎◦

"I think not," a cool voice interjected. A second later, the knight groaned in pain.

Ruth timidly cracked open an eye. The knight was on the

ground, and Oscar stood before him. For some reason, he was holding a black umbrella.

"Huh? Ani...ki?"

"I haven't heard you call me that in a long time. I'm here to take you home, Ruth."

Oscar smiled gently.

For a moment, Ruth's brain couldn't grasp it.

His confusion was understandable. Oscar was wearing strange clothes and carrying an umbrella. More than anything, he didn't seem like his usual lazy, carefree self. No, this Oscar had a sharp glint in his eyes. He looked dangerous. With his graceful features and fashionable glasses, he looked more like the son of a noble than a man who'd come out of an orphanage.

Oscar looked down at the floor in front of Ruth. He stretched his hand out toward the magic circle.

"Oh," said Ruth. "The transmutation didn't work..."

"Yep. That's because of what the bars are made of. Here, let me show you."

Golden mana swirled around Oscar. He hadn't spoken a chant, or used a circle, but he still achieved what Ruth couldn't.

"The bars are made of sealstone. They dissolve mana. Most prisons use it, but even sealstone has its limits. If you put more mana into your transmutation than the ore can handle, you can reforge it."

Oscar transmuted the bars, turning them into ingots of lead.

Then, he kneeled down and looked Ruth in the eye.

"You did good, Ruth. It's because you used transmutation magic that I could find you so quickly."

"Aniki... I..."

Oscar ruffled Ruth's hair. Ruth's face scrunched up. His efforts hadn't been for nothing after all.

Oscar really had come to save them. When he'd reached the sixty-fifth floor, Oscar found the kids' clothes stored in a safe, along with their coins.

They'd been stripped of their possessions when they were kidnapped. It effectively nullified Oscar's tracking. He'd decided to search the rest of the floor before doing anything else, and found multiple templar knights on patrol. He'd grown more suspicious by the minute. Then he'd sensed someone using transmutation magic. One of the knights noticed, too, and went to investigate. Oscar stealthily followed.

Had it not been for Ruth, Oscar would still be searching aimlessly.

"I don't see Dylan and the others anywhere. Do you know where they are?"

Ruth wiped away the tears that had finally fallen.

"No. They brought all of us to this big building in the mines. There were these guys in white, and they made us all stand on this magic circle."

There weren't many buildings inside the Greenway. *And if they were all wearing white, it's obvious they're part of the same organization.* Something very suspicious was going on, especially considering the templars were involved. Oscar narrowed his eyes.

"I don't know what they were doing, but they said I wasn't compatible. They took Dylan and the others further inside, but they brought me here..."

"I see... I get it now. Thanks, Ruth. I'm glad you're safe. I guess I should get you guys out of here first. Come on, everyone. It's time to go home."

Oscar looked behind Ruth at the other children. They were staring at him in awe. His gentle tone helped ease their nervousness, and they began shuffling out.

"We're going home?"

"I can see Mommy and Daddy again?"

The children looked hopefully up at him.

"Yeah, don't worry. You'll get to go home and see your parents again. Just be quiet so the scary knights don't find you."

Ruth looked at the knight Oscar had knocked out. Although Oscar struck the knight with a surprise attack, he'd still downed him in a single blow. Templar knights were strong enough to take on five soldiers at once. No normal craftsman should have been able to take one out so easily.

"......"

Oscar didn't look anything like the loser Ruth was accustomed to seeing. He'd transmuted the bars with such ease, and there was a sharpness to him that he didn't recognize.

"What's wrong, Ruth? We don't have much time. We need to hurry."

❖ ❖ ❖ ❖ ❖ ❖ ❖ ❖ ❖ ❖ ❖ ❖ ❖

"I-I know that!" Ruth snapped back, irked at being interrupted, but Oscar didn't respond. Instead, he just smiled.

That was how he always was. Whenever he was faced with

something unpleasant, he just laughed it off. And yet, the smile Oscar gave Ruth this time felt somehow different.

Questions whirled around in Ruth's head.

Oscar led them through the cavern. Ruth trailed at the end of the line, carefully scrutinizing his brother's back. He was torn between believing in Oscar again and the voice in his mind that told him he'd only be disappointed.

Oscar felt Ruth's burning gaze, but he didn't address it. He focused on avoiding the patrols of knights and led the children to where he'd come down—next to the safe that stored their clothes and Ruth's coin.

However, , "safe" was perhaps too grand a word for what was really just a hollow indent covered with bars. There were spare workers' clothes and a few other miscellaneous tools stored there as well. It was obviously not meant to hold anything important.

Oscar transmuted the bars and walked through.

He put his hand to the wall, and mana the color of sunlight enveloped him. There was a warmth it that made it feel like actual sunlight.

"Wow, it's so pretty!"

"Amazing."

The children watched in amazement. For some reason this made Ruth blush. He kept stealing glances at Oscar's work, but tried to make it look like he wasn't interested.

Oscar's spell only took a few seconds. The wall was transformed into a staircase leading upward.

"Alright everyone, listen up. There's still other kids out there. I need to go save them. This staircase will take you all the way back to the first floor. Can you guys go up it without me?"

Was there a staircase like that on this floor? Ruth puzzled over that while the other kids exchanged nervous glances. They'd been hoping Oscar would take them all the way home. They were scared of going without him.

"Don't worry. Ruth here's my little brother. He's a brave guy. He'll lead you guys out of the Greenway."

"Huh?!" Ruth exclaimed in surprise.

The children turned to him.

He certainly was the only one to try and use magic to escape, so the children were willing to trust him.

Since he couldn't follow them out, Oscar transmuted a few maps. He carved out disk-shaped slabs of rock from the wall and engraved a map of the first floor onto them.

"Ah, my dad sells maps like this to tourists!" said one of the children.

The others crowded around, eager to get a glimpse.

Oscar's maps were so detailed that they could have been drawn by a master artist. Oscar's golden mana faded away as he finished working.

"Take these. I've marked the shortest route to the exit. Follow that and you'll be able to get out. Can I count on you to guide my brother if he gets lost?"

"I-I'm not a kid! I wouldn't get lost on the first floor!" Ruth protested hotly.

However, Oscar's words had reassured the boy. He was less nervous now that he had a role to play.

"I have one last request for you guys. See how there's another map on the back of these disks? That's the map to the Orcus Workshop. I know you all want to go home, but I need you guys to go there first and tell a man named Karg what's going on. I need his help to save the others."

In truth, Oscar wanted Karg to look after them. If the templar knights were involved, then he couldn't trust anyone else to keep them safe.

If the kids went back to their families, their parents would inform the guard. That was the last thing Oscar wanted. The guard would report his actions to the Holy Church.

But he couldn't tell the children not to trust the town guard, either. They'd assume that, even then, they could still trust the Holy Church.

And they wouldn't believe him if he told them not to. If anything, that would make them more suspicious.

So he decided to send them to the one person with authority that Oscar knew he could trust. Karg would handle things discreetly.

Oscar hid his true intentions with an explanation that was easier swallow. Ruth stared at him suspiciously, but the kids were all eager to get going. They puffed out their chests and said things like "Leave it to us!" or "We'll do it!"

"Thanks. You're all really brave."

The kids blushed in embarrassment. Oscar ushered them forward, and they began climbing the steps.

As always, Ruth took the position of rearguard. Although,

this time, he did so because he wanted to talk to Oscar before leaving. Once they were alone, though, he found himself at a loss for words.

"Go on, Ruth. We don't have much time. You know the first floor better than anyone, and you've met the old geezer before."

"I-I know. But...Aniki, you really weren't—"

Oscar knew what Ruth was trying to say, but he interrupted him before Ruth could finish.

"Ruth, get down!"

"Ah?!"

Oscar pulled Ruth close and buried him under his coat. A gust of hot wind blew past them, and there was a loud boom.

Oscar's black coat deflected the attack, but Ruth paled when he turned to look.

"Wh-what the?"

"I had to make sure the kids were safe, but it looks like I wasted too much time..."

The bottom part of the staircase was a smoldering mess.

Ruth realized what must have happened, and his heart sank.

"Stealing an offering to Ehit is an offense punishable by death."

Ten templar knights rounded the corner, their armor clanking. One of them had his arm outstretched.

He was the one who'd shot those flames. Thankfully, the children were already climbing, so they hadn't been hit by the spell.

The knights formed a semi-circle around the cavity. Since it was just an indent transformed into a storage area, it was effectively a dead-end. The knights were blocking the only way out.

Oscar glanced back. For Ruth to escape, he needed to douse the flames and transmute the stairs again. Then, he'd have to create a wall around them using sealstone to keep the knights from chasing after the kids.

"Trying to run away, are we? Let's see you try, you little heretic. We'll end you the moment you turn your back."

Oscar would have to deal with the knights first.

He prepared to fight.

He'd brought this upon himself. From a purely logical standpoint, it would have been better to let Ruth burn. He wouldn't have died, and Oscar could have healed him later. Then, he could go to Dylan and the others right away, and they could escape.

Though I probably couldn't ever forgive myself... Oscar smiled bitterly.

The knights drew their swords. One of them was glowing with mana and stuck a hand out. Judging by the force of the previous spell, Oscar guessed it was the intermediate-rank Crimson Javelin.

Strong enough to melt even their bones.

"A-Aniki, don't! I-If you apologize I'm sure—"

Ruth tugged at Oscar's coat. He still thought they could get out of this. *If only you knew.*

Ruth didn't think they could win a fight. After all, Oscar was up against templar knights. The best of the best, strong enough to kick about normal soldiers with ease. Even if Oscar was hiding his talents, he was still just a Synergist. A blacksmith, not a warrior.

Still, Oscar was determined.

"Don't worry. I won't let them hurt you."

He turned to face the knights. There wasn't a hint of fear in his expression.

Looking at him, Ruth was reassured. He stared at the back of the man he'd thought was a loser.

"You won't let us hurt him, huh? Looks like someone needs to be taught their place."

The knights were irritated. One of them scratched his chin thoughtfully. He came to some kind of conclusion and addressed Oscar, his voice dripping with casual malice.

"Here, I'll give you a choice."

"What do you mean?" Oscar asked suspiciously.

"You raised a hand against a templar knight. On top of that, you stole Ehit's offerings. A heretic like you deserves to be cut down on the spot."

"Your point?"

"Abandon the brat."

Oscar raised an eyebrow. He could see exactly where the knight was going. He didn't like it one bit.

"He's family, right? Well, dump him and beg for your life. Pray for Ehit's forgiveness. If you do, I'll consider letting you live. So, what's it gonna be? Throw away your life, or throw away your pride?"

The knights' shook with barely suppressed laughter. They were enjoying it. They thought they had an overwhelming advantage, and were using it to torment Oscar. They wanted to see him weigh Ruth's life against his own. They wanted to know what kind of person he was.

"Sheesh... I never realized you knights were so rotten."

"What was that? Bastard, I dare you to say that again!"

Oscar just shrugged his shoulders. He didn't look conflicted. He spoke relatively softly, but his voice carried thanks to the c avern's acoustics. The knights hadn't expected this response.

In fact, they were a little shaken by Oscar's unwavering confidence. He gave them a thumbs-up.

"The Holy Church, you templar knights, all of the priests, and even Ehit can suck my dick."

He turned his hand so his thumb was facing down.

"Wh-wh-what was that?! You damned heretic! Die! Be executed! Receive divine punishment!"

The knights' anger was unbelievable. They were so furious that they could barely form sentences. Their leader unleashed his Crimson Javelin.

"Aniki!"

Ruth's scream bounced across the walls.

The flaming spear hurtled toward Oscar. He could feel the heat coming off it.

"I wish you'd just done this from the start instead of trying that disgusting Q&A," he said, his voice completely calm.

"No way..."

The knights staggered backward.

The javelin scattered, blown away by a glowing object in Oscar's hands.

It was his umbrella.

He held it in front of him like a shield, and it completely blocked the intermediate-rank fire spell.

❖ ❖ ❖ ❖ ❖ ❖ ❖ ❖ ❖ ❖ ❖ ❖ ❖

"I'll start with you."

An umbrella that blocked magic. The knights were still strug-gling to comprehend that, but Oscar wasn't going to give them time to get their bearings. There was a soft whoosh, and some-thing shot from his umbrella.

"Guoh?! Was that an arrow?!"

Indeed, Oscar's umbrella fired a small metal arrow. It slammed into the breastplate of their leader.

"But something like this won't even pierce...ah?!"

The arrow possessed quite a bit of force, but nowhere near enough to punch through the knight's armor. So he thought there was nothing to worry about. How wrong he was.

The arrow emitted sparks, and a powerful electric current flowed down it. The knight was struck by an intermediate-rank lightning spell. Even someone as strong as him couldn't take that head on.

"Gah..."

He slumped to the ground, white smoke rising from his armor.

Oscar folded his umbrella. In that state, it looked more like a cane.

There was a moment of silence.

"You bastaaaaaard!"

"Curse you, heretic!"

The knights all charged at once.

Despite being in full plate, they were fast. One of them was mere feet away.

Oscar flung the hem of his coat back, revealing a holster strapped to his thigh. He pulled out the throwing knives and flung them.

They struck the ground inches in front of the knights.

"Hah, fool. You miss—"

The knives exploded, interrupting their taunts and sending them careening backward.

This was another one of his artifacts, Combustion Blades. He'd made his own miniaturized enchanted weapons. Enchanted weapons were, as their name suggested, magical. Most were rare and valuable enough to be national treasures.

And Oscar had just thrown a few like they were nothing. Anyone who knew their worth would have fainted. But Oscar made objects like that in his spare time.

The explosions threw the knights' formation into disarray. Oscar nimbly sidestepped.

"You really should pay more attention to your feet."

He hooked his umbrella around the feet of a knight and tripped him.

"Whoa?!"

The knight fell flat on his face.

The others quickly reformed and charged.

Oscar turned to them. His glasses emitted a blinding flash of light. These were his Obsidian Spectacles. He'd packed a multitude of features into the frame and lenses. A person like him wouldn't wear just any old spectacles.

"My eyeeeeees!"

As the knights stumbled around, Oscar pulled out more throwing knives and lobbed them. These didn't explode. In fact, a single glance was enough to tell that they were different. As they flew through the air, the knives glowed red hot.

These were Heater Knives. They sliced through the knights' armor like, well, a hot knife through butter. The heat melted any flesh it came into contact with.

It looked like their armor had gone through a blast furnace. The heat melted the knives, too, and they screamed in agony as the molten metal burned them to death.

The remaining knights backed away in fear, but Oscar wasn't even looking at them. His focus was on the knight in the very back. The one who was chanting a spell.

"Die, you monster!"

The knight Oscar had tripped earlier got to his knees and sliced at Oscar's feet.

Oscar stretched his left hand toward the chanting knight, and expertly blocked the other knight's blow with his umbrella. There was an unexpected metallic clang as the sword slammed into it.

"What kind of umbrella is that?!"

It was, of course, another artifact. It was enchanted with body strengthening, and made from an alloy of the hardest metals in existence.

Naturally, he didn't tell the knights. And it wasn't just the handle that was super-hard. The canopy was composed of metal mesh as well. The whole thing weighed a solid eight kilograms.

It made for a great blunt weapon. Oscar didn't feel its weight, since he was using body strengthening, but the knight definitely did.

Oscar snapped his wrist, flipping the umbrella around in his hand. Then, he slammed the handle into the knight's neck.

"Uwah, what the?!"

"Guaaah?!"

The blow sent one knight careening into the path of another, who'd been about to stab Oscar. Instead, he ended up stabbing his comrade. Unfortunately, the knight had strengthened his sword with light magic, hoping to finish off Oscar in one blow. His strengthened sword punched through his comrade's armor, killing him instantly.

The knight at the back screamed.

The few remaining knights turned around to see him stripped naked and bound head to toe in slender chains.

There was an ingot of some kind of metal at his feet, and white smoke rose from his body.

Upon closer inspection, the knights noticed electric sparks running down the chains.

The chains were sent by Oscar, of course. When he pointed his left arm at the knight, the chains flew out of his sleeve.

These were Metamorph Chains. Normally, Synergists could only transmute things they were touching, or things that were a short distance away from whatever they were touching. The chains helped overcome that restriction. They were made out of spirit stone, so he could control them remotely, and they allowed Oscar to accurately transmute whatever they touched.

Such a godlike feat was only possible through the combination of Oscar's outstanding transmutation abilities and his artifacts.

Without an incantation, Oscar transmuted the knight's armor into ingots, then activated the lightning magic he'd enchanted into his chains.

"Take him down with magic!"

They realized now that he had a myriad of weapons. Four of their number had already been killed. This was no longer the time to be cocky. They needed to take this seriously.

They fell into a proper formation. The vanguard would hold him at bay while the rearguard prepared their spells.

In the time it took for them to get into formation, Oscar pulled out another three throwing knives and hurled them at the backline.

"Don't think that'll work on us again!"

The vanguard batted away his knives. Since these knives didn't heat up, the knights assumed they were the exploding type. They figured they could withstand the blast and risked hitting them.

Their instantaneous judgment was truly praiseworthy. If these really were the same knives, it might even have been a good plan.

"The forecast for today is localized showers with a chance of hail. Do be careful when heading underground."

Oscar raised his umbrella over his head. It glowed golden with mana and, a second later, water sprayed from its canopy.

It was a strange sight, seeing an umbrella create rain rather than ward against it. But the knights paid it no mind and charged forward.

"Watch your step."

"Ice magic?! When did he cast that?!"

"The knives! They were enchanted!"

Bingo. The knives he'd thrown were Ice Daggers. They froze whatever they struck. The water Oscar drenched them all in amplified their effect.

The three knights in the vanguard had their legs frozen and couldn't move.

"But now you're finished!"

The rearguard had finished chanting their spells.

They held their swords aloft, their bodies surrounded by a radiant halo of mana. Their target wasn't Oscar, but Ruth. That way, Oscar wouldn't be able to dodge.

"Take this, heretic! Tremble before the might of the templar knights' ultimate technique!"

Oscar kneeled in front of Ruth and stuck out his umbrella. It was time to see if his shield could withstand the knights' strongest attack.

"Celestial Flash!"

This was the technique the knights were renowned for. Three shockwaves of Ehit's fury hurtled toward Oscar. Being able to use this skill was the requirement to become a templar.

Celestial Flash was an advanced light spell. It was so powerful that it could shatter through barriers. And Oscar was facing down three at once. Everyone expected him to die.

"Aniki!"

"It's fine."

Ruth was scared out of his wits, but Oscar was calm as always.

Boooooooooom...

The shockwaves smashed into his umbrella. There were furrows in the ground where they passed.

"That spell can take down even advanced-rank barriers. I don't care if you made that umbrella out of azantium. There's no way you can take three of those at...once?"

The knight lowered his sword. At the end, his voice trembled.

"This is the first time I've tested this against a templar knight's Celestial Flash, but I should have known Hallowed Ground could take it. It was worth spending three days enchanting it."

Oscar was completely unscathed. His umbrella wasn't even scratched. In fact, it was shining brighter than the Celestial Flashes.

He'd enchanted it with the strongest barrier spell known to man, Hallowed Ground. He had no aptitude for light or defensive magic, so it took him three days, but the result was the strongest shield ever seen.

And the umbrella wasn't just made of azantium. It was a compound alloy that included sealstone. Combined with a barrier spell, it became truly invincible.

"Impossible... There's no way! What in Ehit's name are you?!"

The ice holding the vanguard in place melted and, in their panic, the knights prepared to charge again. They'd lost their ability to think straight.

Oscar calmly snapped his umbrella shut and stood. Then, he held the handle in both hands and slowly lowered the tip.

❖ ❖ ❖ ❖ ❖ ❖ ❖ ❖ ❖ ❖ ❖ ❖ ❖ ❖

"I'm just your average Synergist," he said as he tapped the umbrella to the stone floor.

Huge cracks spread out from the point of impact.

"R-retreat! Retreaaa—"

The lead knight had a very bad feeling about those fissures, but it was too late. As he'd moved, Oscar transmuted certain points in the floor. Underneath a thin surface layer of rock, the ground was transformed into grains finer than sand.

That thin layer of rock wasn't able to bear the knights' weight, and it crumbled underneath them. They all fell into the sandpit. It was shallow enough for them to stand in, but they were so panicked that they looked like drowning sailors.

"*Cough*... You bastard! Don't think you'll *cough*...be able to *cough*...get away this this!"

"Transmute."

Oscar's voice was pitiless. Golden light surrounded the sand pit. It began to coalesce back into hard stone.

Realizing what was happening, the knights reached out for Oscar.

"N-no, please, forgive—"

"Will you value human life more than Ehit's will? I might consider letting you live if you do."

It was hard to tell if he was trying to get back at the knights for giving him two unreasonable choices, or if he truly wished them to realize the error of their ways.

It didn't matter; the knights were too stubborn to change.

"Nothing is more important than Ehit's will! *Cough...* How can you not realize that?! If you repent your sins now, you might still be—"

Oscar thought they'd been begging for forgiveness, but it seemed they'd actually been trying to say, "Forgiveness is still within your reach."

"Didn't even want to consider it, huh?" Oscar muttered quietly as he sealed the knights into their stone tomb.

Once the deed was done, he breathed a tired sigh. It was his first time facing templar knights, and he'd been rather nervous.

He relaxed now, though, and because of that he didn't notice the figure hiding further down the passage. Nor did he notice when it dashed off.

*/• •/• •/• •/• •/• •/• •/• •/• •/• •/• •/• •/• •/•

Ruth watched in amazement as Oscar buried the templar knights alive.

He wasn't confused by Oscar's unbelievable strength. In fact, a sense of happiness he couldn't quite describe welled up within him.

The brother he'd admired for so long really wasn't a loser. He had the courage to come down here alone, just to rescue his family. And his Synergist skills were even greater than Ruth had thought.

He was so strong that even templar knights couldn't beat him. His abilities far surpassed that of any normal Synergist.

No, surpassed wasn't quite the right term. He'd been able to transmute sealstone, an ore that was supposed to resist magic. Ruth realized that Oscar had made that staircase heading straight to the first floor, too. It must have been how he'd reached Ruth so quickly. *How good do you have to be to make a sixty-five-floor staircase in a few seconds?*

This was what it meant to be a master. All of the various tools Oscar had used to defeat the templar knights were artifact-level masterpieces, and he'd made them all himself.

Ruth didn't know why Oscar hid his talent, but that didn't really matter. *Aniki's even greater than I thought he was!* That was what was important.

"Ruth, are you alright?"

"Y-yeah! Aniki, I'm sorry I misunderstood you all this time..."

Oscar gently patted Ruth's head.

"It's fine, Ruth. It was my fault to begin with. Anyway—"

Oscar fixed up the staircase heading to the first floor.

"I'm sure the kids who went on ahead are worried about you. Go look after them for me."

"But...I want to help... You're going to save Dylan and the others..."

Ruth couldn't just leave his siblings behind. But more than that, he wanted to help his brother, to make up for being mean. He wanted to chase after him like he had in the past.

Just then, the pair heard the familiar clanking of plate armor. The knights were overconfident and hadn't bothered to request backup. That was a real help while he was fighting, but other squads must have heard the commotion.

"Hurry up and go, Ruth."

"But—"

Ruth glanced back and forth between Oscar and the staircase. Oscar smiled fearlessly, something Ruth had never seen him do.

"I'll take care of Dylan and the others, but you need to look after these kids. You're my little brother, Ruth. I know you can do this."

Ruth could tell Oscar was trying to give him a way to keep his dignity, but there was no way he could say no. He bounded up the first few stairs and turned back.

"Aniki. Take a right at the fork we passed. From there, follow the path with a low ceiling made of flamrock. Then, go right where the walls are made of stratified shtar. After that, follow the taur and blastrock tunnel. Then, take a turn at the corner where the green glowstone is chipped! That's how to get to the building where they took us! Keep Dylan and the others safe!"

With that, he turned back around and dashed up the stairs.

Oscar was a little surprised at how detailed Ruth's description was. Still, he quickly closed the entrance, transmuting it to look exactly like the wall around it.

"He really is my younger brother. He'll grow up to be a fine Synergist."

Oscar twirled his umbrella. He smiled, proud at how much his brother had grown, and dashed off down the corridor, following Ruth's directions.

He came across a number of templar knights on his way. Some he defeated with his artifacts, others he buried in stone, and yet others he fled from by transmuting himself through the walls.

Finally, he spotted a glow in the distance. Not the natural light of green glowstone, but the soft glow of lanterns.

"Ah!"

Oscar hid himself behind a nearby boulder.

Ahead, the passage opened into a dome-shaped room twenty meters high. There was an ornate building in the center, and a veritable army of templar knights guarding it.

There were at least thirty of them. Judging by the building's size, the number of storage sheds scattered around, and the fence surrounding the compound, Oscar guessed that it was no ordinary facility.

Makes sense most of them would be here if they've gotten reports that there's an intruder on the loose. I don't regret doing what I did, but I really should have been faster about it... Now then, how to handle this? Should I just transmute an underground tunnel leading directly into the building?

Before he could put his plan into action, however, he was spotted.

"Get out here, heretic. We know you're hiding." An old, grizzled voice echoed through the room.

Guess they found me.

Of course, he had no reason to show himself. He could hear men closing in from behind as well. It was time to make himself scarce. He put his hands on the ground, preparing to transmute a new hiding place.

Sadly, things didn't go as planned. In fact, the worst possible thing happened...

"You came to steal this kid from us, didn't you?"

"Ah!"

Chills ran down Oscar's spine. He poked his head out.

"Oh no—"

One of the men had Corrin by the scruff of her collar.

Why? How? Did they know Corrin was one of his sisters? But when did they find out? And who told them? Those questions whirled around in his mind.

His enemies shouldn't have known who he was. Had they assumed he was here to take all the children back, and picked a hostage at random? No. They wouldn't have said "this kid" if that were true.

Not only did they know who Oscar was, but they also knew who he was close to.

Where did I slip up? He had either defeated every knight he'd come across, or fled from them before they got a good look at his face. Or at least, he thought he had. It seemed his countermeasures weren't perfect.

He clicked his tongue impatiently and stepped out into the open. Corrin smiled when she saw Oscar.

"Ah, Onii—ow!"

The man holding her tightened his grip on her neck. Her face twisted in pain.

"Stop tormenting little kids. Don't you have even a shred of humanity left?"

"What would a heretic like you know about humanity? Know your place, you Orcus Workshop dropout."

They exchanged insults. Oscar was surprised how much information they'd gathered on him. He adjusted his glasses to hide his shock. And, at the same time, he examined the man.

His face had more wrinkles than he could count. However, the flames of ambition still burned brightly in his eyes. Old though he was, it seemed his hunger for power hadn't faded.

His clothes, too, stood out. They were made of high-quality fabric, and were ornately decorated. It was clearly a priest's garment. No low-ranking deacon or curate's habit, either.

These were the robes of a bishop...the bishop of Velka.

"Those clothes, and that face... I remember who you are. So you were behind the kidnappings, Forneus Abyssion."

Although he didn't believe, Oscar had still joined the Holy Church to avoid raising suspicion. But he couldn't stomach their doctrine and rarely showed up. Still, he had a vague recollection of the bishop.

Forneus' eyes narrowed in anger.

"You thrice-damned heretic. How dare you forget the face of your exalted bishop? Such a heinous crime is deserving of death!"

There sure are a lot of crimes punishable by death...

The bishop went on to talk about how dangerous heretics were, how wonderful the Holy Church was, and how he'd been ordained by Ehit for this holy mission. Oscar ignored him.

He'd provoked the bishop to buy himself some time. During the rant, he transmuted the ground underneath them, turning the terrain to his advantage. Then, he quietly sent out his Metamorph Chains, setting up traps in various locations.

Oscar held his umbrella in both hands like a sword, tip pointed at the ground. His pose looked regal, like a knight standing before a challenger. He kept his gaze focused on Corrin.

Don't worry, Corrin, I'll save you.

Okay, Onii-chan!

They didn't need words to communicate. Corrin was scared out of her wits, but she had absolute faith in him. She managed a weak smile.

A panicked, familiar voice interrupted the bishop.

"L-Lord Bishop! Your glorious sermon is wasted on this worthless plebeian! Kill him and be done with it! So long as you hold the child, he cannot fight back!"

On hearing that voice, Oscar finally understood the situation. He knew why Forneus knew so much about him, and why he'd taken Corrin hostage. Most importantly of all, he finally knew exactly why his brothers and sisters had been captured.

It's them. Those adventurers had told Oscar they'd spotted them wandering around the residential district.

"You're the only reason I can think of for them to come down here."

Oscar remembered the words clearly.

So that's how it is. Goldenyellow mana swirled around him.

"So you're the ones responsible for hurting my family."

"Hiii?!"

"Uwaaah…"

"N-no, we're…"

Ping, Torpa, and Raul all took an involuntary step backward.

Oscar's eyes burned with anger as the light wrapped itself around him. His anger hit them like a physical force. Even some of the templar knights balked.

He had too much mana.

Oscar hadn't finished all of his preparations, but he couldn't hold back. He appeared calm, but when he saw Corrin, he was furious. He'd barely held himself in check when Forneus started talking, and the appearance of Ping and his cronies tipped him over the edge. And they'd done it all because of a petty grudge.

Because of these dumb bullies, Oscar's family was in danger. His loser act made them think they could walk all over him. He wasn't only furious at them, but at himself.

"How are you using your mana like that?! Don't tell me you're—ngh, you blasted heretic! Don't you care about what happens to her?!"

Corrin screamed as Forneus dragged her closer. He pulled out a magic stone the size of his pinky finger and held it to Corrin's mouth.

Oscar had no idea what it was, but that didn't matter.

He stuck out his umbrella. Forneus and the knights were still stunned by the monstrous amount of mana coming out of him, so they were slow to react. The umbrella absorbed all of his mana and unleashed an unbelievably powerful gale.

His Black Umbrella artifact had multiple abilities. This was the sixth—Godstorm.

"Nuwaaaaaah?!"

"Kyaaa?!"

The wind was powerful enough to send even the templar knights flying. There was no way Ping, Corrin, and the bishop would be able to withstand it. However, Corrin remained where she was. Oscar's chains snaked out of the ground and kept her from being blown away. Still, the wind swept her off her feet, and she screamed as the gale lifted her into the air.

The chains clanked as they wound back to Oscar's hand.

"It's...well, it's not alright, but you're safe now, Corrin."

"Waaaaaah, O-Onii-chan!"

Oscar retrieved Corrin and hugged her tight. She hugged him back, her head still spinning.

Once the dizziness faded, she looked up at Oscar and smiled. She had no doubt that his arms were the safest place in the world.

"Kill him! I want his head on a pike right this instant! Punish that heretic!"

The bishop and his knights were knocked around by Oscar's Godstorm. The bishop's once-fine clothes were smeared with mud and debris.

The knights charged.

Oscar stomped on the ground, holding Corrin in one arm. The ground glowed, and in seconds it was transmuted into a thick stone wall.

"You're just delaying the inevitable!"

One of the knights raised his sword and began chanting. He could shatter a barrier like that in an instant. Judging from the light running down his sword, Oscar assumed he was casting Celestial Flash. *So he'll just cut right through it.*

"Sorry, but this isn't actually a barrier," Oscar muttered, then thrust his umbrella into the wall.

There was a thunderous roar.

A second later—

"Gwaaah?!"

"Fuck, how did he cast something so powerful in an instant?!"

"Ngh... What in Ehit's name is that umbrella?!"

The knights screamed in pain and confusion.

When he struck the wall, he created a shockwave that shattered it, and sent chunks of stone hurtling toward the knights.

This was his umbrella's second ability—Wall Blast. It utilized a fusion of wind and fire magic to create an explosion. The blast was meant to knock down enemy attacks, but Oscar combined it with his transmutation to make it into an offensive spell. It took him nearly half a month to enchant his umbrella with that.

The fiery shockwave and barrage of rocks destroyed the knights' formation.

"Corrin, hang on tight!"

"O-okay!"

Corrin clung to Oscar's neck as he stabbed his umbrella into the floor.

A few meters away, the ground froze over. This was the fourth of his umbrella's abilities—Flash Freeze. Just a straight port of the intermediate ice spell. So long as he maintained the spell, it would freeze the area he was facing.

"Not this time!"

The knights didn't know what Oscar was up to, but they

weren't waiting to find out. Those still standing launched Crimson Javelins. Oscar found himself facing a crossfire of magical lances.

Using his Onyx Boots to enhance his leg strength, Oscar leaped forward. The javelins crashed into the wall behind him, exploding in a torrent of flames.

The knights fired another barrage, and this time Oscar bent his back right before the javelins struck, letting them pass harmlessly over his head.

Normally, bending so far back would have caused him to fall. Instead, the frozen ground allowed him to keep sliding.

"Curses, someone stop him!"

The knights watched as Oscar slid across the ice field. He was alarmingly fast. Any time he seemed about to run out of ice, his umbrella made more.

The knights pelted him with spells, but he proved difficult to hit. His speed and unorthodox posture helped him avoid them.

Eventually, his wild slide took him right to Forneus.

"Hiii! Get away from me! You fools, do something!"

Forneus' legs gave out, and he fell backward.

"I won't let you—Celestial Flash!"

A shockwave of light split the ground between Oscar and Forneus. It left deep furrows in the ground.

However, Oscar got back to his feet and leaped into the air.

"Fool, you're finished now!"

"You can't dodge midair!"

Two more knights unleashed their Celestial Flashes. They came at Oscar from both sides, catching him in a pincer.

"Actually, I can."

Oscar didn't seem worried.

He leaped up a second time, propelling himself even higher into the sky.

This was another feature of his Onyx Boots, Footholds of Light. He'd enchanted the boots with one of the most basic light spells, Holy Shield. Except he'd reversed the effect, allowing his boots to create platforms to jump off of, even in midair.

"What the?!"

"Impossible!"

The Celestial Flashes crossed paths underneath him and slammed into opposing walls.

Oscar swung his umbrella down at one of the knights, making blades of wind shoot out. The knight's armor saved him from instant death, but the wind blades were still powerful enough to slice through metal.

Oscar landed right next to Forneus.

"You move even a finger, and I cut your head off."

"B-bastard, who do you think—hiii!"

Forneus tried to protest, but fell silent as Oscar transformed the spokes of his umbrella into blades and rested them against his neck.

"You knights don't want your bishop to die, right? Then you better not move. Ping, you too."

The knights froze in place. Ping and his cronies had been trying to sneak away in the confusion. However, they froze in terror when Oscar's chains burst out of the ground in front of them.

After seeing Oscar beat down an entire squad of knights, while holding a little girl in his arms, they were absolutely terrified.

"Now then, Bishop Forneus...tell me."

"T-tell you what?"

"Isn't it obvious? Where Dylan and Katy are. The other two kids you stole from the orphanage. Actually, if you've got any other kids in there, free them as well."

"Free them?"

Forneus had been trembling in fear, but an edge of anger crept into his voice.

"Yeah, you heard me. I have no idea what you're planning to do, but whatever it is, it can't be good. Return the city's children to their parents."

Forneus made to protest, but hesitated. After a second of deliberation, a hateful smile split his face.

"Very well. These children were chosen by Ehit himself. There is nothing to 'free' them from... Still, if you really want to see them that badly, I'll bring them out. Enjoy your little reunion!"

"What are you scheming?"

"I'm just here to watch your touching reunion. See how your family has been transformed into part of Ehit's loyal army!"

Forneus' eyes opened wide. His gaze was directed at one of the knights.

"Don't move!"

Oscar's warning was unnecessary. The knight wasn't trying to move, although his mouth had been moving this entire time. However, as his helmet covered his face, Oscar hadn't noticed.

Nor had he seen the magic circle glowing on the inside of the knight's helmet.

He was using Telepathy to communicate with the people inside.

Unbeknownst to Oscar, they'd already unleashed the ultimate weapon. His warning came too late.

The knight didn't move, but the building's door creaked open.

"Grooooooooorrr!"

A beast's voice echoed through the room.

"What the?!"

Oscar turned to the source of the noise, but a giant clod of metal filled his vision.

"Ah?!"

Fortunately, he managed to get his umbrella up to defend himself.

The metal crashed into his umbrella with a loud thud, and the shock of the impact went down his arm. The force sent him flying.

Had he not strengthened his umbrella, and had it not weighed eight kilos, Oscar doubted it would have been able to block at all. Even if he came out of the impact alive, it could have killed Corrin.

Corrin screamed, and Oscar sent out his chains.

He transmuted the ground below them to cushion their fall. Then, using Footholds of Light and Updraft to adjust his position in midair, he landed on his back, protecting Corrin. His coat further cushioned the impact, making the landing smooth.

He rolled back to his feet, sticking the tip of his umbrella into the ground and grinding to a halt.

"Raaaaaaaaah!"

Another roar, this one much closer.

"Huh?! Ability Ten, Hallowed Ground! Activate!"

Normally, Oscar didn't need to call out the name of his abilities, since he could control mana directly. However, he was so flustered that he forgot.

Whatever they'd brought out was incredibly fast. It managed to keep up with Oscar after blowing him away. Then it followed up with another attack.

Golden light poured from his umbrella, and a dome-shaped barrier surrounded him.

The blows slammed into it, powerful enough to shake the earth.

It seemed there was more than one of whatever Oscar was facing. Swords and maces slammed into his barrier, and small cracks formed at the points of impact.

"Ngh! So strong... Who on earth are you people?!"

On the other side of the barrier, Oscar finally got a good look at his opponents.

They looked human, but unlike any humans he'd seen before. Their muscles bulged, they exhaled plumes of white smoke, and their eyes were bloodshot.

The one directly in front of him was the one who'd sent him flying at the start. He was wielding a giant warhammer, which Oscar recognized as the lump of metal that had tried to kill him.

Their blows were fast, powerful, and well-coordinated. Frankly, they surpassed the templar knights in every way. They were masters of their chosen weapons. Oscar guessed they were Forneus' elite guards.

Oddly, he couldn't shake this strange feeling. For one thing, they all looked too young to be soldiers. *They all look no older than teenagers. Actually—no—they barely look over fifteen.* They were practically boys.

Moreover, everything aside from their weapons was crudely made. They seemed to be dressed practically in rags. The same kind of rags that Corrin and Ruth were wearing...

"Onii-chan!"

Corrin's shout snapped Oscar out of his musings. He looked around and realized the knights were all chanting powerful spells. It looked like they were determined to bring him down.

Stop spacing out! Don't forget you're protecting Corrin! Oscar mentally berated himself.

It didn't matter who he was fighting; he would eliminate anyone threatening his little sister.

"Don't blame me for this!"

A wave of light pulsed out of Oscar's umbrella. He'd activated Wall Burst. The three boys trying to break his Hallowed Ground stumbled back.

After they did, Oscar held his umbrella high and dispelled the barrier. White smoke poured out of its tip.

This was the seventh of his umbrella's abilities—White Prison. The smoke was actually the high level earth spell, Petrification.

"Raaaaaah!"

The three boys' legs were petrified, and they roared in frustration.

Oscar nimbly leaped over them. A second later, a barrage of magic smashed into the ground where he'd been standing.

The entire tunnel shook. Cold sweat poured down Oscar's back. The knights were willing to harm their own allies to get to him. The three kids were close enough to be affected by the shockwave.

Oscar landed a ways away. Two shadows burst out of the dust cloud the knights' spells had raised and dashed toward him.

Although these boys were extremely powerful, and more skilled than he'd expected, Oscar could still deal with them as long as he handled things calmly. At that point, Oscar's only option was to go all out. Crush Forneus' spirit until he was willing to spit out Dylan and Katy's location.

"Wh-what are you doing?"

Oscar didn't even try and hide his surprise. He instantly put up another Hallowed Ground when he sensed the two new assailants, but when he saw who they were, his mind went blank.

Shaken, Oscar shouted again.

"What are you doing, Dylan, Katy?!"

The two people attacking his barrier were indeed his siblings. Dylan was holding a knife, while Katy wore clawed gauntlets.

"Dylan! Katy! What's wrong?! It's me, Corrin! Don't you recognize me!"

Corrin was just as shocked as Oscar.

However, neither Dylan nor Katy responded. Instead, they simply stared at Oscar with blank eyes, bloodlust oozing from every pore.

The knights hurled another barrage of Gale Claws, Crimson Javelins, and Celestial Flashes.

"Shit!"

Oscar thought back to what happened seconds ago. The knights hadn't hesitated to kill those boys along with him.

Oscar dispelled Hallowed Ground and activated his glasses' blinding flash. While they were still disoriented, he used his Metamorph Chains to grab Dylan and Katy and fling them away. At the same time, he leaped in the opposite direction.

He barely managed to get everyone out of the way in time. However, now Dylan and Katy were charging him again.

Their eyesight recovered way too fast! Things weren't looking good. Dylan and Katy closed in on him with polished movements. They definitely hadn't been like that before. Their proficiency with their weapons was unbelievable.

"Gwah?!"

"Onii-chan!"

He obviously couldn't fight back, but dodging would be hard. And he needed to keep Corrin safe as well. In the end, he was forced to take the blows.

Katy's clawed gauntlets scraped his neck, while Dylan's knife plunged into his side, and then his thigh. He only survived because his Metamorph Chains fouled their aim. Still, his wounds were serious. He was bleeding profusely.

"Dylan, Katy, come back to your senses! It's me, Oscar!"

Oscar leaped back with an Onyx Boots jump and tried to communicate with Dylan and Katy.

However, the two of them didn't stop. Ignoring his words, they cut off Oscar's chains. Then, with unbelievable speed and coordination, they chased him down.

It was almost as if they were different people. In Oscar's eyes, there was no way they should have been able to move with such ease.

But still... Dammit, those two are definitely Dylan and Katy! He'd watched over them their whole lives. There was no way he would mistake them for anyone else.

It was then that Oscar noticed something. Both Dylan's and Katy's faces were oddly flushed. Not only that, but their eyes were bloodshot, and their breathing was rougher than before.

Whatever they were doing was taking its toll, but they didn't stop.

"Gah! Dylan, Katy, I'm sorry, but this is going to hurt a little!"

Oscar stuck his umbrella into the ground. It unfurled beneath him, and electricity ran along its canopy.

This was the ninth of his umbrella's abilities—Spark Plasma. One of the strongest lightning spells. Normally it shot bolts of electricity at enemies, but by combining the spell with a metal surface, Oscar had transformed it into an electric barrier. By adjusting the amount of mana, he could control the voltage to stun instead of kill.

But Dylan and Katy reacted instantly, leaping out of the barrier's effective range. Still, the toll of pushing their bodies was beginning to show. They stumbled as they landed, falling to one knee. Blood dripped from their noses and mouths.

"Dylan! Katy!" Oscar cried out again.

He tried to run toward them, but the blood loss had taken its toll. His legs gave out, and he sunk to his knees. He was dizzy. Moving around only made him lose blood faster.

He didn't even have the strength to hold Corrin anymore. She tried to help him up with tears in her eyes.

"Well, are you enjoying your reunion?"

Oscar turned to Forneus, who was smiling sadistically.

"What did you do to them?"

His tone was surprisingly flat. Corrin shivered. She'd never seen Oscar like this.

"This was all thanks to His guidance. These children were chosen. They have become a core part of Ehit's flock. You see, they are the very foundation of what will soon be Ehit's Legion."

"Ehit's...Legion?"

Oscar took stock of the situation. He was surrounded by templar knights, and while Dylan and Katy were no longer bleeding, their faces were still flushed. As much as he hated talking to that fanatical windbag, he needed to squeeze as much information out of Forneus as he could. He'd take any hint that would help his family.

However, Forneus caught on to Oscar's plan and didn't bother answering. Instead, he smiled and switched topics.

"You've surprised me, Oscar. I thought you were just another heretic, but after looking at all those magic items of yours, I've changed my mind! They're all artifact-level! I didn't believe Ping at first when he told me you'd beaten down my knights. I thought those were just the words of a coward...but you've proven me wrong! You made all of those items, didn't you? I can't possibly imagine you being a loser, or a failure!"

Forneus spread his arms wide, carried away by his fervor.

Ping, hiding behind the building, poked his head out and glared.

"What're you getting at?"

"Work for me, Oscar. Kneel before me, and profess your faith in Ehit. Devote yourself, body and soul, to the service of our great lord!"

"And if I refuse?"

Oscar glanced back at Dylan and Katy. They hadn't moved since Forneus starting talking. Their loyalty made Oscar sick to his stomach. At the same time, he knew his answer.

"Can you really bring yourself to?"

Although it irked Forneus how little Oscar thought of Ehit, it did little to temper his joy at having him dancing in the palm of his hand. And so, he continued, making sure Oscar had no escape.

"If you show your sincerity to Ehit, I am sure he'll be willing to grant numbers Forty-Four and Forty-Five his protection. Though, if you refuse, it's possible they will join him in heaven."

In other words, either I join and he brings them back to normal, or he keeps pushing Dylan and Katy until they die.

Oscar ground his teeth. The word "fury" didn't do it justice.

Still, there was nothing he could do. After all, there was no telling what Forneus would do to Dylan and Katy if he attacked.

He could kill all the knights and then threaten to kill Forneus if he didn't turn Dylan and Katy back. However, there was no guarantee that would work. Forneus was a zealot through and through. Oscar doubted threatening his life would be enough. It was a risky gamble.

Besides, can I even beat the knights with my current injuries? His umbrella had a healing spell built in, but even if he could activate the spell instantly, the healing itself would take time.

He doubted his enemies would wait for him to recover. More importantly, the blood he'd lost wouldn't come back.

But, more than anything, he couldn't risk their lives.

"Dylan, Katy..."

They didn't react to his voice. He wasn't confident he could disable them without doing them harm.

He closed his eyes and considered his options. Then, with a dark look in his eyes, he glared at Forneus.

"You have to promise not to hurt Corrin...and the rest of my family at the orphanage. Also, you have to turn Dylan and Katy back to normal and send them home. Those are my conditions."

"Whether I do that or not depends on the depth of your faith."

Oscar gave in. Forneus' lips curled up into a sneer.

"If you don't promise me at least that," said Oscar. "I'll kill you all, even if I have to give my life to do it. At least that way, the other families will be safe. Don't think I've shown you everything I can do yet."

That was a bluff. Oscar was out of trump cards. Still, he was serious about giving his life to kill them. One look at the resolve in his eyes was enough.

Forneus frowned .

"Hmph. Very well, I won't touch the kids at the orphanage. But Forty-Four and Forty-Five stay with me. Who knows what kind of dangerous items you might make? If I turn these two back to normal, what guarantee do I have that you won't turn against me? You can transmute sealstone without trouble, so even a slave collar won't contain you. Until you've proven your faith, those two will stay with me. Don't worry, I promise to keep them alive until then."

"Urgh..."

Oscar ground his teeth, but in the end he nodded. He knew there was no way Forneus would agree without some guarantee. And like he'd said, methods of restraining Oscar wouldn't work.

He swore he'd get his revenge once Dylan and Katy were free.

Forneus called Dylan and Katy back to his side. Then, he ordered Oscar to kneel before him.

"Onii-chan..."

Corrin clung to Oscar's sleeve as he stumbled to Forneus. She knew he was swearing himself to a life of servitude, just to save them.

Oscar patted his clever little sister's head for what might be the last time.

"Don't worry. I promise Dylan and Katy will come back one day. You just wait at home with Mom like a good girl, okay?"

But what's going to happen to you? Corrin couldn't bring herself to say those words aloud.

He'd made his decision; nothing she said would be able to change that. Still, she clung to his sleeve, hoping to convince him to stay.

Oscar gently shook her off, and Corrin didn't have the strength to stop him. Throughout the fight, she hadn't cried even once. Now, big fat tears rolled down her cheeks. It pained Oscar to see her like this, but he turned around and faced Forneus. Then, he walked the last few steps toward him.

"Hee hee, don't worry. So long as you serve Ehit, these two test subjects won't die. I won't do anything to the rest of your family, either."

"You had better not. For your sake."

Oscar knelt before Forneus.

Forneus grinned wider, and he nodded.

"Now, swear your eternal loyalty to Ehit. We mustn't forget the formalities."

You just want to gloat, you old sleazebag. Still, Oscar's expression remained blank. He had never sworn loyalty to Ehit, but he would have to now.

"Almighty, all-knowing lord of creation, Ehit. I hereby swear my fealty to you. I, Oscar, dedicate my life, and my soul—"

All was left was for him to say "to you," but he never got those last words out.

A loud rumbling interrupted him. The tunnel shook so violently that chunks of the ceiling broke off and crashed to the ground.

"Wh-what's happening?! Is this an earthquake?! What is this?!" Forneus yelled out in confusion.

However, no one answered.

The knights looked around, clearly surprised.

And this wasn't Oscar's doing, either. Unlike Forneus, however, Oscar realized something. Because he was a Synergist, he was more in tune with the stone than the others.

"It's coming from inside the building? Shit, don't tell me we've got to deal with another crazy monster."

In a sense, they were about to have another "crazy monster" on their hands. However, it was not of the sort Oscar was expecting.

The vibrations stopped. Silence filled the room. A second later, the building's roof popped off. And from within came...

"Hiyaaah! Everyone's favorite gal, Miledi Reisen, is here to save the day!"

The building's roof floated in the air. There was no visible magic holding it in place, either. Miledi stood on top of it, striking a heroic pose. She made a peace sign in front of her face and winked at Oscar. He could have sworn he saw stars floating behind her.

"Wh-what on earth are you—!"

Forneus, Ping, and the templar knights all exclaimed in surprise. They were surprisingly in sync, and their eyes looked ready to pop out.

As always, Miledi did as she pleased, heedless of their shock.

"Mwa ha ha ha! You, the disgusting old man over there! Too bad, but O-kun's already promised himself to me~! Did you think you'd won? Did you really think you beat him? Hee hee hee!"

Forneus' veins bulged as he looked up at Miledi. Never before had anyone dared to call him a "disgusting old man." What infuriated him even more, though, was Miledi's playful grin.

She'd arrived at the absolute perfect time to save the day. It was almost as if she'd been listening to their conversation and planned her entrance. Oh, also, she'd blown the roof off of Forneus' precious building. He had plenty reason to be angry.

He opened his mouth to yell at her, but before he could say anything, Oscar looked up.

"M-Miledi? Wh-why are you here?"

Miledi looked down and grinned.

"O-kun, I can't believe you. If you'd just asked me for help, you wouldn't have gotten hurt like that, and you wouldn't have made Corrin-chan cry! How pathetic can you get? You even made a little girl cry!"

"That's not true! Okay, well, maybe it is! But still, I thought really hard about what you said and... Wait, this isn't the time!"

Even when she'd just saved his life, she managed to be annoying. The shouting exacerbated his injuries, and Oscar doubled over in pain. Miledi's expression grew serious.

"O-kun, I can't believe you. You should know he'd never keep his promise. They think anything's justified in the name of their god. Even *he* doesn't know how to turn Dylan-kun and Katy-chan back to normal."

"What?"

Oscar's eyes went wide in surprise.

Forneus flushed with anger.

"You bitch, I made that monument for Lord Ehit! How dare you destroy it! Oscar, is she one of your allies?! If that building is completely destroyed, these test subjects will never return to normal! Are you fine with that?!"

"Ah—"

Oscar felt as if he'd been punched in the gut. Forneus glared at him, imploring him to call Miledi off.

Oscar gripped his umbrella. However, Miledi continued cheerfully, unaware of the turmoil in Oscar's heart.

"Hm? Could it be you're worried about me destroying...this?"

She snapped her fingers, and a large object floated out of the roofless building.

"Wh-wh-wh-wh-wh—"

Forneus couldn't even articulate properly anymore.

Floating in the air, with chunks of it crumbling away and falling to the ground, was a section of floor nearly six meters in diameter. A complex magic circle was engraved onto the surface, with an altar of sorts resting above it. The altar was held up by a rectangular pillar in the center of the magic circle, and engraved with an eye.

"O-kun! This is what transformed Dylan-kun and the others. It's an artifact that holds the memories of ancient masters. Not only that, but it can transfer those fighting skills into other people. But this stupid bishop doesn't actually know how to use it!"

According to Miledi, the sheer amount of information was too much for the hosts to handle. Because of that, it suppressed their original personalities. At first, the subjects he'd tested went berserk, but after a while the bishop figured out how to control his super soldiers. However, he still didn't know how to turn them back.

Moreover, to execute the moves of master fighters, the hosts pushed their bodies far past their limits. They couldn't last long in that state, and quickly destroyed themselves. But because their healing abilities had been forcibly increased, their bodies regenerated over and over. Still, there was a limit to how long they could do that. Even with such powerful healing magic, a few battles would leave them dead and broken.

Dylan and Katy started coughing up blood just from moving around a little. It was obvious fighting for longer would be enough to kill them. *So the skills of the best warriors from the past were forcibly implanted into their bodies.*

"I crushed those knights' bones with gravity magic until they talked, so I'm sure of it."

"No...then that means Dylan and Katy won't..."

A despair-filled wail interrupted Oscar's trembling voice.

"My...my artifaaaaaaact... You have Ehit's Eyes! Aaaaaah, how could you?! You accursed, wretched harlot!"

Forneus tore at his hair. He looked completely deranged.

It seemed templar knights had stumbled across the artifact by accident when exploring the sixty-fifth floor.

Forneus received a report on what they'd found, and quickly formulated a plan to create an army of super soldiers dedicated to their god. The floor was also the perfect location to conduct his experiments in secret. His knights weren't skilled enough to carry the altar back with them, so it was practical as well. He'd excavated one of the larger rooms on the floor and constructed the building to serve as a base.

"This was meant to be my greatest offering! I would have created for him a legion of worthy soldiers, loyal to his every command! My achievements would have elevated me to the position of archbishop—no—even to the papacy! Aaaaaaaaaaaaah!"

That's what he sacrificed Dylan and Katy for? Darkness wormed its way into Oscar's heart. Flames of black hatred raged within him. He felt like he was about to go mad. Oscar gripped his umbrella tight and pointed it at Forneus.

"Don't cross that line, O-kun."

"Mi...ledi..."

Miledi floated down and put her hands over Oscar's. He was gripping his umbrella so tightly that his knuckles had turned white.

For some reason, Miledi's touch soothed him. The haze of hate that had been clouding his thoughts dispersed.

Forneus turned to Oscar.

"Oscar, kill that wretch! Don't forget, I hold those miserable childrens' lives in my hands!"

At Forneus' command, Dylan and Katy pointed their weapons at their own necks. With a single word, they would kill themselves.

Oscar ground his teeth in frustration. However, he was no longer fighting alone.

Miledi looked directly into his eyes. There was no cheerful frivolity there anymore.

"O-kun. Even if you join him, you won't be able to protect anyone."

She snapped her fingers again.

At her signal, Dylan and Katy lowered their weapons. Seeing how they were struggling to raise them back up, Oscar guessed that they hadn't lowered them voluntarily.

It was as if their weapons suddenly weighed too much to lift. Forneus watched in dumbfounded amazement.

"It's time for you two to rest," said Miledi.

Her voice was tinged with kindness. Dylan and Katy rose up into the air and floated. They tried to break out of her spell, but there wasn't much they could do. She tapped both of them with a light electric shock, making them lose consciousness. Then she lowered them gently to the floor, and lifted Corrin over to Oscar. Corrin gasped in surprise as she flew through the air.

She was still a little confused, but she hugged Oscar tight. There were still tears in her eyes.

"You weren't born into this world so you could suffer like this."

"Miledi?"

Miledi stroked Dylan's and Katy's hair.

"You focus on healing yourself, O-kun. Those injuries are pretty serious. I'll handle these fools. Okay?"

She stood up and turned to Forneus and his knights.

"The artifact's in my hands. I've rescued all the other children that were in the building. The ones you'd already transformed are unconscious and restrained. O-kun's a master of using artifacts, so I'm sure he can use it to turn everyone back to normal. Do you get what this means, you crazy monster?"

Miledi's voice was so cold that Oscar couldn't believe she was the same person.

The knights chanted their spells. Forneus grasped the crystal hanging around his neck and glared daggers. He opened his mouth to say something, but before he could, Miledi interrupted him.

"You face Miledi Reisen. This is checkmate."

Sky blue mana erupted all around her. It twisted into a spiral, its radiance illuminating the dark room. She floated up into the sky, as if the laws of gravity had no effect on her. Her blonde ponytail fluttered back and forth, and her blue eyes sparkled.

A swirling black sphere appeared between her hands. She set it to orbit around her.

Her mana capacity surpassed even Oscar's.

The knights were stunned speechless. Time slowed to a crawl.

Hovering over them like that, Miledi looked almost divine. Everyone was awestruck.

Forneus was the first to return to his senses.

"Wh-what are you fools doing?! Shoot that woman down!"

The knights came around and unleashed their spells. Oscar made to shout out a warning, but it proved unnecessary.

"Wh-what is that?!"

"My magic just...disappeared?!"

The knights' spells were sucked into the sphere orbiting Miledi and vanished.

This was one of her gravity spells, Spatial Severance. She'd created a black hole that absorbed all spells, regardless of their element. Even the knights' Celestial Flashes couldn't escape. An unbreakable barrier of gravity protected her.

"If I can just take control of her consciousness...!"

Forneus yelled and held up his crystal. It seemed it was imbued with some kind of mind manipulation magic.

The knights began chanting again, hoping to supplement Forneus' attack.

"Too late—Heavensfall."

Countless tiny black spheres popped up around her. They gathered above Forneus and the knights.

A second later, they all sunk to the ground. The knights didn't even have time to scream. They were flat on the ground in the crater Miledi had created, not moving. Forneus was barely conscious.

"Gah! Y-you harlot, what did you do?!"

Blood dripped from his mouth.

Miledi didn't answer, and instead shifted her attention to the knights struggling to their feet. It seemed they'd survived by casting body strengthening.

Miledi silently swung her hand down.

"Gwaaaaaah!"

"Uwoooooooh!"

They were using their swords as crutches, but Miledi's new spell drove them back to their knees. They screamed in pain as they were forced to the ground.

"Something's pushing down on—"

The knight didn't get to finish. With a thud, the crater underneath him grew larger. All of the knights collapsed.

They couldn't even croak out an incantation.

"You accursed heretic! You may break my bones, but you shall never break my faith!"

Although his robes were tattered, the man wearing them was anything but. Oscar fully believed Forneus would take death over renouncing his faith. Oscar guessed he was using some kind of magical barrier from the faint light around him, or a spell that absorbed mana. Whatever it was, it barely let Forneus withstand the weight.

"The heavens belong to the gods! I shall smite you down—Earth Blast!"

Having a large amount of mana was a prerequisite to becoming a bishop. A high-rank earth spell like Earth Blast was well within Forneus' capabilities.

The spell shattered the ground around the caster, and allowed them to use the resulting rubble as ammunition.

A hundred boulders of various sizes all hurtled toward Miledi.

"Miledi!"

Oscar shouted a warning. He was worried the sheer number of projectiles would overwhelm her. Fortunately, he was mistaken.

"Unbelievable... Even mass attacks like that don't work..."

Forneus' voice trembled in fear.

To be honest, even Oscar sympathized. Miledi stopped the boulders in midair, but they hadn't fallen to the ground. They too were orbiting around her.

"How is this possible! First, we have to fight a monster who can make artifacts left and right, and now you?! Why do heretics like you possess such power?! You disgusting, worthless, wretched, deplorable bitch!" Forneus cursed Miledi out with unbridled rage.

Miledi didn't even dignify that with a response. Instead, she raised a hand. The boulders stopped circling. She brought her hand down, and they all moved with her will.

She'd shaped the hundred boulders into a guillotine of rock. If it fell on Forneus, he would surely die. There was no dodging. He could only choose whether he'd be crushed, or have his head cut off.

This was the most bizarre execution Oscar had ever witnessed.

"I remember now. Reisen... Miledi Reisen. You were the daughter of Count Reisen. You're from that family of imperial executioners! Wait, your entire family was supposed to have died a few years ago. Why are you still—"

Miledi wasn't interested in entertaining his questions.

"Don't waste your breath. Like I said, this is checkmate."

Before he could finish, Miledi buried him under a ton of rock.

The floor reverberated with the sound of a hundred boulders slamming into the ground. For a second, Oscar was worried Miledi would bring down the whole cavern.

She protected Oscar and the kids from the shockwaves with a gravity barrier, but he deployed his own Hallowed Ground just in case, then stood protectively over Dylan, Katy, and Corrin.

Eventually, the noise subsided, and the dust cleared. Miledi walked down a flight of imaginary stairs and stopped next to Oscar.

"Phew. That's the end of Miledi-chan's one-sided slaughter. Did you see me, O-kun? I was amazing, right? I was like, super cool out there, right?"

She was back to talking in that same cheerful tone Oscar knew so well. He could hardly believe she'd mercilessly slaughtered so many people.

Oscar smiled at Miledi. It was an awkward smile, but this time it was one hundred percent genuine.

"You're...one hell of a woman, you know that?"

He said the first thing that came to mind.

⁘ ⁘ ⁘ ⁘ ⁘ ⁘ ⁘ ⁘ ⁘ ⁘ ⁘ ⁘ ⁘

Once the battle was over, Miledi waited for Oscar to heal himself.

"But you know, that's a pretty neat trick. You hold up your umbrella and it rains healing light down on you. Is this supposed to be a joke, since umbrellas normally keep rain off you?"

"I just figured the stretcher was the best place to enchant with healing magic. The ore's best suited for the purpose. It's not really a joke or anything."

The healing light of the high-ranked spell Benison Aura poured down on Oscar as he spoke. *Though, now that I think about it, it does make for a pretty good joke. I'm holding up an umbrella that's raining on me.*

His wounds had mostly closed up, and he looked less pale. Corrin snickered at him as he looked away from Miledi, embarrassed by his unintentional bad joke.

"Anyway, Miledi. How long were you inside that building? And how'd you get inside in the first place?"

He decided now was a good time to change the topic.

Miledi's grin faded.

"While you were fighting, I punched my way up through the sixty-sixth floor and snuck into the building from below. I lowered the kidnapped children down to the floor below. My comrades led them to your staircase from there, O-kun. I imagine they must have led the kids to the surface by now."

"By punched your way up...you mean you used that black sphere of yours?"

"Correeect~!"

"Since you know about my staircase, that means you were following me, right?"

"Yep. I know you told me to leave, but I wanted to say my goodbyes to the kids. Though, when I got to the orphanage, Moorin-san looked almost hysterical. When she told me what happened, I thought I had to chase after you, so I asked my comrades to guard the orphanage. When I found you, you were just leaving your house. You had an umbrella, even though it wasn't raining, and you jumped way higher than anyone should be able to."

So she went to the orphanage right after I did, then caught up in the time I was getting my equipment.

"Why didn't you say anything?"

Even if she'd decided to head to the building straight away, she'd had plenty of opportunities to talk to him before that. Considering her personality, he'd expected her to show herself.

Miledi looked around uncomfortably.

"Well... I thought you wouldn't want to see me, O-kun."

"......"

In other words, you're telling me that arrogant, straightforward girl got cold feet at the last minute? Wait. I'm the one who rejected her. No matter how outgoing and cheerful she is, that probably hurt. Oscar thought back to the sad smile she'd given him.

She was afraid of being rejected again, yet she'd still plunged into danger to help. Oscar couldn't even think of what to say. His musings were interrupted by someone tugging on his collar. He looked down to see Corrin staring angrily at him.

"Onii-chan, did you bully Onee-chan?"

"Huh? Uh, no I..."

Does that count as bullying? I guess it does. Oscar trailed off guiltily, unable to fully deny Corrin's words. Corrin looked from Oscar to Miledi, who was smiling awkwardly. That settled it.

"Onii-chan, when you do something bad, what are you supposed to say?"

"Huh?"

"Onii-chan!"

"Oh, uh, s-sorry?"

"Not to me, to Onee-chan!"

"Oh, yeah."

Eighteen-year-old Oscar had just been scolded by a seven-year-old.

Miledi burst into laughter. She'd been holding it in this whole time. She laughed so hard that she had to hold her stomach.

"Haaah... haaah... Oh man, my stomach hurts! O-kun, you just got lectured by a little girl! Aha ha ha hah!"

"Sh-shut up! Besides, you're the—"

"Onii-chan!"

"Guh."

Oscar groaned. Tears leaked out of the corner of Miledi's eyes.

Oscar adjusted his glasses and got to his feet. He had fully recovered. He snapped his umbrella shut, then turned to Miledi.

"Miledi."

"Aha ha ha ha. C-Corrin-chan, you're the best! You guessed it! O-oh man, it hurts to breathe."

"Miledi."

She stopped snickering when she heard the seriousness in Oscar's voice. With tears still in her eyes, she looked up at him.

"Miledi, I don't think the decision I made back then was wrong. You asked me a serious question, and I wanted to give you a serious answer."

"O-kun."

"I won't apologize. Still, there's something I need to say."

Miledi tilted her head in confusion.

"Thank you."

Her eyes opened wide.

"Thank you for saving us. Thank you for lending me your strength. I owe you a debt. Truly, thank you."

"O-oh... Y-you're welcome?"

Miledi hadn't been expecting that. She blushed a little, unused to such straightforward gratitude. The tips of her ears were red.

Corrin glanced between the two of them, her eyes brimming with a child's curiosity.

Oscar and Miledi stared awkwardly at each other.

"Ahem, anyway," said Oscar. "I've recovered now, so we should head back to the surface. You said that artifact was called Ehit's Eyes, right? I need to start analyzing it to figure out how to turn Dylan and Katy back."

"Y-yeah. Let's do that."

They looked away, both painfully aware of Corrin's gaze. Just then, they heard something.

"Gyaaah... Gaaah..."

It sounded like a pained groan.

Oscar and Miledi exchanged disbelieving glances. Miledi cleared a few of the boulders with a wave of her hand. They found Forneus lying underneath them. By some miracle, he was still alive.

"Y-y-y-you bastards... Face E-Ehit's wrath!"

He coughed up blood with every word.

Oscar couldn't believe it.

"How...how on earth did you survive that?" he muttered.

Miledi just stared in slack-jawed disbelief, while Corrin let out a small scream.

His body was crushed from the neck down, and his head hadn't come out unscathed, either. His skull had caved in, and his eyes were nearly falling out of their sockets. Yet, despite all of that, he still drew breath. He glared at Oscar with a look of pure hatred.

"Our lives belong to Ehit... We live for him...and we die for him! That is the only meaning to our existence! How can you not realize that?!"

Faint tendrils of mana began swirling around him.

Is it his fanatical faith that kept him alive? Regardless of how he survived, he looked terrifying.

"Die, die, die! Heretics, enemies of Ehit...you don't deserve life!"

He was no longer sane. Although he was on the verge of death, his expression was ecstatic.

Is he even human anymore?

"Oh Lord Ehiiiiiiiiiiiit, my exalted god! Watch my final moments! Know that until the last, I, Forneus Abyssion, was your loyal servant!"

"This isn't good. Miledi!"

"Die already!"

Oscar had a really bad feeling about the whole situation. Trusting in his instincts, he raised his umbrella and fired a needle at Forneus. At the same time, Miledi cast a gravity spell.

The needle pierced Forneus' head with a wet thud. Miledi drove the point in even further with her magic, to ensure the blow was fatal.

No human should have been able to survive that. Granted, no human should have been able to survive Miledi's first attack, either. However, Forneus' intense hatred kept him bound to mortality for a few seconds longer.

"Glory to Lord Ehit!"

There was a needle stuck through his head, and yet he was still able to talk.

Oscar and Miledi watched as his mana dispersed into mist.

A second later, a massive explosion rocked the chamber— or

rather, the roof. From what Oscar could tell, the explosion had come from the floor above. The tunnel shook from the force of the explosion.

More explosions shook the demolished building. They were smaller than the first, but they still blew out the building's walls.

"Ability Ten, Hallowed Ground, activate!"

Stones rained down from the ceiling. Oscar immediately deployed a barrier to protect him and Corrin.

Miledi's face twisted into a grimace as she saw the cracks growing in the ceiling.

"O-oh no, the ceiling's going to collapse!"

Miledi took to the skies. Surrounded by a whirling tornado of blue mana, she attempted to reverse gravity.

"Gaaah... Th-there's too much to hold!"

It seemed the previous explosion had destroyed the foundations of the entire floor.

Miledi's mana drained away at a prodigious rate as she held five hundred square meters of floor together.

"O-kun, I won't be able to hold it for long! You have to hurry and get Dylan and the others out of here!"

"But what about Ehit's Eyes?!"

"Why do you think I'm trying to hold up the ceiling?! We don't have time to carry that thing out, so you'll have to strengthen it enough that it won't break!"

Miledi could have easily evacuated everyone before the ceiling collapsed, but she'd tried to hold it up instead to buy enough time for Oscar to protect the artifact.

The only way was to transmute a box around it that was strong enough to withstand the impact. They could come back for it later.

"Got it. Just give me twenty seconds!"

"Nnnnnngh. I'll try!"

Miledi lowered Ehit's Eyes next to Oscar.

He put his hands on the ground in front of it and began transmuting.

He regretted not being able to take it back and save Dylan and Katy right away, but he shook off those thoughts.

"I'll make it harder than anything on Tortus."

Oscar's umbrella was crafted from the most resilient alloy on the planet. He'd mixed azantium with sealstone and a few other essential metals. And now he was going to melt it down to coat the rock tomb he'd raised around Ehit's Eyes. That, combined with the activation of Hallowed Ground, would definitely be enough to ward off the ceiling's collapse.

Damn you for making me do this, Forneus. Oscar really didn't want to part with his prized umbrella, but he had no choice.

"Graaaaaaaaah!"

Just before he could transmute it, Oscar heard a peculiar scream.

"What was that?!"

The room shook as something banged against the building.

A second later, an entire wall went flying.

A three-headed earth dragon emerged from the rubble. It was only four meters long, but the danger it posed was immense.

"Wait, what on earth is that monster doing here?!"

The dragon looked up at Miledi, reacting to her voice. She groaned.

"Graaaaaaaaaaaaah!"

The eyes in one of the heads glowed bright red, and it spewed fire at her. Even Oscar could feel the heat.

"W-w-wait, time out! Spatial Severance!"

Miledi's gravity sphere swallowed the flames. But she had to divert some of her power to do it. The cracks in the ceiling deepened.

"Miledi! Damn dragon, stop that!"

Oscar pointed his umbrella at the dragon and cast Spark Plasma. Bolts of lightning hit the dragon deadon. However, it barely made the monster stagger. Spark Plasma was Oscar's strongest instantaneous spell, and the dragon just shrugged it off.

"This isn't good..."

The dragon turned to Oscar. He'd succeeded in grabbing its attention, but he hadn't expected to do no damage.

However, for reasons Oscar couldn't fathom, the dragon didn't fire its breath at him. It simply glared at Oscar with its three heads... before looking away.

"Huh?"

Oscar followed its gaze. It was staring at Ehit's Eyes.

Why's it so focused on that? Either way, Oscar wasn't about to let this opportunity go. He quickly stooped down and told Corrin to get on his back. He belted his umbrella and scooped Dylan and Katy into his arms.

A second later, the dragon roared again.

"Graaaaaaaaah!"

This time it did charge. Oscar could feel his heart thumping.

He activated his Onyx Boots and sped away. He was worried about what might happen to Ehit's Eyes, but there was no time to fortify it now.

He leaped ten meters away, and the dragon crashed into the spot where he had been standing.

"Gaaaaaaaaah!"

"Ngh... Hallowed Ground, partial activation!"

Oscar dropped Dylan and Katy and pulled his umbrella out. He barely got his barrier up in time to deflect the dragon's breath. A second later, the breath's strength doubled.

"Nnnnnngh!"

Oscar was pushed back by the force.

He couldn't see it through his umbrella, but the dragon's second head had added its wind breath to the fire.

If he was pushed back any further, Dylan and Katy would no longer be inside the barrier.

Miledi's strained voice reached Oscar's panicked ears.

"You little...! Take this—Heavensfall!"

A massive wall of gravity pressed down on the dragon.

The breath attack stopped, and Oscar fell to his knees. Plumes of white smoke rose up from the molten ground. The heat was so intense that he broke out into a sweat. Although part of that might have just been panic.

He looked over at the dragon.

"So it can even take Miledi's magic..."

She'd succeeded in pushing it down. However, its legs were still planted firmly on the ground, and it glared fiercely at Miledi, even through the pressure of her spell. Heavensfall hadn't been able to defeat it.

However, Oscar noticed something.

"I knew it—it's protecting the artifact."

Despite the pressure Miledi was placing on it, the dragon didn't thrash around. It kept a careful eye on Ehit's Eyes and kept its distance to ensure Miledi and Oscar's attacks didn't accidentally hit it.

Oscar suddenly remembered an old tale he'd heard as a kid. Supposedly there was a treasure buried deep inside one of the labyrinth-like floors of the Greenway. Any adventurer who defeated the dragon guarding said treasure would go down in history.

Forneus gave his life to create that explosion above them. However, there'd also been an explosion inside the building.

There was only one theory that made sense. This dragon was the original guardian of Ehit's Eyes.

He guessed Forneus and his knights weren't able to kill it, and had sealed it inside that building. With his dying breath, Forneus had undone that seal.

"O-kun, I'm sorry... I can't hold it much longer."

Miledi's strained voice broke Oscar out of his musings.

He looked up and saw her grimacing from the effort of holding up the ceiling. Her eyes were squeezed shut, and sweat poured down her forehead. Even he could tell she was using every last ounce of strength.

She had her back against the ceiling and was somehow keeping it afloat while also putting pressure on the dragon.

She wouldn't be able to keep it up for long.

Suddenly, she smiled.

"Run away, O-kun. I'll keep the dragon and the ceiling at bay until then."

Oscar gasped. She was planning on sacrificing herself.

"I'll protect Ehit's Eyes somehow, too. Leave it all to the invincible...Miledi-chan! But even if I'm invincible... I can't hold this any longer, so run!"

How would she protect Ehit's Eyes while avoiding the dragon, all while the room was collapsing around her? Would she give up her life just to protect it with gravity magic? Even though she was almost completely out of mana? In all honesty, it was unlikely she'd be able to do it, but Oscar believed her. He knew she'd fulfill her promises.

She sounded as frivolously cheery as always, but Oscar knew she was just trying to act tough. Even now, she still hadn't broken. She would save Oscar and his family, even if it cost her life to do it.

Oscar glanced back at Dylan and Ehit's Eyes before making his decision.

"Miledi, could you kill that dragon with your remaining mana?!"

"Huh?! If I used it all on my strongest attack, I-I think I could do it."

Miledi answered the unexpected question almost reflexively.

"Perfect. I'll handle the ceiling. You get that dragon! As long as Ehit's Eyes are here, he won't move!"

"Huh? What? Wait! You can't do that! I swore I'd defend

Ehit's Eyes with my life—"

"As long as they're alive, I'll find a way to save them. Just you watch!"

"B-but!"

"Saving them would mean nothing if you die! If we do this, everyone will be saved! Please, Miledi! Trust me!"

"Ah!"

Miledi gasped, then after a second she nodded.

"Make your move at the count of ten!"

Oscar carried Dylan and Katy to the relative safety of the passage outside the room. Then, he shot the tip of his umbrella at the stone ceiling. It lodged itself into the cracks. Oscar remotely transmuted barbs on it to keep it in place, and thin wires shot out from it.

"Corrin, I know this is scary, but Miledi and I will get you all out safely, so just hang in there, alright?"

"Okay. I'll be fine, Onii-chan."

Oscar detached the wires from the umbrella and tied them to boulders he'd transmuted. After a second, he'd completed a makeshift gondola. He put Corrin and the others inside it. This way they'd be fine even if the ground collapsed.

He patted his brave little sister's head and returned to the battlefield.

As he made his way back to Miledi, he activated another one of his black umbrella's skills.

"Activate skill six—Godstorm, wide area variant! Transmute!"

A violent gale blew through the battlefield.

He'd transmuted the cloth of the umbrella off its frame and turned it into a multitude of metal strings, which flew up to the ceiling. Then, he used remote transmutation to make sure they stuck to the ceiling. It looked like he'd spread a spider's web across it.

"Miledi, now's your chance! Send that oversized lizard to hell!"

"Sheesh, you're such a slave driver!"

Although she was complaining, Miledi was enjoying herself.

The ceiling rumbled as she dispelled the magic holding it up. The dragon made its move as well. It opened all three of its maws, determined to exterminate the thieves who had dared defile the treasure.

"Let me show you my final trump card."

Oscar threw his umbrella, which at this point had been stripped down to the frame, at the three-headed dragon.

When it was directly above the dragon's heads, it exploded in a shower of sparks.

This was his umbrella's final trick, a self-destruct.

He doubted it would kill it, but it would definitely buy Miledi some time.

Miledi rushed toward the dragon, while Oscar leaped up to the ceiling. The two of them crossed paths in midair.

As they passed each other, Oscar gave Miledi the jewel that had been embedded into the umbrella's handle. He'd taken it out before throwing it.

Miledi gasped when she felt the vast amount of mana stored inside it. She glanced at Oscar and smiled triumphantly.

Then, with their backs to each other, the two of them used their most practiced skills.

"Transmute!"

"Nether Burst!"

❖ ❖ ❖ ❖ ❖ ❖ ❖ ❖ ❖ ❖ ❖ ❖ ❖

Golden mana ran across the cracks in the ceiling. At the same time, a pitch black nova descended on the ancient dragon, emitting sky blue sparks.

There was no loud bang, but vibrations from the impact could be felt. Miledi's deadliest attack was also her most silent.

At the same time, the ceiling repaired itself in the blink of an eye. When Oscar looked down, though, he found the ground had vanished.

"......"

The two of them gazed silently at each other.

Oscar hesitantly opened his mouth.

"I know I told you to send it to hell, but I never said anything about *making* a hell..."

"Ugh..."

"What the hell are we supposed to do now? This is way worse than a floor collapsing! You know that, right? There's no way I can fix that even with my Transmutation."

"Y-you don't have to yell at me! Even I know I overdid it a little! Besides, this is all *your* fault, O-kun!"

"M-my fault? You're the one who made a giant abyss! Quit trying to push responsibility on me!"

"No, it's totaaaaaally your fault! What the heck was in that jewel?! I thought it was some kind of artifact that stored mana, so I drew it all out, but there was way more than I thought there'd be! Like, tons more! Not even the rarest of artifacts even come close to that!"

"Uhh, well, it's, uh...a Divinity Stone I made, I guess?"

"Excuse me, I have no idea what you just said."

Or rather, I wish I had no idea.

A Divinity Stone was a legendary crystal that very rarely showed up in nature. It was pure, crystallized mana. Usually Divinity Stones took thousands of years to form. They could store more mana than anything else. It took another couple of centuries for a newly formed Divinity Stone to become fully saturated. Once it was, it secreted a liquid known as Ambrosia. Ambrosia was a miracle drug that could heal any wounds and cure any disease.

And Oscar had just said he'd "made" one. As it was just a crystallization of highly concentrated mana, it could be done. In theory.

"When I learned about Divinity Stones, I figured I might be able to make one, so I tried. Of course, this one doesn't secrete Ambrosia. It's only capable of storing mana. I thought if I kept pouring mana into it, it'd start making Ambrosia on its own, so I've been pouring some into it every day since I was twelve. I put it into my umbrella because it was capable of absorbing a percentage of the mana used in spells directed against me, too."

"I see. I don't get it at all."

Indeed, Miledi's brain failed to comprehend how Oscar had managed to make a mythical crystal at the age of twelve. She smiled, a look of pure confusion on her face.

"I can't believe you used six years' worth of mana in one spell, though... Haaah... Well, I guess we didn't really have time to discuss this, and it's my fault for not warning you, but... Ugh, I can't believe I helped you make a giant hole in the Greenway... I think I'm going to be sick."

Though I guess killing a bishop and his templar knights is an even bigger crime. It's a bit late to be worried about being arrested for vandalizing the Greenway. Oscar shook his head and shifted gears.

"Anyway, let's get out of here. Could you give me my Divinity Stone back, Miledi?"

"Uh, I still don't really get what you're saying," Miledi repeated, that blank smile still on her face. Except now there was cold sweat pouring down her back.

"Miledi, give me back my Divinity Stone."

"O-kun, I'm the kind of woman that never looks back."

"Didn't you tell me your entire life story a few hours ago? Anyway, where's the jewel?"

"D-down there, I think." Miledi pointed down at the bottom of the abyss, averting her eyes.

"Explain yourself. No excuses."

"I was so surprised at how strong my magic was that I accidentally dropped it. The end."

Oscar stared at Miledi with dead eyes. Miledi refused to meet his gaze, as buckets of sweat poured down her forehead.

Oscar glared at her for a few more minutes before sighing and shrugging his shoulders.

"Well, at least we're all safe. One Divinity Stone isn't a big deal."

"You're such a nice guy, O-kun!"

Miledi grinned, and Oscar smiled back. Then, they noticed Corrin standing in Oscar's makeshift gondola and waving frantically at them.

"Guess we should go," Oscar said lightly, and gave Miledi a high-five.

٭ ٭ ٭ ٭ ٭ ٭ ٭ ٭ ٭ ٭ ٭ ٭ ٭

Two days after the incident in the Greenway.

It was still early enough that the sun was yet to rise. Velnika, the capital, still slumbered. Oscar walked down one of the deserted streets.

He had a black coat on, was carrying a large bag, and had an umbrella belted to his waist, even though there wasn't a cloud in the sky. It looked as if he was about to set out on a long journey.

And indeed, he was. Today would be the day he left Velnika.

There were a number of reasons for his departure. The first was obvious. He couldn't remain here after rebelling against the Holy Church and killing Bishop Forneus. Of course, the evidence of his death had vanished into the bottom of the abyss. However, he couldn't be certain *all* of it had been buried.

Moreover, he had a lot of acquaintances in this city. If someone went after him again, it was possible they'd target his friends, just as they'd targeted Dylan and the others.

The second reason he was leaving was to find a cure.

They'd ended up destroying Ehit's Eyes. As they no longer had anyone to command them, Dylan and Katy weren't trying to kill him anymore, but had become empty husks instead. He'd tried all sorts of healing magic and even enlisted Miledi's help, but both Dylan and Katy remained in a coma.

Normal magic had no effect on them, so he needed to search for something new.

Before he left, he convinced Moorin to take the kids out of the capital. They'd be moving to the hidden village that Miledi's organization used as its base.

Miledi promised to protect Moorin and the kids. Even if she wasn't Oscar's friend, she still would have taken them. Dylan and Katy were important witnesses, and Corrin and Ruth now knew the truth about the Holy Church.

It was possible the church wouldn't care. Everything they did was sanctioned by the populace. But it was also possible they'd try and kill the kids to hide the evidence. In which case, an anti-church organization's hideout was about the safest place.

The kids cried when Oscar told them of his plans, but Ruth stepped up to comfort them. With Dylan in a coma, it was his turn to take charge. Ruth looked quite manly when he told Oscar to leave the kids to him.

Furthermore, Oscar saw the kind of comrades Miledi had with her. They were all highly skilled warriors, so he was sure that they'd be able to safely guide Moorin and the children to their village.

Miledi herself vouched for them, which was more than enough.

As she'd had a lot to take care of after the battle, they'd parted ways for the night.

Oscar then spent an entire day replenishing his stock of

equipment and setting his affairs in order. He'd set out early in the morning to avoid being spotted.

Despite the early hour, he avoided the main street and stuck to the back alleys.

"I wanna say my goodbyes to Gramps," Oscar muttered to himself.

Oscar had already talked to Karg. He'd explained what had happened and the reasons why he couldn't stay, but he hadn't really said goodbye. It was true that he was in a rush, but he also felt ashamed, as if he was letting Karg down.

However, what would really be shameful would be not saying goodbye to the man who'd done so much for him.

And so, Oscar found himself heading to the Orcus Workshop.

Normally, Karg wouldn't even be there this early.

But Oscar needed to leave soon. If Karg didn't show up, he'd leave his farewell letter and be on his way.

He continued walking.

"Ah..."

As he approached the gates, he spotted a man leaning against them with his arms folded.

It was a man he'd recognize anywhere.

"So you came after all, Oscar."

Karg spoke as if he'd expected Oscar to come from the beginning.

"How did you..."

"I knew you wouldn't be able to leave without saying anything."

He'd been Oscar's surrogate father for years, so Oscar's thoughts were as clear as day to him.

Oscar smiled awkwardly.

"You're going, then?"

"Yeah. I need to find a way to cure Dylan and Katy."

"Will you be coming back?"

"I'm not sure. Not for a while, at least. It's going to be a long journey."

"I see..."

The silence stretched. Karg could tell at a glance that Oscar's black boots, black coat, and black umbrella were no simple traveler's garb. He knew they were all powerful artifacts. That brought a smile to his face.

"Damn, boy, you're good."

He praised Oscar in his customarily coarse fashion.

Oscar blushed and smiled.

"I guess."

He was unable to hide his joy.

Karg walked up to Oscar. His expression was dead serious, and filled with conflicting feelings.

"Oscar. It's not really much of a parting gift, but will you take what this old man has to offer?"

"What is it?"

Oscar tilted his head in confusion. Karg nodded and spoke solemnly.

"I want you to inherit the name Orcus."

"Gramps... I'm quitting the workshop, so—"

"I know, but I still want you to take it. I told you before, you're the only one fit for it. You're the best damn Synergist I know. I refuse to pass the name down to anyone else."

"But then..."

Who's going to be the next head of the workshop? Besides, I might become a wanted man soon. Worse, the Holy Church'll probably brand me a heretic. What'll happen to the workshop if I inherit its name?

Oscar tried to say as much, but Karg cut him off. He was prepared for the consequences. He had been since he made his decision.

"Us craftsmen are a stubborn, peculiar lot," he went on. "Sure, we get jealous of each other's skills, but any craftsman worth his salt also knows shame, boy. None of them will ever be the next Orcus, and not just 'cause I won't give them the title. They all know you deserve it, and they'd be ashamed to take it from you."

Oscar's eyes went wide with surprise. He was sure all of the craftsmen thought he was a loser. However, the truly skilled members of the workshop had always known. Even if it grated them to admit it, they knew it.

Sure, Oscar never made any weapons, but the Orcus craftsmen were professionals. They could tell from the quality of his household products alone.

I really do have a lot to learn...not just in terms of my transmuting skill, but as a person.

Although he'd worked alongside them for years, Oscar didn't understand one thing about them. Not their pride, nor their feelings, nor their love for their craft. He didn't understand a craftsman's soul at all. Oscar closed his eyes, sinking into deep thought.

They understood how much trouble this would bring the workshop. Despite that, they'd still chosen him. At that point, he wouldn't be a man if he didn't take up the mantle.

He opened his eyes and stared back determinedly at Karg.

"I'll do it, then. From today onward, I'm the new Orcus. Oscar Orcus."

Karg's face lit up in a beaming smile.

⁂ ⁂ ⁂ ⁂ ⁂ ⁂ ⁂ ⁂ ⁂ ⁂ ⁂ ⁂ ⁂ ⁂

Oscar walked to the capital's main gate with a new spring in his step.

However, worry colored his face as the gate guard scrutinized him. Fortunately, he was waved through without incident.

Forneus' disappearance was public knowledge, and the city was conducting a full-scale search. The guards were on high alert, so they weren't especially suspicious of Oscar. It was only a day since Forneus' disappearance, and it was entirely possible he'd left on some secret mission with his templar knights. A man in his position wasn't required to report his comings and goings.

Only Oscar and Miledi knew he was resting at the bottom of the abyss, so a single craftsman heading out on a journey, likely to the next town, didn't seem suspicious.

Oscar walked silently down the main road. Before long, Velnika was no more than a dot on the horizon. Just as he thought he was far enough away that he could activate his Onyx Boots without attracting suspicion, he spotted a familiar figure sitting on a boulder.

Her blonde ponytail fluttered in the chill morning breeze. She swung her legs back and forth, as if bored.

Oscar adjusted his glasses. Then, with hurried steps, he walked up to her.

"Morning, O-kun. It's nice out today."

"Yeah, though you still look pretty bored."

Once Oscar drew close enough, Miledi hopped off the boulder.

"I'm not really the waiting type. I prefer action."

"Then why didn't you act? Don't you think it's kinda late to ambush me here? I was expecting to see you crawl out of somewhere ages ago."

"Hey, that's rude!"

Miledi puffed out her cheeks, and Oscar smiled. The two talked about what they'd done since parting two nights ago.

Miledi updated Oscar on Moorin and the children's travels, while Oscar told Miledi he'd closed off the staircase he'd made. Miledi also explained that, thanks to the false rumors her comrades had spread, the search for Forneus was headed in the completely wrong direction.

When he told her he'd inherited the Orcus name, Miledi congratulated him. Oscar blushed and adjusted his glasses, but Miledi saw right through him and grinned. She'd been around him enough to know his mannerisms.

Oscar cleared his throat and changed the subject, his expression serious.

"You've helped my family so much. Thank you. I owe you a

debt bigger than I can ever hope to repay. If you still want me to, I'll join your—"

"What's important isn't what I want, but what you want, O-kun."

Miledi cut him off with a smile.

"Forget all that crap about debts. Your future is for you to decide. You have to choose what you want to do. If the path you want to walk is different from mine, then that's fine. I won't abandon your family just because you won't join me. Don't you dare think I'd ever try and blackmail you like that!"

"Miledi..."

He didn't doubt her words. She wouldn't abandon his family over something so petty. Of that, he was certain.

The sun crested the horizon, and the world grew lighter. Miledi's hair sparkled in the sunrise.

✦ ✦ ✦ ✦ ✦ ✦ ✦ ✦ ✦ ✦ ✦ ✦ ✦

"But my wish is still the same..." Miledi whispered. Her sky blue eyes perfectly matched the color of her mana. Right now, the only thing they reflected was him.

"This will be the last time I ever ask you this."

Miledi sucked in a huge breath and held out a hand.

"You're an exceptional Synergist, Oscar Orcus. Don't you wish to see a world where people can live freely? A world where anyone can decry an ideology, where no one's values reign supreme, where those who call out oppression are not punished for it? Would you like to come with me and change the world?"

Oscar held his breath. Her words pierced right through him. He thought back to the day they'd first met. She'd captivated him right from the start, that night in the orphanage's backyard.

◦ı◦ ◦ı◦ ◦ı◦ ◦ı◦ ◦ı◦ ◦ı◦ ◦ı◦ ◦ı◦ ◦ı◦ ◦ı◦ ◦ı◦ ◦ı◦ ◦ı◦ ◦ı◦

He already knew the answer to the question he was about to ask, but he had to ask it anyway.

"Who...are you?"

The sun continued its slow rise.

Miledi could guess why he'd asked. She smiled, exuding a radiance brighter than the sun, and puffed out her chest.

"I'm Miledi Reisen the Liberator. One who fights against this world's gods."

I knew it. This is what it means to be captivated by someone.

He couldn't make this decision halfheartedly. The world couldn't be changed by resolve alone. Fighting the gods was paramount to suicide. Even a cat didn't have enough lives to survive that. If he followed her, he'd surely see hell.

But if it's with her, I don't think I'd mind.

That was what he truly thought, from the bottom of his heart.

Oscar looked away. He didn't want to let Miledi see him like this, but for a completely different reason than when he'd first refused.

He poured all of his feelings into his voice.

"I'll follow you for life, even if the path you walk takes us to hell and back."

He'd walk forward together with this unbelievably reckless girl.

Miledi's response was completely unexpected.

"Uh, well, hell and back is kinda...creepy, you know? I know you've fallen head over heels for me, but I'm not really into yanderes. Sorry, O-kun!"

Birds chirped nearby as the morning sun blazed down.

Aside from the birds, there was silence.

Oscar's glasses glowed, and his face turned beet red. He trembled, then pulled out his umbrella.

"Milediiiiiiiii! I'm going to kill you, you biiiiiiiiiiiiiiiiiiiiitch!"

"Kyaaaaaa, O-kun's snaaaaaaaaapped!"

Miledi turned tail and ran.

Oscar chased after her, fueled by anger and embarrassment in equal measure. Lightning, flames, and blades of wind shot out of his umbrella.

Miledi dodged each of them, screaming all the while. There wasn't even a hint of fear on her face, though. In fact, she was blushing.

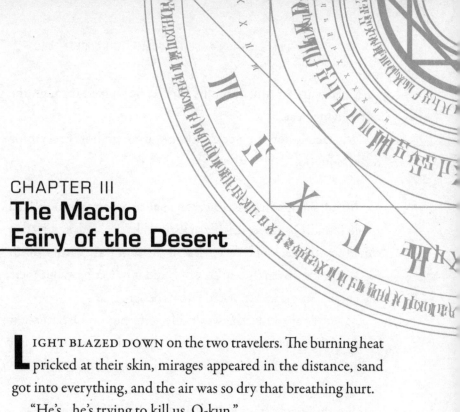

CHAPTER III
The Macho Fairy of the Desert

LIGHT BLAZED DOWN on the two travelers. The burning heat pricked at their skin, mirages appeared in the distance, sand got into everything, and the air was so dry that breathing hurt.

"He's...he's trying to kill us, O-kun."

"Personify the sun all you want, that's not going to make him any less hot."

A pair of footsteps trudged through the burning sand.

"It's so hoooooot. Hoooooooooot. I'm sweating so much I'll dry out."

"At least you're wearing my coat."

Sand stretched out as far as the eye could see. Oscar and Miledi were walking through the Crimson Desert, located on the western part of the Northern Continent. It was named such because of its striking red sand. The grains were all so fine that even a slight breeze would whip them through the air, turning the sky crimson.

Oscar carried Miledi on his back as he walked through the unforgiving heat.

"My face is hot, my neck's hot, my arms are hot. Everything feels hoooooot."

"......"

Miledi slumped against Oscar and flailed her arms around like a spoiled child. Oscar's jet-black coat looked like the kind of thing that would absorb heat, not reflect it. But of course, it was an artifact with metal threads woven into it. Not only did it reflect heat, but there was cooling magic incorporated into its design.

Miledi looked like she was really suffering, so Oscar gave it to her and decided to carry her on his back. In other words, not only was Oscar wearing a single sweat-drenched shirt, but he was forced to lug a heavy object.

"I'm thiiiiiirsty. If we keep going like this, I'll dry up."

"......"

"I hate being all sweaty like this."

"......"

"And the sand's getting everywhere."

"......"

"O-kun. O-kun. Hey, O-kun. Glasses-wearing O-kun. I mean, glasses—"

"Gaaaaaah, just shut up!"

Oscar finally snapped. He grabbed Miledi by the ankles and started spinning. It looked like he was swinging her around like a giant bat. The pair of them spun in circles in the middle of the desert.

"Hyowaaaaaaaaaah!"

Miledi's skirt flipped up, her panties clearly visible as she spun through the sand, her hands outstretched.

"Take thaaaaaaaaaaaat!"

With a spirited yell, Oscar flung his partner. Miledi screamed as she flew through the air. She landed a short distance away, and kicked up a cloud of dust.

Oscar wiped the sweat off his brow and smiled.

"Bleh... Pwah... Sand got in my mouth! Why'd you do that, O-kun?! You brute! Devil! Four-eyes!"

"Can you stop making fun of my glasses?!" Oscar said, walking over. "For crying out loud, the sand and the heat are bad enough without you complaining about it every five seconds. If you're really that hot, then why don't you make an ice block or something with your magic?"

"Ah..."

Miledi gazed up at Oscar, her mouth a small O in surprise. After a second, she snapped back to her senses and glared at him.

"I could say the same to you, O-kun. You can use that umbrella of yours to block the sun and make water, too, can't you?"

"Ah..."

The two gazed at each other underneath the blazing sun.

A cloud of dust blew past. They were quiet for a good ten minutes.

Miledi summoned a giant clod of ice, floated it above them with gravity magic, and summoned a breeze to waft past them.

At the same time, Oscar unfolded his umbrella and raised it above them. The cloth expanded to many times its normal size.

Then, he activated the new ability he'd installed with Miledi's help. With the combination of the spirit stone and Miledi's gravity magic, he was able to make the umbrella float above them. A veil of wind covered them, protecting the pair from the sand. The two were now pleasantly cool, and free of sand.

"This is all the sun's fault for being too hot!"

"Seriously. It should learn some humility from the moon and quit trying to show off!"

"Yeah, no one cares how bright you're shining! This is why no one likes guys like you!"

"You're not some street thug from Velnika, so stop acting like it, you damned sun!"

The pair vented their frustrations at the sun. They'd underestimated the heat, which took a bigger toll on their mental fortitude than they'd thought. They were rather embarrassed that such simple countermeasures hadn't come to them earlier.

In response, the sun almost got hotter. Like it was angry.

They walked onward for another hour, berating the sun.

"Hm? Miledi. Look, there's a small oasis over there. I think it's meant to be a rest stop on the way to the city. Should we stop for a bit?"

"Yeah, let's do it! I was just getting tired."

Miledi happily bounded forward, her ponytail swishing behind her.

"You've got really good eyes, you know that? I can't even see it from here."

Oscar smiled proudly.

"Did you think these glasses were just for show?" he asked.

"I mean, they totally are, aren't they? I know you're the kind of guy who'd wear them to make himself look smarter. I mean, even in Velnika I could tell you were just pushing up your glasses all the time because you knew the girls thought it looked cool. You were totally going for an intelligent gentleman look, right?"

"We really need to have a talk about how you see me."

Oscar glared at Miledi. Her words hurt even more since she'd said them all with a straight face.

Oscar cleared his throat.

"These glasses are an artifact, too. I've enchanted them with a lot of different spells. The lenses can emit a powerful flash of light, and they make me immune to dark magic... I've also enchanted them with Farsight."

He did his best to explain that they weren't just a tool for him to be popular with the ladies.

Miledi looked up at him in shock.

"Heh," said Oscar. "I knew you'd be surprised. But now you know these glasses aren't just—"

"Your glasses sparkle?! They can shine?!"

"Wait, that's what you're amazed about?"

Miledi's eyes were glittering with excitement. For whatever reason, it really impressed her.

"I wanna see it!"

"I get the feeling you're trying to make fun of me somehow, so no."

"Why not?! I wanna see Sparkly O-kun!"

"Sparkly O-kun? Now I *know* you're making fun of me."

Miledi continued begging, but Oscar ignored her.

"Come on, O-kun. Make your glasses sparkle for me. Pleaaase O-kun!"

A frigid wind blew against Oscar's face, frosting the rims of his glasses. However, Oscar didn't reply, and the wind grew even colder.

I can't let myself get angry. I'll just be playing into her hands. I need to stay calm and compos—

"Remember when you went to visit Aisha-chan before you left, O-kun? She was crying and clinging on to you and told you that—"

Glasses Beam!

"Higyaaaaaah?! My eyes! My eyeeeeees!"

Miledi clutched her eyes as his flash hit her at point-blank range.

As a side note, the continuation of that sentence would have been, "She'd heard from an adventurer that O-kun liked girls in aprons."

Oscar was only human. He drank with his acquaintances occasionally, too. Naturally, girls were one of the things they talked about while drunk. And it seemed Aisha grilled those acquaintances to tell her more about him. After that, she requested one final job from Oscar and set up a surprise drinking party. By the end, Oscar was terrified of women.

There were some things in the world better left unknown.

"Look, Miledi. There's even a cabin at the oasis. We might as well stop there for lunch."

"You know, O-kun. I still can't see anything."

Miledi was still groaning in pain and pawing blindly at the air. She'd experienced firsthand the fearsome power of Oscar's glasses. In all honesty, they scared her a little.

Oscar commanded his umbrella closer and used it to cast healing magic on her. This was the eleventh of his umbrella's abilities, Benison Aura. Healing light rained down from the spokes.

"Aaah, I can see again. The world isn't black!"

"Haaah... Stop fooling around, Miledi. Let's go."

Miledi raised her hands up to the light, as if offering a prayer to heaven. Oscar sighed and carried her in his arms.

The oasis had a number of trees growing around it, and the shade was pleasantly cool. The cabin seemed to be in good condition as well. *Someone probably comes and cleans it regularly.* Clean though it was, it was still just an empty cabin. It kept the sun and sand out, but it was still hot inside.

In fact, it was more comfortable under Oscar's umbrella. And so, the pair decided to stay outside and sat next to the shore.

Oscar brought his umbrella back to the ground, just in case anyone else showed up. He didn't want people to suspect what magic they were capable of.

"Everyone needs an O-kun in their house."

Miledi washed her face and hands in the oasis.

"You could at least make it sound like I'm a person, not an object. Besides, I'm not here to make everyone's life more convenient."

Oscar bent down and started washing his face as well.

They'd gotten pretty dirty. The cool water felt great on their hot, sweaty skin.

Oscar felt refreshed, but this wasn't enough for Miledi.

"Ugh, it got in my hair, too."

She undid her ponytail and ran her fingers through her hair. They came back gritty. Her clothes, too, were filled with sand. Her sweat caused them to stick unpleasantly to her skin.

"We're just going to have to deal with it until we make it to the city. We'll get there by the end of the day, and you can just take a shower there. I wonder if I can enchant my clothes to keep sand off... Is something like that even possible? Hmm..."

Oscar trailed off, and Miledi spoke up.

"Can't I just strip and jump in the oasis?"

"Bwah?! Are you kidding me?! This is a public place! What if someone comes here?! Actually, forget that, *I'm* here! Don't you have any shame?!"

Oscar hurriedly stopped Miledi from stripping down.

Normally this would have been the part where Miledi started teasing him, but she just stared at the oasis instead, a dangerous look in her eyes.

She was still a girl, after all. They may have been in the middle of a journey, but she still wanted to be clean.

At this rate she'll probably jump in fully clothed if she has to.

"Calm down, Miledi. Think about this rationally."

"I need to jump in there so I can start thinking rationally again. A famous person once said something like, 'Why do I leap into oases? Because they're there.'"

"Whoever this person was, they probably only became famous because everyone thought they were a pervert. Either that, or you got the quote wrong."

Miledi edged closer to the water. Any more and she really would fall into the oasis.

Oscar sighed.

"Alright, alright. You want to wash up, right? I'll make you a shower room in the bushes over there, so just use that."

"I love you, O-kun!"

"Yeah, yeah."

Oscar held Miledi back as she tried to hug him, and pulled one of his artifacts out of his pocket.

It was his Silver Slate. Originally it was just made to track people, but he'd added a second function. It could now detect the presence of mana within a certain radius.

They were hunting for other people with ancient magic. It was likely such people would have mana reserves as large as Miledi's and his own. Moreover, it could sense the approach of any threat, or just anyone with abnormal strength.

As beastmen didn't possess any mana, it couldn't sense them, but it was good enough for the time being. Oscar definitely wanted to improve it before they reached Haltina, though.

Still, it made a good alarm.

"No one around in a three-hundred-meter radius. Perfect."

There were only two dots on the plate, Miledi and himself, both glowing brightly.

Oscar walked over to a surprisingly dense thicket, and

transmuted. He did his best to not harm the local flora as he scrounged materials from underground to craft his makeshift shower.

An average Synergist would have fainted in awe at Oscar's unbelievable skills. However, he was taking no chances. This was a shower room for his beloved partner!

"Miledi, this is just to ensure your privacy, so the walls aren't that tough. Don't go wild in there, okay?"

"Wow, you actually put a shower in there!"

Before Oscar could even tell her to get her own water, she'd scooped out a huge quantity of it with gravity magic and poured it into the tank he'd prepared. He left the ceiling open, so she could bring in more if she needed it.

The shower had a faucet and everything, but before he could explain how it worked, Miledi jumped in.

"O-kuuun!"

"Yeah?"

"Thank youuu~!"

"Uh, yeah. You're welcome."

Oscar scratched his cheek awkwardly and walked away.

"I'm not that far, so if you need anything just yell for me. Though I think we'll be fine."

"Mmm, got it. No peeking~!"

"Don't worry, I won't."

"You better not. Like absolutely, definitely better not. I'm serious, O-kun. Don't you dare—"

"Are you trying to hint at something?! Or do you really not

trust me at all?!"

Oscar could hear Miledi's laughter through the walls. A second later, the sound of falling water replaced it. Miledi seemed to be in a good mood.

"Seriously..."

Oscar adjusted his glasses in exasperation.

"Come to think of it, I'm pretty sweaty, too. Plus, there's sand all over my clothes..."

He was just as dirty as Miledi. He looked down at his Silver Slate. It appeared there still wasn't anyone nearby.

"Hmm... I guess I could wash up too..."

He wasn't planning to strip down and take a full shower, just take his shirt off and wipe himself down. He didn't need to make a separate changing room for himself.

Oscar took his shirt off, soaked a towel, and started wiping himself. He scrubbed hard, making sure he got all the sand and sweat off.

Just then, he noticed someone looking at him. Instantly wary, he turned to see who was staring.

"Gulp..."

Miledi was peeking over the shower room wall.

"What are you doing?" Oscar asked, his eyebrows twitching.

"You know, I realized this back when you were carrying me, but... O-kun, you're surprisingly buff. You look like a thin scholar, but you've got a lot of muscles."

"I had the adventurers teach me how to fight, just in case. Also, those eyes of yours are scaring me. What happened to not peeking? Don't you have any tact?"

"I left it back in the Reisen Gorge."

"Then go get it back!"

And she's the one who said not to peek on HER! I never knew she was such a hopeless pervert. Just then, Oscar saw something out of the corner of his eye.

"M-Miledi, let's just drop this. Get away from the wall."

"Hee hee hee. Are you embarrassed, O-kun? That embarrassed to be seen naked by a girl? Well, are you?"

"I won't even complain about how annoying you're being, so please just get away from that wall. I told you before, the shower room wasn't built to last."

"Hm? It's not?"

"Yes, so—aaah, wait! Don't lean against it! If you do—"

There was a sharp crack. Then, the walls of the shower room crumbled.

"Huh?"

Miledi's weight was too much, and they collapsed.

"Whoa..."

"Ah..."

Miledi fell forward. Her naked body flew toward Oscar. He got a good view of her slender back, her beautiful curves, and her smooth legs.

"Gah, I can't believe this—"

Miledi stood up, realizing too late what kind of view that would give Oscar.

"O-O-kun, don't look!"

"Way ahead of you!"

Oscar pivoted on the balls of his feet and turned straight around.

"Ugh, he totally saw. There's no way he didn't... I mean it's my own fault, but... Maybe I should hit him with Nether Burst anyway..."

Oscar didn't like the sound of that. There wouldn't even be a speck of him left. It had caved in an entire floor of the Greenway.

"I-I didn't see anything! Promise!"

"Liar. You're a big fat liar, O-kun! Your voice is shaking!"

"Guh. Okay, so maybe I saw a little... Sorry."

"Ugh. It's my fault, so you shouldn't be the one to apologize... It feels wrong."

It was kind of novel, seeing Miledi genuinely embarrassed. Oscar found it quite cute.

"Anyway, the changing room should be fine still. Go hide in there. I'll repair the shower, if you want to finish up."

"Nah, it's fine. I'll just go change."

She was acting uncharacteristically meek. When she was like this, she seemed like any other girl. Oscar preferred her annoying version, since he didn't have to feel bad about hitting her when she was like that.

Putting those thoughts aside, Oscar found his shirt and got dressed.

The two of them spent some time sitting by the oasis under the shade of Oscar's umbrella.

"......"

"......"

They didn't say anything. Miledi's ears were still red.

Oscar rifled through his pack for their food. He'd brought a lot of non-perishable goods. They were stored in containers that he used to make for adventurers. The airtight seals meant food lasted even longer than usual.

The versions he'd made for himself were, of course, a lot more impressive. If word of his improved inventions spread, he'd probably be flooded with requests. Logistics for supplies was the hardest part about organizing an army.

"We sweat out a lot earlier. Need to get some salt back in us."

He handed Miledi some food.

"Y-yeah, you're right!"

She took it excitedly. It seemed she was still trying to shake off her embarrassment.

Oscar was also at a loss for what to say, so he focused on eating.

Today's lunch was beef. He used a lot of seasoning and spices in the sauce, so it made for a surprisingly delicious meal. That was the other reason Oscar's food containers were in such high demand. The food he packed into them was good. On top of that, because the cans were well-sealed, he could keep perishables in perfect condition.

"Mmm, this is great! This is the same dish that was at Aisha-chan's restaurant, right?"

"Yep. Remember how there were always a bunch of adventurers there whenever we went? They like that place because it serves spicy food like this."

"I see. No wonder our lunches were so delicious. Wait, that means you bought all this from Aisha-chan's restaurant, didn't you? That's how she found out you were leaving and started crying!"

"Pretty much."

Oscar stuffed his face full of meat. He clearly didn't want to talk about that. Unfortunately for him, he'd piqued Miledi's curiosity, which at least meant she was back to normal.

"Hey, O-kun. What did Aisha-chan say to you? Come on, tell me. And what'd you tell her? Come on! It's no big deal, right?"

She grinned and ribbed him gently with her elbows.

"Miledi. You're being annoying again. Unbelievably annoying. I'm kind of relieved. Please stay like that forever, so I don't feel guilty about blowing you halfway across the planet."

"H-huh? That wasn't the reaction I was expecting... What's that even supposed to mean? Here I am making fun of you and you look almost...kind. I don't even know what I'm supposed to say to that."

It was rare for Oscar to show Miledi any kindness, so she was taken aback.

"Uh, umm... Oh yeah! About the city we're going to!" she said, forcibly changing the topic.

Oscar went back to his food.

"The city's called Chaldea, right?" he asked. "It's the biggest city in Polvora, I think. They're part of the Sharod Federation."

Miledi chewed and nodded. The desert was ruled by the Sharod Federation, a loose alliance of small independent fiefdoms.

They were more large tribes than properly organized regions. Each tribe had its own culture, customs, and laws. Even Sharod, the most powerful member, didn't have the power to influence another region. These small tribes had joined together to show a united front against the larger powers.

Polvora was on the southeastern tip of the desert, and the closest to Velka. Its largest city, Chaldea, was famous for its textiles.

"We're going to start by gathering information," said Miledi. "And since we're there anyway, we might as well spend some time checking out their clothes."

"We're looking for the 'Fairy of the Desert,' right?"

"Yep," she agreed. "The Fairy of the Desert. I was actually on my way to Polvora originally. I just stopped by Velnika because it was on the way."

"Turned into a pretty big detour, huh?"

"It turned into the best detour of my life."

"Mhm," Oscar replied, and swallowed his food. "You said you've been searching for more wielders of ancient magic ever since you joined the Liberators, right? You and your comrades have supposedly been scouring the globe."

"Most of our leads have ended up being dead ends, but yeah."

She'd told most of this to him back in Velnika.

There weren't too many people like Oscar and Miledi, who could use ancient magic and possessed ungodly amounts of mana. It stood to reason that those few who existed would stand out, which meant rumors would spread. However, Oscar hadn't heard any such rumors. He assumed they were like him, hiding their talents. That was why Miledi and her comrades had leaped on even the most outlandish of rumors. It was all they had.

Most ended up being false leads, but every now and then they hit the jackpot. Oscar was the first person Miledi found capable of using magic from the age of the gods, but they'd still picked up a number of insanely talented people.

Since chasing outlandish rumors had borne some fruit, they continued. And the Fairy of the Desert was one such rumor.

According to legend, there was a wandering fairy who patrolled the Crimson Desert and guided lost travelers home. It sounded pretty fake to Oscar. He tilted his head.

"Why a fairy, of all things?"

"Because she's a pretty, dainty little girl, maybe?"

Miledi tilted her head. She wasn't sure, either.

They didn't have enough information, so they were headed for the largest city to gather more.

"It would be nice..." said Oscar. "If they could use ancient magic too."

"Healing magic specifically, right?" Miledi replied gently.

Miledi wanted to find someone who could help her fight against the gods. However, while Oscar wanted to help her achieve her goal, he also wanted to find someone who could cure his brother and sister. For him, that took precedence.

Oscar pushed up his glasses, embarrassed that she'd seen through him.

The hidden village where Oscar's family had been sent, and where all the non-combatant members of Miledi's group lived, was deep in the Reisen Gorge. Back when she'd worked as an executioner, Miledi chanced upon a cave deep within it. There were a few other places Miledi had considered, but this was the easiest to defend and the least likely to be discovered.

Oscar had entrusted the orphans, and a few Liberators, with some of his artifacts, so the village was better defended now.

Once they found a way to heal Dylan and Katy, Oscar was planning to go back and see them. Whenever that was, he'd be sure to bolster the village's defenses with the most heinous physical traps he could come up with.

Anyone who dared to hurt his family deserved only the most painful of deaths.

"Hey, O-kun? You're smile's starting to creep me out. You look kinda evil."

"Oh, whoops."

Miledi had finished eating. She stared at Oscar, shivering in fear.

Oscar hurriedly finished his own meal.

"Well, that's a long enough break. If night falls before we get into the city, it'll be harder to find an inn."

"At least this time the journey will be nice and cool."

Miledi and Oscar walked into the harsh desert, their floating ice cube and umbrella providing perfect air conditioning.

⁕ ⁕ ⁕ ⁕ ⁕ ⁕ ⁕ ⁕ ⁕ ⁕ ⁕ ⁕ ⁕

Sand stretched on as far as the eye could see. The wind shaped the dunes, undulating like waves. It really felt like they were traversing a sea of sand.

"Hm? Miledi, we've got something coming from the right. Five of them."

"I don't see anything. They must be underground."

Miledi scanned the area.

Oscar counted down. As he reached one, five crimson scorpions shot out of the ground.

Miledi struck at almost the same time.

"Heavensfall!"

The scorpions were slammed back into the sand. Gravity magic pinned them in place. The scorpions screeched in pain. However, they were in the desert. Below the scorpions was just sand. Instead of being crushed against the ground, the scorpions sunk deeper in.

"Hmm, deserts and I really don't get along."

Miledi cast a combination of earth and wind magic to summon a blade of sand, and cut the scorpions in half. They screeched again as they died.

"You've been using gravity magic an awful lot lately. Any reason?"

"Practice. It's pretty hard to use, and it takes up a lot of mana. I want to get better at controlling it, and hopefully reduce the amount of mana it drains, so I've gotta keep practicing."

She puffed her chest out proudly.

Although she appeared skilled at first glance, Miledi still couldn't fuse other elements with her gravity magic. Furthermore, there were spells even she couldn't control.

Nether Burst was one such spell. Once activated, it would

drain all her mana unless some external factor forced the spell to cut off.

She wasn't happy that her most powerful spell was one she couldn't fully control. Worse, if she wasn't careful, she was liable to kill herself with it.

"I see. It certainly does seem difficult to use. So even you're not able to use it perfectly..."

"Hey, O-kun. I've been the only one fighting for a while now... Do you really plan on making a girl do all the work?"

Miledi glared at him.

Like most places, the Crimson Desert was rife with monsters. In fact, it was one of the more dangerous regions on the continent.

The scorpions were known as the assassins of the desert. Travelers feared them because of their deadly poison and ability to move through the ground undetected.

Since leaving the oasis, they'd been attacked rather frequently. However, Oscar was always able to detect them ahead of time, and Miledi crushed them in seconds, so there was no sense of urgency.

Still, as strong as she was, Miledi was still a girl. She was tired of being the only one fighting, and wanted her partner to pull his weight.

Oscar just stared at her blankly. Almost if he didn't understand.

"Okay, now I'm mad. I'm mad, O-kun! I'm a girl, too, you know?! I know this is child's play, but you could still say something like, 'Oh, leave it to me' or 'I'd feel bad making you do all the hard work' or something!"

"You just said yourself that this is child's play. You're better suited to fighting than I am. Besides, just thinking about you acting like a normal city girl is...ha ha."

"Hey, why'd you laugh? O-kun, you better explain yourself."

Miledi glared at Oscar, a dark look in her eyes. But just then, Oscar's Silver Slate reacted again. There was a giant monster headed their way. It was fast, too.

"Miledi, behind us. It's fast. I'll count down for you."

"......"

"Ten, nine, eight, seven, six, five, four, three, two, one. Go!"

A giant earthworm, known as a Sandworm, burst out from directly under their feet.

Oscar and Miledi jumped in different directions, just barely avoiding the creature's circular maw. Its razor-sharp teeth ground the sand it was chewing. It almost looked like it was grinding its teeth in frustration.

"Hm? Huh?"

Oscar looked over in confusion.

Normally, Miledi would have crushed the worm to the ground with her gravity magic.

Is she charging up a really powerful spell or something? Oscar flicked his left hand. Thin chains flew out of his sleeve. His Metamorph Chains. Before, he'd had to physically fling them, or snake them along the ground to his target by using the spirit stone contained within. However, he'd enhanced them with Miledi's gravity magic, and now they floated freely in the air.

He could control all five at once since they'd become easier to handle. Furthermore, the pouch at his waist had a huge carrying capacity, so he'd lengthened each one to a hundred meters.

His chains wound their way around the Sandworm. They were powerful enough to bind it in place.

He sent a second chain burrowing through the ground, then remotely transmuted the ground underneath the Sandworm into stone.

"Miledi, how much longer is this going to take?!" Oscar shouted.

There was no reply. *Don't tell me she got injured?!* But when he looked over, he saw that she'd dodged just fine. Her actions baffled him.

"Miledi? What are you doing?"

She was lying in midair, her hands behind her head. High enough that the Sandworm couldn't reach her.

Miledi grinned.

"I thought I should give you a chance to train your skills, too. That monster is a gift from me. Oh, what's that? No need for thanks! We're partners, after all."

Guess she's holding a grudge. She'd lifted herself high enough that she was in no danger.

A vein pulsed in Oscar's forehead. He tightened the chains around the Sandworm, and it screamed in pain.

"Miledi. Doing in this in the middle of a fight is not funny. What you're trying to say doesn't even make sense. Listen up, in the first place—"

He stalled as he looked at his Silver Slate. A number of huge enemies were headed their way. Oscar guessed they were this Sandworm's friends.

"M-Miledi. There's six more coming. Stop playing around and get rid of them."

Miledi made no move to get up.

"No," she said, like a spoiled child, and smiled.

Six Sandworms popped out of the ground, surrounding Oscar. They looked at their trapped buddy, and then at Oscar. Their anger was palpable.

Oscar's expression stiffened, but he remained calm.

"Miledi, I understand that you're frustrated. I'm willing to listen, so let's talk this out, okay? But first, could you please get rid of these—giyaaaaaaaaaaaaah!"

Before he could finish, the Sandworms converged. Six gaping maws bore down on him.

Oscar screamed, and a cloud of dust rose up where he'd been standing. The Sandworms' heads were all stuck in the ground. They looked like giant upside-down Ns.

"A-are you really just going to sit there?!" Oscar demanded.

As the dust cleared, Miledi saw him on one knee, with his umbrella thrust out before him.

He'd activated Hallowed Ground to keep himself alive. The sheer weight of six massive creatures should have buried him in the sand, even with a barrier, but he'd transmuted the ground into metal. His Transmutation abilities were truly impressive.

"You're my partner, aren't you, O-kun? You're not going to be much help against the gods if you can't beat monsters like this."

Oscar finally snapped. Miledi didn't notice.

"What's wrong, O-kun? Come on, you can do it! Don't give up! Stay light on your feet! Believe in yourself! I know you can do better than this! Come on, get back up!"

Oscar stood up. He extended the umbrella's shaft toward the Sandworms, then pulled out a single black glove and put it on. He took out a few of his enchanted weapons.

Finally, he took a deep breath and looked up at Miledi.

"Milediiiiiiiiiiiiiiiiiiiiiiiiiii! I'm going to fucking murder you!"

His voice carried pretty far.

At the same time, there was an explosion, and one of the monsters flew back. The Sandworm that he'd suppressed with his chains was a smoking husk. He'd used lightning to kill it.

The explosion tore huge chunks out of a few of the remaining Sandworms. He'd hit them all with Combustion Blades. The resulting blast was pretty powerful.

Chunks of meat rained down on him, which he fended off with his umbrella. He bent one of his gloved fingers. There was a loud whistling noise, and one of the Sandworms was split into five.

This was another one of his artifacts, the Sable Glove. It was crafted from superfine threads of metal, enchanted with gravity magic. The threads were made of spirit stone, so he could also control them freely. While his chains were made for binding and restraining targets, those were made to kill. The threads of spirit stone were sharp enough to cut flesh.

The remaining Sandworms tried to burrow back underground. This opponent was too much for them to handle.

"You're not going anywhere."

Oscar transmuted the ground around him. The sand, which should have been their domain, turned into their tomb.

Oscar closed his umbrella, lifted it up, and slammed it into the ground. Blades of wind bisected two of the Sandworms, while electrified chains and metal wire made mincemeat of the rest.

It hadn't even taken a minute.

After finishing up, he glared at Miledi. She was clapping happily.

"I knew you could do it if you tried, O-kun!"

To ensure they had a good working relationship going forward, Oscar decided to teach her a little lesson. He aimed his chains at her. But before he could fire them off—

"Hm?"

"Huh?"

The air shook. A second later, the ground began to shake, too.

Something a few hundred meters out was running right at them. It was kicking up a cloud of dust so big that it looked like a sandstorm. That something turned out to be an entire herd of Sandworms.

Oscar looked down at his Silver Slate. The whole thing was glowing with light. There was easily more than a hundred of them, spanning an area over three hundred meters wide. One of the Sandworms looked a lot larger than usual.

It appeared the ones he'd killed had a *lot* of friends.

He couldn't fight such a large group. He'd be blown away by their sheer mass before he even had a chance.

"Miledi-san? If you're telling me to fight *that* all on my own, too, I'm going to have to rethink my decision to travel with you."

Oscar looked up pleadingly.

"E-even I wouldn't be that cruel. Actually, let's get out of here! I don't think my magic's gonna be enough for that!"

"Y-yeah."

Oscar attempted to leap into the air with his Onyx Boots.

The Sandworm army was almost on top of him. They were fast. Up close, he realized the giant one was even bigger than he'd first thought. It was like a living mountain.

Crap, I might not make it. Miledi must have been thinking the same thing, as she lightened him with gravity magic.

"Huh?"

"Huh?"

Just then, Miledi and Oscar looked down in shock.

This was hardly the time, but what they saw was simply unbelievable. A man had appeared between him and the monsters.

He had rust-red hair and eyes as sharp as a hawk's. His eyes were the same color as his hair. He wore a faded gray robe, with a white sash over it. He was massive, standing a formidable two meters tall. Oscar guessed he was in his mid-twenties.

From his clothes, it seemed likely that he was a resident of the Crimson Desert, but neither Oscar nor Miledi sensed him coming.

He dashed over to Oscar, completely unconcerned about the

army of Sandworms.

"Huh, wait, who are—"

"Don't worry about that."

Oscar faltered as the heavily muscled man towered over him. He grabbed Oscar's arms, his voice utterly emotionless.

A second later—

"Wha?"

"O-O-kun?"

Miledi was directly in front of him. They blinked.

With his free hand, the man grabbed hold of Miledi.

A second later, they vanished.

"Huh?"

"Wha? Wait, all we've been saying for the past minute is 'huh' and 'wha'..."

And reappeared on a sand dune somewhere else. A giant city rose up in the distance.

The two of them exchanged looks and turned back around.

"Please forget all about me."

He let go of their hands and looked into their eyes.

"A-are you the Fairy of the Desert?" Miledi blurted out.

"Huh?"

"Huh?"

Both the man and Oscar looked at her in surprise.

Oscar turned back to the man.

"Fairy?" His sharp eyes refused to meet Miledi's gaze. "F-fairy?"

A blush spread up his chiseled face. It looked like he'd only just realized. He must have been embarrassed.

❖❖ ❖❖ ❖❖ ❖❖ ❖❖ ❖❖ ❖❖ ❖❖ ❖❖ ❖❖ ❖❖ ❖❖ ❖❖

The man returned to his senses and coughed.

"Anyway, please don't tell other people about me."

Mana swirled around him.

"O-kun, don't let him get away!"

"Huh? Oh, got it!"

Oscar wrapped his chains around the man, and used them to disperse his mana. The man let out a gasp of surprise.

"Wow, that was amazing, O-kun! And it looks like we hit the jackpot right off the bat! I can't believe this! I spent years searching fruitlessly before I found you, and now we've got another falling right into our laps! Looks like my luck's finally turning around!"

"Uh, sure."

Miledi got herself hyped up. She pumped a fist into the air and leaped with joy. Oscar was honestly a bit put off.

Meanwhile, the man tried to free himself.

"Hee hee hee," Miledi laughed. "Don't even bother. O-kun's chains are made of sealstone. You won't be able to emit mana easily with those around you."

"What do you plan on doing to me?"

He stared warily at the two of them. When he narrowed his eyes, he looked positively terrifying.

Cold sweat poured down Miledi's forehead.

"Th-thanks for saving us back there, but we can't have you leaving just yet. We actually came here to find you. But man, I can't believe we ran into you before we even got around to gathering info!"

"What do you plan on doing to me?" he repeated.

His tone was even fiercer than before. It seemed Miledi had only made him more suspicious. Oscar sighed and removed his chains.

The man looked at him in surprise.

"Sorry," said Oscar. "It's true that we came all this way to meet you, so I panicked a bit when you were about to leave. Also, I apologize for my partner's attitude. I'm truly sorry."

The man looked away, clearly uncomfortable.

"And what's that supposed to mean?!" Miledi screamed. A second later, she looked back at the man and bowed. "Sorry."

The man tried to look anywhere but at the two of them.

Oscar held out a hand.

"Thanks for saving us back there, really. My name's Oscar. Oscar Orcus."

The man looked at Oscar's outstretched hand. He made no motion to take it. After a brief moment of silence, he shook his head.

"Sorry, but I'm not interested."

Mana started swirling around him once more.

Miledi tried to stop him.

"Wait, please listen!"

"......"

"We're like you!" she yelled out as he was about to vanish. "We can use magic from the age of the gods!"

His mana dispersed again. This time, Oscar hadn't done anything. He'd stopped casting of his own accord. Judging by his stunned expression, he probably hadn't meant to.

Miledi breathed a sigh of relief. Her expression was serious now.

"You're the same, aren't you?"

The man's expression gave nothing away.

"You just popped up out of nowhere," she went on. "And then you touched O-kun and showed up next to me with him. After that, you brought us here in an instant. You must have some kind of teleportation magic, correct? Something normal mages can't possibly use."

"You're wrong. My power is nothing special. It comes from an artifact I found."

The man pulled a necklace out of his robes.

Miledi glanced over at Oscar, who gazed intently at the necklace for a few seconds. He shook his head.

"That's just a normal necklace."

"You simply cannot see its power," said the man. "I'll say this now: I won't lend it to you. If you plan on stealing it—"

"Sorry, but those lies won't work on us," said Miledi. "I told you before, we can use ancient magic, too. O-kun over here's probably the only Synergist alive who can make artifacts. No one's more knowledgeable about them than him."

The man turned to Oscar, clearly at a loss for words.

Oscar made his chains and umbrella float in the air. Electric sparks flew off of them. They were obviously not your average magical tools.

"By the way," said Miledi. "I was floating using gravity magic earlier, not wind magic."

She showed off her powers as well. Sky blue mana swirled around her, and a second later, a massive segment of sand flew up into the air.

"We're on a journey to find other people with powers like ours. Please at least hear us out."

She gazed silently at the man. For a while, he just stared at the floating umbrella and sand. Neither Miledi nor Oscar could read his expression, although Oscar thought he caught a hint of jealousy.

"My answer remains unchanged," he said at last. "I have already decided how I wish to live my life. I have no desire to join any group."

His sharp gaze pierced Miledi.

"Why? You're using that power of yours to help people, aren't you? So why do you want to be alone?"

"This power is nothing more than a curse."

What kind of things happened in his past? Oscar was surprised at the darkness in his eyes.

"That's all I have to say," said the man with a flat tone of finality. "Please don't trouble yourself any further with me."

Miledi hung her head. She was trembling. The man felt a little guilty. Oscar spared Miledi a glance before giving the man a look of sympathy. He knew where this was going.

"No!" said Miledi. "I'm not giving up that easily! I managed to seduce O-kun eventually, too! Don't underestimate me!"

"Can you please stop using suggestive words like that?" asked Oscar.

Miledi ignored his protests. After throwing a mini-tantrum, she closed in on the man.

Flustered, he took a step back. Miledi's menacing demeanor, or perhaps just her overbearing presence, were enough to disturb him.

"I'll make you listen to me, even if I have to force you!"

"Wh-wha?!" said the man. "I told you I don't—Cosmic Rift!"

Miledi disappeared into a glowing ring of light. Just before she vanished, she let out a confused yell.

The man was breathing heavily, and looked like he'd just faced down some kind of demonic monster.

"Sorry about that," said Oscar. "Our leader's a little excitable. Just making sure, but she's okay, right?"

"Haaah... Haaah... Y-you'll see in a moment."

The man waved his hand. Another ring of light appeared at Oscar's feet. Oscar yelled in surprise and vanished into the portal.

A very exhausted man remained alone on the sand.

⁎⁎ ⁎⁎ ⁎⁎ ⁎⁎ ⁎⁎ ⁎⁎ ⁎⁎ ⁎⁎ ⁎⁎ ⁎⁎ ⁎⁎ ⁎⁎ ⁎⁎

There was a huge splash in a small oasis some distance away.

"*Ack... Hic...* I swallowed too much water..."

The oasis was empty, but had anyone been there, they would have seen someone appear seemingly out of thin air right above the water.

Oscar splashed about in the shallows, still trying to get his bearings. He slicked back his hair and looked around. His glasses were missing.

"Looks like an oasis... That guy's got some impressive magic.

Anyway, did he also send Miledi..."

There she is. She was sitting at the edge of the water, sobbing and cradling her knees.

Upon closer inspection, Oscar realized that her clothes and hair were muddy, and her face was dripping with water. Her nose was red, as if it had scraped across the ground.

Off to the side, the oasis turned into a marshy swamp. There were skid marks where someone had slipped into it.

That told Oscar everything he needed to know. When Miledi was teleported, she'd been running. If he'd teleported her near the oasis, it stood to reason that she would have slipped on the slick mud. And because she'd been waving her arms around wildly, she wouldn't have been able to stop herself from falling.

Oscar walked over to her.

"Should I make you another shower?"

"Please."

Miledi sniffled and nodded meekly.

A short while later, she returned to Oscar's side. Her nose was still a little red, but she was clean. Oscar sat cross-legged at the edge of the oasis and was staring at his Silver Slate.

"O-kun, thanks for the shower."

"You're welcome."

Miledi sat next to him. She hugged her knees and stared into the water.

"All the wielders of ancient magic are a huge pain the ass," she said at last.

"I hope you realize that includes you."

She ignored him, as usual.

"That was teleportation magic he used back there, right?" she asked instead.

"Seems like it," Oscar agreed. "That ring of light... It's some kind of portal, I guess? You pass through, and end up in a completely different location. It seems he can transport himself even without that portal, though. Either way it's pretty impressive. It's going to be a real pain."

"Anytime we're close, he can just send us away, or teleport himself. We won't even have a chance to talk to him."

"I'm pretty sure he only teleported us away that time because you were scaring him." Oscar was, once again, ignored. Still, he cleared his throat and continued. "At any rate, he refused our offer. Quite firmly, too. I imagine that won't be deterring you, though."

"Of course not! I mean, he didn't refuse us completely. You could tell there was something else in his eyes, right?"

So you won't stop until you hear what he really thinks, huh? Oscar smiled. Like she'd said, that was how she seduced him, too.

He almost felt a twinge of sympathy for the poor man.

"Though, I have no idea where we are or where he went..." said Miledi. "And since he can teleport wherever he wants, it's going to be hard to gather information on his whereabouts... Urgh, what are we supposed to do noooooow?"

Miledi rolled around and pounded the sand angrily. She was back to acting like a spoiled child.

Oscar smiled. His Silver Slate began to glow.

"Finding him will be a piece of cake, actually."

"Huh? How?!"

Miledi looked up in surprise, and Oscar showed her his slate.

"The moment he transported you, I figured I'd be next. So while we were talking, I attached one of my trackers to a thread and hid it under the ground. I managed to get it onto him before he dropped me."

The slate showed Miledi and Oscar in the center, two dazzling pinpricks of light. Some distance away was a third pinprick of light, equally as bright.

"Oh, and from the looks of it," Oscar went on, "he's transported us two days east of Chaldea. I found a signpost near the oasis while you were taking your shower. Judging by the distance, he's probably somewhere near the city still."

Miledi trembled.

Is she going through some weird withdrawal? Oscar thought. A second later, she hugged him with all her might. His head felt like it was in a vice.

"Nice job, O-kun! I knew I could count on my partner! Those glasses really aren't just for show after all! I'm sorry I thought you were a weirdo for wearing a black coat in the middle of the desert!"

"Can you give it a rest about my glasses already?! Wait, hey, you were really thinking that?! And get off of me! Let me go!"

"Come ooon~! Let me hug you a little longer!"

"Daaaaaaaaaaaaaaaah! Gods, you're so annoying!"

Oscar finally managed to push Miledi away. Although it

might not have been because he thought she was annoying, but for a different reason entirely. Oscar's face was bright red as he adjusted his glasses.

"Alriiight! Thanks to your quick thinking, we know where he is. Let's hurry back to town!"

She pumped her fist in the air energetically, already over being pushed away.

"Roger," Oscar said with a nod. He was still blushing.

⁂ ⁂ ⁂ ⁂ ⁂ ⁂ ⁂ ⁂ ⁂ ⁂ ⁂ ⁂ ⁂

One day after, Miledi and Oscar left the oasis.

The man who'd sent the terrifying girl and her glasses-wearing companion away led a herd of four iraks into Chaldea.

Iraks were large four-legged mammals that the desert folk used in place of horses. Normally, the beasts were lazy creatures. They were often too lazy to even find food, and could survive a month without eating. As long as they drank water every few days, at least.

They shambled along at a brisk walking speed. Rarely could their riders urge them into anything faster. But if they felt their lives in danger, they could gallop across the dunes for hours on end without tiring. They often spit at people who annoyed them, too.

Still, iraks were valued by the desert people and sold for high prices.

This man was an irak herder, and made his living selling them.

He'd sold quite a few at the nearby villages already, and was planning to sell the remainder in Chaldea. After that, all that remained was to deliver supplies to a few other villages.

Chaldea's main street was a cacophony of noise. Travelers and merchants haggled over prices, hawkers called out the names of their wares, and people shouted to be heard over the din.

The man gently led the iraks down the street and turned at an intersection. Before him stood a large pillar with many iraks tied to it. This was the main irak market.

"Oh, it's you. I was expecting you."

The owner smiled and walked up to the man. He was well-built, but a slight paunch bulged out from behind his white robe. His clothes were of fine quality, and had clearly been sewn by a master. You could tell easily that he was a prospering merchant.

"I've brought three to sell. What's your price?"

"Curt as always, I see. I haven't seen you in months, my friend. Surely you can spare some time to share a tale or two."

The man looked away, troubled. The merchant clearly meant no harm, though.

"Well, I won't force you. I certainly wouldn't want to lose your business... Marvelous. As always, the iraks you've brought me are of exceptional quality."

The merchant tied the three iraks to the pillar and nodded in satisfaction. He asked the man to sit inside his shop while he performed a more thorough inspection. And so he sat down, and an apprentice brought him some tea.

The apprentice had seen the man quite a few times, and wasn't nervous around the silent giant. The man smiled slightly and gave the boy his thanks.

He didn't know if the merchant had sent the boy to keep him

company while he examined the iraks, or if it was the boy's own curiosity that kept him there. Regardless, the boy was clearly intent on making conversation.

"Mister, the master's been complaining a lot recently."

"Huh?"

"The Holy Church has started monopolizing the irak trade... Of course, that means master was able to sell his whole herd to them, but then he was out of stock. An irak trader is nothing without iraks, so he went around looking for more to buy, but the other big irak traders sold to the Holy Church as well, and all he could find were dregs no one else wanted."

"Why would the Holy Church want iraks?"

"Beats me... Anyway, that's why master's so happy to see you. I don't suppose you'd be willing to sell all four of them?"

"I'd have a hard time getting home if I did."

In truth, he'd have no trouble at all, but it would raise suspicion. The merchant was convinced he lived far away, since he only came by every few months. It would be odd not to take an irak over such distance.

Besides, he'd had that one irak a long time, so it was practically family. He wouldn't sell it even if he could.

The boy knew he wouldn't part with it, either. He smiled in understanding.

"I thought as much. Well, did you have any trouble getting here? Like a run-in with monsters or something?"

The man looked up in surprise, wondering what had led the boy to that conclusion.

"You just look tired, is all."

This boy is quite sharp. He'll make a good merchant someday. The man thought back to his strange encounter yesterday.

That boy and girl had possessed the same kind of abnormal powers as him. They claimed they'd come looking for him.

Neither seemed like bad people, really. Furthermore, they'd both seemed proud of their abilities.

The boy claimed he could create artifacts, even. *The power to create...* Truly, he was a little jealous. Especially of their relationship.

Although the girl seemed to lead him by the nose quite often, the pair clearly trusted each other. Neither was the other's servant.

"Umm, Mister?"

He snapped back to the present. The boy was looking at him with worry.

The man gave him a small smile.

"Ah, sorry. It's nothing."

In a sense, he had encountered monsters, and he told the boy as much. He took another sip of his tea and—

"Miledi-chan's here! I've finally found you!"

"Bwah?!"

He spotted Miledi hurtling down from above. The man spit out his tea. The boy, whom she'd landed on, rolled across the ground, covering his eyes.

"Wh-why? How did..."

How did she find me? In fact, how is she even here? I sent her two days away just one day ago.

Miledi looked down at the man and grinned.

"I won't let you escape that easily!"

Miledi frightened him, but that grin also irked him.

The man hesitated. Meanwhile, the young boy whimpered.

"Mister, why did this happen to me? Did I do something wrong?"

He was still rubbing his eyes, which Miledi had hurt. The man was worried about him of course, but right now he needed to find a way out of this predicament.

He couldn't open a portal here. The risk that someone might see it was far too great. That left running. But he hadn't been paid yet, and he didn't want to leave his irak behind.

"Hey, what's going on in there?"

The merchant came to see what all the noise was about. An idea came to mind. The man turned to him.

"Sir. Please put the money in the pouch tied to my irak. I'll come back for it later."

"What? But then how... Hey, wait!"

The man dashed off without waiting for a reply.

"Aaah, get back here!"

Miledi ran off after him.

"Master? Master! What's going on? I still can't see."

The young apprentice blinked a few times to clear his sight.

"Sorry about my companion. She's rather boisterous. Anyway, could I ask you a few questions about the man who was in here?"

A young man in a stiflingly hot black coat appeared in the doorway. For some reason, he was carrying an umbrella.

"What on earth is going on?"

The merchant scratched his balding head.

❖ ❖ ❖ ❖ ❖ ❖ ❖ ❖ ❖ ❖ ❖ ❖ ❖

"*Sniffle...*"

A young girl cried at the edge of an oasis. She was soaked from head to toe, and covered in mud. Her nose was red.

Suddenly, there was a blinding flash of light in front of her.

A second later, Oscar fell into the water with a huge splash.

The water and wind magic embedded in his clothes cleaned and dried him off, and he walked out of the water looking none the worse for wear.

When he saw the state of Miledi, he guessed what had happened.

"O-kun, he threw me away like I was trash..."

"Ah... I see," Oscar replied noncommittally.

As Miledi chased after the man, she ran straight into a portal. However, she'd managed to dodge over it with gravity magic.

Certain he'd be willing to at least listen now that she'd rendered his traps ineffective, Miledi let her guard down. Just as she'd started talking, the man grabbed her by the scruff of the neck and threw her into his portal. She was so shocked that she'd lost her concentration and fallen into the mud.

"Ugh, damn that man! I can't believe he'd throw a girl like that!"

"In your case, I can see why he'd do it... Also, it's Naiz, not 'that man.'"

"Huh? What do you mean?"

"That's his name. While you were wasting your time running after him, I talked to the merchant. Turns out he's an irak herder. He comes by every few months with a few well-bred iraks to sell."

Unfortunately, that was all he'd been able to find out. Even the merchant, who seemed close to Naiz, knew very little about him. He'd described Naiz as a taciturn but sincere man.

After Oscar was done talking, he'd noticed that Naiz's irak was missing. The merchant wondered when Naiz had time to get it, but assumed he'd missed Naiz while talking to Oscar.

On the other hand, Oscar guessed what must have happened.

He'd thanked the merchant and decided to head back. When he'd stepped into an alleyway, though, he'd fallen through one of Naiz's portals.

Still, they'd gotten some more information on him.

"You're amazing, O-kun! No matter what happens, you still come away with something useful!"

"Meanwhile, you just keep charging in like an idiot."

She went to hug him, but Oscar restrained her with his Metamorph Chains. He didn't want to get smeared in mud, too. He sighed and made another shower room for Miledi. Then, he threw her into the changing room.

"I feel like I'm being thrown around a lot lately..." she muttered.

He ignored her.

⋅⁍⋅ ⋅⁍⋅ ⋅⁍⋅ ⋅⁍⋅ ⋅⁍⋅ ⋅⁍⋅ ⋅⁍⋅ ⋅⁍⋅ ⋅⁍⋅ ⋅⁍⋅ ⋅⁍⋅ ⋅⁍⋅ ⋅⁍⋅

Two days later.

Naiz finished his business in the surrounding villages and

started home. He led his irak from the village on foot until he was out of sight. Only then did he teleport.

He'd gone to the village to deliver stillstone, which only grew in the wastelands to the north, or within the Red Dragon's Mountain. When he was on his way to Chaldea, he'd heard the villages were suffering from a stillstone shortage, so he'd teleported north and gathered some.

Although those two had somehow found him at the irak trader's place, he was certain he'd be safe in the surrounding villages. His business there wasn't planned, and no one knew he was there. Still, he looked around restlessly.

He had a nagging feeling that girl who came and went like a storm would somehow appear anyway, followed by that respectable young man.

"I'm just being paranoid..."

This time he'd teleported them a whole five days away. That was the furthest distance he could manage. There was no way they'd catch up to him in just two days.

The irak tilted its head at Naiz, wondering what he was worrying about. Its droopy eyes were trained on him.

"It's nothing. Don't worry about it. Let's go home, Suzanne."

"Gweeeh."

Suzanne lost interest in Naiz after hearing his reply, and turned her half-dead eyes forward. She seemed to be staring at something, far off in the distance.

"Suzanne?"

"Gweeeeeeh."

Naiz had been with Suzanne for years and could read her grunts.

"What is it, girl? What do you see?"

Naiz squinted at the horizon. All he could see was the sun, the sand, and—

"Hm? What's that..."

Naiz felt a sense of foreboding. He spotted something far off in the sky.

"Is that a black...dot? No, it seems to be a..."

Naiz's voice was trembling.

The steadily growing black spot turned out to be two people.

"Found youuuuuuuuuu!"

"Impossible."

Miledi's voice rang loudly through the desert. He was stunned. This was becoming his worst nightmare.

As they got close, Naiz could see that Miledi was holding Oscar by the collar. Oscar looked exhausted, and would have slumped on the floor if they'd been standing on it.

"We found you again, Nacchan!"

"N-Nacchan?"

Miledi landed lightly. The moment her feet touched the ground, she doubled over and panted. Her chosen method of travel had exhausted her.

Naiz was amazed at her nickname for him. He looked over at Oscar, whom she'd deposited at her side.

He was lying face-up on the ground. It didn't look like he'd be getting up anytime soon, either.

"Is he...alright?"

"Haaah... Haaah... He's fine! He's O-kun after all!"

I'm not quite sure how that's a proper reason. Still, Oscar raised his hand and waved it weakly, so Naiz left it at that.

"I gotta say though, using ancient magic for two days straight really wears a girl out. Even with all of O-kun's mana, I was barely able to make it. If monsters found us now, we'd be dead!"

"That's not really something to be excited about..."

Naiz stared at her as if he was looking at some alien creature.

"How'd you find me?"

"That's a secret!"

She brought her finger to her lips and winked. Although there was no wind, her ponytail bobbed back and forth.

For a few short seconds, Naiz lost it. He could kill at that moment. Once he'd calmed down, he repeated his question.

"How'd you find me?"

"Hee hee. Well, I *suppose* I could tell you. But not for free. You've gotta listen to what I have to say fir—"

Naiz opened a portal beneath them. His retribution was merciless. Oscar vanished into it.

"Ah, O-kuuuuuuuuuuuuuuuun?!"

Miledi dropped to all fours and stared into the portal.

"Come to think of it," said Naiz, "he can't move... Oh no. I hope he doesn't drown..."

"Wait, O-kun's in trouble?! Damn you, don't think this is over yet! Even if I leave now, I'll keep coming back as many times as it takes!"

With those parting words, Miledi jumped into the portal.

The desert was quiet once more.

Although for some reason, with the disappearance of the girl, the silence felt oppressive.

A slight breeze ruffled Naiz's hair.

"Gweeeeeeh."

"You're right, Suzanne. Let's go home."

Naiz started on the road home.

⁕ ⁕ ⁕ ⁕ ⁕ ⁕ ⁕ ⁕ ⁕ ⁕ ⁕ ⁕ ⁕

A few days later.

Naiz was back home. Although whether his living space really qualified as a house was up for debate.

Currently, he lived in a cave. It fell straight down, and ended at a terraced base. There, he'd carved out rooms from the rock. There was a spot for his bed, a table in the center, a storage room, a kitchen, and so on. But what was truly strange about his dwelling was that it was lit by magma.

His cavern was at the heart of the Red Dragon's Mountain, a massive volcano at the heart of the Crimson Desert. No people lived near the volcano, nor was it somewhere people should have been able to live.

The volcano had earned its name because its eruptions were like a red dragon's breath, burning hot and always unpredictable.

The nearby villagers believed a red dragon truly did sleep in the depths. Not only did no one live at its base, but people didn't even dare approach it.

Despite that, Naiz had no problems. The extreme heat didn't bother him in the slightest. He stepped out on the terrace and looked at the river of magma below.

"Everything looks fine..."

He turned and returned to his room, then sat down at his table and reached for the basket atop it. In it was the food he'd bought by selling iraks. Bread, cheese, and fruit.

He pulled a sheet of parchment from a nearby rack and started writing something.

"The Holy Church has been buying up iraks..."

He muttered quietly to himself. That was what the merchant's apprentice said. He was curious about what they were planning, but it didn't really matter. He was basically retired from irak herding.

Although it would be a problem if their actions made iraks vanish from the desert. They were the preeminent beasts of burden here, and used in many different aspects of life. The rural villages depended on them for trade, and would die without them. Transporting as many goods as possible was of paramount importance, because of how frequent monster attacks were.

Oftentimes traders lost their iraks to monsters. Unless they were able to find a replacement instantly, they were forced to move their wares by foot. If the Holy Church had taken all of those spares, there was reason to be concerned.

"Maybe I should see what they're scheming..."

Naiz finished off his bread, downed a pitcher of water, and stood.

He thought back to the two who'd been chasing him this whole time. He was certain they wouldn't be able to chase him into the volcano, but once he left, chances were they'd pop up again.

"Nah, it's impossible... This place is too far from where I sent them. They definitely won't find me here."

He'd encountered Miledi and Oscar in the southeastern fringes of the desert, but the volcano was to the north. Moreover, he was planning to make his trip using teleportation. There was no possible way for them to keep up.

At least, that was what he kept telling himself. He was still terrified of running into them. *Next time I'll force them to tell me how they're tracking me and promise to leave me alone.*

Unwilling to even step foot outside of his house, he left using teleportation. He spent the day checking up on the outlying villages, finally starting down the road home as the sun set.

He breathed a sigh of relief. The pair of troublemakers hadn't appeared all day.

Once he was safely hidden behind a pair of dunes, he teleported back home.

"Ah, welcome back, Nacchan!"

"Sorry for barging into your house without asking. We brought you some gifts, though."

Miledi and Oscar were sitting at his table, sipping tea. Naiz couldn't believe it.

"How?" he croaked out.

◦|◦ ◦|◦ ◦|◦ ◦|◦ ◦|◦ ◦|◦ ◦|◦ ◦|◦ ◦|◦ ◦|◦ ◦|◦ ◦|◦ ◦|◦

"D-don't be so mad. I-I'm sorry I came in without asking. Please forgive us, Nacchan."

"I'm not mad. Just amazed. Also, quit calling me Nacchan," he said, as he sank down into a chair.

Idly, he noticed there were two more chairs than there had been before.

In truth, he almost admired their persistence. At the same time, he couldn't believe they'd managed to track him down here. Or had the guts to come into a magma chamber. More than anything, he really wished she'd stop calling him Nacchan.

"You might as well give up... That nickname's there to stay. She's crazy—I mean, stubborn. Oh, these are for you, by the way. They're baked sweets made with the local fruit. You don't dislike sweets, do you?"

"Hm? Yeah, they're fine."

"Hey, did you just call me crazy, O-kun? Did you? Hey! Answer me—"

"You won't teleport us away again, will you?" Oscar asked Naiz.

"Now that you've found this place, it won't matter. I have only two options. Find out how you're tracking me and destroy whatever means you're using, or..."

"Hear us out and refuse our offer," said Oscar. "Right?"

"Yes."

"Hey, why're you two leaving me out?" said Miledi. "Don't you think that's mean? Also, O-kun, you totally did call me cra—"

Oscar and Naiz stared at each other, completely ignoring her. They probed each other's intentions. An epic battle of wills played out between them in the span of a few short seconds.

After a while, they heard sobbing from under the table. The two men blinked as they returned to reality. They looked underneath the table simultaneously, and found Miledi curled up in a ball, crying.

They ignored her completely and resumed staring at each other. Oscar took a sip of his tea.

"By the way, your place is amazing. As far as I can tell, you're not using any artifacts, but the place is still perfectly insulated against the magma. Are you doing this with your ancient magic?"

"You could say that."

"But why make a place like this your home? Well, I guess if you want to avoid people, the middle of a volcano is perfect."

"Are you going to tell me what you came for," said the man. "Or just ask me about my life?"

"Whoops, my apologies. Your design choices just piqued my interest as a Synergist."

The two of them were actually carrying on a conversation. Still in tears, Miledi crawled out from under the table and sat with them.

"Okay, I'll be serious now, so can you please stop ignoring me?"

Her tone was uncharacteristically contrite.

Naiz and Oscar sighed simultaneously.

"How are you two in sync like that?" she asked.

"Probably because of you."

"It's definitely because of you."

"*Hic...*"

Miledi blew her nose.

Once she'd composed herself, she gave Naiz the same speech she'd given Oscar. She talked about the tyranny of the gods, the Holy Church's madness, and the twisted way of the world. She spoke about the fate that awaited those who stepped out of line, as well as the horrors that accompanied blind fanaticism. She also briefly explained her past and how she came to meet Oscar.

Finally, she came to the organization she belonged to—the Liberators.

When she was finished, all she could hear was their soft breathing.

Then Naiz broke the silence and explained his powers. "My magic allows me to interfere with space. I can connect two different points, teleport somewhere else in the blink of an eye, and create spacial barriers to block things off, even insubstantial things like heat...but I don't have the ability to heal."

Oscar could guess why he'd brought up healing.

"Don't worry about it," Oscar said with a smile, and shook his head.

Miledi looked warmly into Naiz's eyes.

"You're a good person," she told him with conviction. What pained Naiz the most wasn't the truth about the gods, or the wretched state of the world, but the fact that Oscar's siblings were hurt. And he lamented his own powerlessness.

Come to think of it, he was like that the first time he saved us, too, Oscar thought. Judging by his actions, and the fact that he'd chosen a volcano for a home, Oscar knew he was trying to hide his powers. Despite that, he hadn't even hesitated to use them to save the two of them from the Sandworms.

The only reason rumors about him had spread was because he broke cover to help those in need. However, Naiz didn't seem happy to be called kind. He twisted his face into a grimace.

"No, I'm not. I'm just—"

He cut off. Whatever he couldn't say pained him to no end.

Miledi looked straight at him.

"Just what? Tell us."

She knew it was rude, but she asked anyway. Even if it hurt him to speak, they couldn't help until they knew.

"I have no way of knowing what kind of things you're dealing with," Oscar chimed in. "But at the very least, you've saved enough people in the desert that rumors have spread. And for that, I respect you. We'd really like to have someone like you in our group."

Naiz could tell they were being sincere, but his expression hardened. Then, he delivered his ultimatum.

"As you wished, I listened to your story. However, my answer remains unchanged. Nothing you say can convince me otherwise."

In the end, he said no. At the same time, he opened up another portal. It was obvious he wanted them to leave. Miledi and Oscar could tell from his grim expression that he would say no more.

They exchanged glances. Oscar shook his head. Miledi's shoulders drooped, and she smiled sadly at Naiz.

"Okay. Bye then, Nacchan."

She stepped into the portal of her own accord. Oscar nodded to Naiz and followed.

Silence filled the room.

For some reason, he felt cold as he stared at the chairs Oscar had transmuted.

Naiz spent a long time staring at those two chairs.

⁕ ⁕ ⁕ ⁕ ⁕ ⁕ ⁕ ⁕ ⁕ ⁕ ⁕ ⁕ ⁕ ⁕

The next day.

"We're baaack. Nacchan, are you here? I've come over to hang out!"

"Hey, it's been a while. A whole day, in fact. We brought you some cheese this time."

Miledi and Oscar returned to Naiz's house.

He stared at them in shock, as he'd been certain he wouldn't see them again.

"Oh? Did you think we'd leave you alone because of how we parted yesterday? Puha ha ha! I never said anything about leaving you alone forever! You just assumed that all on your own, Nacchan!"

Miledi cackled, her serious demeanor from yesterday nowhere to be seen. A vein pulsed in Naiz's forehead, and he opened a portal underneath Miledi.

However, she used her gravity magic to dodge out of the way. She sidestepped every other portal Naiz opened, too.

"How many times do you think you've done that now? I've got the timing of your portals down pat!"

Naiz wanted to knock that smug smile off her face. For first time in his life, he actually wanted to hurt someone.

"We brought our own cups, too," said Oscar. "Seems like we'll be coming here pretty often, so do you mind if we leave them here? This is your cupboard, right?"

Oscar put not just cups, but a few plates and spoons into Naiz's cupboard as well.

I thought he was suffering under Miledi's tyranny, but he's just as brazen.

Had Oscar realized how much Miledi had influenced him, he'd have been so shocked he'd stay huddled in bed for a week.

⁕ ⁕ ⁕ ⁕ ⁕ ⁕ ⁕ ⁕ ⁕ ⁕ ⁕ ⁕ ⁕

Another week passed.

Oscar and Miledi started taking their meals with Naiz. Sometimes they'd talk about the Liberators; other times they'd just make small talk.

Whenever Naiz tried to tell them he wasn't interested, Miledi would wave him off and change the topic. He couldn't get rid of them. Miledi was too used to his portals.

Oscar found himself fascinated by the ore contained in the volcano, and started exploring its depths. At one point he rode his umbrella like a miniature boat down the magma streams.

In doing so, he'd figured out the real reason why Naiz had chosen this volcano.

The Red Dragon's Mountain was an active volcano that erupted once every fifty years or so. It had been fifty-five years since the last eruption, and most of the desert dwellers expected another any time.

However, Naiz was forcibly keeping the volcano dormant. He'd calmed the magma by dumping a massive quantity of still-stone into it. He'd also carved a side channel with his spatial magic for the magma to flow into when the pressure grew too great.

That told Oscar that, unless something serious happened, Naiz wouldn't leave the volcano.

So far, neither threats, nor escape, nor even a blunt refusal had gotten Miledi or Oscar to leave. He was at his wits' end. Still, though he didn't realize it, he had started to look forward to their visits. Eating meals together, talking to Oscar about his various inventions, and discussing iraks with Miledi had taken on a certain charm.

Naturally, Oscar and Miledi picked up on the shift in his attitude.

The fact that he genuinely seemed to enjoy their company was the main reason that they hadn't given up.

Although Naiz still stubbornly refused to join them.

❖ ❖ ❖ ❖ ❖ ❖ ❖ ❖ ❖ ❖ ❖ ❖ ❖ ❖

Eight days had passed since Miledi and Oscar found out where Naiz lived. They were currently eating breakfast at a restaurant in the small oasis village of Liv.

Although it was classified as a village, the settlement was the size of a small town. It was located in the southern Doumibral domain, the closest human settlement to the volcano.

The two rented an inn here because of its proximity to Naiz.

At present, Miledi was flopped over their table and groaning. The two of them were meant to be hashing out a plan to convince Naiz.

They were eating their breakfast early, and there was still a chill in the air. The sun hadn't risen yet, and nights in the desert were frigid. For the people who lived here, this cool time period between the freezing nights and scorching days was their favorite. Despite the early hour, many others were eating their breakfast as well.

Most of the other patrons' gazes were locked onto Miledi, whose loud groaning attracted their attention. Oscar, meanwhile, was perusing a local brochure and paying his partner no mind.

"Miledi, according to this, the greengrocer to the east distills his own wine. What do you think of bringing some to Naiz as a gift? He seems like a heavy drinker, but I don't think he liked the dry sake we got him last time."

"O-kun, can't you see how distressed I am? As my partner, shouldn't you be more concerned?"

Oscar looked up from the brochure.

"Sorry. I figured you were just complaining about breakfast. You're always whining about how you don't have enough to eat."

"Excuse me, I'm no glutton. Besides, what I'm worried about is how we're going to convince Nacchan. I know you two get along now, but we still haven't gotten any closer to convincing him."

"Well, he's definitely interested in all of my inventions. He's liked all the ones I showed him. Whenever I talk about what I'm working on, he pulls out the alcohol, and we talk for ages. Anyway, as for changing his mind... I think we should just take it slow. First we've got to build trust."

"So Nacchan can tell us what's burdening him, right?"

"Exactly. Even you had to warm up to me before you were willing to tell me about your past."

"You've...got a point there."

Oscar set the brochure aside. He entwined his fingers together and spoke carefully, choosing his words.

"Life is...difficult. For everyone, really. But especially if you have scars so deep that they're still hurting. His problems aren't something he can tell just anyone, nor are they things we can ask about just because we're curious. That's why I want us to get to know each other better. We have to get closer if we want to help him. And making lasting friendships is something that takes time, right? If we push him, it'll only end up driving him into a corner."

Oscar gulped down some water. He turned away from Miledi and looked over at the sparkling oasis, watching the sun crest the horizon.

"So let's take it slow," he went on. "I'll follow you forever, so long as you haven't given up. There's no need to rush."

He'd promised her he'd follow her to the depths of hell, and he meant it. Miledi didn't reply. The sounds of other customers eating filled the silence.

Oscar turned back to Miledi, wondering why she was so quiet.

"What's with that expression?" he asked.

"Hmmm? What do you mean?"

Miledi was grinning from ear to ear. Oscar's mood suddenly soured. He busied himself with cleaning up the remnants of their breakfast.

"You're totaaaaally in love with me, aren't you, O-kun?"

"Leave the sleep-talking for when you're asleep, and help me clean up."

Oscar narrowed his eyes and jerked his chin at Miledi's plate.

"Oh, are you blushing?" Miledi teased, still grinning. "You *are,* O-kun!"

Oscar debated throwing his coffee into Miledi's face, but he decided to be civil. As the days passed, he was getting better and better at handling Miledi.

And so he simply adjusted his glasses and changed the topic.

"Naiz said he'd be busy this morning. He's probably delivering iraks to the villages that are running low, so I'm thinking we should head over in the afternoon."

"He's out helping people again? I can't tell if he's just a good person, or if..."

"Hopefully we'll find that out eventually, too," said Oscar. "Though I am a little worried. Sure, he tends to hide his abilities, but he'll use them if necessary to help people. After all, he didn't hesitate to save us. And rumors have spread so far that even you'd heard of him, all the way in the east. It's only a matter of time before his powers are exposed."

"You're right. One thing I don't get, though... Why does everyone call him a fairy?"

The rumors had all said that the "Fairy of the Desert" had saved them. With his bulky frame, taciturn expression, sharp eyes, and red hair, Naiz was the furthest thing from a fairy that Oscar could imagine.

"Bwah."

Oscar nearly spit out his coffee, as he imagined Naiz trying to look like a fairy.

"W-well, it doesn't look like he's the one who came up with it, and rumors have a habit of going wild. A wandering fairy of the desert who helps lost travelers makes for a much better story than a buff dude doing the same."

Still, I really want to know how anyone came to associate the word "fairy" with Naiz. Both Miledi and Oscar were burning with curiosity.

As they cleaned up, a young girl interrupted them.

"Umm...have you met the Fairy of the Desert?"

Miledi and Oscar turned to see two girls looking up at them.

They appeared to be siblings. At the very least, they resembled each other. Both had dark brown skin and jade green eyes. The older one looked to be around twelve or thirteen, while the younger couldn't have been over eight. The younger girl wore her long hair loose, while the older sister had her shoulder-length hair in braids. They were both wearing white robes and sandals, and seemed to be local residents.

"Umm, are you talking to us?"

"Ah, y-yes. We're sorry for interrupting you!"

The older sister bowed her head. It seemed they'd overheard.

Miledi smiled reassuringly at them.

"He certainly didn't look like a fairy to me, but we have met him~! We were just wondering why everyone calls him a fairy... Would you two happen to know?"

The girls' expressions changed when Miledi mentioned that they'd met him. They exchanged furtive glances. It was obvious they knew something. However, the two didn't speak. They weren't sure whether or not it was safe.

After a few seconds, the older sister replied.

"Are you two from the Holy Church?"

"Hell no."

Oscar and Miledi answered in sync, their contempt obvious. Such an open display of malice would have been dangerous if they were talking to devout believers. Fortunately, the two girls seemed relieved. The younger sister leaned forward.

"Onii-san, Onee-san!" she blurted out. "Do you know where the guardian deity is?! Me and Sue-nee really like him! We've been looking for him this whole time! We really want to see him again!"

The older sister hurriedly tried to cover her younger sister's mouth, but it was too late.

Miledi and Oscar exchanged glances. She'd called him a guardian deity, not a fairy. They needed to know more.

"Sue-nee is really popular with the boys," added the younger sister, who didn't know when to shut her mouth. "But she turned them all down because she's in love with him!"

Poor Sue blushed as she tried to shut her sister up.

Oscar and Miledi nodded to each other.

"Would you like to join us for breakfast?"

"We'll treat you to dessert, too."

They bribed the sisters with food.

❖ ❖ ❖ ❖ ❖ ❖ ❖ ❖ ❖ ❖ ❖ ❖ ❖ ❖

The sisters loaded their plates, the younger with gusto, the older with a little more hesitation. She was still embarrassed.

Over the course of breakfast, Miledi and Oscar learned that the older sister's name was Susha Liv Doumibral and the younger's was Yunfa Liv Doumibral. They were, as Oscar had guessed, residents of the village.

It was customary for people in the desert to take the name of the region and village they were born in, which was why their middle and last name were Liv and Doumibral, respectively. They were from Liv village, in the Doumibral fiefdom.

That reminds me, where's Naiz from? As Oscar hadn't known much about the desert customs, he hadn't given it much thought. He asked Susha if she knew, but she hadn't even known that his first name was Naiz.

When Oscar told her, she repeated it like some kind of charm. *Damn, this girl's serious about him.*

Miledi asked how the girls had met Naiz, and it turned out their first encounter was pretty much the same as Miledi's.

They were under attack by monsters when he showed up and teleported them to safety.

However, one of the monsters caused Yunfa's mana to go berserk. When Susha told Naiz that, he vanished and came back with stillstone.

They'd been so surprised by Naiz's constant teleporting that they couldn't even thank him before he'd disappeared with his customary "Don't tell anyone about me."

"Since then, we've been looking all over for him. I still haven't been able to give him my thanks."

"And you want to confess and marry him, too!" said Yunfa. "I'm fine with being his mistress!"

Susha blushed again. She wrapped an arm around her sister's mouth and gagged her.

"We actually spread the rumors that he was the Fairy of the Desert on purpose. I thought that since Naiz-sama didn't want people to know about him, the least we could do was say that the person who saved us looked completely different. I knew word would spread eventually, so I made sure to tell all the adventurers and bards my version of events first."

"I see. So your way of thanking him was turning the guardian into a fairy."

Miledi nodded in understanding. However, Oscar noticed something off about Susha's story. Yunfa's next words solidified his suspicions.

"I helped Sue-nee out, too! I told everyone exactly what Sue-nee told me to!"

So this was definitely all her idea... Oscar came to a conclusion. He pushed up his glasses.

"Sorry for asking such a sudden question, but do your parents run this bar?"

"No. Our parents were killed by monsters when we were young... Right now we're living with their friends."

"And they run this bar?"

"Yes." This time she didn't deny it. Now Oscar was certain. Susha was the start of the rumors.

"You were the one behind the fairy rumors?"

"Yep." Susha grinned.

Oscar and Miledi exchanged glances. According to Susha, Naiz saved them around two years ago. In other words, she'd come up with this elaborate plan to create the Fairy of the Desert when she was just ten. All on her own.

And it worked. At the very least, everyone talked about a Fairy of the Desert, and not a guardian.

"Th-that's pretty impressive."

Miledi spoke her honest opinion. Susha blushed.

"It's all for Naiz-sama's sake."

Considering her age, it was conceivable that she would have hit puberty already. Still, the fact that she was so set on Naiz from the age of ten was rather impressive. She was really serious.

"What kind of relationship do you two have with Naiz-sama? You said you'd met him."

Susha definitely wouldn't let any leads out of her grasp. Yunfa stared expectantly.

"Hmm... You could say we run into him a lot these days."

"R-really?! Where is he staying?!"

Susha leaned forward excitedly. Neither she nor Yunfa had expected them to meet him at will.

"We'll have to ask him if it's okay to tell you first," Miledi replied. "We're going to see him again today, too, so we'll ask him then. I promise you'll get to meet him soon, so just wait patiently, okay?"

"Miledi-san... I suppose we'll have to. Yeah, we'll wait."

Although she was a little disappointed, Susha had to admit Miledi was right. She nodded.

Yunfa looked from Oscar to Miledi. After a few seconds, she dropped another bombshell.

"By the way, are you two a couple?"

Susha turned back to her sister in a panic. *You can't just ask that!*

Miledi stared blankly at Yunfa, while Oscar grinned.

"Ha ha ha... That's a good joke, Yunfa-chan," said Oscar.

"O-kun? What's that supposed to mean?"

Even if you're not going to admit it, you could at least not deny it so cleanly! As Miledi glared at Oscar, Yunfa continued dropping bombshells.

"You're not? It would have been better if you were, though~!"

"Huh? Why's that, Yunfa?" asked Miledi.

"Because you said you're always talking to the guy Onee-san's in love with. And you're going to meet him again today... If you two aren't lovers, then maybe you're seducing him!"

"......"

Susha fell silent. Her expression was thunderous. There was a dangerous glint in her eyes.

"It's a misunderstanding! I don't have any interest in that guy, promise!"

Miledi hurriedly tried to explain herself. Susha's glare was absolutely terrifying. Miledi broke out in a cold sweat.

Oscar watched the whole exchange with a grin. Miledi turned her reproachful gaze onto him.

"Besides, O-kun's been with me the whole time! I promise it's really not like that. We're going to see him about something a lot more serious than that."

"A lot more...serious? You mean your future together?"

"Shit. I should have known it would end up like this!"

This was the first time Oscar had seen Miledi, who was always teasing others, so flustered. It was the most fun he'd had in ages. Plus, Yunfa wasn't done.

"It's okay, we have Sue-nee anyway! Her boobs are way bigger than yours! Once he sees them, he'll totally fall for her!"

"Huh?"

"Huh?"

Miledi looked at Susha's chest. Susha looked at Miledi's.

It was hard to make out the shape of Susha's body through her bulky robe. Despite that, her chest still stuck out.

Miledi compared that to her own chest. She ran her hands over her washboard-flat boobs. Her head drooped. She looked crestfallen.

Oscar was honestly impressed.

"Yunfa-chan, you've got a bright future ahead of you. Not many people can say they've made Miledi cry..."

"Huh? Umm, ehe he, it was nothing."

Yunfa didn't really get what Oscar was saying, but she could tell she was being praised.

The real question is, was she doing it all by instinct, or was that planned? Seeing as Yunfa's older sister was a master of information manipulation at the age of ten, Oscar was certain she had a lot of potential.

He had a sneaking suspicion that Yunfa tore Miledi down just in case she was thinking of taking Naiz from Susha, but he didn't want to stir up a hornet's nest by asking.

Oscar watched Susha console Miledi and wondered how the presence of these sisters would change the relationship between himself and Naiz.

⁎⁄⁎ ⁎⁄⁎ ⁎⁄⁎ ⁎⁄⁎ ⁎⁄⁎ ⁎⁄⁎ ⁎⁄⁎ ⁎⁄⁎ ⁎⁄⁎ ⁎⁄⁎ ⁎⁄⁎ ⁎⁄⁎ ⁎⁄⁎

The Red Dragon's Mountain was a dome volcano. That meant its eruptions were usually just outpourings of viscous lava instead of violent explosions. It also meant the mountain itself was shaped like a gently sloping trapezoid. It was a mere three kilometers tall, but five kilometers wide.

After parting ways with the sisters, Miledi and Oscar headed over to the volcano. They could feel the heat as they landed on the summit. White smoke rose up from holes, and it really looked as if a red dragon might live there.

There was an entrance to Naiz's house at the top. They approached the glowing orange crater that doubled as Naiz's front door. The heat was kept at bay by Naiz's barriers.

"Let's go, O-kun."

"No matter how many times I do it, I'll never get used to jumping into the mouth of an active volcano."

"Says the guy who rode his umbrella down a lava river."

The pair bantered with each other as they leaped in. Miledi sped them up with her gravity magic as they headed down to the terrace.

As they drew closer to the ground, the air grew cooler. Naiz's barriers kept the heat out around his house more effectively than elsewhere. It was quite an impressive achievement. Oscar had learned over a night of drinking that it had taken Naiz a lot of time to master barriers that precise.

"Nacchaaaaan! You home? We've come back to play~!"

"Sorry for coming over all the time," said Oscar. "We brought you some wine today. It's still mid-afternoon, but how about a drink?"

They waltzed into Naiz's house like it was their own. The pair found him sitting cross-legged on the floor, grinding something down with a pestle and mortar. He sighed and turned to his unwanted house guests.

"It's already been more than a week... How long are you planning on doing this?"

"Until you agree to become our comrade."

"So you'll keep coming for the rest of your life?" he asked.

"Aha ha, I feel like someone else said that to me before, too!"

"That'd be me."

Oscar gave Naiz a sympathetic look and helped him clean up his workspace.

"Is that stillstone?"

"Yes. It's difficult to harvest, so most villages are always short."

"Except you live where it grows, so it's a piece of cake for you.

I've taken the liberty of harvesting some for myself, too."

Oscar eased himself into his chair. Miledi sat down next to him and idly swung her legs. She seemed bored. Whenever Oscar and Naiz started talking about these kinds of things, Miledi found herself left out.

"I wanted to see if I could grind the powder so fine it would turn into a liquid."

"You what?"

"There's a lot of monsters around here that make people's mana go berserk. Stillstone is considered the only cure, since it suppresses mana."

"I mean, yeah, but why would you need to liquify it?"

"I'm not sure yet, but maybe it'll be easier to ingest. Also, you could change the concentration. And if you're trying a dangerous magical experiment, you could make your magic circle out of it."

"Hmm... So basically, you're looking for ways to use it other than as medicine."

"Precisely. So—"

As the conversation grew more technical, Miledi interrupted them with a yell.

"Gaaaaaaaaaaaaaaaaaaaaaah! I can't believe you two are ignoring me and having fun on your own! It's not good to ignore your friends like this!"

Miledi crossed her arms.

Oscar and Naiz shared a knowing smile. Miledi always sulked when she saw them getting along so well.

She muttered something angrily.

"I'll tell Sue-chan that Nacchan's more into O-kun than he is into me."

"Hey, don't make it sound like we're gay. Also, I get the feeling she'll take you seriously, so please don't say that."

Oscar shivered. Naiz looked over at Oscar with a questioning gaze. Oscar and Miledi exchanged glances.

"Sue-chan's this girl who lives in Liv," said Oscar. "She has a little sister called Yunfa."

"Hmm?"

"They're the ones that spread the rumor that you're the Fairy of the Desert."

"What? What does..."

Naiz suddenly looked interested. He was always interested in the rumors. He looked puzzled as to why anyone would change them.

Oscar chimed in with an explanation.

"You saved a pair of sisters from monsters two years ago, right? The younger had her mana go berserk, and you healed her. Remember them?"

Naiz combed through his memories for a minute.

"Those two, huh?"

"So you do remember them?" Oscar asked.

"Hee hee hee hee. You're one smooth operator, Nacchan," said Miledi. "The older sister's totally head over heels for you, and she's a real cutie."

"She's what now?"

Naiz didn't recognize the expression. He tilted his head in confusion. After having been so thoroughly demolished, Miledi was dying to tease someone.

"Well, you see, ever since you saved them, those two girls have been looking allllll over for you. They said they want to thank you for saving them. But the truth is, the older sister's in love with you! Even though she's only thirteen!"

Miledi didn't mention that despite her age, Susha had bigger boobs than her. She wasn't a masochist, after all.

"The little girl from back then is in love with me?"

Naiz remembered how young the children were. He found it hard to believe that in just two years, that girl had run a mass misinformation campaign because she'd fallen in love with him.

For her part, Miledi found it hard to believe that she'd been beaten by a girl many years younger. Worse, Susha was still in the middle of her growth spurt, while Miledi had long since passed through puberty.

"Since you said you didn't want people to know about you," Oscar continued, "she made up a story that the person saving travelers was a dainty fairy. All because she loves you."

Naiz grimaced.

Miledi grinned and pointed at him.

"Hey, how does it feel? Hey, Nacchan, tell me. How does it feel knowing a thirteen-year-old girl's totally in love with you? Come on, Nacchan, you can tell, I won't spill your sec—"

Naiz grabbed Miledi's face in an iron grip.

"Oscar, do you mind if I throw your partner out of this volcano?"

❖ ❖ ❖ ❖ ❖ ❖ ❖ ❖ ❖ ❖ ❖ ❖ ❖ ❖

Oscar pulled his chains out of his sleeves.

"Owwwwwwww! Hey, Nacchan, could you loosen your grip a little?! I can feel my skull cracking! And O-kun, you're *my* partner! You're supposed to be helping *me*, not him!"

"This is your fault!"

"Why are you two always in sync like thiiiiiiiiiiiis?!"

There was a loud crack, and Miledi's body went limp. When Naiz let her go, she fell into her chair with a thud. After that, Oscar and Naiz ignored her and began drinking the wine.

Some time later, Miledi awoke to find Oscar's umbrella raining healing light on her. Once her headache was gone, Oscar returned to the topic of the two girls.

He explained their sincere wish to meet Naiz. Oscar expected that Naiz, who made helping people such a big part of his life, wouldn't mind meeting them. However, he looked troubled.

"She already knows about your powers," said Oscar. "Plus, they're trying harder than anyone to make sure no one finds out about you, so what's the problem with going to see them?"

"Even if you don't have much to say," Miledi added, "I think you should go see them. If you don't, I'm pretty sure Sue-chan will keep searching for you for the rest of her life. She's that serious about you."

"Those girls think I'm some kind of hero or guardian deity," Naiz said in a despondent voice. "Don't they?"

"I think some of the other locals think you're a guardian deity, too, but yes."

"Well, they're wrong. I'm no guardian. I'm only doing this for myself...to atone for my mistakes."

Oscar and Miledi looked at each other. Miledi sat up straighter.

"Did something happen in the past? Is that why you can't meet Sue-chan, or come with us?"

"......"

"Nacchan. You asked how long we're planning on stay. I won't leave until you at least tell us why you won't come with us. That's how much recruiting you matters to me. I know this is a rude thing to ask, and I know it probably hurts to talk about, but that's precisely why we can't leave."

Her implacable gaze pierced Naiz. He turned to see Oscar wearing the same serious expression. His quiet eyes held a deep resolve. They knew what they were asking, but this time they wouldn't back down.

These are the most troublesome friends I've ever made. However, he'd already heard Miledi and Oscar's tales. He knew from the start that they wouldn't be shaken so easily. He understood now why a flat refusal wasn't enough. Unless he gave them a reason, they wouldn't back down. No, they couldn't back down. It was his own fault for dragging things on this long. Naiz smiled bitterly.

"Do you know of a village called Gruen?"

Miledi and Oscar shook their heads. Naiz took a deep breath.

"It's the village I was born in...and the village I destroyed."

Oscar and Miledi gulped.

Eyes downcast, Naiz began his tale.

"My full name is Naiz Gruen Caliente."

"Caliente's the region furthest to the north, isn't it?"

Naiz nodded.

"Gruen was the village closest to the capital. My father was a soldier in the fiefdom's army. I always looked up to him, and wanted to be just like him. Me, my best friend Yogun, and my little brother Est would always practice swordplay together. My mother was the kindest person I'd ever known. Not only that, she was also a talented mage. Thinking back, I was truly blessed."

He'd had a loving family, and friends who shared the same dreams. Not only that, he'd been a rather talented young boy.

Oscar glanced over at Miledi. Although she was born into a wealthy household, her family hadn't shown an ounce of love. Miledi noticed his gaze and looked over. She guessed what he was thinking, but didn't seem the least bit depressed. In fact, she flashed Oscar a warm smile.

Seeing as he didn't have to worry about his partner, Oscar returned his gaze to Naiz.

"My dad was usually away for work, but he'd come back for a few days every month to spend time with us. Mom always told us not to bother him because he was tired, but Yogun and I would always beg him to train us. My dad was the strongest warrior in the village, and I was always eager to show him how much I'd grown," Naiz said wistfully. He'd obviously been very fond of his friends and family.

"Yogun had a saying: 'No true hero meets their end in a backwater village.' He wanted to fight for important people in important places and rise up in the world. His ambitions were always greater than mine, always looking toward the future. And even though he was a talented fighter, he was always jealous of my skills."

Unlike Naiz, who only wanted to be a soldier, Yogun dreamed big. And Naiz envied that.

Naiz smiled briefly, reminiscing. But before long, his dark expression returned. Oscar couldn't tell if it was anger or regret.

"I never realized just how deep that jealousy ran. Even though I was always with him, I never noticed what he was really thinking."

On a day like any other, Naiz's father Solda returned home and started sparring with Yogun. The hour grew late, and Solda was planning on returning home, when a bunch of the villagers ran up. Their faces were pale, and they were screaming about a monster.

The village had its own guards, of course. They dealt with most of the threats that showed up. But this time, the monster was too powerful.

Solda knew his duty, and immediately agreed to go help. The monster was too powerful for the guards, but a professional soldier like Solda should have had no trouble.

"Yogun and I begged my dad to take us with him. We were already fifteen by then. In one year, we would have been eligible to join the army. My dad thought it would make good training, so he agreed."

The two of them happily followed Solda to the gates...and that was where everything went wrong.

"There were more monsters than the villagers had mentioned

in their report. We'd just finished dealing with the ones the villagers had told us about, so we let our guard down, which was why neither me nor Yogun noticed them burrowing behind us."

By the time they heard Solda's warning, they were nearly in the monster's jaws.

There wasn't even enough time to cast a barrier. Even if there was, Yogun and Naiz were too terrified to move. However, the crisis awoke a slumbering power inside Naiz, and he moved entirely on instinct.

"That was the first time you used spatial magic, right?"

Naiz nodded silently.

"My dad couldn't believe what had just happened. Neither could I. I'd shredded the monster in front of everyone's eyes. I'd unconsciously opened a rift in space. No incantations, no magic circle."

"When your dad and Yogun found out you could use magic from the age of the gods, what did..."

It was obvious the awakening of his powers was directly linked to the destruction of Naiz's village. Miledi scrunched up her face. Oscar took a deep breath, mentally preparing himself.

"My dad made me and Yogun promise to keep it a secret. Though the people of the desert believe in Ehit now, we used to worship nature. Everyone pays lip service to the Holy Church, but most people aren't devout. There are many people who still follow the old ways in secret."

"And your dad was one of them?" asked Oscar. "That was why he wanted to keep your powers a secret. Your father really loved you, but then..."

Oscar furrowed his brows. He could guess what must have happened next. Naiz's secret had gotten out. And since it was clear Solda loved his son, that only left...

"The next year," Naiz continued. "Me and Yogun joined the army. At first, we worked together, aiming to rise up the ranks... but then things changed. Yogun started to act odd, and he often looked at me with barely concealed contempt. I tried to pretend I didn't notice..."

With the awakening of his powers, an unbridgeable gap had been created between them. Furthermore, Naiz discovered he had an aptitude for all kinds of magic. To keep his powers a secret, he used fake magic circles and incantations, but he continued honing his ability to manipulate mana directly. Naturally, his skill with spatial magic grew, too.

Yogun burned with jealousy. He grew to resent Naiz. And so, in the end, he broke his word and spilled Naiz's secret. He told his lord that he knew someone who could use ancient magic. He went to his lord and not the Holy Church, because he knew the church wouldn't reward him. They would have said serving Ehit was reward enough.

However, the results of his betrayal were disastrous. Yogun didn't realize how far someone in power would go to get their hands on ancient magic.

The lord of Caliente, Bolemos, decided to adopt Naiz as his own son, and then step aside to make him the new lord. He wanted his region, Caliente, to be the predominant member of the Sharod alliance, and making an ancient magic wielder the lord was the best way to achieve it.

"So Bolemos would have found your original family...a hindrance."

"That's right. There was a big rainstorm that day. My dad barged into my house, told me to take my brother and mother, and run. Bolemos had sent people to arrest my entire family. In order to let the rest of us escape, my dad..."

Naiz would never forget that stormy day. The sight of his father, yelling at him to save Est and his mother, facing down the soldiers sent to kill him, was burned into his skull.

Warriors of the desert were taught to never show tears, but Naiz cried that night. He wept, cursed his own helplessness, and left his father to die.

He would never forget what happened right after, either. Another unit of soldiers ambushed him as he left his house. He was too distraught to fight back, and was nearly captured. But then, someone came to save him.

"It was Yogun. Yogun came to save me. In the fight that followed, he was mortally injured. With his dying breath, he told me everything."

"He said, 'I'm sorry. I'm so sorry, Naiz. I-I've done something terrible. Please forgive me.' He died begging for forgiveness."

But Naiz couldn't give it.

Even now, he wasn't sure how he felt.

Naiz hated Yogun for destroying his family, but he couldn't deny that he shared some of the blame. He'd spent the most time with Yogun, and yet he couldn't see how his strength was eating away at his best friend. No, he'd pretended not to see it. When he thought about things that way, he wasn't sure he should hate Yogun.

"I ran all the way back to my village. I couldn't teleport as freely as I can now. If I could have, maybe things wouldn't have ended up the way they did."

When he'd arrived, he knew he was too late. His mother and brother were dead. Hundreds of Bolemos' soldiers had stormed the village, with Bolemos at their head. The corpses of Naiz's brother and mother were at the center of the town. They were surrounded by the other villagers.

"He killed them? He didn't try to take them hostage?"

That would have been the smart decision. The only way to keep control of someone as powerful as Naiz.

"According to Yogun, Bolemos was planning to kill them all along, and just say he had them hostage. He told the other villagers that my mother and brother were heretics and ordered them brought out. That was why Bolemos went in person. His words were backed by authority. If he was there, the villagers couldn't disobey."

Bolemos wanted to remove any trace that his soon-to-be-adopted son ever had a real family.

He'd planned to capture Naiz, kill his father, and condemn his mother and brother as heretics. That way, there would be no one to question his story. Anyone who knew the truth wouldn't speak out in fear of being silenced.

Oscar and Miledi looked at each other again. There was one part of Naiz's tale that didn't make sense: Naiz said that Bolemos ordered the villagers to bring Naiz's family to him.

Bolemos needed Naiz to believe his family was still alive to hold any power over him, so he would never have killed them with witnesses around.

It would have made more sense to take them away and quietly dispose of them later. That way, even if Naiz questioned the villagers, they wouldn't know.

Chances were, the people who really killed Naiz's family were the villagers themselves. They'd done it to save their own skins. Having been told that Naiz's family were heretics, they would have wanted to show that they had nothing to do with them. That they were pure. They'd killed Naiz's family to prove their loyalty.

After all, Bolemos had brought hundreds of soldiers with him just to capture two people. The villagers weren't fools. They knew the soldiers had come to destroy their village.

Bolemos claimed Naiz's family were heretics, but he hadn't brought a single priest to confirm that.

It was obviously suspicious. The villagers knew their lives were forfeit once they gave up Naiz's mother and brother.

So, as a drowning man tries to drag others down with him, they'd killed Naiz's family. At least that way, Bolemos couldn't claim that they had been harboring heretics.

Of course, Naiz must have noticed that, too, which was why—

"When I came to, there was nothing around me. I was holding my family's corpses in the empty desert. Bolemos, the villagers, and even the village itself had vanished."

Naiz remembered how the villagers looked at him near the end. They'd worn the guilty expressions of men and women who knew they'd done something wrong, but had felt they had no choice. He remembered how Bolemos just looked annoyed that his plan was ruined. He remembered the soldiers looking warily at him, scared of what he might do. But more than anything, he remembered the rage.

What did my family ever do to deserve this?! You want power that badly?! Fine, I'll let you taste it!

He'd let his anger fuel him, and cast the most powerful spell he was capable of. He'd utterly destroyed a section of space. In other words, he quite literally wiped Gruen off the map, along with the villagers and Bolemos.

As Naiz finished, Miledi and Oscar let out breaths they hadn't even known they were holding.

He looked up at them for the first time since starting his tale.

"Even if Bolemos was guilty, I'm sure many of the soldiers following him were just doing their duty. They might have been good people, with families to return home to. I'm still not sure whether I hate the villagers for what they did, but it wasn't a good reason to kill them all. What I did was horrible."

So that's why he said he's helping people to atone. And because of that, it's not something he wants to be praised or thanked for.

A monster like Naiz didn't deserve to be loved. That was what he believed. He couldn't live with himself if he was surrounded by people thanking him.

"This is the last time I'll say this," he said.

Miledi gulped. Oscar furrowed his brow.

"I won't join you guys. I swore to never again use my powers to fight, even if that means my death."

Naiz had decided to only ever use them to run or protect. His refusal this time was absolute.

"But, Nacchan—"

"Please," he said. "Let this be the end. Don't come see me ever again. If you do, I'll leave. If I keep running, you'll have a hard time chasing after me and continuing your own journey."

He's right. Even if I can track him, there's no way we can keep up with the speed of his teleportation. The only reason they'd been able to chase him thus far was because he never strayed out of the desert.

If he really tried to run, they'd never catch him. Unless they restrained him somehow, anyway. If they did that, they'd be no different from Bolemos.

Naiz waved a hand, and a gate appeared behind them.

"It was a pleasure meeting you, Miledi Reisen, Oscar Orcus. I doubt we'll see each other again, but I wish you luck in your travels."

Miledi opened her mouth, but no words came out.

"Let's go, Miledi."

"O-kun..."

Oscar put a hand on her shoulder. Miledi sighed and stood up. The two of them walked to the gate.

Miledi hung her head for a moment, then turned back to Naiz.

"Nacchan...no, Naiz Gruen. Is this really what you want?"

What saddened her wasn't that Naiz refused. Rather, it was the path he'd chosen.

"It is."

"I see..."

Miledi gave him a small smile and walked through the gate. Oscar didn't turn around, but he had some parting words.

"Someday, when our journey is finally over..."

"What?"

"Can we come visit you again, as just friends?"

"I'll think about it."

Satisfied, Oscar nodded and stepped through the gate.

Naiz stared at the empty space where his friends had sat.

"What happened to 'I doubt we'll ever see each other again?'"

His tone was full of self-derision.

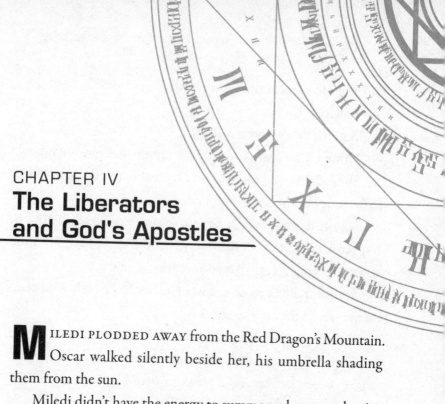

CHAPTER IV
The Liberators and God's Apostles

MILEDI PLODDED AWAY from the Red Dragon's Mountain. Oscar walked silently beside her, his umbrella shading them from the sun.

Miledi didn't have the energy to summon a breeze or her ice block, so the umbrella was all that staved off the heat. However, ice lined its edges, and a slight breeze wafted from its canopy.

Oscar looked over at Miledi. She was clearly depressed.

This must be how she felt when I refused. Even now, Oscar didn't think he was wrong back then. However, that didn't make him feel any less guilty. It hurt to imagine Miledi wandering Velnika's streets looking so depressed.

When she was happy, she was a handful. When she was sad, she was still a handful. Oscar breathed a small sigh.

"Are you depressed because he didn't join us? Or because of how sad his story was?"

"Both."

"You can't accept the choice he made, can you?"

"I can't."

"But he's the one who made it."

"I know. That's why I won't try and convince him anymore."

She didn't sound the least bit happy about it, though. Miledi puffed out her cheeks and pouted.

Naiz had given them a reason, so they had no choice but to respect his decision. Pushing any harder would have been the same as forcing their will on him. Miledi knew that.

Still, that didn't mean she liked it. Her feelings showed plain on her face as they walked back.

Naiz's berserk rampage had caused irreparable damage. He'd killed the villagers, and hundreds of soldiers.

However, he was also a teenager who'd just seen his family killed. Even a fully mature adult would have been hard-pressed to act rationally.

Despite that, Naiz blamed himself. And he would spend the rest of his life atoning for it, forever alone in the cave. Oscar knew even if they tried to go back, he'd run away and help people somewhere else.

Isn't that just too sad?

"Haaah..."

Miledi let out a heavy sigh. She looked utterly wretched.

Oscar adjusted his glasses, a conflicted expression on his face.

"Before I left, I asked him if we could visit again as just friends."

"Huh?"

Miledi instantly perked up.

"He didn't exactly say yes, but he at least said he'd think about it."

Oscar watched Miledi's eyes widen in surprise.

"We still have our own journey to complete," he said. "But one day, we'll come back to see him again. Not to convince him to be our comrade, but to help him out. We're his friends now. Surely he won't mind...right?"

The original goal of the Liberators was to save those crushed by the injustices of the world. It would be well within their scope to help a friend who'd enforced such a strict lifestyle on himself. In fact, they couldn't call themselves Liberators if they didn't.

"O-kun!"

"Whoa?!"

Miledi flung herself at Oscar. Flustered, he somehow managed to catch her.

"That's it! You're right! Absolutely right! We're Nacchan's friends!"

"Uh, yeah, we are. Anyway, that's why you don't have to feel so down about it. We'll just say the Fairy of the Desert incident ended with us gaining a friend instead of a comrade. Now, please get off me."

"I knew I could count on you, O-kun! You're the greatest partner ever! Now we're friends with someone amazing! And if he needs our help, we can go back to save him anytime! Man, I feel way better!"

"Great. Now quit clinging to me."

Despite his best efforts, Oscar was unable to peel Miledi off of him. She was quite beautiful, and Oscar found himself troubled by her proximity. Especially since he'd seen her naked. When he saw her smiling innocently at him, though, he berated himself for having such indecent thoughts. What mattered was that she wasn't depressed anymore.

Oscar gave up on getting Miledi off him and stroked her back until she was satisfied.

After a while, the two started walking again. There was a new spring in Miledi's step. Oscar, too, walked with a lighter heart.

They crossed a number of sand dunes before the town of Liv came into sight.

"Hmm? Hey, O-kun?"

"Yeah, I see it. Something's definitely not right."

Oscar activated his glasses' Farsight spell.

"There's an awful lot of iraks in the town. A bunch of wagons too. They all look pretty ornate... Miledi!"

"Huh, what is it? What'd you see?"

"It's the Holy Church!" Oscar continued in a strained voice.

Miledi's eyes narrowed dangerously.

⁂ ⁂ ⁂ ⁂ ⁂ ⁂ ⁂ ⁂ ⁂ ⁂ ⁂ ⁂ ⁂

The members of the Holy Church arrived late in the afternoon.

At first, the villagers thought the herd of iraks and wagons was a merchant caravan. Hoping to trade for supplies, the villagers eagerly crowded the main gate.

But when they saw the opulence of the wagons and the knights, they realized their mistake. It was not merchants, but the bishop of Doumibral who had come to visit.

The bishop, Agares Myurie, stepped out of the lead carriage. He was accompanied by his priests and the templars. All told, he had brought sixty knights with him. Either he was here to threaten the village, or he wanted to impress them with the church's power.

Agares was a young bishop, still in his twenties. His blond hair was swept back, revealing a handsome face. He spoke softly and always seemed to have a gentle smile on his face. All things considered, he looked like the very embodiment of a pious, humble man.

However, one did not rise to the position of bishop at such a young age by being humble. The Holy Church only had thirty bishops, one for each major city on the continent. There were only seven archbishops, four cardinals, and the pope who ranked above them, so few seats opened up because a previous bishop was promoted.

The primary reason was because a current bishop had lost their position. There were various reasons a bishop could be stripped of their rank. Some retired because of age or failing health, and others were demoted for failing to fulfill their duty. Yet more were excommunicated because their faith was found lacking, or perished in unexpected "accidents." Agares' predecessor was deemed a heretic and executed. He'd been known as a very pious man, so it came as a shock.

Moreover, the inquisitor who unveiled the heresy was none other than Agares.

Agares had made quite a name for himself as an inquisitor, so the town could more or less guess why he'd come to Liv.

"Good citizens of Liv, there is but one reason as to why I have come here today. We have heard there is a heretic in this town who dares declare themselves a god. Such an act is an affront to Lord Ehit. Are there any here who know of the Guardian of the Desert?"

Susha and Yunfa paled.

Someone must have told the Holy Church. Although Yunfa and Susha had tried spreading rumors of the Fairy, the number of people he had saved was so large that his old nickname was making a comeback.

Still, his existence was nothing more than a rumor. To most, he was just a fairy tale. The Holy Church shouldn't have had any reason to send an inquisitor, especially because Susha and Yunfa worked so hard to misdirect the rumors.

And yet—

We didn't do enough! Susha grit her teeth.

These past two years, she'd done everything in her power to keep Naiz's a secret. Plenty of adventurers, minstrels, and travelers Naiz had saved also helped out, but it wasn't enough. The Holy Church was after him.

"Sue-nee..."

Susha wanted to reassure her younger sister, but she couldn't. All she could do was tightly hold on to Yunfa's hand. Agares smiled at the villagers, looking absolutely harmless. That smile terrified them.

Naiz had saved many in Liv. Of them, a good number knew what he looked like. None of them believed they would be able to survive Agares' torture.

"All of the clergymen within the federation are looking for the heretic known as the Guardian of the Desert. We will bring this accursed man to justice no matter the cost. Anyone who claims there is any god but Ehit deserves nothing but death. The same goes for all who try to hide him from us."

Agares gestured with sweeping motions as he gave his speech, almost like an actor.

"There have been more and more reports of this godless heathen appearing in the desert. In order to keep this blessed world pure, we must weed out all heretics. To bring in this one, we have decided to launch an inquisition. The archbishops have granted the authority to execute anyone they deem suspect."

As he said that, the knights unloaded a number of wooden beams and a giant blade from the wagon, then began fitting them together.

"A-a guillotine?" one of the villagers muttered.

Agares fondly patted the scaffolding and swept his gaze over the villagers. They flinched back in fear.

"There is no reason for you to feel indebted to this Guardian of the Desert. Had he been a true believer, he would have used his powers in the service of Lord Ehit. The fact that he did not proves his guilt. Now then, let the inquisition commence."

Agares sat down on a magnificent chair that one of his priests brought out for him. His knights fanned out and dragged the villagers to him one by one.

Surprisingly, when the villagers told Agares they knew nothing, he simply said, "I see," and let them return home.

An hour passed. The sun was about to dip under the horizon, and the curtain of night was falling.

The villagers, who had been expecting to be tortured, started to look hopeful. This almost seemed like a formal, proper interrogation.

A middle-aged man was brought up to Agares, and the bishop asked the same question.

"Do you know the Guardian of the Desert?"

Susha let out a barely audible gasp. The man had actually met Naiz.

Apparently Naiz had gotten him some valuable and rare medicine to cure his son. The man swore he would one day repay the favor. He was also one of Susha's conspirators, and had helped her spread rumors about the Fairy of the Desert.

The man, Porukka, stared unflinchingly at Agares.

"No, Lord Bishop. I do not."

His voice didn't stutter. His poker face was perfect.

Agares smiled and responded in a calm, cold manner.

"It's not good to lie."

The villagers exchanged worried glances. Porukka's expression stiffened.

"Wh-what do you—"

"You have met this man before, have you not?"

"N-no, I haven't!"

"That's a lie, isn't it? You have a child, correct?"

"Yes..."

"Now see, that is the truth. Is your child a girl?"

"Yes."

"And that is a lie. You have a son, not a daughter. This Guardian of the Desert met with your son, did he not?"

"No, Your Eminence."

"Another lie. He saved your son's life, did he not?"

"No he didn't! I've never even—"

"More lies. He saved your son's life, which is why you're lying to protect him."

"You're mistaken, Lord Bishop! Please, believe me!" Porukka shrieked, terrified.

Agares' smile didn't waver. He repeated the question.

Those that knew Porukka trembled in fear. Agares guessed everything despite Porukka's answers. No matter what the man said, Agares somehow divined the truth.

"It seems you really don't know any more than this. Hmm, well, I was at least able to ascertain this man's appearance. A step in the right direction."

"Wh-why? How..."

Porukka looked at Agares with lifeless eyes. Still smiling, Agares explained.

"Because I am an apostle, one who carries the blood of Ehit in my veins."

The villagers muttered to each other. Agares basked in their fear for a few minutes before addressing them.

"I have the power to see into people's souls. You cannot lie to me. No matter how good a liar you are, your soul shall show your falsehood."

In other words, this was his special magic. Like Oscar and Miledi, he possessed inhuman powers. It was also what made him such a good inquisitor.

"Now then, it's time for your divine punishment. For the sin of lying, you and your entire family are condemned."

Even now, there was still a smile on Agares' face. He hadn't hesitated.

"Wait! Please wait! Spare my family at least!"

However, it was too late. The templars dragged his family up to the scaffolding.

"The inquisition is not over yet. We must hurry the process along, or it will be dark before we're finished. Surely you good people would not want to force the templar knights to do something as menial as create light for us?"

Even though Agares had just condemned a man to death, he was lecturing Porukka as if *he* was the unreasonable one for not agreeing to die quickly and quietly. Agares' gaze didn't hold even a hint of remorse. There was no hope for Porukka or his family.

Tears sprung to the villagers' eyes as they watched Porukka and his family get dragged to the guillotine. Many of them couldn't bear to watch. However, one brave soul was different.

"Is it a sin to thank someone who helps you?"

Her voice rang out clearly through the crowd.

The knights stopped and looked for the voice's owner.

The crowd hastily parted, leaving two young girls standing alone. Susha didn't try and hide. She stood firm and met Agares' gaze, her eyes glimmering with resolve.

"I'm sorry, I didn't quite catch that. Could you say it again?"

His gaze seemed to be saying, "Say that to my face, if you dare." However, neither Susha nor Yunfa flinched. This time it was Yunfa who replied.

"You don't know? When someone helps you, you say thank you. And when you do something bad, you say sorry. I'm eight and even I know that. How come you don't, Bishop?"

Yunfa's words dripped with venom. They echoed clearly through the night.

For the first time since he'd arrived, Agares' smile slipped.

The priests and knights were amazed. The villagers watched in abject horror.

"Bishop, please forgive our desire to help this man who has done so much for us. Our faith in Ehit is not false. We simply wish to show our gratitude. That's all. Please allow us this shred of humanity. I'm sure Lord Ehit would show us mercy."

Now it was Susha's turn to speak. She knew that once her turn came, she wouldn't be able to keep hold of her secrets. Not in front of this man who could use ancient magic.

She had a rough idea of where Naiz lived because of the two odd strangers she'd talked to that morning. They told her they met Naiz relatively often, and the two of them were staying at Liv's inn. In other words, Naiz's house was somewhere in the area. There was only one place you could hide yourself nearby. The Red Dragon's Mountain.

Perhaps if they confessed, Susha and Yunfa's lives would be spared. But neither of them would, even if lying was futile.

No matter what happened, their lives were forfeit. They decided not to beg, but to go down fighting. And now was the time. Porukka had done his best to protect Naiz. They would do what they could, too.

Susha and Yunfa clasped each other's hands and walked forward.

"Please forgive Porukka-san and his family. At the very least, spare their lives."

Susha looked more mature than any other thirteen-year-old. Yunfa, too, bowed her head and begged for Porukka to be forgiven.

While everyone else looked on, stunned, Agares grinned. His smile was far more sinister than before.

"I see. Such splendid children. To think you would lecture me on morality. Hee hee hee, it has been some time since I enjoyed myself this much. Indeed, this is wonderful. As thanks for bringing me such joy, allow me to explain something."

"Explain what?"

"You seem to be misunderstanding morality. It is certainly very important. Indeed, almost as important as worshiping Ehit."

Susha gulped. She knew where Agares was going.

"However, there is nothing more important in this world than Ehit's will. Compared to that, something as trivial as human morality means nothing. In fact, what you're doing is not truly moral if it contradicts the word of god. Besides—"

Agares raised his hands to heaven and brought his face close to Susha's, his movements like a broken doll's. Susha was terrified by his bulging pupils.

"What right do you have to speak of Ehit's will?"

Out of everything Susha said, that was what irked him the most.

A ball of glowing fire appeared in Agares' hand. He hadn't used a magic circle and spoke no incantation, yet he had cast one of the strongest fire spells known to man, Solar Blast. Normally, the spell created a sphere of fire over eight meters wide, but Agares had compressed it into the size of his hand and made it far more powerful. This was the power of God's Apostles.

Originally, Agares was planning on questioning Yunfa and Susha first, but their blasphemy drove him over the edge. He would wipe them off the face of Tortus.

"You are not even worthy to breathe the same air as me. Disappear."

No one moved. The sight of such a powerful spell left them rooted.

Only Susha, hugging her little sister, still had the courage to glare back.

"Then Ehit's will is wrong."

Her voice didn't waver.

As the girls looked on and accepted their fate, Agares unleashed his fireball. It was powerful enough to blow through the whole crowd and leave not even ashes behind.

"Ability Ten, Hallowed Ground, Partial Activation!"

A black shadow interposed itself between Susha and the fireball. He was holding something no one expected to see in a desert—a black umbrella.

He thrust it forward, and it glowed with a vibrant light. The fireball smashed into it head on. At the same time—

"Miiiiiiiiiiiiiiiiiiiileeeeeeeeeeeeeeeeeeeeediiiiiiiiiiiii..."

A girl's voice rang out from somewhere far away. Then, a second later—

"Kiiiiiiiiiiiiiiiiiiiiiiiiiiiiick!"

A girl's foot slammed into Agares' face.

She struck him from the side, and the force of the kick nearly shattered his cheekbones.

He flew out of his chair. The villagers watched as Agares sailed through the air. He flew straight through a number of buildings and skidded across the ground. His legs slammed into a tree, flipping him around, and he kept going. He skipped across the oasis and finally came to a halt on the far bank.

No normal kick could generate that much force. It had looked like the attacker was almost falling sideways.

Miledi—for that's obviously who the girl was—alighted atop the chair Agares had been sitting on. She looked down at the dumbfounded templar knights and winked. Her ponytail fluttered behind her as she made her characteristic peace sign.

"It's everyone's favorite magical girl, Miledi-chan!"

Miledi posed for the crowd.

A second later, Agares' fireball flew off into the sky. Oscar had deflected it with his umbrella. It exploded safely above the heads of the villagers, illuminating the early night sky with its radiance.

The light framed Miledi perfectly, making her look like a goddess.

"Nice one, O-kun! I never knew you were such a good showman!"

"That was actually just a coincidence."

Oscar swung his umbrella over his shoulder and adjusted his glasses. Whether it was on purpose or just a coincidence, he struck quite a theatrical pose.

The templar knights finally returned to their senses.

"L-Lord Bishoooooop!"

"Agares-samaaaaaaaaa!"

"We need a healer! Quick, bring a healer over to the bishop!"

A detachment of knights ran over to where Agares fell. Most of them expected to find him dead.

Oscar ran a finger over the edge of his glasses and nodded to himself. He had wanted to make sure.

"Miledi, you broke his neck. He's definitely dead."

"Can you really see that well in the darkness?"

"These glasses have night vision, too."

Just how many features did you put inside those glasses...?

"Wh-who on earth are you guys?! And what have you done?! Accursed heretics, prepare to face Ehit's wrath!" one of the priests yelled, pointing a finger at them.

Killing a bishop of the Holy Church was one of the worst crimes imaginable. Harming a member of the clergy was the equivalent of besmirching Ehit's name. Declaring the entire human world your enemy.

However, Miledi didn't seem worried.

"Good grief," she said, and shook her head sadly. She pointed at Susha and Yunfa. "Clean out your ears and listen up, all of you! You see these two girls over here? See how cute they are?! *That* is the truth of this world! Cute is justice! Screw your god!"

"I'm not sure I like this world order any more than Ehit's," said Oscar.

Miledi ignored him.

The priest, shocked by the blatancy of Miledi's blasphemy, could only splutter.

"Sue-chan's right. Any god that would dare hurt a pretty girl like her is totally wrong!"

"U-umm, that wasn't exactly what I meant."

Susha was the kind of person who could articulate her opinion regardless of the circumstances. Even now, she managed to speak through her tears.

"O-Oscar-san, Miledi-san. Do you realize what—"

"Oh yeah, don't worry. We're prepared for the consequences."

Yunfa and Susha looked worriedly up at their saviors. But Oscar gently patted their heads.

What do they mean, they're prepared for the consequences? Susha thought.

Oscar saw the question in her eyes.

"We're here to fight against people like this," he said. "We're here to liberate those oppressed by madness, by malice, and by this unreasonable world."

"To liberate people?"

Oscar smiled at Susha. Before he could explain further, Miledi called out to him.

"O-kun, let's go!"

"Yeah, yeah. Go ahead, I'm ready whenever."

Suddenly, the templar knights charging Miledi were thrown into the sky.

She'd used the gravity spell Inverse Square. It reversed the gravitational pull of anyone she targeted.

Far off in the distance, the sun's last rays shot across the sky. They illuminated the dozens of knights as they fell upward. Miledi manipulated their fall so that they came back to earth outside of the village. She wanted to move the battlefield away from the townspeople. She remembered all too well how Forneus had blown himself up at the end.

Miledi and Oscar leaped to where she'd deposited the knights.

The villagers slumped to their knees, defeated. A few of them glared at Susha and Yunfa. They probably blamed the two girls for sowing the seeds of their doom. The villagers were too scared to point fingers at Miledi or Oscar, so they vented their frustration on the helpless girls instead.

Susha and Yunfa exchanged glances, and ignored them.

"Sue-nee."

"Yep."

They were satisfied with how things had turned out.

With angry glares at their back, they dashed out of the village.

⁘ ⁘ ⁘ ⁘ ⁘ ⁘ ⁘ ⁘ ⁘ ⁘ ⁘ ⁘ ⁘

"Impossible... How are you..." one of the knights groaned, his body sunken into the ground.

He was the last to be defeated. He watched as Oscar and Miledi tore through the squad of templars like they were nothing.

Most of the knights were skilled magicians, and could soften their landing enough to avoid injury. The priests hadn't been so lucky. The only reason they hadn't died outright was because the sand cushioned their fall.

Perhaps it would have been luckier if they *had* died. The slaughter that followed was merciless.

None of the knights could mount any kind of resistance. They were mowed down.

"Why? You're God's Apostles as well, aren't you?! Why do you oppose us?!"

"Actually we're god's enemies~!"

It was one of the most dangerous things you could say, but Miledi said it lightly.

The knight was stunned. He couldn't believe anyone could blaspheme so casually. Once he recovered, he spat, "Heretics!" Those were his final words before Oscar crushed him to death.

"Always leaves a bad taste in my mouth when I kill people from the church," said Miledi.

"Is there any kind of killing that doesn't leave a bad taste in your mouth?"

Miledi sighed as she surveyed the destruction.

She smiled sadly and chose not to answer Oscar's question.

"Now then, what are we going to do about Liv? Even if they tell the Holy Church they had nothing to do with us..."

"I'm sure if the townspeople cooperate, the Holy Church

won't kill them out of hand. Unlike Naiz, we're not even from here. They have no reason to protect us. If you're worried, we can hide out at a nearby oasis after this and see what happens."

"Yeah, you're right," said Miledi. "We can totally do that. Do you think we should tell Nacchan, too? Although it feels kind of awkward to go back right after we said we'd leave. He probably won't like it, either."

"W-well, you're not wrong. But I think we should still tell him."

This is something that affects him directly. He'll probably find out on his own eventually, but the sooner he knows, the better.

"Anyway," said Miledi. "What about Sue-chan and Yun-chan?"

"They sure went off on that bishop. The whole town heard them, too."

Oscar doubted they could continue to live in the village. *The next time a bishop comes to interrogate the town...*

Chances were, they'd be taken.

"I want them to join the Liberators."

"They certainly have the courage for it," Oscar agreed. "The real question is whether or not they'll leave the desert when Naiz is still here."

Oscar and Miledi looked at each other.

Just then, they heard a voice behind them. They turned to see Susha and Yunfa heading their way. The two of them were riding an irak stolen from the knights. They waved at Oscar and Miledi.

"And now they've stolen the Holy Church's irak... " Oscar muttered. "They've got guts, and the ability to manipulate information on a large scale. I'd say they're a pretty valuable asset."

"I bet Nacchan would have been caught ages ago if it wasn't for them."

The two girls gulped as the sixty dead knights came into view, but quickly recovered.

"Thank goodness we made it in time... I was worried you two might leave before we got here."

"Thank you so much for saving us, Onee-chan, Onii-chan!"

Yunfa hopped off the irak and skipped over to them. Susha slipped off the irak as well, and bowed.

"Miledi-san, Oscar-san," Susha said with a look of determination. "I know this is an unreasonable request, but please take us with you!"

"Please!"

Yunfa bowed her head as well.

Miledi and Oscar exchanged another look.

"Unfortunately, we weren't able to convince Naiz to join us. If you come with us, you won't get to see him."

"I see. Even so, we'd like to come. I may just be a burden when it comes to fights, but I'm sure I'll be able to help in other ways. I'll do my best to be useful!"

"I'll try hard, too! So please let us come!"

Neither Oscar nor Miledi missed the few seconds they spent gazing longingly at the Red Dragon's Mountain.

They really were clever. With just the limited information Oscar gave them, they'd figured out where Naiz lived. And despite that, they still chose to go with Miledi.

Harsh though it may be, they were facing reality. Even if they went to see Naiz, there was no guarantee he'd meet with them. Furthermore, as long as they stayed here, their lives were in danger. If they wanted to survive, their best option was to go with Miledi and Oscar.

Their unbending will and tenacity to stay alive was impressive. Miledi and Oscar respected them for it. The two girls swallowed their complaints and their dissatisfaction, and kept struggling to survive. Their determination was dazzling.

"Umm, it's true that we're here because we can't go back home anymore, but that's not all."

"Huh?"

"Hm?"

Miledi and Oscar were surprised Susha had guessed what they were thinking, and were curious what else could be motivating the two girls. Yunfa sighed.

"When someone saves your life, you're supposed to thank them. That's the right thing to do."

And so the Liberators were lectured on morality by an eight-year-old girl.

"O-kun, I never realized I'd turned into such a calculating person."

"Don't say it, Miledi. That just makes me feel even worse."

"U-umm! We were also thinking that if we went with you, the chances of us meeting Naiz-sama would be higher than if we left on our own. So we're calculating, too!"

Susha's attempt at cheering them up only made them more depressed.

That reminds me, even though Susha's in love with Naiz, the main reason she was looking for him was to give him her thanks. That was why she'd started spreading false rumors, even though she couldn't meet him.

It seemed that a desire to repay their debts drove them even more than a desire to survive.

"Okay, okay, we got it. But it'll be too dangerous for you to come with us, so—"

So we'll take you to our headquarters, and you can help our organization from there. However, Miledi wasn't able to get the second half of her sentence out.

Susha and Yunfa looked curiously at her, wondering why she hadn't finished. Miledi broke out in a cold sweat.

"O-Oscar-san, Miledi-san's—"

Susha didn't finish her sentence, either. Oscar looked just as surprised as Miledi. He gulped.

The two of them panted.

They turned around, their necks creaking like badly oiled machines. Susha and Yunfa followed their gaze, wondering what had them so terrified.

"To think you would notice me despite my attempts to erase my presence..."

They heard a voice from above. It was a beautiful voice, one that rang out like a bell. At the same time, it was completely devoid of emotion.

The sun dipped below the horizon, and darkness fell.

Floating in the night sky above them was a beautiful woman.

She was wreathed in silver light, and looked like a miniature moon.

Even in a shapeless nun's habit, her stunning figure was clearly visible. Her clear blue eyes and silver hair looked like they'd come from a painting. A pair of glowing silver wings sprouted from her back.

Her beauty was beyond mere mortals.

"Hiii!"

"Uwaaah!"

Susha and Yunfa squealed in terror as they slumped to the ground.

Although the woman looked like a divine creature, she was terrifying.

Those eyes staring down at them were inhuman.

The sisters were wise beyond their years, and understood at once how dangerous she was. However, Miledi and Oscar's presence bolstered their courage.

"Miledi!"

"Got it!"

The woman vanished the instant Oscar deployed his barrier.

A second later, there was a thunderous boom. A shockwave spread out from his umbrella.

"Ngh?!"

Oscar grunted and fell to his knees. He'd managed to block the woman's radiant sword with his Hallowed Ground, but it was a near thing. The woman's vertical slash left deep cracks in his barrier. In a single attack, she'd done more damage to his Hallowed Ground than a squad of templar knights.

Still, Oscar managed to buy the time they needed. Miledi successfully sent Yunfa and Susha flying back to the village. Or rather, unceremoniously flung them to safety. It was a pretty bumpy ride, but she didn't have time to give them a controlled landing. The best she could do was throw them in the relative direction of the oasis so the water would cushion their fall.

And not a moment too soon.

"Gah?!"

There was another boom. When Miledi turned around, Oscar was nowhere in sight. The strange woman held her twin swords aloft, prepared for any counterattack.

Something slammed into the dunes a good distance away.

Putting the pieces together, it was obvious that the woman had sent Oscar flying. But Miledi couldn't spare the time to worry about him. She had her hands full dealing with the next attack.

"Ah?!"

Miledi barely dodged the diagonal slash by "falling" backwards.

The woman's longsword grazed her hair as it swung past. Had she spent even a half-second longer getting Susha and Yunfa to safety, Miledi's head would be rolling on the ground.

Cold sweat poured down Miledi's back.

She continued falling backward, parallel to the ground, but the woman chased after her with a speed that surpassed Miledi's own.

"So annoying!"

"Your struggle is futile."

This time, Miledi dodged by falling into the sky.

With one flap of her wings, the woman caught up. This time, there was no escape.

Miledi paled as she saw the sword close in on her. Even if she countered with a spell, at this distance it wouldn't avail her.

Five small daggers came out of nowhere, deflecting the woman's death blow. They came from such an angle that at even the slightest change in trajectory, they would have hit Miledi instead. But Oscar had enchanted all of his blades with gravity magic as well, which allowed him to freely control them.

The woman faltered. It should have been impossible for throwing daggers to have such speed and accuracy. She noticed that one of them was glowing red-hot, while another was emitting sparks. *These daggers are enchanted.*

The woman struck down the burning and electric daggers with her sword, then swatted the rest away with her wings. One dagger emitted a powerful gale as it spun away, while another spewed petrifying smoke. The last froze the air.

The woman was easily able to defend against all three with a barrier of light, but that gave Miledi enough time to get away.

"Nice save, O-kun! Heavensfall!"

Miledi summoned a massive black sphere and crushed the woman to the ground.

At the same time, Miledi flew over to where Oscar was waiting.

"Sorry. I nearly hit you with those."

"It's all good. It's only thanks to you that I'm still alive."

The two kept a watchful eye on the cloud of smoke in front of them.

"What on earth *is* that?"

"Remember what I told you?"

A silver-haired nun. Oscar remembered now. Miledi met her after destroying her family. According to Miledi, she'd barely escaped with her life.

"It's not a person, whatever it is. It has no future, no destiny. And it's quite a handful."

"Told you."

Although their voices were playful, their expressions were grim.

They watched as a massive pillar of silver light rose up to the sky. It spiraled away into the heavens, and blew away the dust cloud. The night sky blazed with its light.

"The ability to manipulate gravity..." said the woman. "So that is your special—no—your *ancient* magic. I remember you. You escaped from me once before."

The sky quaked. The earth trembled. The very heavens cowered in the face of her might. The woman unleashed a wave of pressure so potent it was palpable. Oscar could hardly breathe. If his focus slipped even a little, the woman's aura would knock him unconscious.

"To think my opponents would be humans who have inherited a fragment of my lord's powers. I suppose it is only proper to introduce myself, then. I will be using my full strength against someone of your caliber."

The sand surrounding the woman blew away. Her nun's habit vanished, replaced by a white battle uniform. A helmet, gauntlets, greaves, and a waist plate.

She flapped her wings, and swung her swords in front of her. A declaration of war.

"I am one of God's Apostles—Hearst. My duty is to rid my lord's game board of undesirable pieces."

Why's a "God's Apostle" here? thought Oscar.

By undesirable pieces, does she mean us? Has she been chasing after us this whole time? But if she only just remembered she fought Miledi before, then she couldn't have been. Does that mean she came here to eliminate someone else?

There was only one other person she could have come for. That foolish, kind man who'd consigned himself to repentance.

Oscar and Miledi would have to make good on their promise to help Naiz, and sooner than they thought.

They were clearly outmatched, but the two of them grinned fearlessly.

"Bring it on."

"Do your worst."

Their voices melded together as they roared out a challenge. "Just try and kill us!"

They wouldn't let anything stand in their way.

◦⃫◦ ◦⃫◦ ◦⃫◦ ◦⃫◦ ◦⃫◦ ◦⃫◦ ◦⃫◦ ◦⃫◦ ◦⃫◦ ◦⃫◦ ◦⃫◦ ◦⃫◦ ◦⃫◦

Meanwhile, Susha and Yunfa managed to crawl out of the oasis. Fortunately, neither of them were hurt.

They coughed out the water, and heard a deafening boom.

"Sue-nee. What should we do? That lady was scary."

"Yeah. Even Miledi-san looked like she was having trouble. And she defeated all those templar knights like it was nothing."

The two sat silently on the sand for a few seconds. Water dripped from their soaked clothes. Their breath misted in the air. Desert nights were freezing. However, neither of them seemed the least bit bothered.

As they sat there, they noticed the sound of fighting was growing further and further away.

"Are they leading her away from the village so it doesn't get caught up in the battle?"

Although she had no proof, Susha was certain.

She hadn't known them for long, but she felt as though she understood them.

"Sue-nee. I don't like this. We can't just leave them."

But they were less than useless when it came to fighting. Yunfa bit her lip and clung to her sister's arm. Susha was proud to have such a brave little sister. Despite seeing firsthand how terrifying the enemy was, she still wanted to help. Susha wracked her brains, trying to think of something.

Her thoughts turned to the man who'd saved their lives. After their mom and dad died, Susha and Yunfa found it difficult to stay with their parents' friends. They'd tried to run away. Not long after heading into the desert, they'd been attacked by monsters. Susha cradled her sister's poisoned body, thinking all hope was lost, when Naiz came to save them. She'd been able to help him; surely she could help her two new friends as well.

"That's it! I know what we can do! Let's go find Naiz-sama!"

"Yeah! Naiz-sama should be able to help them!"

Yunfa nodded in agreement. The two sisters exchanged glances and stood up.

•/• •/• •/• •/• •/• •/• •/• •/• •/• •/• •/• •/• •/•

Naiz sensed a massive outpouring of mana, one greater than any he'd felt before.

He dashed out of his cave and saw bursts of mana flashing intermittently in the direction of Liv. *Whoever's fighting over there, they're not normal people.*

Oscar's and Miledi's faces appeared in the back of his mind.

"I should see what's happening."

Naiz created a tiny portal the size of a small window and surveyed the village.

The first thing he noticed was the villagers' confusion. Next, he saw the abnormal amount of iraks and carriages in the town square. A closer look revealed that they belonged to the Holy Church. However, he didn't see any templar knights or priests. He moved his portal to the outlying desert.

"Wh-what on earth happened...?"

He saw an army of templar knights lying dead on the sand. Wisps of residual mana covered the battlefield, the remnants of a few extremely powerful spells.

A great battle had taken place here. Only Oscar and Miledi could have defeated such a large contingent of knights.

But then, who could they possibly be struggling with? More importantly, why did someone so strong come to Liv? Were they chasing after the Liberators? A pair of young voices interrupted his thoughts.

"Naiz-sama! Naiz-sama!"

"You have to help Onii-chan and Onee-chan!"

How do they know my name?

He moved his portal closer to the voices and saw two girls shouting his name.

They were asking for his help. The way they talked, they were certain he'd come to their aid.

"......"

Naiz hesitated. But he remembered those girls from two years back. Miledi mentioned she'd told them a little bit about him. Seeing as they already knew his name, and what his magic could do, he decided there would be no harm in revealing himself.

A second later, Naiz was standing behind them.

"What's wrong?"

"N-Naiz-sama?!"

"Naiz-sama!"

The two started and turned around. After a moment's surprise, tears spilled from their eyes. They'd finally met him again.

Naiz panicked when he saw the two girls cry. But, before he could say anything, Susha wiped away her tears.

"Naiz-sama, thank you so much for saving us before. Forgive us for asking your help again, before we even had a chance to thank you for the last time."

"Naiz-sama. Onii-chan and Onee-chan are in trouble! They're fighting this scary person who looks like a person but isn't a person!"

"What do you mean, looks like a person but isn't a person?"

The sisters hesitated. They didn't know how to explain.

Regardless, Naiz could tell from the urgency in their voices that Oscar and Miledi were having a hard time. From Susha's fragmented explanation, Naiz gathered that it was likely the Holy Church's trump card.

Susha brought her hands together, like she was praying.

"Please, please, I'm begging you. Help them! You're the only one who can!"

"Naiz-sama!"

The two of them had absolute faith in the Guardian of the Desert. He was far more reliable than Ehit, who they couldn't even see and whose servants had brought them nothing but misfortune.

Although he had never hesitated to help someone before, Naiz paused.

"Naiz-sama?"

He had sworn never to fight. Would he even be of any use? Whatever they were fighting was stronger than any monster. Wouldn't he just get in their way?

Sure, he could help them flee. But for how long? The Holy Church had sent this powerful creature after the two of them. Even if he teleported them to safety, it would just chase after them.

Would he help them escape again, then? How long would he keep that up? So long as he wasn't fighting, would he be of any help? Besides, he'd told himself he'd never meet with them again.

More than anything, though, this situation brought back unpleasant memories. His mind flashed back to that day.

He'd obliterated his village and everyone in it. Not even a trace had remained.

His powers were too dangerous. There was no telling what he might accidentally destroy.

Which is why, I...

Over and over, he repeated his excuses.

"I'm sorry, Naiz-sama."

"Huh?"

He looked down, confused by her apology. Yunfa, too, bowed her head and apologized. They weren't berating Naiz for hesitating; in fact, they looked almost sad.

"I don't know what exactly happened, but I do know my request is causing you pain. I'm sorry. I never wanted to force my savior to make that kind of face."

"I'm sorry, too, Naiz-sama..."

"What face?"

What kind of face am I making?

Naiz unconsciously brought a hand up to his cheek.

"We'll go ourselves."

Susha and Yunfa turned around.

"Go where?" Naiz asked automatically.

"To help Miledi-san and Oscar-san."

"Wh-what are you—"

"We know we'll just get in the way. But maybe we can distract that woman, even if it's only for a second."

"I can do a little magic. Maybe if I make some sparks it'll surprise the not-person."

They spoke lightly, but their resolve was the real deal. Naiz could see it in their eyes. They wanted to help, even if it meant their death.

"Why would you go so far for them? You can't have known them for more than a few days..."

"Because they saved our lives."

"Yeah!"

Susha and Yunfa jumped onto their irak. Susha took hold of the reins. She didn't even look back.

Naiz couldn't believe it. They said it like it was the most obvious thing in the world.

If someone saved your life, it was only natural to risk yours to save theirs. Anyone would agree. But few people could actually follow through with that.

Suddenly, Naiz realized something.

In their explanation, Susha and Yunfa mentioned why the Holy Church came to their village. The bishop, Agares, had launched an inquisition. Oscar and Miledi saved the two girls just before the bishop executed them for heresy.

But why were they suspected of heresy in the first place? There was only one possibility.

"Wait! Wait a second, you two. Why did the Holy Church declare you heretics?"

"Well..."

"Please tell me."

Susha hesitated. She and Yunfa shared a look. But when Susha saw the sincerity in Naiz's eyes, she sighed and told the truth.

"Because I told the bishop there was nothing wrong with wanting to help the Guardian of the Desert."

"Ah—"

So it is my fault after all.

Even Miledi and Oscar only got wrapped up in this because of me.

Although he told himself that he was keeping his distance to protect them, he'd only been protecting himself.

And now he was making excuses, trying to pretend this had nothing to do with him. Could he really let these two girls throw away their lives because he was too cowardly to help? *I'm an embarrassment!*

"I hope we can meet again one day, Naiz-sa—"

"Wait. You don't have to go."

The words spilled out of their own volition.

These girls had risked their lives for him, and they were about to do the same for Miledi and Oscar.

He was done making excuses for himself.

Powerless as they were, these two girls were trying to do the right thing. Yet he was trying to shirk his duty.

He didn't want to shame himself any further.

How could I have forgotten? I'm a warrior's son. I'm Solda Gruen's son. My job is to defeat anyone who threatens our people!

The chains of his sin still bound him. His guilt would never disappear. His power was repulsive. He didn't want to hurt anyone ever again. But did that mean he could abandon these two brave girls who were begging him for help? Absolutely not. He was done running from his past. If he abandoned them here, he'd never be able to face his family in the afterlife.

Naiz made his decision.

"I'll go."

"Naiz-sama!"

"Naiz-sama!"

Susha's eyes went wide with surprise, while Yunfa's sparkled in admiration.

"Thank you so much for trying to protect me. Wait here for me. I'll be back. With Miledi and Oscar."

The thought of fighting still pained Naiz, but his mind was made up. His resolve wouldn't waver.

The two girls looked up at Naiz in wonder.

"Good luck!"

"We'll be waiting, Naiz-sama!"

They waved farewell to their reliable Guardian of the Desert.

•/• •/• •/• •/• •/• •/• •/• •/• •/• •/• •/• •/• •/•

A localized thunderstorm raged a few kilometers south of Liv.

"Gah?!"

"Ah?!"

Flashes of lightning illuminated the torrential downpour. Oscar and Miledi were in the middle of it, trying to dodge the deadly rain.

Oscar's umbrella groaned with the abuse. Miledi put out multiple Spatial Severances, and each had absorbed so much energy it collapsed.

They didn't even have time to grumble. Even a moment's lapse in concentration would lead to their deaths.

"You better not underestimate me."

Oscar flung a volley of daggers at Hearst. He controlled their flight freely, closing in on Hearst from all sides.

"I have seen that trick already."

Her silver wings smacked down Oscar's missiles before they could reach their target.

They burned, scorched, and froze the air as they fell.

"But now you're wide open!"

Miledi fell upward into the sky. Once she was above Hearst, she unleashed a powerful gravity sphere.

Hearst crossed her swords above her head and blocked it. Normal swords would have been crushed to a pulp, but Hearst's weapons were made of sterner stuff.

Miledi's lips twitched, but she wasted no time in increasing the sphere's pressure.

Oscar jumped up next to her using his Onyx Boots and thrust his umbrella at Hearst.

"Ability Nine, Thunderlord's Judgment! Full power!"

Originally, Spark Plasma was the ninth ability. It was the most cost-effective lightning spell he had. But now he was fighting with Miledi, and his own skills had improved. So he swapped out the ninth ability for the most powerful electric spell known to man.

His umbrella turned inside-out, and concentrated balls of lightning formed at the tips of each rib. They combined into one massive lightning sphere at its ferrule. That massive sphere of lightning hurtled toward Hearst.

There was a blinding flash of light. For a few seconds, all Oscar could see was white. Hearst vanished into it.

The recoil sent Oscar flying backward, but he was able to recover in midair thanks to his Onyx Boots.

"O-kun!"

"I'm sure that hit! But—"

He wasn't able to finish.

There was a dull thud, and both Miledi's gravity sphere and Oscar's lightning were blown away.

Hearst leaped at Oscar and crossed her swords around his neck.

It was only thanks to the heightened perception provided by his glasses that he was able to bring up his umbrella in time.

Her swords bit into his umbrella. He could feel them cutting into his neck.

He avoided being decapitated, but only by a hair's breadth. The swords digging into his skin reminded him that his head could fly at any moment. That one attack shaved a decade off his life just from the fright.

"You're surprisingly tenacious."

Hearst's lifeless eyes bored into Oscar. They were the same blue as Miledi's.

He knew this wasn't the time to be comparing eyes, but Oscar couldn't help it. While Miledi's looked like a clear blue sky after a storm, Hearst's resembled empty glass spheres.

There was only the tiniest hint of light in those glass globes. Up close, it felt as if her gaze was piercing right through him.

"O-kun!"

Miledi fired a barrage of wind blades.

Hearst turned to face the onslaught, and sent Oscar flying with a roundhouse kick. Then she cut down the wind blades with her swords.

Oscar slammed into the ground faster than he could blink.

"*Cough. Cough.* Gah, this isn't good."

Coughing up blood, he struggled to all fours. Despite his coat's protection, one kick was enough to knock the wind out of him. If it wasn't for his Ebony Coat, he'd be dead right now. As he struggled to his feet, he heard a scream above him.

"Kyaa?!"

"Miledi!"

Oscar willed his wounded body into action, and leaped to where Miledi was falling.

He caught her in midair, swallowed down the bile and blood that threatened to spill out of his mouth, and landed on his back. He wasn't going to let her go, no matter what.

"Ugh. Th-thanks, O-kun."

"Looks like you're...not okay."

There was a deep gash running from the top of Miledi's shoulder to the tip of her breast. Though she was pressing on it with her hand, blood still dripped between her fingers. The wound wasn't fatal, but it was certainly grave.

Oscar looked down at his umbrella. Despite the fact the cloth was made from the hardest material in existence, the earlier scissor cut had hacked it nearly in two.

He reviewed his remaining trump cards.

He knew his chains had no hope of binding Hearst. If she had the strength to cut through his umbrella, his chains wouldn't last. The same held true for the threads in his gloves. *Just what is her body made of?* They hadn't been able to scratch her. Oscar was out of enchanted daggers.

Even his strongest spell, Thunderlord's Judgment, hadn't been able to touch her.

"What kind of monster is she?"

"Aha ha, don't ask me."

The two smiled bitterly at each other. No matter what attack they threw out, it was nullified by that barrier surrounding her. Even if they could get past that, her body was so tough they couldn't dent it.

Not only could she fly, but her physical specs were through the roof. She had a seemingly inexhaustible supply of mana, and her combat skills were unparalleled. She was an absolute monster.

"Have you finally given up?"

The woman who called herself God's Apostle looked down at Oscar and Miledi.

"No way."

"I'm not sure I understand the question. The word 'give up' isn't in my dictionary."

The two of them glared at Hearst. Their wounds had left them pale-faced, but neither of them felt the pain.

Hearst observed the two of them dispassionately.

"Even though my charm spell is supposed to be quite powerful, it seems it's not working on you at all."

Her eyes shimmered. She'd been using brainwashing magic on them this whole time.

"Hmph, don't even bother. These glasses of mine—"

Are enchanted to defend against dark magic. Except he never got to finish his sentence.

"You're trying to charm my O-kun?! You little thief! Too bad, O-kun's so head-over-heels in love with me that your feminine wiles won't work! How does it feel knowing I'm way prettier and way better than you? Huh? You mad? Are ya?"

Despite their perilous situation, Miledi continued taunting Hearst. *Is it just me, or is she acting even more annoying than usual?* It seemed Hearst had really ticked her off. Hearst raised her twin swords.

It looked like this was it.

"With your wounds, you won't be able to dodge anymore. Pitiful creatures who could not even become my master's pawns. I will grant you a painless end."

Silver feathers fell from her wings. They hung in the night sky like stars.

"I'll block the next attack. You try and finish her with your strongest spell, Miledi."

"Looks like I'll have to. Even if I can't control it, it's the only option left."

The two bumped their fists and steeled themselves.

"Disappear!" shouted Hearst.

Thousands of glowing feathers plunged to the earth like a meteor storm.

Oscar transmuted the sand around his feet and stuck his umbrella into the newly worked earth. Once again, he activated his Hallowed Ground.

All noise vanished.

Or at least, Oscar was so focused on the attack that no sound reached his ears. The feathers demolished everything beyond Oscar's barrier.

"Gaaaaaaaaaaaah!"

Oscar screamed and poured more mana into his tattered umbrella. He was simultaneously maintaining the spell while also repairing his umbrella with transmutation. Sustaining both at the same time was a herculean task, and his mana drained away at a prodigious rate.

His damaged body cried out in pain, and he felt more blood fill his mouth. Still, he managed to hold out. He'd bought enough time for Miledi to cast her most powerful spell.

"It's over! Nether Burst!"

A two-meter sphere of pure destruction formed around Hearst.

"This is..."

For the first time, there was emotion in Hearst's voice. Surprise. The feathers vanished.

"Gah!"

Oscar spat out a mouthful of blood and grinned triumphantly.

Miledi's sphere closed in around the apostle. She still wasn't able to regulate the spell. Once she cast it, it wouldn't stop until it drained all of her mana.

So she had to make sure it would hit. Hearst was too strong

for them to force an opening. They'd had to wait for her to use her ultimate attack. That was the only time this would work.

"Wait, Miledi. Is it just me, or is it smaller than last time?"

"Shut up! This is...the biggest I can...make it right now!"

Miledi's words were punctuated by sharp gasps. Casting such a powerful spell left her drained.

Her Nether Burst was so much larger last time because Miledi had also used the six years' worth of mana stored in Oscar's Divinity Stone.

"I see. But this should still be more than enough to—"

"N-no way! She's trying to break out of it!"

"What?!"

The walls of Hearst's gravity prison grew thin in places, making it possible to see inside. Hearst had her eyes closed and seemed to be concentrating on something. What surprised Oscar most was that she'd been able to maintain her form. Anything stuck inside Miledi's Nether Burst was crushed.

Miledi groaned.

It was taking all of her concentration just to keep the skill going. Hearst's mana and Miledi's warred inside the gravity prison. For the moment, they appeared evenly matched.

"Shit. The only thing I can think of is throwing this in there—"

Oscar twisted his umbrella's handle. Before he could do any more—

"O-oh no!"

There was a huge explosion, and Miledi's Nether Burst was ripped apart.

A huge cloud of dust blossomed where Hearst had been standing. Oscar and Miledi were both sent flying.

Oscar managed to keep them together with his chains, but couldn't mitigate the force of the blow.

Their bodies were battered to begin with, but now they didn't even have the strength to get back to their feet.

"You really don't know when to give up," said Hearst.

Oscar couldn't tell if she was impressed or just exasperated. There was too little emotion in her voice to be sure.

Oscar and Miledi couldn't do any more than raise their heads.

There was a massive ball of fire burning as hot as the sun above her.

Still glaring at Hearst, Oscar took Miledi's hand. She squeezed his back.

Just then—

"Void Fissure!"

Space itself warped.

"Ah?!"

The burning sun vanished, and Hearst was blown backwards. She quickly recovered, but was battered by a series of invisible explosions. Unable to defend herself, God's Apostle was sent flying off into the distance.

"You're still alive, right?"

"Nacchan?!"

"Naiz?!"

⁎⁄⁎ ⁎⁄⁎ ⁎⁄⁎ ⁎⁄⁎ ⁎⁄⁎ ⁎⁄⁎ ⁎⁄⁎ ⁎⁄⁎ ⁎⁄⁎ ⁎⁄⁎ ⁎⁄⁎ ⁎⁄⁎ ⁎⁄⁎

Naiz smiled and lifted each of them up with one arm. A few hundred meters away, there was an explosion of silver light. Even after Naiz had ripped apart space, Hearst was still fine, it seemed.

Still, he'd bought them a few precious seconds.

"Let's regroup."

Naiz opened a portal and retreated from the battlefield.

Hearst returned to find everyone had vanished. She swept her gaze back and forth, before stopping at a point some distance to the south.

* * * * * * * * * * * * *

"Th-this is..."

"We're about one hundred kilometers south of the volcano. This is as far as I can teleport in one go."

Naiz sounded tired. Miledi cautiously looked around. When she didn't see any silver-haired women chasing after her, she raised her arms in joy. Except she was still injured.

"Owww?!"

"What are you doing, idiot?"

Tears sprang to Miledi's eyes, and she writhed in pain.

Oscar deployed his umbrella's Benison Aura to heal their wounds.

"O-kun...we're sharing an umbrella."

"Uhh, yes?"

Miledi purposely snuggled closer. Oscar was too tired for a proper retort.

"It looks like I'm interrupting something. Should I just go back?"

Naiz stared pointedly at the two of them. He pulled some mana potions out of his pouch and tossed a few over. The rest he downed himself.

Oscar and Miledi thanked him and gulped down their potions.

"Why did you come?"

"Those girls begged me to help you."

"Sue-chan really knows what she's doing," Miledi said, smiling.

"At any rate, you saved our lives. Thank you. I know how hard it must have been to make this choice."

"Yeah, thanks for saving our hides again, Nacchan."

"Don't mention it..."

Miledi and Oscar knew he must have agonized over his decision.

Naiz did his best to keep a straight face while they thanked him.

This was the first time he'd used spatial magic offensively since that day. Attacking Hearst brought back unpleasant memories, and even now he felt like he might puke. Still, he was glad he'd come to save them.

"Now then. If there's a hundred kilometers between us, I think we have enough time to strategize at least... What should we do? Keep running? I don't think we'll be able to escape for long."

"No, no running."

"Yeah, we wouldn't be able to get away."

Naiz groaned as he heard their reply.

"But how are we going to beat her?" said Naiz. "Even my Void Fissure couldn't scratch her.

"And that's exactly why we can't run," said Miledi. "Assume it's impossible to get away. I was able to do it once before, but the situation was completely different."

She'd infiltrated the head chapel to ascertain whether or not Belta had told her the truth. Back then, she just scouted the area. She only got close enough to monitor the building with Farsight. When she was discovered, she tried to flee. She kept the apostle busy by firing wide-area elemental spells at the chapel and had only used her gravity magic to flee.

Back then, the apostle mistook her flight for wind magic and hadn't realized what Miledi was. Hearst, however, knew Miledi and Oscar were Atavists. Furthermore, they were a threat to her lord. She'd stop at nothing to eliminate them.

Hearst would chase them down forever. Miledi doubted they'd ever be able to escape her notice.

"Besides, you'd stay even if we ran."

Naiz started. He remembered why the Holy Church had come here. It hadn't been to chase down Miledi and Oscar. It was purely by accident that Hearst had discovered they were Atavists.

Her original goal was to eliminate Naiz.

"Remember, back when I asked if we could come visit again as friends?" asked Oscar. "You said you'd think about it."

"As your friends," Miledi added. "There's no way we'd leave you to die on your own."

Even though I never once actually called you guys my friends. Still, they were both willing to lay their lives down for him. Naiz couldn't help but be moved.

Ah, it's the same as last time. Once again, other people are protecting me.

"Alright," he said. "How do we defeat her? Void Fissure's my strongest spell."

He was sure if he thanked them, he'd become a blubbering mess. So instead he focused on the enemy. At the very least, he'd share his friends' fate.

Miledi and Oscar understood and smiled.

"She even broke out of my Nether Burst... I'm not sure we've got any cards left to play."

Miledi rubbed her forehead.

Naiz's expression grew grim, and he lapsed into thought.

Only Oscar didn't seem defeated. He looked at his two companions, then looked up at the sky.

"I do have *one* idea. I have no idea if we can actually pull it off, though. The odds are going to be stacked really high against us, and even if we make it work, we might end up killed along with her."

"R-really, O-kun?!"

"At this point," said Naiz, "I'll take anything. It's still better than rolling over and dying."

Miledi's eyes shone with renewed hope, and the corners of Naiz's mouth twitched up in a faint smile.

Oscar nodded. Just as he was about to explain his master plan—

"Ah?!"

All three of them looked up.

Oscar activated his glasses' Farsight ability. A shining silver meteor shower was headed toward them.

"She's here!"

"Are you kidding me?! This is one hundred kilometers away! Just how fast is that thing?!"

"I'm starting to realize now that I didn't escape last time. She *let* me run away!"

Despite their complaints, all three of them prepared to intercept her.

Oscar talked as fast as he could.

"I need an opening to stab her with my umbrella! Then when I give the signal, hit her with another Nether Burst, Miledi!"

The storm of silver feathers reached them the moment he finished.

The three of them scattered in different directions.

The feathers slammed into the ground with more force than any feather should rightfully have. Dust clouds puffed up one after another.

Hearst flew out of the dust with such speed that the air groaned. Oscar was her first target.

He backed out of the way and tried to counter with Spiral Blaze, one of the strongest fire spells. A tornado of flames erupted out of his umbrella.

Hearst didn't even bother to dodge. She crossed her swords in front of her and powered right through.

"Uwaaah?!"

The force of her charge pushed Oscar's umbrella up into the

air. Hearst tried to ram her sword through his now-exposed chest.

"Not on my watch."

Naiz suddenly appeared behind her. He grabbed her head, and they both disappeared. A second later, they appeared high up in the sky. Naiz pushed Hearst in front of him as they fell. She took the brunt of the impact as they hit the ground.

"Void Fissure!"

Naiz followed up with his strongest attack. A huge shockwave spread out from Hearst's helmet.

She turned her head to the side and glared at Naiz.

"Ah!"

His magic wasn't powerful enough to kill her, but he'd hoped to at least give her a concussion. It seemed even that was too optimistic. Hearst fired a barrage of feathers at him at point-blank range.

"Gaaah?!"

Naiz managed to teleport away fast enough to avoid being turned into a pincushion, but she'd scored a few good hits. His entire body was covered in blood.

"Naiz?!"

"Don't worry about me! It wasn't fatal!"

Hearst flew up after Naiz. Miledi cast six Heavensfalls to box her in from all directions. All six sheets of gravity pressed in on the apostle. Hearst attempted to weaken one of the sides, planning to break out from there.

"?!"

However, her body was pushed in an unexpected direction.

"Even if I can't crush you, I can mess with your sense of gravity! Good luck flying now!" As Hearst was tossed this way and that, she gathered her mana. Her body glowed with an intense silver light. She held out her hand, and waves of fire exploded in every direction. She'd just cast the strongest area of effect fire spell in existence, Hellfire Tsunami.

Miledi, Oscar, and Naiz all dealt with the flames in different fashions.

"Shit—"

However, just as Oscar blew away the wave of fire, Hearst appeared next to him. She drew one of her swords and thrust it at him.

Oscar's Hallowed Ground cracked with the blow. A second later, it shattered.

Her sword kept going and stabbed Oscar through the chest.

"Gaaah?!"

The flames dispersed. Both Miledi and Naiz saw Oscar floating in the air, stabbed through by Hearst's sword.

"O-kun!"

"Oscar!"

Miledi and Naiz screamed in horror.

"One down."

Hearst brandished her second sword. The first missed Oscar's heart by a paper-thin margin. Hallowed Ground held just long enough for Oscar to deflect the blow by a few centimeters.

There was no way he could dodge the second sword, not with the first already stuck in his chest. Nor would Hearst give him the any time to recover.

"It's not over yet!"

Oscar poured a huge amount of mana into his boots and hugged Hearst. Greatswords were useless at close range. As long as Oscar was sticking to her, she wouldn't be able to swing.

Of course, that also meant he drove the first sword deeper. The pain nearly caused him to black out.

"Futile—"

"Miledi, Naiz, now!"

Oscar sent out all of the threads in his gloves. They wound around both him and Hearst. He threw his umbrella. It flipped around in midair, the point aimed directly at Hearst. Once more, he activated Hallowed Ground. This time, the barrier covered both of them. He used the defensive spell as a cage to trap Hearst. The greatsword in Hearst's hand vanished, and she made to strike Oscar with her bare hands.

Before she could hit him, Miledi acted.

"Nether Burst!"

The black sphere covered both Hearst and Oscar. Even an apostle of god needed focus to shatter it. It would hold for at least a few seconds.

Of course a mere human like Oscar wouldn't last even a second. Fortunately, Naiz opened a portal and saved Oscar just as the sphere formed.

"Gah!"

"Do you have a death wish or something?!"

Although it was only for a split second, Oscar's body had

been put under Nether Burst's immense pressure. Blood poured out of his mouth, his nose, his eyes, his ears, every orifice that he had. The hand Naiz had grabbed was bleeding as well.

"But we got her."

Oscar raised a hand, and his umbrella flew into it. He thrust his left hand forward and pulled his right hand back, like he was drawing a bow. His pose was similar to the one Hearst took when she'd stabbed him.

"Naiz, give me a portal!"

"R-roger!"

Naiz opened a portal in front of Oscar. Its exit point was directly behind Hearst's heart. Oscar transmuted the ferrule into a razor-sharp point and flung it as hard as he could.

Hearst had no armor protecting her there. When he'd hugged her, Oscar had transmuted it away.

The umbrella's point pierced the apostle's white skin.

But it didn't drive in much further. Hearst's ridiculously sturdy muscles prevented it from reaching her heart.

"But can you handle this?"

Oscar snapped his fingers, and the ferrule ejected from the end of the umbrella. The propulsion drove it even further into Hearst's body.

A second later, a jolt of electricity traveled down the umbrella.

"Let's get out of here."

Naiz teleported Oscar, along with the umbrella, down to the ground. The only thing left near Hearst was the ferrule and its connecting wire.

"Gaaah!"

"Oscar, don't die on me!"

He'd paid a steep price for his reckless antics. Rivulets of blood poured out of the gaping wound on his chest.

"Don't worry, I'm fine."

He gritted his teeth and cast a fire spell on his umbrella. Once the metal cloth was red-hot, he pushed it against his chest, cauterizing the wound. He screamed in pain.

"O-kun, are you okay?!"

Miledi looked like she was about to cry. Oscar didn't have time to reassure her.

"What about her?! Did we get her?!"

"Huh? Well... Wait? I think my spell is winning?"

Last time, Hearst had overpowered Miledi and broken free. This time, Miledi's mana was winning out.

"Haaah, haaah, think you'll be able to kill her with this?"

"No way! This just means she'll be trapped for longer."

"Figures," Oscar said with a grim smile. "But still, we managed to restrain her for a little bit. That means we can move on to stage two. Naiz."

"I'm here. What do you want me to do?"

He didn't ask for details. He had absolute trust in Oscar.

"Teleport me to the mouth of the volcano."

"Understood."

Naiz put a hand on Oscar's shoulder.

"Miledi, I'll be right back! Just hold her until I return!"

"You got it! I'll show her what I'm made of!"

The next second, Naiz and Oscar were standing on the terrace overlooking the magma chamber.

"Naiz, recover as much mana as you can. You're going to need to cast two more long-distance teleports."

Naiz nodded and gulped down as many mana potions as he could.

Oscar pushed away the blackness gathering at the edge of his vision and brought out his Metamorph Chains.

"It's time we try a new vector of attack."

He dropped all five of his chains into the magma.

Every second, a little more of Miledi's mana drained away. That mana was her lifeline. Once it ran out, the reaper would come for her. But she wasn't worried.

Hearst stared at Miledi through her black prison.

Miledi smiled fearlessly.

"Looks like you've gotten a lot weaker. Did O-kun's hug get you so flustered you couldn't fight back?"

Her mana may have been running out, but she still had unlimited snark.

Miledi knew it was Oscar's ferrule that had weakened Hearst and not the hug, but she still wanted to say it.

Her Nether Burst creaked ominously. It wouldn't be long before her prison failed.

"O-kun, Nacchan..." she whispered.

Just then, a bright light appeared directly above her.

"Is that a star? It looks too bright to be one..."

Miledi looked up. She hadn't recalled any star existing in that spot before. It was also far brighter than the others. Before she could question it any further, she noticed it was growing larger.

"Wait? Is it just me or—"

Cold sweat poured down her back. Her lips twitched.

Unable to believe her own eyes, Miledi stared at the burgeoning light.

"Wait wait wait wait wait wait wait! No way! A star's falling down!"

This wasn't just a meteor shower. A giant burning hunk of rock was hurtling toward the earth. By Miledi's calculations, it would land in twenty seconds. She'd seen a lot in her life, but this was far beyond anything she'd experienced.

A voice broke her out of her stupor.

"Miledi!"

Oscar and Naiz had returned. Oscar looked white as a sheet, and Naiz was so exhausted he couldn't even speak.

"Guys, a star's falling from the sky!"

"We know! Control its descent so it lands directly on her!"

Oscar started transmuting the ground. He dug a hole big enough for the three of them and surrounded it with as many layers of metal as he could.

You've gotta be kidding me! Still, Miledi flew over to Oscar and started working her magic.

There was a sharp crack, and her Nether Burst shattered.

"Unbelievable..."

Hearst looked up at the massive blazing boulder of lava

bearing down on her. Even a God's Apostle was stunned.

She beat her wings, trying to fly out of the way.

"It's over!"

Oscar's chains were waiting right outside Nether Burst's sphere of influence. The moment it shattered, he sent them flying at Hearst. Hearst expected she would be able to shake them off easily, but the chains glowed golden and wouldn't budge. Oscar had enchanted them with one of Naiz's spells—Spatial Anchoring.

Ten seconds until impact. Great gouts of golden mana pulsed out of the chains. Hearst used all of her strength to try and shake them off. The chains creaked.

Five seconds until impact.

"You're not getting away!"

Naiz burned the last of his remaining mana to cast as many Void Fissures as he could. The impacts left Hearst rooted to the spot.

Oscar cast Hallowed Ground around their makeshift bunker. Miledi gave him the last dregs of her mana to bolster his barrier.

Two seconds until impact.

Miledi—"Don't you ever underestimate humans!"

Naiz—"Looks like we win."

Oscar—"Rot at the bottom of the earth, you puppet of the gods."

Their voices were far too quiet to be heard through the din of battle. Still, at the last second, Hearst turned towards the three of them...

Impact.

The world went white.

The force of the meteor knocked Miledi and the others out, even through all of their barriers.

❖ ❖ ❖ ❖ ❖ ❖ ❖ ❖ ❖ ❖ ❖ ❖ ❖

The first thing Naiz felt was pain. His whole body hurt.

He grimaced, ears buzzing, and pushed himself to his knees.

"Ngh. Did it work...?"

He looked around. He spotted Miledi and Oscar right away. They were half-buried in the sand, and neither of them were moving.

"Oscar! Miledi!"

He was so drained that he couldn't even walk. He crawled over to the two of them. Oscar's umbrella was still in his hand. It was so battered, it hardly resembled an umbrella anymore.

Naiz somehow managed to get them both out of the sand and lay them down. Fortunately, they were still breathing. They were alive. Barely, but they were.

"Ugh. Where am I...?"

"Nhaaah."

He slapped their cheeks a few times, and they woke up. Miledi groaned in pain as she opened her eyes.

"Are you two alright?"

"In what world do we look 'alright,' Nacchan?"

"Heh. I suppose so. You look especially bad, Oscar..."

"Fortunately, I'm pretty tough. Owwwwww..."

Oscar took Naiz's hand and rose to a sitting position.

"How long were we out for?"

"I'm not sure. A few minutes at most. Your blood's still wet."

The three of them somehow managed to stand, leaning on each other's shoulders. There was a huge crater in the earth a good distance away. White smoke still rose from it.

They nodded to each other and walked over. They reached the lip of the crater and looked down. There was still a huge pool of lava at the bottom, bubbling and smoldering.

After a few minutes, Miledi raised her hands. Oscar and Naiz silently followed suit. The three of them exchanged high-fives.

"So what exactly did you do?" Miledi asked.

"While you were keeping her trapped, we went back to the volcano. I turned a bunch of magma into a kind of magma boulder. Then I had Naiz teleport that into the sky above her."

"Not only did I have to teleport it a hundred kilometers away, but I needed to put it a few kilometers in the air as well. Then I had to teleport the two of us back. I thought I was going to pass out."

That was Oscar's last-ditch plan, to turn a giant sphere of lava into a mini-meteor. He'd taken the idea from the huge Nether Burst Miledi had used to obliterate part of the Greenway.

"Th-that's pretty extreme. Oh yeah, what did you do that weakened the Apostle anyway?"

"Oh. I stuffed the tip of my umbrella with liquified stillstone."

"Ah, that was what Nacchan was making last time!"

He'd liquified and compressed as much stillstone as he could into the tip of his umbrella. Honestly, he'd wanted to use it on a monster and see what happened when it tried to use magic.

"Even with the stillstone and the lava meteor, I wasn't sure we'd be able to pull it off properly... I'm glad it worked."

Despite all of the barriers they'd put up, it was a miracle they'd survived. Oscar breathed a sigh of relief, and Miledi and Naiz smiled. Just as they were about to say something, the three of them heard a rumbling from inside the crater.

"There's no way, right?"

No one responded to Oscar's muttered comment.

They watched as something began to rise up.

The burning hot lava fell away to reveal Hearst, surrounded by a nimbus of silver light.

She'd lost an arm, her armor was completely melted away, and her clothes were burnt to cinders. Her entire body was covered in burns. But her mana burned as brightly as before.

She lifted what remained of the boulder with one hand and tossed it into the air.

As it fell back down, she jabbed up with her hand and broke it to pieces.

Despite her wounds, she was still raring to go.

Miledi, Oscar, and Naiz exchanged despairing looks. Grudgingly, they readied themselves for a fight. They had no mana and no weapons. Their chances of winning were less than zero.

But that was no reason to give up.

However, it looked like fate was on their side for once.

"Ah. But Noint, these irregulars must... Yes, ma'am. Understood. I shall return immediately."

Hearst took to the sky. She glanced down one last time at Miledi and the others.

"Rejoice. I have been summoned to my lord's game board."

She flew off to the northwest, a silver meteor shooting through the sky.

"What...just happened?"

"I don't know, but it looks like we were spared."

"I thought we were dead for sure."

All three of them sighed in relief and fell backwards.

They lay there on the sand, looking up at the starry sky.

"We need to get stronger," Miledi mumbled after a while.

"Yeah," Oscar and Naiz said in unison.

"Hey, Nacchan."

"Yes?"

"Come travel with us."

Miledi had exhausted all of her well-formed, eloquent arguments. Her final attempt at solicitation boiled down to a single sentence.

Naiz closed his eyes. He thought back to the village he'd destroyed. The pain of his sins weighed down on him even now. Would he really be able to protect people without going berserk? Now that Oscar and Miledi meant so much to him, he was worried he might accidentally...

"Don't worry. If it looks like you're going to lose it, we'll stop you."

Oscar's voice was quiet, but filled with conviction.

Of course. If I'm with these two, then there's nothing to worry about...

"Besides," Oscar followed up, jokingly. "This tomboy's too much for me to handle on my own. I need someone to help me with her."

"Heeey! What's that supposed mean, O-kun?!"

The two started trading insults again. Naiz found the noisy atmosphere pleasant.

He smiled, his eyes still closed.

"I want to be worthy of calling myself a Gruen again one day."

"......"

"And I get the feeling that if I keep traveling with you, that day will definitely come. So—"

"I'd be glad to join you."

Naiz raised a fist into the air. Miledi and Oscar followed suit. Three tiny fists joined together under the vast starry sky.

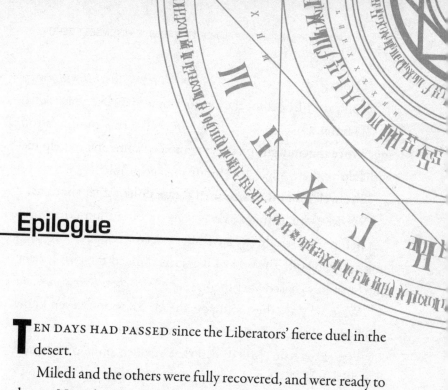

Epilogue

TEN DAYS HAD PASSED since the Liberators' fierce duel in the desert.

Miledi and the others were fully recovered, and were ready to depart. Now that their business in the desert was concluded, their next destination was the western ocean.

Susha and Yunfa showed up to see the party off. They were accompanied by a few of the Liberators. Miledi had seen to it that Susha and Yunfa would be guided to their secret base.

The two sisters accosted Naiz, while Oscar thanked the Liberators for bringing him a heap of ore he could use to transmute new artifacts.

"Naiz-sama. No matter how far apart we are, my feelings for you won't waver."

"I-I see."

"We're going to train hard so we can travel with you too someday!"

"O-okay."

"I promise I'll be come the kind of woman you like, Naiz-sama!"

"U-umm..."

"We're the only girls you can marry!"

"I think there might be a bit of an...age problem—"

"Farewell for now, Naiz-sama! Please don't forget about us!"

"We love you, Naiz-sama!"

Before Naiz could say anything, the two hopped onto their irak and rode off. The other Liberators noticed the girls leaving and hurriedly chased after them.

"Wait, why are they going on ahead? They don't even know where the village is, do they?!" they yelled as they rode off.

"Hey, Nacchan." Miledi had that devilish smile on her face that Naiz had come to dread. "Hey, how do you feel right now? You just got proposed to by two preteen girls. You gotta tell me, does that make you happy? Did Sue-chan's knockout body make your heart skip a beat? Even though you're in your twenties? Come on, don't be shy now—"

Naiz grabbed Miledi's head in a death grip. Her skull creaked from the pressure.

"Oscar. Looks like it's going to be just you and me."

"Perfect. We'll move faster that way."

"I'm sorry! I'm sorry! I won't do it again! Please forgive me! My head's—"

"Sorry."

He let Miledi go.

She fell limply to the ground.

"Our next target is the 'Saint of the Western Ocean,' right? What do you think of the rumors Susha and Yunfa heard at the bar?"

"No clue," Oscar replied. "But the Fairy of the Desert rumors turned out to be real. So I think it's at least worth checking out. From the start, our journey had little chance of success. It's like chasing after mirages."

"So you go into each new lead expecting to come away disappointed?" Naiz asked.

"Let's just have fun and get stronger on the way," said Oscar. "I don't know about you, but I've never been to the ocean before. I want to try the seafood."

"Likewise."

Oscar and Naiz chuckled.

"Umm, did you guys forget about me again?"

Miledi was still lying on the floor like a discarded piece of trash.

Oscar and Naiz looked at each other. Then they walked off without a backwards glance.

"Heeeey, wait for me! Stop ignoring me! People can die from loneliness, you know that?!"

Miledi hurriedly chased after them.

Despite what she was saying, there was a smile on her face.

Because Oscar and Naiz had left enough space between them for her.

The three off them walked off into the desert, toward their next journey.

❖❖ ❖❖ ❖❖ ❖❖ ❖❖ ❖❖ ❖❖ ❖❖ ❖❖ ❖❖ ❖❖ ❖❖

The Holy Church's great cathedral sat eight thousand meters above the ground, atop the Spirit Mountain.

A single woman kneeled before the altar, raised atop a massive limestone pillar.

She was missing an arm and had burns all over her body.

"Are you certain, my lord?" Hearst's voice echoed through the large cathedral. "As you wish."

Although she appeared to be talking to herself, the pillar radiated divine energy.

"I am not worthy of such praise. Yes...their powers clearly marked them as Atavists. At present, however, they are not much stronger than regular men."

Hearst, who had kept her eyes closed and her head bowed low until now, looked up in surprise.

A second later, her arm was restored, and her burns vanished. Even her clothes were restored to their former glory.

"My humblest thanks, lord. As always, I live to serve."

Hearst bowed low. When she finally rose to her feet, the divine presence was no more.

She turned on her heel and walked out of the cathedral. The cathedral opened up to the elements. A steep staircase cut directly into the mountain descended into the distance. Only a few were allowed to climb this hallowed staircase.

Although normally devoid of people, there were quite a few here today.

Although perhaps it was wrong to call them "people."

Each and every one of them looked exactly like Hearst.

They said no words. But the light in their eyes spoke volumes. That was all they needed to converse.

Hearst stretched out a hand. She pointed to a boulder in the distance.

Silver light gathered in her fingertips. Once she'd gathered enough, she fired a silver burst at the boulder. It vanished without a sound. There was no impact. It was as if the boulder had never existed. Tiny particles of dust flew off in the wind.

Satisfied, Hearst turned back to her doppelgangers. Without a word, all of them flew off in separate directions.

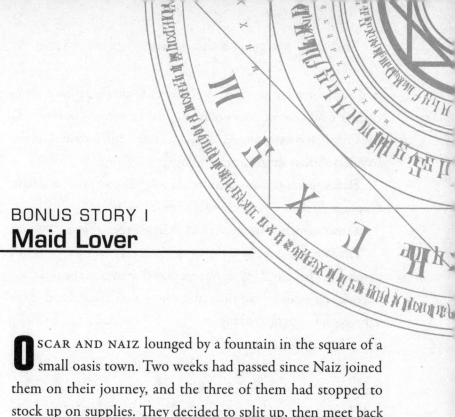

BONUS STORY I
Maid Lover

OSCAR AND NAIZ lounged by a fountain in the square of a small oasis town. Two weeks had passed since Naiz joined them on their journey, and the three of them had stopped to stock up on supplies. They decided to split up, then meet back up at the fountain. Over an hour had passed since Oscar and Naiz returned, but there was still no sign of Miledi. Naiz frowned.

"Miledi's late."

"Well, she is still a girl. It's no surprise her shopping's taking longer."

Naiz nodded in understanding. He'd heard that girls took longer to shop than guys, too. But still, he was getting tired of waiting. He looked over to his partner, who didn't seem the least bit impatient.

"You seem rather knowledgeable about women, Oscar."

"Please don't make it sound like I'm some kind of skirt chaser."

Oscar frowned. Although it was true that back in Velnika,

he'd been forced to accompany girls in their shopping more times than he could count. Many of his regular customers, or their relatives, or their friends would "coincidentally" run into him on the street, and then strong-arm him into going along.

If those outings count as dates, then I guess I've been on dozens. Can't say I actually wanted any of them, though.

Oscar adjusted his glasses and changed the subject.

"Anyway, it's not like we're in any hurry. I made a new board game the other day. How about we play that to pass the time? It's a mock-war game where you order your pieces around and try to capture the opponent's king."

"Oh, sounds interesting."

Naiz's interest was piqued. However, before they could start their magic chess, Miledi arrived.

"Sorry I took so long, guys! But I'm back now~!"

Oscar and Naiz exchanged looks, and turned toward the overly energetic voice. When they saw what Miledi was wearing, their jaws dropped open.

"Miledi, what on earth is that outfit?"

"Hee hee. Impressed? You're impressed, aren't you? Have you finally fallen for my charms too, Na—"

Annoyed, Naiz grabbed Miledi's face in a death grip.

"Miledi, what on earth is that outfit?"

"Okay, okay, I'll quit joking around, so please stop crushing my skull!"

Miledi hurriedly took out a letter and a photo from her pocket. She flung them both to Naiz, who caught them with ease.

His expression stiffened as he examined the picture.

"Hee hee. Hey, Nacchan, how does it feel?" she asked. "Those two sisters took pictures of themselves in maid outfits just for you. As a grown man, how does that make you feel? Come on, tell—"

Naiz clamped down even harder. The picture showed Susha and Yunfa wearing revealing maid uniforms. Both of them were striking sexy poses. If anyone found out a grown man like Naiz was carrying around a picture like that, they'd certainly think him a pedophile. Ignoring a growing headache, Naiz opened the letter. It was quite long, but the gist of it was this:

Naiz-sama, remember how much you were talking about the maid uniforms of that restaurant before? We thought you might like them, so we tried wearing them, too. I hope you like the picture. Love, Susha and Yunfa.

Naiz definitely knew what restaurant Susha and Yunfa were talking about. In the last town they'd stopped at, they'd had dinner there. Naiz really liked their food, so he'd asked one of the waitresses for the recipe. The question was, why did Susha and Yunfa know about that?

"One of the Liberators delivered that to me. Then, on my way back, I saw a similar outfit in one of the shops, so I figured, why not?"

Naiz wasn't even listening anymore.

"Ha ha ha… Look, Oscar. I can't stop shaking."

He was terrified. Terrified of the fact that Susha and Yunfa seemed to know his every move. Oscar, however, didn't respond. In fact, he'd been completely silent since Miledi returned. Wondering what was wrong, Naiz turned to look at him.

"O-O-kun?"

Oscar's attention was completely taken up by Miledi. She was actually somewhat scared by the intensity in his gaze.

"Glorious..."

Oscar looked Miledi up and down, his eyes sparkling.

"O-O-kun? What's wrong? You're starting to scare me a little..."

"Miledi, you're the most annoying person I know. Even when you do those dumb cutesy poses of yours, they just make you look like you're trying too hard."

"Hey, are you *trying* to make me mad?"

Miledi went from scared to angry in a heartbeat.

Oscar ignored her and continued his speech.

"But still, that maid uniform suits you perfectly. I suppose if I had to critique your outfit, your skirt could be a bit longer, and folded better."

Oscar inched toward her.

"You're still a novice maid, so it's understandable that you're not an expert with the uniform yet. Listen up. First of all, a maid is supposed to be prim and proper. So no peace signs and definitely no cutesy crap. If you're going to strike a pose, then you have to do it right. Keep your arms demurely in front of you, and when you walk, keep your gait graceful. Never, under any circumstances, act like an excited little child. Keep your eyelashes long, and don't look too arrogant."

"Okay, I get it, you have a maid fetish. C-can I go change now?"

Miledi slowly backed away. Oscar's fanaticism terrified her.

Once she'd put some distance between them, she spun around and dashed off down the street.

"Where do you think you're going?"

"Hiiiiii?! O-kun, snap out of it! You're really starting to scare me!"

Oscar grabbed her shoulder before she could go more than a few steps, then spun her around.

"Miledi, right now you look more amazing than you ever have."

"Thanks so much for that! But you know, you're still scaring me! So I'm gonna go change!"

"Don't be ridiculous! If you change, you'll just go back to being your regular, annoying self! Without that maid uniform, you're nothing!"

"Hey, now that I can't let slide! I never knew you were such a pervert!"

"Excuse me! I am not a pervert! I'm simply a gentleman who loves maid uniforms!"

"I'm changing out of this right now!"

"Don't you dare!"

"Just try and stop me!"

"Oh, it's on!"

Their back and forth exchange continued for a few minutes. Meanwhile, Naiz sighed deeply as more and more people came to watch the spectacle. It didn't help that he was still holding a picture of two underage girls.

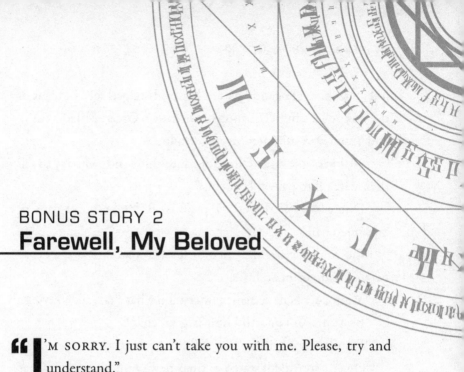

BONUS STORY 2
Farewell, My Beloved

"I'M SORRY. I just can't take you with me. Please, try and understand."

Despite the man's pleading, she didn't listen. The forlorn look she gave him tore at his heart. He was just as sad to be leaving her as she was. They had weathered good times and bad together, supported each other in sickness and in health, braved both poverty and riches, and sworn to be together until death did them part. They loved each other, so of course neither of them wanted to part.

Unfortunately, the man had to embark on a journey. One that had no end, which would be filled with hardship and danger. That meant he would be forever walking in darkness.

"Don't make that face, please. This is hard for me, too, you know? Please, Suzanne, just try and understand."

"Gweeeh."

Indeed, Naiz was tormented over parting with his beloved

irak, Suzanne. He gently patted her oval-shaped face in front of the irak seller's hut. The shop's apprentice, Oscar, Miledi, Susha, and Yunfa were all watching, incredulous.

"He looks like one of those deadbeat husbands who try to sell their wife off to pay off his debts."

"Don't worry, Mister... I promise I'll take good care of Suzanne-chan."

The young apprentice tried his best to placate Naiz, an exasperated expression on his face.

"Wait, does Naiz actually understand what that irak is saying?"

"Beats me, O-kun. All I hear is 'gweeeh.'"

"Don't worry, Miledi. That's all I'm hearing, too."

Oscar and Miledi stared at their new comrade with exasperated expressions.

Meanwhile, the dramatic farewell between Naiz and Suzanne continued.

"Gweeeh."

"That's not true. I don't hate you!"

"Gweeeh."

"What? You think I'm leaving you because I found someone else? Don't be ridiculous, I'd never do something like that!"

"Gweeeh."

"Bring you with me? I can't, it's too dangerous."

"Gweeeh."

"Will I ever come back...? I'm sorry, I'm not sure if I will."

"Gweeeh."

"Wait. Wait, Suzanne!"

Miledi snickered to herself.

"Even I could understand that last 'gweeeh.' It sounded like 'Hmph, I don't care about you anymore!'"

"Yeah, it sounded like that to me, too."

Suzanne huffily turned away from Naiz and walked over to the apprentice boy. He seemed at a loss for what to do. Naiz crumpled to the ground as he watched his beloved Suzanne go off to another man. Oscar had never seen such a look of profound despair on his face before. Susha suddenly butted into Oscar and Miledi's conversation with a completely unexpected remark.

"I want to become an irak."

"Sue-nee?!"

Even Yunfa was surprised by that. Oscar and Miledi turned to Susha, shocked. Her eyes were dead, and there was a mirthless smile on her face. Both of them backed away a few steps.

"Hey, Miledi-san, do something."

"O-okay! Umm, what's wrong, Sue-chan?"

"Is there any magic from the age of the gods that can turn me into an irak?"

Oh crap, she's serious...

"W-well, the world's a big place, so maybe? But I think you're a lot cuter the way you are, Sue-chan."

Susha turned her dead gaze to Miledi, who squealed in terror and clung to Oscar for safety. Unfortunately, he too was trembling in fear.

"What good is being cute, if it's not the kind of cute Naiz-sama wants?"

"You're right, I'm sorry!"

The leader of the Liberators kneeled and bowed her head to its newest member. Yunfa sighed and muttered.

"Haaah, Sue-nee's gone over to the dark side again. Bringing her back takes so much time."

Yunfa set about consoling Susha, her practiced mannerisms making it evident that she was used to dealing with this. Oscar and Miledi were once again reminded that Yunfa was just as amazing as her older sister. No one else had been able to stand up to Dark Susha. In that moment, they both thought the same thing: *There's no way Naiz is ever gonna escape those two.*

AFTERWORD

HEY EVERYONE, Ryo Shirakome here.

Thank you so much to everyone who picked up this book.

How did you like this *Arifureta* side story? It's a completely original prequel, one that's never been uploaded as a web novel. To be honest, I never thought a day like this would come, not even in my wildest dreams.

Still, it has, and now I'm finally able to tell the story of how the Liberators came to be.

I tried to make this as chuuni as possible, too, and my only hope is that it entertained you enough to be worth the purchase. As long as you enjoyed it, that's all I could have asked for.

Now then, we're going to go off topic for a bit, but this is something that needs to be said. Who on earth is that girl on the front cover?! I'm sure many of you thought that when you first picked it up, right?

To be honest, I kind of thought the same thing.

I'm sure no one expected that super annoying golem Miledi to have originally been such a beautiful girl. There is actually one description of her human form up on Syosetsu, so those of you who've read that probably weren't as surprised as the rest.

Her whole thing is supposed to be that she's cute, but annoying as hell.

At any rate, my never ending thanks to Takayaki for drawing her so well.

By the way, I'm sure some of you might have guessed where Oscar's umbrella comes from. What can I say, I'm an easily influenced guy. If something tickles my chuuni instincts, I can't help but use it.

For those of you who are still wondering what it's a reference to, Google "manners maketh man." You will learn what it means to be a true gentleman.

A lot of the events in this book tie in directly to the seventh book in the main series, which is why the two came out at the same time. For those of you who are interested, I definitely recommend checking out the connections.

Finally, it's time for the acknowledgments.

I'd like to thank Takayaki-sensei for doing all of the novel illustrations, as well as Roga-sensei for drawing one very kick-ass manga. I'd also like to thank my manager, Morimisaki-sensei, all of my wonderful editors and proofreaders, and all the people without whom this book would not be possible. And as always, a big thank you to my readers.

Praise for Maria Reva's

GOOD CITIZENS NEED NOT FEAR

One of *The Guardian's* Best Fiction of 2020

"Creative, poignant, and darkly hilarious, *Good Citizens Need Not Fear* is full of relevant questions about resistance, corruption, and maintaining dignity against the dehumanizing power of the State. This is an outstanding first book."
—Anthony Doerr, author of *All the Light We Cannot See*

"*Good Citizens Need Not Fear* is the funniest, most politically astute book I've read in years. Reva's pitch perfect tone—especially at that comic junction where the absurdity of a system rigged to control human beings collides with actual humans—is bang-on brilliant."   —Miriam Toews, author of *Women Talking*

"Luminous. These stories speak with humor yet real emotion of the heaviness of totalitarian systems and show how the light of our humanity still shines through. Terrific stuff."
—Yann Martel, author of Man Booker Prize–winning *Life of Pi*

"Dazzling. . . . With their big, delightful dollops of surrealism and absurdity, these stories conjure up from the old Soviet-era Ukraine a world that feels, with its hall-of-mirrors twists and torques, uncannily—alarmingly!—on point and up-to-date. *Good Citizens Need Not Fear* marks the beginning of what is sure to be a long, strong career for the brilliant Maria Reva."

"Fantastically, winningly weird . . . Witheringly incisive and consistently pitch-perfect, Maria Reva's *Good Citizens Need Not Fear* is nothing short of a comic triumph."

"Bitterly hilarious. . . . Reva's satire spares no one, though many get a little sympathy. . . . Maria Reva is a new voice in fiction, but already on the basis of this great collection a dominating one."

"Who needs kindling when writing like this throws off sparks?! Good citizens need read this book! Hilarious, absurd, and ultimately tender stories from a building that doesn't exist. This is seriously so good. Maria Reva is a wonder of this world."

"Deliciously wry . . . [A] clever novel about survival in tough times."

"A magic trick of a book: a dark and scathingly funny set of interconnected stories, each one alive with originality, that nonetheless leave the reader immersed in the very wholeness of these characters and their place in the world. Erased and ground down, Reva's good citizens rise up and shine, insisting that their existence matters in harrowing and surreal and sometimes hilarious detail, as she proves the importance of writing toward the light, even—or especially—in the darkest times."

MARIA REVA

GOOD CITIZENS NEED NOT FEAR

Maria Reva was born in Ukraine and grew up in Canada. She holds an MFA from the Michener Center at the University of Texas. Her fiction has appeared in *The Atlantic*, *McSweeney's*, *Best American Short Stories*, and elsewhere, and she has won a National Magazine Award. She also works as an opera librettist.

www.mariareva.ca

GOOD
CITIZENS
NEED
NOT
FEAR

GOOD
CITIZENS
NEED
NOT
FEAR

GOOD
CITIZENS
NEED
NOT
FEAR

Maria
Reva

VINTAGE CANADA

PUBLISHED BY VINTAGE CANADA

Copyright © 2020 Maria Reva

Published in 2021 by Vintage Canada, a division of Penguin Random House Canada Limited, Toronto, and simultaneously in the United States by Anchor Books, a division of Penguin Random House LLC, New York. Originally published in hardcover by Alfred A. Knopf Canada, a division of Penguin Random House Canada Limited, in 2020. Distributed in Canada by Penguin Random House Canada Limited, Toronto.

www.penguinrandomhouse.ca

Vintage Canada with colophon is a registered trademark.

Several stories originally appeared, some in slightly different form, in the following publications: "Novostroïka" in *The Atlantic* (December 2016); "Little Rabbit" as "Unsound" in *McSweeney's Quarterly Concern* (August 2018); "Letter of Apology" in *Granta* (November 2018); and "The Ermine Coat" published by the Writers' Trust of Canada and winner of the RBC Bronwen Wallace Award in 2018.

Library and Archives Canada Cataloguing in Publication data is available upon request.

ISBN: 9780735281967

Text design by Maria Carella
Cover design by Emily Mahon
Cover art by Shout

Printed and bound in the United States of America

10 9 8 7 6 5 4 3 2 1

Penguin
Random House
VINTAGE CANADA

To my family

CONTENTS

PART ONE
Before the Fall

PART TWO
After the Fall

PART ONE

Before
the
Fall

NOVOSTROÏKA

The statue of Grandfather Lenin, just like the one in Moscow, 900 kilometers away, squinted into the smoggy distance. Winter's first snowflakes settled on its iron shoulders like dandruff. Even as Daniil Petrovich Blinov passed the statue and climbed the crumbling steps of the town council behind it, he felt the Grandfather's 360-degree gaze on the back of his head, burning through his fur-flap hat.

Inside the town council hall, a line of hunched figures pressed against the walls, warming their hands on the radiators. Men, women, entire families progressed toward a wall of glass partitions. Daniil entered the line. He rocked back and forth on the sides of his feet. When his heels grew numb, he flexed his calves to promote circulation.

"Next!"

Daniil took a step forward. He bent down to the hole in the partition and looked at the bespectacled woman sitting behind it. "I'm here to report a heating problem in our building."

"What's the problem?"

"We have no heat." He explained that the building was a new one, this winter was its first, someone seemed to have forgotten to connect it to the district furnace, and the toilet water froze at night.

The clerk heaved a thick directory onto her counter. "Building address?"

"Ivansk Street, Number 1933."

She flipped through the book, licking her finger every few pages. She flipped and flipped, consulted an index, flipped once more, shut the book, and folded her arms across it. "That building does not exist, Citizen."

Daniil stared at the woman. "What do you mean? I live there."

"According to the documentation, you do not." The clerk looked over Daniil's shoulder at the young couple in line behind him.

Daniil leaned closer, too quickly, banging his forehead against the partition. "Nineteen thirty-three Ivansk Street," he repeated, enunciating each syllable.

"Never heard of it."

"I have thirteen, no, fourteen people living in my suite alone, who can come here and tell you all about it," Daniil said. "Fourteen angry citizens bundled up to twice their size."

The clerk shook her head, tapped the book. "The documentation, Citizen."

"We'll keep using the gas, then. We'll leave the stove on day and night." The stove offered little in the way of heating, but Daniil hoped the wanton waste of a government-subsidized resource would stir a response.

The woman raised her eyebrows; Daniil appeared to have rematerialized in front of her. "Address again?"

"Nineteen thirty-three Ivansk Street, Kirovka, Ukraine, USSR. Mother Earth."

"Yes, yes. We'll have the gas-engineering department look into it. Next!"

—

Was it fourteen now? Had he included himself in the count? Carefully avoiding the ice patches on the sidewalk on his way home, Daniil wondered when he had let the numbers elude him. Last month twelve people had been living in his suite, including himself. He counted on his fingers, stiff from the cold. In the bedroom, first corner, Baba Ola slept on the foldout armchair; second corner, on the foldout cot, were Aunt Inaya and Uncle Timko and their three small children (but Uncle Timko promised they'd be assigned their own place soon because of his job superintending the municipal square's public restroom— a government position); third corner, Daniil's niece and her friend, but they hardly counted, since they ate little and spent most of their time at the institute; fourth corner, Daniil himself, bunking under Uncle Timko's mother, (Great) Aunt Nika; in the hallway, someone's mother-in-law or second cousin or who really knew, the connection was patchy; on the balcony camped Second Cousin Glebik and his fiancée and six hens, which were not included in the count but who could forget the damn noisy birds? That made thirteen. He must have missed someone.

Daniil's name had bounced from wait list to wait list for three years before he'd been assigned to his apartment by the Kirovka Canning Combine, where he worked as a packaging specialist. The ten-story paneled *novostroïka* was newly built and still smelled of mortar. His fifth-floor suite was no larger than the single room he had shared with his parents in a communal apartment, but he could call it his own. The day he'd moved in had been nothing short of sublime: he'd walked to his sink, filled a glass of water, guzzled it down, then lay on the kitchen floor with his legs squeezed into the gap between the stove and table. Home was where one could lie in peace, on any surface. He felt fresh and full of hope. Then came a knock at the door. Daniil's grandmother burst into the apartment, four mildewy sacks of grain and a cage full of hens strapped to her back. She spoke Ukrainian, which Daniil barely understood, having been raised and educated in Russian. She cursed her neighbor, who either was in love with her or had it in for her and had threatened to poison himself, or her, or perhaps both. Daniil simply nodded, ashamed to ask for clarification. And so Baba Ola stayed.

Two. Two had been fine. Until two became fourteen.

———

Minimum Dimensions of Space Necessary for Human Functioning, 85 processes: Sleeping (based on average Moscow male, head to toe) = 175 cm. Standing (gravitational effect included) = 174.5 cm. Opening oven (based on average Moscow female, buttocks to baking tray) = 63.5 cm. Washing face (elbow to elbow) = 52 cm. Opening refrigerator (door span area) = $\pi(55 \text{ cm})^2 \div 4$. Lacing up boots (floor space) = 63.5 cm x 43 cm. Pulling out dining chair (floor space) = 40 cm x 40 cm. Mending clothing, shoes, other (floor space) = 40 cm x 40 cm. Child rearing (floor space for corner time) = 30 cm x 30 cm. Watching educational television programs = 64.5 cm x 40 cm. Listening to educational radio programs = 64.5 cm x 40 cm. Evacuating bladder (volume) = 400 ml. Mental training (based on average Moscow male, brain volume) = 1260 cm^3. Dreaming = 1260 cm^3 . . . or ∞? Breathing (torso expansion) = 1.5 cm. Yawning (torso expansion) = 3 cm. Sneezing (torso retraction) = 3–4 cm.

Stretching (limb extension) = n/a. Etc. Etc. Minimum dimensions necessary for human functioning (TOTAL) = 9 m^2.

—

Daniil stuffed his hands back into the damp warmth of his pockets as he climbed the narrow set of stairs to his floor.

Suite 56 greeted him with its familiar smell, boiled potatoes and fermenting cabbage. "Daniil, is that you?" Aunt Nika hollered from the kitchen. At sixty-five, her voice retained its cutting timbre, perfectly suited for her job hawking seed oils at the bazaar. "Come look, we get barely any gas."

Daniil cringed. He had wanted to remain unnoticed by his relatives for a few seconds longer. When he opened the closet to hang his coat, a pair of gray eyes stared back at him, round and unblinking. Daniil started. He had forgotten Grandfather Grishko, who slept standing, as he used to do while guarding a military museum in Kiev. This was the fourteenth member of the Blinov residence. Daniil closed the door softly.

"Took me three hours to boil potatoes," Aunt Nika told Daniil when he stepped into the kitchen. She wore a stained apron over a floor-length mink coat inherited from her grandmother. Its massive hood obscured her face. She turned the knobs to maximum; the burner heads quivered with a faint blue. "Did you go to the town council? They should look into it."

"It seems they already have," Daniil said. "But they're better at turning things off than on."

A pigtailed girl, Aunt Inaya and Uncle Timko's, jumped out from under the kitchen table singing, "May there always be sunshine / May there always be blue skies." She air-fired at the lightbulb hanging from the ceiling. Aunt Nika gently scratched the nape of the girl's neck, and the child retreated back under the table.

"What did they tell you at the council?" Aunt Nika asked.

"The building doesn't exist, and we don't live here."

Aunt Nika's mittened hand brushed a strand of dyed red hair off her forehead. "Makes sense."

"How so?"

"I had a talk with the benchers last week." She meant the group of pensioners who sat at the main entrance of the building, ever vigilant, smoking unfiltered cigarettes and cracking sunflower seeds day and night. "They told me this block was supposed to have only two towers, but enough construction material had been discarded to cobble together a third—ours."

A series of barks blasted through the thin walls of the bedroom. Daniil glanced in alarm at Aunt Nika. He hadn't approved of the hens, but they were at least useful—now a dog?

Aunt Nika cast her eyes down. "Vovik. Bronchitis again, poor boy. What are you going to do about the gas?"

Aunt Nika's granddaughter bellowed from under the table, "May there always be mother / May there always be me!"

"I don't know," said Daniil.

Uncle Timko appeared in the doorway to announce that he needed a glass of milk. Daniil and Aunt Nika evacuated the kitchen and waited in the hallway while he opened the refrigerator.

The human shuffle complete, Daniil resumed inspecting the stove. Aunt Nika followed, her fur hood falling over her eyes until she flung it off, releasing a cloud of dust.

"Grandfather Grishko's telling everyone he hasn't seen

his own testicles in weeks," she said. "We're tired of the cold, Daniil."

As if in agreement, Vovik's coughing started up again, deeper in pitch, as though it came not from the bedroom but from beneath the floor. Daniil couldn't imagine the dainty four-year-old producing such sounds. He stroked the smooth enamel of the stove, never having felt so useless.

"And we're tired of hearing about the testicles."

The memo on Daniil's desk the next morning unsettled him. It was addressed from Moscow:

> In accordance with General Assembly No. 3556 of the Ministry of Food Industry, Ministry of Meat and Dairy Industry, and Ministry of Fish Industry on January 21, 1985, the Kirovka Canning Combine has been ordered to economize 2.5 tons of tinplate per month, due to shortages. Effective immediately.

At the bottom of the memo, his superior's blockish handwriting:

THIS MEANS YOU, BLINOV.

The telephone on his desk rang.

"You've read the memo?" It was Sergei Igorovich, his superior, calling. Daniil turned to look across many rows of desks. Sergei Igorovich stood in the doorway of his office, receiver pressed to his ear, watching Daniil.

"I have, Sergei Igorovich."

Daniil went on to inquire about testing alternative tin-to-steel ratios for containers.

"None of that, Blinov. Just stuff more food into fewer cans. Use every cubic millimeter you have," his superior said. "I see that you're not writing this down."

Daniil pulled up an old facsimile and set about doodling big-eared Cheburashka, a popular cartoon creature unknown to science.

"Good, very good," Sergei Igorovich said. "But don't think of pureeing anything."

"No?"

"The puree machine's on its way to Moscow. Commissar's wife just had twins."

Daniil examined the diameter of Cheburashka's head, making sure the ears matched its size. "Sergei Igorovich? May I ask you something?"

"If it's quick."

"I was looking over the impressive list of goods our combine produces, and couldn't help wondering—where does it all go?"

"Is that a philosophical question, Blinov?"

"All I see in stores is sea cabbage."

Sergei Igorovich let out a long sigh. "It's like that joke about the American, the Frenchman, and the Soviet guy."

"I haven't heard that one, Sergei Igorovich."

"A shame," Sergei Igorovich said. "When I have time to paint my nails and twiddle my thumbs, I'll tell you the joke."

Daniil resisted the temptation to roll himself into a defensive ball under his desk, like a hedgehog. He straightened his shoulders. "Sergei Igorovich? May I also ask about the pay."

Daniil watched his superior retreat into his office, mumbling into his phone about the shortages. Surely the pay would come through next month, Sergei Igorovich said, and if not then, the month after, and in the meantime don't ask too many questions. He hung up.

Daniil reached into his desk drawer, extracting a new sheet of graph paper and a T-square. He ran his fingers over the instrument, rich red, made of wild pearwood. When he was a child, his parents had awarded him the T-square for top marks in school. At the time, he'd thought the pearwood held some magical property, a secret promise.

He set to work drawing diagrams of food products in 400-milliliter cylinders. Chains of equations filled his graph paper. Some foods posed more of a packing problem than others: pickles held their shape, for instance, while tomatoes had near-infinite squeezability. Soups could be thickened and condensed milk condensed further, into a mortar-like substance. String beans proved the most difficult: Even when arranged like a honeycomb, they could reach only 91 percent packing efficiency. In the middle of every three string beans hid an unfillable space. By lunchtime, Daniil had submitted a report titled "The Problematics of the String-Bean Triangular Void" to Sergei Igorovich's secretary.

For the rest of the day, Daniil pretended to work while the combine pretended to pay him. He drew Gena the Crocodile, Cheburashka's sidekick. He pondered the properties of dandruff, specifically Grandfather Lenin's dandruff. Could a bald man have dandruff? Unlikely. What, then, about the goatee?

—

Canning for civilian consumption: sausages in pork fat sausages
in tomato sauce kidneys in tomato sauce hearts in tomato sauce
roast brains roast pork and rice pressed meat liver paste tongue
in jelly fried meat macaroni with beef pork or mutton beans
peas with beef pork or mutton meat pies sweet and sour meat
mixed offals udder liver heart kidneys head cheek tail ends and
trimmings fat salt onions plus one bay leaf whitefish in vegetable
oil sturgeon in vegetable oil with the occasional bone to be
retracted from esophagus in one of many district clinics available
to citizens mackerel in vegetable oil fried red mullet in vegetable
oil sheatfish in vegetable oil sprats in vegetable oil pike perch
in vegetable oil plaice in vegetable oil sardines in vegetable oil
bream in vegetable oil goby in vegetable oil sturgeon in natural
juice of the fish salmon in natural juice of the fish Caspian roach in
natural juice of the fish whale meat in natural juice of the mammal
anchovies in vinegar sprats in vinegar sardines in vinegar also in
fish cakes ground or mixed in vegetables tuna cod crab carp caviar
sliced eggplant vegetable marrow sliced vegetables tomato puree
tomato paste tomato catsup pureed sorrel pureed beet plus one
bay leaf green peas in natural juice of the legume asparagus in
natural juice of the vegetable cauliflower in natural juice of the
vegetable beets in natural juice of the vegetable carrots in natural
juice of the vegetable sliced eggplant in tomato sauce with
vegetable oil eggplant paste in tomato sauce with vegetable oil
pepper and tomato in tomato sauce with vegetable oil eggplant
and squash in tomato sauce with vegetable oil vegetable marrow
in tomato sauce with vegetable oil sliced vegetables in tomato
sauce with vegetable oil tomato puree tomato paste tomato
catsup spinach puree sorrel puree red pepper puree green pea
puree beet puree carrot puree vegetable soup puree vegetable
marrow vegetable marrow stuffed with rice vegetable marrow

in tomato to lower national risk of gastrointestinal disease sliced apricots in natural juice of the fruit sliced apples in natural juice of the fruit apricots in sugar syrup quince in sugar syrup grapes in sugar syrup cherries in sugar syrup pears in sugar syrup raisins in sugar syrup apricots pureed pears pureed peaches pureed plums pureed apples pureed for the toothless young and old condensed and dried milk constitute the most common canned milk products cylindrical oval rectangular pyramidal cans are packed in wooden boxes made of dry wood with a water content of not over 18 percent and if one or all of the above food products is unavailable: potatoes

—

Daniil reached the entrance to his building in late evening. His eyelids were heavy with fatigue, but his feet resisted going inside. Perhaps it was the hacking coughs, the endless questions, the innumerable pairs of shoes he'd have to dig through just to find his slippers. With his index finger he traced the red stenciled numbers and letters beside the main entrance. Nineteen thirty-three Ivansk Street. The building was a clone of the other two buildings on the block: identical panels, square windows, and metal entrances; identical wear in the mortar; identical rebar under the balconies, leaching rust. Nineteen thirty-three Ivansk was solidly there, in front of his nose. He blinked. But if it wasn't? He stepped closer to the stenciled numbers, felt the cold breath of the concrete. Was he the only one who could see it? It was there. Or it wasn't.

"Fudgy Cow?" a voice behind him asked.

Daniil jumped, and turned. He discerned the hunched silhouette of one of the benchers. From the spot the man occupied—right bench, left armrest—he knew it was Pyotr Palashkin, retired English teacher, loyal Voice of America listener. Palashkin lit a cigarette, illuminating his mole-specked face, and handed a candy to Daniil. The chubby cow on the paper wrapper smiled up at him dreamily. Daniil hadn't seen candy like this for months. He pocketed it for later.

"What are you out here stroking the wall for?" Palashkin asked.

Daniil shrugged. "I was just on my way in." He stayed put.

Palashkin looked up at the sky. He said in a low voice, "It's all going to collapse, you know."

"Oh?"

"Whispers are all we hear now, rumors here and there, but give it a few more years. Know what I'm saying? It's all going kaput."

Daniil gave the concrete wall a pat. "Let's just hope none of us are inside when she goes."

"What are you, cuckoo in the head? We're already inside. And I'm not talking about that building."

"I don't know about you, but I'm outside," Daniil said, now feeling unsure.

"Go eat your Fudgy Cow, Daniil." Palashkin extinguished his cigarette between his thumb and his index finger, stood up, and disappeared into the dark.

Daniil bent so close to the glass partition, he could almost curl his lips through the circular opening. The woman in booth number 7 (booths 1 to 6 were CLOSED FOR TECHNICAL BREAK), Kirovka Department of Gas, wore a fuzzy yellow sweater that Daniil found comforting, even inviting. He gazed at her and felt a twinge of hope.

The woman shut the directory with a thud. "What was it, 1933 Petrovsk, you said?"

"Ivansk."

"Look, I've heard rumors about that place, but it's not on any of the lists. Nineteen thirty-three Petrovsk is, though."

"That doesn't help me."

"Don't be hostile, Citizen. You are one of many, and I work alone."

"I know you know 1933 Ivansk exists. It exists enough for you to fiddle with the gas when you feel like it," Daniil said.

"What are you accusing us of, exactly?"

"Us? I thought you worked alone."

The woman took off her reading glasses, rubbed the bridge of her nose. "Refer to the town council with your questions."

"Already did. They said you'd fix it."

"Refer to the factory in charge of your suite assignment."

"What do they know? The whole combine is in a state of panic." Daniil was referring to the problem of the string bean.

"Best wishes with your heating problem," the woman pronounced. "Next!"

—

Candies Available for Civilian Consumption: Masha and Bear / Bear in the North / Little Bear / Clumsy Bear / Stratosphere / Strike! / Brighter! / Little Squirrel / Thumbelina / Moscow in Evening / Kiev in Evening / Fantastic Bird / Little Lemon / Little Lenin / Snowflake / Jelly / Fuzzy / Iris / Fudgy Cow / Little Red Hat / Alyonka / Little Miracle / Solidarity / Leningrad / Bird's Milk / Red Poppy / Mask / Meteorite / Vizit / Red Moscow / Dream / Caramel Crab Necks / Goose Feet / Duck Beaks / Kiss Kiss / Golden Key / Snow / Crazy Bee . . . And So Many More!

—

Daniil entered his apartment to find every square centimeter of shelf and bed space covered in stacks of red bills. His relatives had squeezed themselves into corners to count the money.

Daniil backed out of the apartment, closed the door behind him, stood on the landing until he had counted to thirty, and reentered. The red bills were still there. All right, he thought, so the hallucination continues. Run with it. Let the mind have its fancy.

The children's shrieks and snivels and coughs rang out from the kitchen, yet seemed warped and far away, as though they were coming from inside a tunnel.

Uncle Timko, the only grown-up not counting bills, sat cross-legged on Daniil's bunk, hacking away at a block of wood with a mallet and chisel. "Your grandfather's disappearing testicles saved the day, Daniil," he said, without looking up.

"I can't stand lamenting them anymore," said Grandfather Grishko, cocooned in a comforter. "Back in my district, they enjoyed quite a reputation. The girls would come from far and wide—" He went on to say a few things Daniil chose to expunge from his hallucination.

"The *children!*" Aunt Nika exclaimed from the depths of her fur.

Grandfather Grishko tossed a red stack at Daniil, and Daniil leafed through the crisp bills, half-expecting them to crackle and burst into pyrotechnic stars.

"This is my life's savings, Daniil," his grandfather said. "I've been keeping it for hard times, and hard times have arrived. Take the money. Don't ask me where I've been stashing it. Put it in for heating, bribe someone—anything."

Daniil mustered a weak thank-you.

Uncle Timko held up his mangled block of wood. "Does this look like a spoon or a toothpick?"

"Neither."

"It's supposed to be both."

"You're getting wood chips all over my sheets," protested Daniil.

Uncle Timko ignored him. "Spoon on one end, toothpick on the other. A basic instrument of survival."

When at last the counting was done, Grandfather Grishko's savings, along with money the other relatives had scrounged up, came to a hefty 8,752 rubles and 59 kopeks.

Daniil did a quick calculation in his head, imagining what 8,752 rubles and 59 kopeks could buy. He took the rabid inflation into account, and recalled the prices he'd seen at the half-empty state store the week before. Then he looked up from the stacks of bills into the expectant eyes of his family.

"We've got enough here to buy one space heater," he declared. He quickly held up a cautionary finger to stop the dreamers in the room. "If I can find one."

The next day, Daniil found another memo on his desk, this one from Sergei Igorovich:

TO FILL UNFILLABLE STRING-BEAN TRIANGULAR VOID,
ENGINEER TRIANGULAR VEGETABLE.
DUE FRIDAY.

Daniil rubbed his temples. An irresistible desire to stretch came over him. He wanted his body to fill the office, his arms and legs to stick out of the doors and windows. He wanted to leap and gambol where wild pearwood grew. His great parachute lungs would inflate, sucking up all the air on the planet.

The phone rang.

Sergei Igorovich was calling from his office again. He stood in his doorway, coiling the powder-blue phone cable around his index finger. "Is that a Fudgy Cow on your desk?"

"Just the wrapper, Sergei Igorovich."

"I haven't had one in months."

The line filled with heavy silence.

"I should get back to the triangular vegetable, Sergei Igorovich."

"You should." Sergei Igorovich kept the receiver pressed to his ear. "Blinov?"

"Yes, Sergei Igorovich."

"Was it good?"

"The candy? A bit stale."

Sergei Igorovich let out a brief moan before glancing over at his own superior's office, to find that he was being observed as well. He hung up.

Daniil placed the wrapper in his drawer, beside the T-square and his drawings of the Cheburashka gang. He turned to the diagram lying on his desk: a tin can containing exactly seventeen black olives. Seventeen was the maximum capacity, provided the olives were a constant size. The ones in the middle compacted into cubes, with barely any space for brine. Good, thought Daniil. No one drinks the brine anyway.

The heater was set to a lavish High. Its amber power light flickered like a campfire. Fourteen figures huddled around the rattling tin box and took turns allowing the warm air to tickle their faces. A few disrobed down to their sweaters. A bottle of *samogon* appeared from its hiding place, as did a can of sprats. Daniil felt warmth spread to his toes, to his chilliest spots. Aunt Nika took off her hood; her cheeks had gained a lively red. Grand-father Grishko sat on a stool like a king, knees spread, about to bite into a piece of *vobla* jerky he claimed predated the Great October Revolution.

"Let's hope the jerky has fared better than Ukraine," toasted Aunt Nika.

A knock came at the door.

Everyone fell quiet.

Another knock.

Aunt Nika poked Daniil's arm.

Daniil took another swig of home brew, slid off his chair (which Uncle Timko immediately occupied), and opened the door.

Two tall men in black beanies stood in the narrow hallway, holding a coffin.

Daniil felt himself teeter as his relatives crowded behind him. "If you're here to collect me, I'm not ready yet."

"We need access to your apartment, Citizen," the square-jawed man on the right said.

"Why?" Daniil asked.

The man on the left, endowed with wet meaty lips, rolled his eyes at his colleague. "God dammit, Petya, do we have to give an explanation at every landing?"

"An explanation would be nice," Daniil insisted.

"The guy on ninth croaked, and the stair landings aren't wide enough to pivot the coffin," Petya said. "So we need to do it inside the apartments."

"Yet somehow you got it all the way up to ninth." Daniil knew the cabinet-size elevator wouldn't have been an option.

"When the coffin was empty, we could turn it upright."

"And now you can't."

Petya narrowed his eyes at Daniil. "Some might find that disrespectful, Citizen." In agreement, Baba Ola flicked the back of Daniil's neck with her stone-hard fingers. Petya said, "Look, this thing isn't getting any lighter."

"You sure you aren't here to collect anyone?" Daniil asked.

"As you can see, we've already collected. Now let us in."

Daniil stood aside and the men lumbered in with the coffin, trampling on shoes without taking off their own, scratching the wallpaper.

"Yasha, we'll have to move the cot to make room," Petya said.

"Which one?"

"Pink flower sheets."

"Keep holding your end while I set mine down," Yasha instructed. "Toasty in here, eh?"

"Yes, mind the heater by your feet," Daniil chimed in.

"I'll have to step out on the balcony while you pivot."

Baba Ola lunged at the men, yelling something about the balcony, but no one understood exactly what.

A panicked brood of hens stormed the room.

Aunt Nika clutched at her chest. "Sweet Saint Nicholas."

"We'll have to report this poultry enterprise, Citizens," said Petya.

Daniil was about to tell them these strange hens must have hopped over from another balcony when everything went dark.

The heater's rattle ceased. The hens were stunned silent. Through the window, Daniil could see that the neighboring buildings were blacked out as well.

"Electrical shortages," Yasha said. "Heard about it on the radio. Said to stay tuned for scheduled blackouts."

"Setting the coffin down," Petya said, voice strained. "It's about to slip out of my hands—"

"Slow, slow—"

A delicate, protracted crunch—the sound of slowly crushed tin—filled seventeen pairs of ears. Daniil had counted: seventeen, if you included the man in the coffin. For a few seconds, no one said a word.

"Well, looks like we're going to be here awhile." Yasha sighed and shuffled, and the stale smell of socks wafted through the air. "Wasn't there some jerky going around?"

Daniil's head whirled. Seventeen humans in one room, arms and legs and fingers and toes laced together. Plus one bay leaf. The crunch of the space heater replayed in his mind, even as the cold seeped in. A small clawed foot stepped on his. Seventeen olives. Daniil would die just like this, stuffed and brined with the others, their single coffin stuck in someone else's bedroom. No one drinks the brine anyway. A brush of feathers huddled on his feet, shivering. Daniil took a step forward, and the feathers swished past. In the dark he felt for the coffin, yanked out the crumpled space heater from underneath it. The corner of the coffin slammed against the floor. The children screamed.

Daniil stepped onto the balcony, flung the heater over the ledge. For a second he felt weightless, as if he himself had taken to the air. A hollow crash echoed against the walls of the adjacent buildings.

He stepped back inside and sank down on his bunk. Wood chips scratched between his fingers.

Grandfather Grishko was the first to speak. "Daniil, go down and get it." The whispered words were slow, grave. "We'll get it fixed."

What was his grandfather hoping for? Still, Daniil would

do as he was told, if only to get out of the crowded suite. Then he felt the cold steel of his uncle's mallet and chisel among the wood chips. He grabbed the instruments and descended to the ground floor. A gruff voice offered caramels but Daniil snatched the bencher's cigarette lighter instead. He lit its flame, illuminating the red stenciled numbers on the front of the building.

And then he knew what he had to do. He had to get heating, because heating meant Number 1933 Ivansk existed. And if the building existed, he and his family had a place, even in the form of a scribble buried deep in a directory. He would show them proof. He would show the ones behind the glass partitions—he would bring the stenciled numbers to them. Daniil positioned the chisel. The first hit formed a long crack in the concrete, but kept the numbers whole.

LITTLE RABBIT

Sometimes they arrive in vans from the maternity ward. Sometimes in strollers, or inside shawls wrapped around waists. Sometimes from the village, sometimes from the town. Few of the babies have names. If they arrive healthy, they were born unwanted; if wanted, then unhealthy.

The baby house sits tucked behind a hill, out of sight of the village and the town.

It's bad luck to talk about or show pictures of the babies living at the baby house, much like it's bad luck to talk about or show pictures of a train wreck or a natural disaster.

The main hall of the baby house has bright windows and three rows of beds, and a *sanitarka* who makes rounds with a milk bottle. She strokes the babies, talks to each in turn.

She says, "My kitten."

She says, "I wish I could keep you for myself."

She says, "They told your mother to try again."

The director of the baby house is young, eager, and progressive. He's the darling of the Ministry of Health. The beam of light piercing the fog. The broom battling the cobwebs. Within the first year of his tenure, he urged the Ministry to take a holistic approach to the issue of invalid care. Since adult invalids are classified as Group Ones, Twos, and Threes according to labor capacity, the director believes each baby's group number can be predicted—projected—at birth. That way the Ministry can anticipate the resources necessary for lifelong collective care.

According to the director's classification of infants, the Threes have a minor defect. It may be cosmetic—webbed fingers, a misshapen ear—but when has that helped a person land a job? Even the outwardly normal babies pose a risk. Abandonment is taxing, and there is always the chance of a depressive mother, an alcoholic father lurking in the genes. So the director deems the healthy but abandoned babies Threes, just in case.

Twos are blind and/or deaf. Skin disorders and ambiguous genitalia fit the criteria, too.

Ones simply lie there.

An aerial view of the baby beds looks like this:

[ ] [ ] [ ] [ ] [ ] [ ] [ ] [ ]
[ ] [ ] [ ] [ ] [ ] [ ] [ ] [ ]
[ ] [ ] [ ] [ ] [ ] [ ] [ ]

This year, the Ones, Twos, and Threes sleeping in their beds look like this:

[3] [3] [2] [3] [2] [3] [3]
[2] [1] [1] [1] [1] [1] [2]
[3] [2] [3] [3] [3] [2] [3]

The director would deny any pattern to the distribution of the babies. If the healthier babies lie next to the great bright windows where they can chatter with the magpies, and next to the doors where the occasional Ministry inspector can see them best, it's surely a coincidence. Pick any other room, where the older children sleep—though they rarely sleep, not all at once—and try to find a pattern in that jumble.

And anyway, it's the *sanitarki* who assign the babies to their beds, not he.

In this particular batch of babies, the loudest voice comes from row three, bed seven. The puzzle pieces of her face hadn't sealed together in her mother's womb. A cleft begins at her right nostril, plunges down the upper lip and into the hole of her mouth. A boisterous Three, just on the edge of invalidity, this girl is one of the favorites. She coos and babbles and peekaboos, flirts with the *sanitarki*, grips their fingers with an iron strength when they peer in at her.

At six to ten months, the babies begin to crawl. Hands and knees patter on the vinyl floors. Today the distribution of the crawling babies looks like this:

3   2   3   2 33
3   2 3   3
3 2 2   3 2   3

On the far right, the lone baby: she's the lively Three. Faster than the others, the girl has slipped out of the baby house. She's cruising along the wooden picket fence, eyes set on a gap wide enough to squeeze through. Pine trees tower beyond it, beckon

her with their syrupy smell. Four pickets to go, three, two ...
The same *sanitarka* who found the girl inside the medicine cabinet yesterday, an overturned dustbin the day before, catches up
to her now. As the girl sticks her head through the gap—the
air feels different on the other side, less dense—she feels her
romper tighten around her neck, pull her backward. The pines
slide away.

The *sanitarka* is doubled over, panting. "You'll be the end of
me." She lets go of the romper. The baby looks up at her and a
flutter of giggles escapes her mouth, wins her captor over like it
did yesterday and the day before.

A small, secret relief for the overworked attendants: not all
the babies learn to crawl. This failure is only natural for those
with clubfeet or spinal conditions. And if some of them aren't let
down from their beds, it's because they'll never be able to walk
anyway. Beds take up most of the space, and there aren't enough
sanitarki eyes to watch over everyone. If all the babies learned to
crawl, where would they go?

The older children name her Zaya. Little rabbit. Her mouth is a
crooked assemblage of teeth and gums. As the teeth grow, they
poke through the slit in her lip. At breakfast, half her porridge
oozes from her nose.

The name starts with a letter she can't pronounce, and the
other children delight in hearing her try. There are many letters
the girl can't pronounce, because they require both sets of lips
and a complete upper jaw.

Whenever a *sanitarka* goes for a smoke in the courtyard,
Zaya follows. Most of the time the woman sits in silence, staring at the wall opposite, taking grateful pulls on her cigarette.

On good days she reads a magazine; on the best days she reads aloud to Zaya, who learns to follow the words. Topics covered: newly released books, home remedies, the latest five-year economic plan, hat etiquette.

Every New Year's Eve, the baby house receives a donation from the Transport Workers' Union. A six-wheel truck sighs to a stop in front of the gates, enveloping the waiting children in a great diesel plume. Grandfather Frost—whom a recently orphaned boy calls "Saint Nicholas" before receiving prompt correction—descends from the passenger side. He wears a tall boyar hat, a long white beard, a blue velvet coat, and felt boots.

Grandfather Frost beams down at the children. "Who's been good this year?"

The children shrink back, alarmed by the question.

Grandfather Frost recoils, too, unaccustomed to children afraid of the prospect of gifts. He whistles up to the pock-faced man behind the wheel, who wears a plastic crown festooned with a shiny blond braid—Snow Maiden. The bed of the truck lifts, dumps a pile of old tires over the fence. Grandfather Frost uses shears to cut the tires into swans.

"It's a miracle," says a *sanitarka*, and so it is. The children keep silent, watch the miracle unfold. This is how Grandfather Frost does it:

1.   2.   3.   4.

Soon the courtyard is littered with dusty brown swans. The children paint the swans red or blue or yellow. At first Zaya mixes red and yellow in her tin to make a radiant orange, but an experimental dab of blue turns the mixture brown.

When the director of the baby house comes to Zaya's swan, he says, "That's a shame. Grandfather Frost gave you three bright colors to choose from."

Zaya invents an explanation, one the director would find very clever, and would surely repeat to his colleagues at the Ministry, who would find it very clever also—but of the sounds that slosh out of Zaya's mouth, the director understands none.

So he asks, "Why not just paint the swan yellow?"

Every spring, the *sanitarki* trim the hedges along the building, pull weeds around the tulips. They bleach and starch the curtains, pour ammonia over the floors, shine the doorknobs, wipe the babies down.

And every spring, the Psychological-Medical-Pedagogical Commission of the Ministry of Education arrives in a procession of three cars. Zaya and the other four-year-olds press themselves against the windows of the baby house, watching the procession in a quiet panic. They are about to be redistributed.

The Threes shouldn't worry. Unless they freeze up during the test, they'll move on to the children's house.

The Ones don't yet know they should worry. They can't even get out of their beds, and no one can do anything about that now, so they'll be transferred to the psychoneurological *internat*.

"What's at the *internat*?" asks a pudgy-cheeked boy, twice caught wearing a dress in the laundry room.

"It's a delightful place where children run barefoot, pick berries," says the director, who has popped in for the day. "Communicate with nature, and so on."

A *sanitarka* starts to weep.

"Happy tears," the director explains.

The Twos are the wild cards. Sometimes the Commission sends them to the children's house, sometimes to the *internat*.

Zaya, our solid Three just a few months back, has regressed to a Two. She has abandoned speech in favor of writing, but few of the children know how to read yet, so most of the time she points and grunts.

When it's Zaya's turn with the Commission, the director escorts her to the back of the building, to a small room that smells like moldy onions. The Commission members sit at the head of a long table. They've arranged themselves in descending order of height, like nesting dolls. The largest man, who has a thick mustache cascading from his nostrils, asks Zaya to confirm her name.

Zaya hopes this isn't part of the test, but knows she must answer every question, without exception. She fears that her bottom is about to give out like a trapdoor, jams her knees together, afraid of wetting herself. To deflect, Zaya does what she saw a *sanitarka* do once, with the director, to get an extra day off. She twists her finger in her curls, peeks at the men through her thick lashes. She leans in, coy, as if she wants to tell them a secret. The men lean in, too. First she raises three fingers, then seven. When no one says anything, Zaya forces out a giggle: Silly, can't you understand?

The largest man looks down at the file in front of him and laughs. "Row three, bed seven. Her sleeping assignment." This answer satisfies the Commission.

The man in the middle, with oily porous cheeks, pushes four puzzle pieces across the table. Zaya fits them together. It's a picture of a cat, dog, and parrot.

"Can you tell us what you see?"

Zaya stares at the cat, dog, and parrot. She feels the shape of the first word inside her mouth, whispers it into her hand. It doesn't come out right, so she moves on to the next word, then the next.

CAT

DOG

PARROT

BIRD

THING

WITH

FEATHERS

PETS

ZOO

ANIMALS

FLUFFY

FRIENDS

The Commission watches the clock above the girl's head. The inside of Zaya's palm is warm and wet from her breath. At last the smallest of the men says, "One more question and you're free to go. What's the weather like outside?"

Zaya swivels around, looks out the window. All she wants is to run out of the building, out to where the weather is. Instead, she turns back to the Commission, presses her hands to her ears to keep from hearing herself, starts pushing the first word out. Its mangled syllables resonate between her palms. She wishes the Commission wouldn't look at her. She shuts her eyes, bangs her fist against the table, louder, louder to keep from hearing herself, until the pressure in her chest breaks and the words fire out. "How bright and beautiful the sun," she cries, "not one cloud can cover it up!"

The psychoneurological *internat* stands at the edge of a cliff, overlooking the Dnieper River. Patches of white plaster flake off the walls to reveal pink brick underneath, as if the building suffers from a skin condition. Long ago, before its gold-plated cupolas were dismantled and its eighteen copper bells melted down to canteen pots, before its monks were shot, it was a monastery. An iron fence, a recent addition, surrounds the grounds, its spiked rods rising high enough to keep in the tallest of the children, the space between the rods narrow enough to keep in the smallest.

The fresh batch of five-year-olds arrives in the back of a decommissioned camo truck, hair and faces dusty from the road. A tall woman in a dark green suit—their new director— orders the children to gather round in the courtyard. Her large smooth forehead emits a plastic sheen. One hand rises in greeting as the other does a head count. The children who can stand prop up those who can't against the fence.

Zaya watches a group of teenagers blow dandelion fluff at each other in the distance, two of them barefoot, just as the previous director promised. She scans the courtyard for tire animals, sees in their stead fresh mounds of earth.

The woman points to a sheet-metal sign nailed to the arched entrance of the decommissioned monastery. "Can anyone tell me what that says?"

When no volunteers come forward, she reads the sign herself: "THERE IS NO EASY WAY FROM THE EARTH TO THE STARS."

The reedy boy beside Zaya asks what stars are.

"To reach the stars you need to build a rocket. And we did that," the new director says. "But let me tell you a secret." She lowers her voice, and the circle of children tightens around her. "To build a rocket you need parts, and sometimes you get a crooked bolt, a leaky valve. These have to be thrown away. If they aren't, the rocket won't launch. Even if it does launch, it might explode into a million pieces."

The children nod along.

"That's just the way it is, when you're reaching for the stars." She casts a magnanimous gaze over the group. "Sometimes you get defective parts."

The children nod along.

"But we don't throw people away. We take care of them. You can bet on that for the rest of your life." She straightens up. "Something to think about, when you're feeling blue."

The children follow the director into the building. They file along a corridor, past the canteen; past a storage room containing a blackboard; past the latrine where a bald boy squats in the shadows, gargoyle-like, his shoulder blades jutting out; past a pair of twin girls balancing on one leg each; past a door with a tiny square window too high for Zaya to see through. They reach a cavernous hall crowded with beds and children. The painted walls are crowded, too, with scenes of wrath and deliverance: flames rise from the floor; a red snake coils up a wall and wraps its tongue around a thrashing figure; above are curly clouds, men with wings, men without wings, disembodied wings twisting around each other, stretching to the domed ceiling, at the center of which is a woman cradling a baby. The baby stares down at Zaya day and night wherever she is in the hall, its hand up, on the verge of uttering something important.

In the following months, Zaya adds to the pictures to pass the time. Using a sharp stone, she scratches the men's mouths open to let them speak. She wishes she could reach the never-sleeping baby, but it sits too high.

When winter comes, cold whistles through the cracks in the windows and into the lungs of the children.

It begins with a cough. The tickle in Zaya's throat burrows into her chest, blossoms into double pneumonia. She drifts in and out of a fevered fog. Noises filter into her dreams—the ruffle of sheets, snot bubbling up and down endless nasal passages, the distant cowbells from a village, the clack of trains from a rail yard.

Outside the window, a couple of older, healthier children chatter as they dig another pit. When she hears them shoveling earth back into the hole, Zaya feels for damp soil on her own hot face. But it isn't there; it's for someone else.

Green buds erupt on the branches outside. Sunrays on bed-sheets shine brighter.

When Zaya wakes between fevers, she sees a pair of with-ered arms and legs on her bed. She tries to move; the matchstick limbs answer. She covers them with her sheet.

Zaya looks at the beds around her. The room is hushed, so she's surprised to find most of her neighbors awake, blinking at the ceiling. She's in a different room than before, a white-tiled room—the room on the other side of the door with the tiny square window.

[1] [1] [1] [1] [1] [1] [1]
[1] [1] [1] [1] [1] [1] [1]
[1] [1] [1] [1] [1] [1] [1]

Zaya could try walking again, but where would she go? Everything aches, as if a fire has ravaged her insides. She lays her head down and goes back to sleep.

She wakes when a pair of fingers press on her wrist, checking for a pulse.

She wakes when the corners of her sheet lift and she floats in the air for an instant. She screams and falls back down on the mattress.

She wakes writhing in hot wet sheets. Something hard slams into her side. When she disentangles herself, she is on the floor. Her sweaty palms slip on pale pink vinyl as she crawls to the door with the square window. She tries the knob, beats her fists against the door. She slumps back down to the floor, a heap of bones. Coughs erupt through her mouth and nose in painful spasms, expelling a frothy pus—not into her hand, but in the crook of her elbow, as she has been taught. Two limp-faced girls gaze down at her from their own beds, peaceful. All she needs to do is let it happen, their heavy-lidded eyes tell her. Give in, melt into the floor. Isn't that what this room is for—a long rest? Her lungs will unclench, fill to the brim like two bottles of milk, and the *sanitarki* will take her away. That's when the parents come at last. Zaya has seen them visit once their child is safe in a small box. A nurse might even sew up her lip for the occasion.

Her head rolls to the right. In the corner of the room, a crack in the vinyl floor glows.

What she has to do is crawl toward that crack. The need is bodily, instinctual. She has seen it in every moth and mosquito bewitched by a flame.

Right hand, left knee, left hand, right knee. Her joints grind painfully, her elbows buckle, but she keeps moving.

Zaya lifts the corner of the vinyl. It peels away easily, revealing a pair of short loose planks. The glow beckons her from beneath them. Panting, she pulls the planks aside. A small hole in the floor opens up to a set of stone steps leading underground. The tunnel's cool breath gives the girl a burst of strength. She stands on shaky legs. Strings of cobweb cling to her arms and face as she follows the light down the cold steps, which level out into a chamber. Long narrow shelves are carved into the stone walls. Broken candles and vases litter the floor—remnants of pillage. The air smells sweet, like a baby's mouth after feeding.

The glow emanates from a corner of the chamber, from underneath a gray pile of robes. Zaya unwraps them—the cloth's folds retain a bluish luster—and the unsettled dust brings on another coughing fit. Inside is a mummified body. Or, half of one. The legs appear to have been snapped off. The brown leathery face squints up at Zaya. Its mouth, petrified midscream or midyawn, suggests the creature met its end in wretched terror or sublime repose. Its hair and beard are the yellow of dead grass, but its teeth gleam white. The hands cross at the chest, skin stretched between knuckles like a bat's wings. Beside the creature lies a dark red cylindrical hat Zaya has seen before, atop the bishops painted on the monastery walls—but on this hat, the jewels have been picked out.

Zaya beholds the shriveled face, and determines from its

gaze that something awaits her, something important. The saint, she knows, doesn't want to be buried at the *internat* any more than she does.

Zaya tugs the hat over its shiny forehead. The hat is fetching. A waste indeed, to be a saint stuck underground with such a hat.

She gathers the saint in her arms. Centuries of desiccation have made its body very light. The saint pulls forward, as though tied to a string. The pair make their way through the tunnels, turning right here, left there, the bundle leading her through the dark, urging her toward the miracle of escape. They totter up a set of steps, toward an opening. Zaya smells the leaves before she sees them. Gripping the saint with one hand, pulling the branches and weeds apart with the other, she climbs over a clutch of tree roots.

The blue sky greets them.

Zaya leaps forward, ready to run from the *internat*, run as far as her aching legs will take her. But then she stops.

They're outside the building, but still inside the tall iron fence.

Before Zaya can feel the blow of defeat, the bundle pulls her back into the tunnel—and Zaya follows.

Down the tunnel they go, then to the left, right, left again. They reach an opening in the cliff face. The only way down here is a fall to the jagged rocks below. Back into the tunnel they go. The saint's pull is stronger now, the pruney creature in Zaya's arms frantic to perform its marvel, and she frantic to witness it. Right, left, another left.

They're outside again, but still inside the fence, this time just a few steps shy of the forest beyond.

Zaya waits for direction. The saint, now inert, gives none. She shakes it. In the daylight, its parched features look exhausted, accepting their fate. At least one of them can escape, Zaya thinks. She thrusts the bundle over the fence. The saint lands faceup on the wild grass, hat uncapped in salute.

Zaya hears a *sanitarka* call her name, turns to see the woman racing toward her. Just a few meters away now, the woman's creamy arms are spread wide enough for an embrace.

When Zaya slides her leg between the rods of the fence, she doesn't expect the rest of her body to follow—but it squeezes right through. She picks up the saint, and runs for the pines.

LETTER OF APOLOGY

Don't think.
If you think, don't speak.
If you think and speak, don't write.
If you think, speak, and write, don't sign.
If you think, speak, write, and sign, don't be surprised.

News of Konstantyn Illych Boyko's transgression came to us by way of an anonymous note deposited in a suggestion box at the Kirovka Cultural Club. According to the note, after giving a poetry reading, Konstantyn Illych disseminated a political joke as he loosened his tie backstage. Following Directive No. 97 to Eliminate Dissemination of Untruths Among Party Cadres and the KGB, my superior could not repeat the joke, but assured me it was grave enough to warrant our attention.

One can only argue with an intellectual like Konstantyn Illych if one speaks to him on his level. I was among the few in the Kirovka branch of the agency with a higher education; the task of reeducating Konstantyn Illych thus fell to me.

Since Konstantyn Illych was a celebrated poet in Ukraine and the matter a sensitive one, I was to approach him in private rather than at his workplace, in case the joke had to be repeated.

Public rebuke would only be used if a civil one-on-one failed. According to Konstantyn Illych's personal file (aged forty-five, employed by the Cultural Club), the poet spent his Sundays alone or with his wife at their dacha in Uhly, a miserable swampland 30 kilometers south of town.

Judgment of the quality of the swampland is my own and was not indicated in the file.

The following Sunday I drove to Uhly, or as close as I could get to Uhly; after the spring snowmelt, the dachas were submerged by a meter of turbid water and people were moving between and around the dachas in rowboats.

I had not secured a rowboat for the task as the need for one was not mentioned in Konstantyn Illych's file, nor in the orders I was given.

I parked at the flood line, where five rowboats were moored: two green, two blue, one white, none black. Usually, our mode of transportation was black. I leaned on the warm hood of my car (black) and plucked clean a cattail as I deliberated what to do next. I decided on the innocuous white; I did not want to frighten Konstantyn Illych, and cause him to flee, by appearing in a black rowboat.

The dachas were poorly numbered and I had to ask for directions, which was not ideal. One man I spoke to was half-deaf and, after nodding through my question, launched into an account of his cystectomy; another elderly man, who clearly understood Russian, rudely responded in Ukrainian; one woman, after inquiring what in hell I was doing in her brother's rowboat, tried to set her Rottweiler on me (fortunately, the beast feared water). I was about to head back to the car when an aluminum kayak slid out of the reeds beside me, carrying two knobby-kneed girls. They told me to turn right at the electric transformer and row to the third house after the one crushed by a poplar.

A few minutes later I floated across the fence of a small dacha, toward a shack sagging on stilts. On the windowsill stood a rusted trophy of a fencer in fighting stance, and from its rapier hung a rag and sponge. When no response came from an oared knock on the door, I rowed to the back of the shack. There sat Konstantyn Illych and, presumably, his wife, Milena Markivna, both of them cross-legged atop a wooden table, playing cards. The tabletop rose just above water level, giving the impression that the couple was stranded on a raft at sea. The poet's arms and shoulders were small, like a boy's, but his head was disproportionately large, blockish. I found it difficult to imagine the head strapped into a fencing mask, but that is beside the point.

"Konstantyn Illych?" I called out.

The poet kept his eyes on the fan of cards in his hands. "Who's asking?"

I rowed closer. The wood of my boat tapped the wood of the table. "My name is Mikhail Ivanovich. Pleased to meet you."

Konstantyn Illych did not return my politesse, did not even take the toothpick out of his mouth to say, "You here for electric? We paid up last week."

His wife placed a four of spades on the table. Her thick dark hair hung over her face.

I told Konstantyn Illych who I was and that the agency had received reports of how he had publicly disseminated wrongful evaluations of the leaders of the Communist Party and Soviet society at large, and that I was here to have a conversation with him. Konstantyn Illych set his cards facedown on the table and said in a level tone, "All right, let's have a conversation."

I had conducted dozens of these conversations before and

always began from a friendly place, as if we were two regular people—pals, even—just chatting.

"Quite the flood," I remarked.

"Yes," confirmed Konstantyn Illych, "the flood."

"I'll bet the children love it here."

"No children."

Usually there were children. I stretched my legs out in the rowboat, which upset its balance, and jerked them back.

"No parents, grandparents, aunts, or uncles either," said Milena Markivna. Her upper lip curled—the beginning of a sneer, as if to say, But you already knew that, didn't you?

There had indeed been mention in the file of a mass reprimand of Milena Markivna's relatives in the fifties, but amid all the other facts about all the other residents of Kirovka, with all their sordid family histories, the detail had slipped my mind. Still, did the woman need to dampen the spirit of the conversation?

Konstantyn Illych broke the silence. "So what's the joke?"

"I hadn't made a joke," I said.

"No, the joke I supposedly told about the Party."

Already he was incriminating himself. "The term I used was 'wrongful evaluation,' but thank you for specifying the offense, Konstantyn Illych."

"You're welcome," he said, unexpectedly. "What was it?"

"I cannot repeat the joke." I admit I had searched Konstantyn Illych's file for it, but one of the typists had already redacted the words.

"You can't repeat the joke you're accusing me of telling?"

"Correct." Then, before I could stop myself: "Perhaps you could repeat the joke, and I'll confirm whether or not it's the one."

Konstantyn Illych narrowed his eyes, but said nothing.

"We aren't moving any closer to a solution, Konstantyn Illych."

"Tell me the problem first," he said.

A brown leaf, curled into the shape of a robed figurine, floated by Milena Markivna's foot. She pressed the leaf into the murky water with her thumb before turning to her husband. "Just say sorry and be done with it."

I thanked her for her intuition—an apology was precisely what was in order, in the form of a letter within thirty days. Milena Markivna advised me not to thank her since she hadn't done anything to help me; in fact, she hated officers like me and it was because of officers like me that she had grown up alone in this world, but at least she had nothing to lose and could do anything she wanted to: she could spit in my face if she wanted to. This, I did not recommend.

Konstantyn Illych was tapping his fingernails on the table. "I'm not putting anything in writing."

It is usually at this point in the conversation, when the written word comes up, that the perpetrator becomes most uncomfortable, begins to wriggle. Few people grasp the simple logic of the situation: once a transgression occurs and a case file opens, the case file triggers a response—in this case, a letter of apology. One document exposes the problem, the second resolves it. One cannot function without the other, just as a bolt cannot function without a nut and a nut cannot function without a bolt. And so I told Konstantyn Illych, "I'm afraid you don't have a choice."

He reached for the small rectangular bulge in his breast pocket. "Ever read my poetry?"

I expected him to retrieve a booklet of poems and to read from it. Dread came over me; I had never been one to understand verse. Fortunately he produced a packet of cigarettes instead.

"Come to my next reading," he said. "You'll see I'm as ideologically pure as a newborn. Then we'll talk about the letter."

Normally I had a letter of apology written and signed well under the thirty-day deadline. I took pride in my celerity. Even the most stubborn perpetrators succumbed when threatened with loss of employment or arrest. The latter, however, was a last resort. The goal these days was to reeducate without arrest because the Party was magnanimous and forgiving; furthermore, prisons could no longer accommodate every citizen who uttered a joke.

In Konstantyn Illych's case, next came gentle intimidation. If Konstantyn Illych stood in line for sausage, I stood five spots behind him. If Konstantyn Illych took a rest on a park bench, I sat three benches over. He pretended not to see me, but I knew he did: He walked too fast, tripping on uneven pavement; bills and coins slipped from his fingers regularly. His head jerked right and left to make sure he never found himself alone on the street. He needn't have worried—there was always the odd pedestrian around—and anyway, I did not intend to physically harm or abduct Konstantyn Illych, though that would have been simpler for both of us. My older colleagues often lamented the loss of simpler times.

Four days passed without a word exchanged between us.

On the fifth day, I attended Konstantyn Illych's poetry reading at the Kirovka Cultural Club. I took a seat in the front row of the lectorium, so close to the stage I could see the poet's toes agitate inside his leather shoes. In the dim light, I was able to transcribe some of his poetry:

>Helical gears, cluster gears, rack gears,
>bevel and miter gears, worm gears, spur gears,
>ratchet and pawl gears, internal spur gears,
>grind my body
>meat grinder
>grinds
>gr gr grrr
>ah ah ah
>aah aah aah
>ah haaaaaah!

And also:

>The bear
>bares his flesh
>skinless, bears the burden
>of the air wooooooooooooooooosh

And also:

>Dewy forget-me-not
>not me forgets.
>Stomp.

I cannot guarantee I transcribed the onomatopoeic bits with accuracy; Konstantyn Illych's reading gave no indication of the number of *a*'s and *o*'s, et cetera.

At the end of the reading the poet placed his pages at his feet, unbuttoned his faded blue blazer, addressed the audience: "Time for some trivia. I'll recite a poem and one of you will guess who wrote it. Get it right and everyone here will admire you, get it wrong and you'll be eternally shamed." A few people laughed.

Throughout the challenge poets such as Tsvetaeva, Inber, Mayakovsky, Shevchenko (this one I knew), and Tushnova were identified. The audience expressed their enjoyment of correct answers by whooping and clapping between names.

Konstantyn Illych waited for the lectorium to quiet down before he leaned into the microphone. "Who, whom."

This, apparently, was also a poem; the crowd erupted in fervid applause. I made a mental note to alert my superiors that local culture was going down the chute.

Konstantyn Illych scanned the audience until his eyes met mine. "The gentleman in the front row, in the black peacoat," he said. "Who wrote that poem?"

Once more the hall fell silent.

I turned right and left, hoping to find another man wearing a black peacoat in my vicinity. That's when I saw Konstantyn Illych's wife sitting behind me. She crossed her arms, her great bulging eyes on me, beckoning me to answer. One of her hands, nestled in the crook of her opposite arm, resembled a pale spider waiting to pounce.

Konstantyn Illych's voice boomed above me. "The greatest poet of all time, Comrade, and you do not know? I'll give you three seconds. Three . . ."

I froze in my seat. The middle-aged man to my right, whose nose looked like it had been smashed many times, nudged me in the ribs.

"Two . . ."

The man whispered "Grandfather Lenin!"—a mockery that I found in poor taste.

"One!" Konstantyn Illych bellowed. "Who was it, esteemed audience?"

The words rose from the crowd in a column. "Grandfather Lenin!"

Konstantyn Illych looked down at me from the stage, tsked into the microphone. Each tsk felt sharp, hot, a lash on my skin.

It was around this time I began to suspect that, while I had been following Konstantyn Illych, his wife had been following me. I forced myself to recollect the preceding week. Milena Markivna never figured in the center of my memories—the bull's-eye had always, of course, been Konstantyn Illych—but I did find her in the cloudy periphery, sometimes even in the vacuous space between memories. If I stood five spots behind Konstantyn Illych in line for sausage, the hooded figure four spots behind me possessed Milena's tall narrow-shouldered frame; if I sat three benches away from Konstantyn Illych, the woman two benches over had the same pale ankle peeking out from under the skirt. I began to see my task of retrieving the letter of apology in a new light.

What I suspected: My mission was not about the letter, but about the lengths I would go to retrieve it.

What I suspected: I was being vetted for a position of great honor.

What I knew: "Who, whom" had been a simple test, and I had failed it.

What I knew: My mother had been subjected to the same tests as a young woman, and had succeeded.

When I was a child, my mother was invited to join the

Honor Guard. According to my father, she had always been a model student, the fiercest marcher in the Pioneers, the loudest voice in the parades. She was the champion archer of Ukraine and had even been awarded a red ribbon by the Kirovka Botanist Club for her Cactaceae collection. One evening, an officer came to our door and served my mother a letter summoning her to the Chief Officer's quarters. Within six months she was sent to Moscow for special training, as only special training would suffice for the Guard that stands at the mausoleum of Lenin. Since our family was not a recognized unit—my parents hadn't married because my paternal grandparents (now deceased) didn't like my mother—my father and I could not join her in Moscow. I was too young to remember much about this period, but do have two recollections: one, I could not reconcile the immense honor of the Invitation with the grief that plagued the family; two, my father assumed care of my mother's cactus collection, and every evening, when he thought I was asleep on the sofa bed beside him, wrapped his fingers around the spines of the plants and winced and grit his teeth but kept them there until his whole body eased into a queer smile. For many months his hands were scabbed and swollen. Within a year my father was gone also; he had at last been able to join my mother in Moscow. My grandparents told me that one day I, too, would join them.

Now that Milena Markivna had entered my life, I felt I had finally been noticed. The vetting process for the Honor Guard was still possible. My reassignment to Moscow to see my mother and father was still possible. I believed it was possible to make gains with hard work.

From that point on I followed Milena Markivna's husband with greater vigilance, and in turn Milena Markivna followed me with greater vigilance. If Konstantyn Illych rifled his pockets for a missing kopek for the newspaper, Milena Markivna's voice behind me would say, "Surely you have an extra kopek for the man," and surely enough, I would. If I dropped a sunflower-seed shell on the floor while pacing the corridor outside the couple's apartment, behind the peephole of Suite 76 Milena Markivna's voice would say, "It's in the corner behind you," and surely enough, it was. She was a master observer, better than I.

(It should not go unsaid that, beyond mention of the reprimand of Milena Markivna's family, and of her employment as a polyclinic custodian, her file contained little information. On the surface, this was because she was born in the province surrounding Kirovka and not in the town itself, but I suspected it was a matter of rank: if Milena Markivna were indeed my superior, tasked with the evaluation of my conduct and aptitude for ceremonial duty, of course I would not have access to her full history. Information is compartmentalized to mitigate leaks, much like compartments are sealed off in ships to prevent sinking.)

Konstantyn Illych grew accustomed to my omnipresence, even seemed to warm to it. Once, after a bulk shipment to the Gastronom, I watched him haul home a 30-kilogram sack of sugar. By the time he reached his building, Number 1933 Ivansk (at least, this was the theoretical address indicated in his case file—the building number appeared to have been chiseled out of the concrete), the sack developed a small tear. Konstantyn Illych would be unable to haul the sack up to the tenth floor without losing a fair share of granules. The elevator was out of the question due to the rolling blackouts, and so I offered to pinch the tear as he carried the load over his shoulder, and he did not decline. Many minutes later we stood in front of Suite 76, Konstantyn Illych breathless from the effort. Since I was there I might as well come in, he said, to help with the sack.

He unlocked the steel outer door and the red upholstered inner door, then locked the doors behind us—all this with an excessive jingling of numerous keys. Here was a man with a double door, he wanted me to take note: a Man of Importance.

The apartment was very small, surely smaller than the sanitary standard of 9 square meters allotted per person, and only marginally heated. After we maneuvered the sack to the balcony, I scanned the suite for a trace of Milena Markivna—a blouse thrown over a chair, the scent of an open jar of hand cream, perhaps—but saw only books upon books, bursting from shelves and boxes lining the already narrow corridor, books propping up the lame leg of an armchair, books stacked as a table for a lamp under which more books were read, books even in the bathroom, all of them poetry or on poetry, all presumably Konstantyn Illych's. A corner of the main room had been spared for a glass buffet of fencing trophies and foils, and on top of the buffet stood a row of family portraits. I tried to find Milena Markivna in the sun-bleached photographs but these, too, belonged to Konstantyn Illych—the large head made him recognizable at any age. I wondered if she lived there, if she was even his wife.

Milena Markivna entered the apartment a few minutes later, with a soft scratch of keys. After shrugging off her long black raincoat to reveal the bleach-flecked smock underneath—a marvelous imitation of a custodial uniform—she appraised me as I imagined she might appraise a rug her husband had fished out of a dumpster. Would the piece be useful, or would it collect dust and get in the way? Her expression suggested the latter, but her husband was leading me into the kitchen, the point of no return. Once a guest steps into the kitchen, to let them leave without being fed and beveraged is of course unconscionable.

Milena Markivna leaned her hip against the counter, watching Konstantyn Illych mete out home brew into three cloudy shot glasses. "Lena, fetch the sprats, will you?"

Milena Markivna indicated she needed the stool, which I immediately vacated. She stepped up on it to retrieve a can from the back of the uppermost cupboard, then set the can down on the table, with some force, and looked at me, also with some force, presumably daring me to do something about the unopened sprats. I produced the eight-layer pocketknife I always kept on my person. In an elaborate display of resourcefulness, I flicked through the screwdriver, ruler, fish scaler and hook disgorger, scissors, pharmaceutical spatula, magnifying lens, hoof cleaner, shackle opener, and wood saw, before reaching the can opener. Its metal claw sank into the tin with so little resistance, I could have been cutting margarine. Milena Markivna must have noticed the surprise on my face. She asked if I knew about the exploding cans.

I conceded I did not.

"It's something I heard," she said, "something about the tin, how they don't make it like they used to. People are getting shrapnel wounds." After a pause, she gave a dry mirthless laugh and so I laughed as well.

Before Konstantyn Illych passed around the shots, I laid a sprat on my tongue and chewed it slowly to let the bitter oil coat the inside of my mouth and throat, minimizing the effects of the not-yet-ingested alcohol.

I took note that Milena Markivna also chewed a sprat before the first shot.

Three rounds later, Konstantyn Illych was speaking of the tenets of futurist philosophy. He was about to show how he employed them in his poetry when I jumped in to ask about the letter of apology, due in fifteen days.

"Mikhail Ivanovich," he said. "Misha. Can I call you Misha?"

"You may." The home brew was softening my judgment and there was only one sprat left.

"Fuck the letter, Misha. What is this, grade school?"

I told him about the possible repercussions, that he might be fired or arrested. "You're lucky," I said. "In earlier times, a political joke meant ten years."

Konstantyn Illych set his empty shot glass upside down on his index finger like a thimble, twirled it in languid circles. "Once upon a time," he began.

I wanted to shake the letter out of him.

"I got the flu," he continued. "Ever get the flu?"

"Sure."

"The flu turned into bronchitis and I ended up in the hospital. Not only did I get my own room, but by the end of the week the room was filled, and I mean floor-to-ceiling filled, with flowers and cards and jars of food from people I didn't even know, people from all around the country."

Milena Markivna placed the last sprat between her lips and sucked it in until the tip of the tail disappeared into her mouth.

Konstantyn Illych leaned in. "Imagine, Misha, what would happen if you tried to get me fired."

Another week passed without success. My superior remarked that I was usually quicker at obtaining a letter, and was I not dealing with someone who specialized in the written word, who could whip up a heartfelt apology in no time? I considered bribing the poet, but the mere thought felt unnatural, against the grain, against the direction a bribe usually slid. I began to neglect other tasks at work but still believed my persistence with Konstantyn Illych would be rewarded. I admit I thought of Milena Markivna as well, and often. She followed me into my dreams. Throughout my life, she would tell me in those dreams, I had been watched over. She would award me with a certificate signaling my entry into the Honor Guard, would place on my head a special canvas cap with a golden star on its front. I cannot say if this image is true to the initiation ceremony, but it was how I imagined it had happened with my mother. I would wake at night to find myself alone in my dark room but felt no fear. I knew I was being watched over.

The day before the deadline I stood at the back of the town cinema, watching Konstantyn Illych watch *Hedgehog in the Fog*. Eventually my attention turned to the animated film itself. I had already seen it a number of times and always found it unsettling—similar to the way heights are unsettling. En route to visit his friend for tea, Hedgehog gets lost in the fog that descends on the forest. It isn't the fog or the forest that troubles me, although they trouble Hedgehog; what troubles me is this: Hedgehog sees a white horse and wonders if it would drown if it fell asleep in the fog. I've never understood the question. I suppose what Hedgehog means is: If the white horse stops moving, we would no longer see it in the white fog. But if we no longer see it, what is its state? Drowned or not? Dead or alive? The question is whether Hedgehog would prefer to keep the fog or have it lift only to discover what is behind its thick veil. I would keep the fog. For instance, I cannot know the whereabouts of my parents because they are part of me and therefore part of my personal file and naturally no one can see their own file, just like no one can see the back of their own head. My mother is standing proud among the Honor Guard. My mother is standing elsewhere. She is sitting. She is lying down. She is cleaning an aquarium while riding an elevator. Uncertainty contains an infinite number of certainties. My mother is in all these states at once, and nothing stops me from choosing one. Many people claim they like certainty, but I do not believe this is true—it is uncertainty that gives freedom of mind. And so, while I longed to be reassigned to Moscow and look for my parents, the thought of it shook me to the bones with terror.

When the film ended, I felt a damp breath on the back of my neck. Milena Markivna's voice whispered: "Meet me at the dacha at midnight. I'll get you the letter."

It was a weekday, a Wednesday, and so the dachas were empty of people. The swamps were still flooded, but this time a sleek black rowboat waited for me. It barely made a seam in the water as I rowed. Northward, the overcast sky glowed from the lights of the town. My teeth chattered from cold or excitement or fear—it is difficult to keep still when one knows one's life is about to change. Already I could feel, like a comforting hand on my shoulder, the double gold aiguillette worn by the Guard. The tall chrome leather boots tight around my calves.

I tried to retrace the route I had taken the first time I visited the dacha, but found myself in the middle of a thicket of cattails. The glow of the sky suddenly switched off. (Normally electricity is cut not at night but in the evening, when people use it most, and thus the most can be economized—this is the thought I would have had had I not been engulfed in panic.) Darkness closed in on me. I circled on the spot. The cattails hissed against the edge of the boat. Willow branches snared my arms and face. A sulfurous stench stirred up from the boggy water. Milena Markivna had given me the simplest of tasks and I was about to fail her.

A horizontal slit of light appeared in the distance, faint and quivering. I lurched the boat toward it. Soon I recognized the silhouette of the shack on stilts, the light emanating from under its door. I scrambled up the stairs, knocked. The lock clicked and I waited for the door to open, and when it did not, I opened it myself.

A figure in a white uniform and mask stood before me, pointing a gleaming rapier at my chest. The figure looked like a human-size replica of the fencing trophies I had seen inside the glass display in Suite 76.

"Close the door." The voice behind the mask was calm, level, and belonged to Milena Markivna.

I tried to keep calm as well, but my hand shook when it reached for the handle. I closed the door without turning away from her, keeping my eyes on the rapier. The ornate, patinated silver of its hilt suggested the weapon had been unearthed from another century.

"Down on the floor. On your knees."

I had not imagined our meeting would be like this, but did as I was told. I inquired about the utility of having my ankles bound by rope and Milena Markivna explained it was to prevent me from running away before she was done. I assured her I wouldn't think to run from such an important occasion and she, in turn, assured me she would skewer my heart onto one of my floating ribs if I tried. Before she stuffed a rag inside my mouth, I told her I had been waiting for this moment since I was a child, and she replied that she had been waiting for it since she was a child as well. I told her I was ready.

She said, "I'm ready, too."

I do not know how much time passed with me kneeling, head bowed, as Milena Markivna stood over me.

I tried to utter a word of encouragement, perhaps even mention my admiration for the canvas cap with the golden star on its front, but of course I couldn't speak through the rag in my mouth. All I could do was breathe in the pickled smell of the fabric.

She knelt down in front of me, one hand on the hilt of the rapier, its tip still quivering at my chest. With the other hand she took off her mask. Hair clung to her forehead, moist with sweat. I searched her face for approval or disappointment but it was closed to me, as if she were wearing a mask under the one she had just removed. I wondered how this would all look if a stranger barged through the door: she almost mad and I almost murdered.

At last Milena Markivna stabbed the rapier into the floor, which made me cry out, and said there was really no hurry. She brought over a stout candle that had been burning on the table and dipped my fingers into the liquid wax, one by one, as she named her relatives who had been executed, one by one, thirty years ago. The burning was sharp at first—although I dared not cry out or make another sound—but soon felt like ice. Milena seemed calmer after this. She removed the rag from my mouth, unlaced her boots, set her bare feet on top of them, and gave me a series of instructions. As I bowed my head and enveloped her warm toes in my mouth—they had a fermented taste, not unpleasant, like rising dough—she reminded me how she hated me. I removed my lips from the mound of her ankle long enough to tell her that we were not so different, she and I; that I, too, had grown up alone, even though my solitude would end soon. As she picked up a second candle and began to tip it over my scalp, she asked how it would end. Barely able to speak now, I told her that it would end when she inducted me into the Honor Guard and I would go to Moscow and see my family again. She laughed as if I had told a joke. My head pulsed with pain; tears blurred my vision. The smell that greeted me was of singed pig flesh, sickening when I realized it was my own. Milena Markivna set the candle down and asked how I knew of my family's whereabouts. I said it was what I had been told. As she slid her fingers along the blade of the rapier, she said the neighbor who had taken her in had promised that her family had gone to a better place, too, but never specified where or explained why they never wrote. The darkness of the night filtered in through the cracks of the shack and into my mind, and I began thinking of things I did not like to think about—of my mother and father and where they really might be. Milena Markivna wrapped her hand around the hilt of the rapier again and told me to take off my coat and shirt and lie facedown on the floor.

As I did so, one thought knocked against the next, like dominoes:

There was a possibility I was not, at present, being recruited.

If not, there was no Honor Guard waiting for me.

If not, my parents' rank did not matter.

If not, my parents did not have rank.

If not, Mother was not in the Guard.

If not, they were not in Moscow.

The blade dragged from my tailbone up the thin skin of my spine, searing my mind clean. I screamed into my mouth so that no one would hear. When the blade reached between my shoulders it became warm, and from its point a sweet numbness spread through my arms. I thought of my father with his bleeding hands, understood that queer smile. My head spun and the walls began to undulate. My voice came hoarsely. "How do you know what happened to your family?"

After a moment she said, "They disappeared. That's how I know."

"They could be anywhere."

"Do you believe that?"

"Yes." My body shook against the damp floorboards. "No."

It was when I welcomed the blade that it lifted from my skin. I felt a tug between my ankles, then a loosening. She had cut the rope.

"You can go."

"You're not done."

"No," she said, but still she pushed my shirt and coat toward me with her foot. I lay limp, spent. Through the window I could see the glow of the town flicker back on. I remembered why I had come to the dacha, but could not rouse myself to bring up the letter. I found I did not care about it much myself. I would be the one who would have to issue an apology to my superior tomorrow, giving an explanation for failing to complete my task. I would write it. My superior would read it. I would be dismissed. What next? I would stop by a news kiosk on my way home, search my pockets for the correct change. If I did not have it, a voice behind me might ask if someone has a kopek for the man. Surely enough, someone would.

Before leaving, I asked Milena Markivna, "What was the joke your husband told?"

"Oh." She said, "███████████████████████ ███████████████? ███████████████████████."

"All this trouble for that?"

It was the first time I saw her smile. "I know. It's not even funny."

BONE MUSIC

The first time Smena's neighbor knocked on her door, she asked to borrow cloves. The woman stood in Smena's doorway, clutching a canvas sack to her chest. Her diminutive frame barely reached the latch. "I'll bring the cloves back," she promised. "You can reuse them up to three times."

This neighbor, Smena knew, associated with the building's benchers. The woman never sat with them but did spend a good deal of time standing beside them, cracking sunflower seeds, no doubt gossiping, and Smena would often hear the metallic clang of her laughter through the bedroom window. Smena had placed the woman in her mid-sixties, around Smena's age, but up close her wet lips and bright caramel eyes made her look younger. Her cropped hair, dyed bright red, reminded Smena of the state-made cherry jam she used to see in stores.

She did not let the neighbor in, but made sure to leave a crack between the door and its frame so as not to shut it in the woman's face—word got around if you were rude, especially to a bencher or bencher affiliate. Smena rummaged in her kitchen drawers for the cloves, then continued the search in her bathroom cabinet, which contained the kitchen overflow. There, the cloves rattled inside a newspaper pouch; they'd lost their peppery tang.

Smena stepped out of the bathroom and blurted "Oi." The neighbor was sitting in her kitchen. The woman had taken off her clogs, and a grayish middle toe poked through a hole in one of her socks.

Neighbors rarely visited each other, and if they did, it was to complain about a leak in the ceiling or to spy out who had better wallpaper and why. Smena tossed the pouch of cloves on the table, hoping the woman would take what she'd come for and leave.

"I'm Nika, from fifth," the neighbor said. "Have a biscuit." From her canvas sack she produced a small plastic bag, rolled down its rim, and Smena felt a pang of delight: inside were the same cheap biscuits Smena used to buy at the bazaar, the ones that had the shape and consistency of a fifty-kopek coin and had to be soaked in tea to save teeth from breaking. This gesture meant her guest wanted tea, which she, the host, should have offered long ago, upon greeting.

Nika craned her neck for a better view down the corridor. "Say, this a one-room or two-room?" Nika pronounced her words with a dawdling slur that was at odds with her quick movements. Smena wondered if the woman was recovering from a stroke.

"Two-room."

"For one person?"

Smena tensed. Anything she said, already she could hear being repeated around the block. "My husband snored." This was true: Smena had shared the sofa bed with her daughter, in the other room, until the girl had moved in with her fiancé's family many towns away.

To occupy herself, Smena set the kettle on the stove. When she turned back to the woman, beside the biscuits lay a black plastic sheet. An X-ray scan. Smena recognized it instantly; she had a stack of them in the cupboard beside the refrigerator.

"I hear you make a nice ruble copying vinyl records onto X-rays," said Nika.

Smena's brows lifted in mock surprise. "Who told you that?"

"A friendly worm in the ground."

"The friendly worm is mistaken."

"I used to own a few bone albums myself, a long time ago," Nika went on. "Only played them a couple times before they got worn through. Didn't compare to vinyl, of course, but that's how you got the real music." By "real" she meant banned music. American rock 'n' roll, decadent capitalist filth, the stuff with sex and narcotics. Smena's specialty. She had begun copying bootlegged albums in the postwar years, when she and her husband were desperate for money and radiographic film was the cheapest, most readily accessible form of plastic. Now, with the national shortage of reel cassettes—the national shortage of everything—Smena was back in business.

"I hear your records are the best," said Nika. "Can play for days."

Smena hunched her shoulders in an attempt to make her broad frame appear small, innocuous. "I don't know what you're talking about. I'm a simple pensioner, just like you."

"A simple pensioner like me doesn't have a two-room all to herself."

Smena detected judgment in Nika's voice—it was uncouth for a woman, especially one far along in her years, to take up so much space—but also envy.

When the kettle whistle blew, Smena was wary of turning her back to the woman again; she imagined discovering a pile of X-rays, or the woman's entire family, in the kitchen. She reached a hand behind her hips to turn off the gas, fumbled with the cutlery drawer for a spoon—then stopped. This was the same drawer that contained the lathe for engraving X-rays. Smena used her fingers to pinch tea leaves into cups, and stirred the tea by whirling each cup in a circle.

"I hope you can help me," said Nika.

"Sugar in your tea?"

"Please. Say, ever got an X-ray done yourself?"

"Everyone has."

"The radiation alone is enough to kill you, just slower than whatever it is they're checking for." Nika paused, as though waiting for Smena to say something. "What were they checking for?"

"A bout of pneumonia, a couple years ago," said Smena, distracted. She'd remembered the sugar jar lived in the same cupboard as the record player—which was a perfectly mundane object in itself, but not if seen in conjunction with the lathe. "I forgot, I'm out of sugar."

The two women drank their tea bitter. Smena observed that once, when Nika made to dip her biscuit, she missed the cup, tapped the table instead, noticed the error, and dipped the biscuit into her cup with vigor. Before her guest left, Smena tried to push the X-ray back into her hands, but Nika refused. "I'll be back with your cloves," she said from the doorway.

"Keep them."

"You can reuse them up to three times. I read about it."

"Keep reusing them, then."

"Oh, I couldn't."

Smena forced a smile. "It's a gift."

"I'm the one who should be gifting you gifts, for helping me."

"I haven't done anything to help you."

"But you will," said Nika. "I can always pick out the good people. Like good watermelons." She was about to head off at last, then paused and turned to face Smena again. "You said your husband snored. What fixed it?"

"He died."

Nika winked. "I'm divorced, too. They say our building is cursed."

Smena closed the door on the woman, to hide her own blush. She shoved the X-ray in the garbage bin under the sink. Her underground business made Smena vulnerable to extortion. If Nika visited again, she might ask for more than cloves.

But the X-ray did not stay in the bin long.

Smena's worst traits, her mother had once informed her, were her height and her curiosity.

It was the golden hour, the best time of day to inspect new X-rays, when sunbeams shot directly through Smena's kitchen window, illuminating each feathery detail of the bones. Smena lived on the tenth floor, and the neighboring building was far enough from hers for the X-ray viewings to be conducted in privacy. She secured Nika's scan onto her window with suction cups.

The profile of a skull shone at her. The architecture of a human head never failed to shock Smena, or make her wonder how such a large bulbous weight balanced on the thin stack of vertebrae.

Smena couldn't help but feel excitement: a head X-ray did not come her way as often as those of other body parts. And heads were the most popular with the buyers, fetched the most money. A shame she couldn't use this one. She would not be lured into Nika's trap.

The small white letters on the bottom right-hand corner of the film, easily overlooked by the untrained eye, read VERONIKA L. GUPKA, TUMOR. Smena noticed a thinning at the base of the skull, a shadow overtaking it from inside. The thing looked contagious, like a curse. She didn't like the tumor hanging on her window, projecting its tendrils onto her kitchen wall.

She understood then: the woman was dying. Whatever she wanted from Smena stemmed from this fact.

Smena hid the scan, but this time, despite herself, she did not try to dispose of it.

Megadeth's growls and screams, banned in all fifteen Soviet republics, came from Smena's cupboard record player—at minimal volume, of course.

"I'm with the Kremlin on this one," said Milena, Smena's dealer. "If these are the latest tunes from the West, maybe the place really is rotting." As usual, Milena stood leaning against the windowsill, ignoring the vacant stool in front of her. She seemed to prefer heights, like a cat, Smena had noticed.

This was their biweekly meeting. Milena brought wads of cash from selling bone albums at subway stations, public squares, and parks, and Smena counted the profit, taking the largest cut for herself. Next, Milena presented her with an array of X-ray scans procured through her job as a polyclinic custodian, and Smena picked out the most desirable designs. Today's winning selection included a foot that had been subjected to an asphalt roller; a handsome pelvic girdle; a torso with what looked like a prominent colon but was really the spine of a fetus; a child's hand curled into an obscene gesture.

Smena had recruited Milena because of her proximity to X-rays, but also for her proximity to Smena herself. Milena lived two doors down in a one-room she shared with her poet husband, and Smena didn't even need to cross her own doorway to coax her neighbor in for a chat. From the first, Smena had known Milena would be perfect for the position; no one would suspect the pale middle-aged woman with drab clothes and uneven bangs of dealing illicit albums. At first Milena had refused, recounting how just last month she'd had to shake off a government lackey who had been trailing her husband, and was not sure she would be able to get rid of another, but after a second round of shots Milena confessed she could use the extra money. She was saving up—what for, she didn't say.

Seated across the kitchen table from Smena was Larissa, the style hunter who supplied hits from the West. "Megadeth is a deliberate misspelling of the English word 'megadeath,' one million deaths by nuclear explosion," she explained. Unlike Milena, who wore only black like a perpetual mourner, Larissa was a carefully choreographed explosion of color: red-and-yellow checkered dress, tangerine tights, peacock-blue heels (which she hadn't taken off at the door). She sewed most of her clothes herself, copying styles from British and French magazines, complete with embroidered duplicates of the most prestigious logos. Thirty-one years old, Larissa lived with her mother and two daughters in the suite below Smena's. From the fights Smena overheard through the heating vent—typical topics raised by the mother: Larissa's low-paying job at the chemical plant two towns over, Larissa's expensive tastes, Larissa's failure to keep a man—Smena had gauged that her downstairs neighbor, like Milena, could not refuse a second income. It had only taken

Smena two nights of thumping her floor with a broom handle before an irate Larissa paid her first visit.

Smena closed her eyes, taking in Megadeth's restless rhythms. She couldn't understand the lyrics, of course, but the singers' screams were so wrenching, they seemed to be dredging up bits of Smena's own soul. She wondered how Megadeth would sound at full volume, the power of the screams unharnessed.

"I think there's something to this," she said.

Milena's and Larissa's eyes swiveled to her in surprise.

Smena glared at the women in return. "Oh, come off it. I'm old but I'm not obsolete."

"The group's aesthetic is contextual. People scream a lot in America," offered Larissa, adjusting her horn-rimmed lensless glasses. "They have screaming therapy for terminal patients. Very expensive. I read about it. Doctors drop patients off in the middle of the woods and get them to hurl their lungs out. Barbaric, yes, but most come back happier."

"The last time I made a person scream they didn't seem any happier," Milena remarked with a smirk, "and I did it for free." Smena nodded without comment, assuming Milena was referring to one of her fencing tournaments.

When the meeting ended and Milena left, Smena found herself alone with Larissa as she gathered her effects into a quilted faux-leather purse. Smena leaned across the table toward the woman and stretched her lips over her teeth into a smile. This felt awkward, so she unstretched them. "You're doing a fine job, Larissa."

Larissa simply nodded, without deflecting the compliment. Another of her imports from the West: a lack of modesty.

Smena produced two bills from her pocket. She did not look

at the money as she slipped it into Larissa's breast pocket. She wanted the action of touching money to look easy, as if it was something she did a lot, something she barely noticed anymore. "I hear the bakery by the chemical plant is better than the one around the block. Mind picking up a loaf sometime this week?" she said. And added, "Keep the change."

A child's whining cry reached them from the suite below. Larissa gave a weary smile. "I'd be happy to."

"And a dozen eggs, if you see them."

"At the bakery?"

Smena slid a few more bills across the table, many more than necessary.

"Brown or white?" asked Larissa.

"White bread, brown eggs." The pricier options.

Smena had asked Milena to bring potatoes two weeks prior. If Milena and Larissa picked up an item or two of food for her every now and then, with her small appetite she would be fine. She did not want her neighbors to suspect that, combined, they were part of a greater pattern. She hadn't been to the bazaar in over a year, hadn't even ventured past her front door. Each time Smena opened the door, she felt the dank air of the outer hallway cling to her skin, as if she were being pulled into a tomb.

Smena's fears had begun with a newspaper article: a boy had tripped over exposed rebar and broken both wrists. For years, the townspeople had been privately griping about the poor state of roads, sidewalks, bridges, but this was the first time the consequences of decaying infrastructure were publicized. Soon more and more reports came, from all over the country, each more outlandish than the next. A sinkhole trapped a commuter bus. A family of five plummeted to their deaths in an elevator malfunction. A gas leak gently poisoned preschoolers for weeks before being discovered. Pedestrians were advised to avoid underpasses.

Even previously privileged information was released, about how the town had been built on a not-quite-drained marsh that was slowly reliquifying. Smena's daughter, and her daughter's university friends, had cheered on the liberation of the press, which was taking place in their respective towns, too. But Smena had felt safer under the maternal hand of censorship.

Smena's building, her entire town, now felt like a death trap, but she convinced herself that the concrete walls of her own apartment were secure. After a yearlong renovation, none of the windows or doors creaked. The new checkerboard linoleum felt smooth and sturdy under her feet. As long as she stayed in her space, twelve by twelve steps, she would be safe.

The X-ray of Nika's skull lay on the kitchen table. Smena admired its smooth round shape. No matter how penetrating the radiology waves, the thoughts and desires within that doomed chamber remained secret. There Nika lived, and there she would die.

Smena felt no pity. Pity masked itself as kindness, but was rooted in condescension. Smena would not want to be pitied herself.

She turned Megadeth back on. Screaming therapy, she thought. Now there's something useful.

She lit a cigarette, and paused to appreciate the scratchy vocals and pulse-raising tempo before hitting Stop, resetting the needle to the beginning. Using manicure scissors, Smena cut the radiograph into a circular shape. She made a hole in the middle of the circle with her lit cigarette, right where the ear would be, and the acrid smell of burning plastic rose from the film. She positioned the film on the phonograph, attached a spidery metal arm from the record player's needle to the cutting stylus on the phonograph, and hit Play on both machines. As the grooves on the vinyl vibrated the needle and produced music, the metal arm transmitted the vibrations to the cutting stylus and reproduced the grooves onto Nika's skull.

The evening before the next meeting, Larissa's eleven-year-old daughter knocked on Smena's door. Given Larissa's talent for fashioning replicas, Smena found it fitting that Dasha should look just like her wide-eyed mother—down to the cowlick, and the platoon of bobby pins enlisted to flatten it. The girl informed Smena that her mother couldn't make it to their biweekly study session on dialectical materialism—Smena couldn't help smiling—because her mother was so sick with the flu she couldn't crawl up two flights of stairs to tell Smena Timofeevna so herself.

Smena dropped her smile, remembering. "Eggs? Bread?"

Dasha tilted her head, confused. "No thank you." She turned on her heel and skipped down the corridor, purple dress rustling.

Smena spent the next hour scouring her kitchen, making a mental inventory of the remaining food: three potatoes, two bread heels, nine walnuts, one thimble-size jar of horseradish. Her millet and rice stocks had run out the month prior. If she cut down her already meager consumption, she estimated the supplies would last less than a week.

The smell of boiling chicken now wafting from the heating vent did not help calm Smena's nerves.

One thing Smena would not do was call her own daughter. After the grandchildren started coming, occasionally the daughter called to suggest Smena come live with her and her family in Crimea. They could sleep on the sofa bed together like old times, her daughter would joke, figure out a cot for the son-in-law. Smena would hear the shrieks of the grandchildren at the other end of the line and try to imagine herself as the babushka depicted in children's folktales: stout, puffy-cheeked, bending over a cauldron of bubbling pea soup with a wooden spoon in hand, ready to feed, bathe, rear an entire village.

"The time isn't right for a move," she had told her daughter the last time they spoke. "I'm too busy."

"Busy with what?" Her daughter didn't know about the bone business. "You're all alone over there!"

Smena took this to mean, "You're going to die alone over there," which was where the conversation always headed, and promptly hung up.

Smena's mother had birthed six other children before she had Smena, and had made a point of telling her that a husband and children were the best insurance against dying alone. The family had lived in a crumbling clay house. One day, when Smena's father was at work and she and her siblings were at school, Smena's mother took her metal shears and slashed away at the tall grass outside the window. The blades crunched into an electric cable. Smena was the one who found her mother's body in the weeds. Smena remembered how her own throat had contracted in shock, how her scream had come out as a hiccup. For a long time Smena had studied her mother's face, which was set in a wild openmouthed grin, as if she were biting into the sweetest happiness on Earth. Seven children, eighteen years of cleaning, chiding, spanking, loving, pea soup making, and what did it matter? Smena's mother had died alone, and seemed to have fared all right. Before the accident, Smena had imagined death as a send-off, a majestic ship to board while your party of relatives crowds at the port ledge, waving goodbye. The higher the attendance, the more valued your life. Now, she imagined something more private. Once you got past the ugly physicality of death, you were left with a single boat, a cushion. Room to stretch out the legs.

The second time Nika knocked on the door, she returned the cloves in their newspaper pouch. From the doorway she beamed up at Smena, as though she had proven herself by fulfilling her ridiculous promise. She produced a baking tray of buns from her cloth sack. Fragrant, buttery, they bulged out of the tray in a tight grid, ready to spring into Smena's mouth. Each had a neat hole on top, from a clove.

"Borrower's interest," Nika joked. Her speech had slowed since the last visit, her syllables become more labored.

Smena didn't know whether it was the hunger, or the shock at this small act of kindness—albeit suspect kindness—that made her say, "Come in for some tea?" before she could stop herself.

"Oh no, thank you. I couldn't." But already Nika was kicking off her clogs. "Just for a minute." She was wearing the same faded socks, with her toe sticking out. Smena offered a pair of furry dalmatian-print slippers, ones Milena usually wore during their meetings.

As Smena brewed tea, Nika separated the buns and arranged them in a circle on a glass platter—also conjured from the magical sack. "Got any butter?" She was quick, antlike, and before Smena could intervene, she opened the refrigerator. The expanse of white gaped at her, empty. With horror Smena imagined this detail registering in the neatly categorized inventory of Nika's mind, and wanted to snatch it back out.

Without comment Nika turned and marched out of the apartment, leaving Smena to wonder if the state of the refrigerator had offended her. But a few minutes later Nika returned bearing not only butter, but also bread, eggs, and a pat of lard wrapped in a plastic bag, for frying. She began piling the supplies into the refrigerator.

"You don't have to do that," said Smena. "I was going to go to the Gastronom tomorrow."

"So was I. We'll go together?"

Smena pretended to consider it. "Actually, tomorrow's no good."

"The day after."

"I'm tied up."

Nika shut the refrigerator, gave its handle a conciliatory stroke. "The benchers told me they haven't seen you leave the building in months," she said softly. "They only see your visitors, not you."

Blasted benchers, Smena thought. Nothing better to do. "Most of those old stumps are half-blind," she said. "And I move very fast." She pulled a bill from a metal tin on the counter, knowing she risked insulting the woman. But Nika only laughed, swatted the money away. "Please," she said. "*Kak auknetsja, tak i otkliknetsja.*" Do as you would be done by.

The women sat down together. Smena's discomfort melted away when she took her first bite of bun. Its thin caramelized crust, where egg whites had been painted on in crisscross, protected a warm flaky interior. The best bun she had ever tasted.

Nika ran her hand along the chrome length of the table. "This is nice. Quiet. Where I live it's a zoo. Fourteen people, another one in my daughter-in-law's belly. Imagine! Despite his position, my son and his family still haven't been assigned their own peace."

Smena wondered if she meant "place," and if the tumor was pressing a fibrous finger on just the wrong spot. "Which factory does he work for?"

"Timko works for the government." She let the last word fall heavily, significant.

Perhaps this was a threat? Working for the government meant anything from licking envelopes to spying on high-profile citizens.

"A nice two-room, is that so much to ask?"

Smena wasn't sure to whom, exactly, the woman was directing the question. But there it was: the dying woman's motive. A lovely two-room for her lovely family. Her legacy secured. If Smena were to be imprisoned for the bone business, Nika's growing, government-affiliated family would be next in line for her apartment. Smena wanted to jump up, scream "Gotcha!" like she'd seen a man do at the bazaar once, after he'd stabbed his finger into a vendor's pot of golden honey to reveal the cheap sugar syrup underneath.

Before Nika left, she placed a second sheet of black film on the table, without inquiring about the first.

An hour later, the new scan glowed on the kitchen window. Smena wanted to track the progression—again, for curiosity's sake.

The sun's rays showed more thinning of the bone as the

tumor burrowed toward the spinal column. Smena couldn't help being impressed by the thing—an organism living by its own will, clawing for space in the tight dome of the skull.

The next meeting, Larissa forgot about the bread and eggs, but did bring two albums by John Coltrane.

"Never heard of him," said Milena, who stood at the window, left thigh resting on the sill.

Larissa straightened the velvet lapels of her blazer and looked up at Milena. "John Coltrane," she explained, "was one of the most prominent jazz musicians of the twentieth century." Her nose and cheeks were red and puffy. Despite her best efforts to appear composed, she looked in danger of crumpling to the floor any moment.

"How am I supposed to know? No one's ever asked for a Coltrane," said Milena. She eyed the tray of buns poking over the top of the refrigerator, then glanced at Smena for permission. Smena nodded—she regretted not having offered them herself.

"You're supposed to *know* what you're selling," said Larissa, hoarse voice rising. Smena shushed her. "How else do you test for fake clients, impostors?" Larissa whispered.

"Speaking of," Milena said through a mouthful of bun.

Smena and Larissa turned to her.

"It's probably nothing," Milena tried.

"Tell us the nothing," said Smena.

Milena scratched a spot of grime off the window with her fingernail. "I was at the park, my usual spot by the thousand-year oak, when a guy came up to me. Skinny, with a sad attempt at a mustache. Asked for a KISS. Like the group. The music group."

"Very good," said Larissa, rolling her eyes.

"I started to grill him," Milena continued. "Year the band got together, band leader's middle name, year of their breakout single, whichever useless facts Larissa shoves down my ear." She winked at Larissa, who turned away in a huff. "The guy was doing well, seemed to know everything. Then he started grilling *me*. Asked why Ace Frehley added eyeliner to his iconic 'Space Ace' makeup design. What was I supposed to do, look stupid? I played along, answered best I could, but when I asked, 'So are you buying the album or not?' he only said, 'Nah, I got what I came for.'"

"And then?" asked Smena.

"He just walked off."

Milena helped herself to another bun. She mashed the entire thing into her mouth, and Smena watched her masticate it without any apparent enjoyment. There were only four buns left, and she imagined what would happen once they were all gone, how she'd gnaw on laurel leaves, suck peppercorns for taste.

After a while Milena said in a low voice, "It's what *they* do. Play with you first, see you flail, knowing you have nowhere to go."

"Play is all it is," countered Larissa. "No one gets sent to the camps anymore. Human rights," she proclaimed, chin tilted up, "are in vogue."

"My sweet thing," cried Milena. She sank down to the stool beside Larissa, grasped the young woman's hand. At first Smena took Milena's outburst for sarcasm, but Milena seemed genuinely shocked by Larissa's innocence, as if she'd discovered a kitten playing in a dumpster. Larissa blushed, but did not retract her hand before Milena let go.

When Smena had starting making bone records, in the fifties, the risks were clear, the boundaries stable. Now an invisible hand was loosening the screws, but it was impossible to tell which screws, and for how long the loosening would last. Although no one got sent to the camps (for now), every citizen was able to imagine more clearly than ever before what might await them in those very camps; the newspapers had begun publishing prisoners' accounts, down to the gauge of the torture instruments.

"Camps or no camps," Milena said, "prison wouldn't be fun either." She turned to Smena. "So what do we do?"

"You didn't show the man any of the albums?" Smena asked. "You kept them inside your coat the whole time?"

Milena nodded. "He saw nothing."

While the possible punishment was unclear, something else was not: they all needed the money.

Larissa turned to Milena. "When the man asked why Ace started using eyeliner, what did you say?"

"To keep the silver face paint out of his eyes. He's become allergic."

Larissa smiled proudly.

Now Nika visited Smena every week. She would bring soup or cabbage pie, and the pair would sit down for a midday meal followed by tea. Each time Nika knocked, Smena vowed to confront her. If Nika really was looking to extort her, Smena was willing to preempt, negotiate, even give her a cut of the bone music profits. But confronting Nika would also mean admitting to the business, and what if the woman wasn't willing to negotiate? And, a distant possibility: What if Nika wasn't trying to extort her at all? More and more, Smena was willing to believe it.

In truth, she didn't mind Nika's visits. The woman's chatter offered a lens into the outer world that the newspapers—which Smena had mostly stopped reading anyway—could not. From Nika, Smena learned that the irises were blooming, the flowers floppy as used handkerchiefs; that it was the time of year when woodpeckers drummed on utility poles down by the river, to woo their mates. Nika exclaimed, "Can you imagine the ruckus?" Yes, Smena could.

Week to week, Smena watched the change in Nika over the rim of her teacup. One visit, Nika's slur was so pronounced Smena could barely understand her, and the pair sat in silence, pretending nothing was wrong. Another visit, Nika regaled Smena with jokes, but as she spoke her face lacked expression, as though she were posing for a government identification photo.

"You keep giving me a funny look," Nika remarked on that occasion.

Smena tried to brush it off. "I'm impressed. You tell a joke but keep such a straight face."

"I'm losing feeling in my face."

"Oi."

"My daughter-in-law says it'll do wonders for the wrinkles."

"The brat."

"I'll look all the better when they bury me." A strand of hair fell over Nika's eyes and her hand pecked at her forehead, trying and failing to find the strand.

"You should be in the hospital, Nika."

The women locked eyes.

"So you've looked at the scans," said Nika.

"I don't know why you keep giving them to me."

Nika shrugged. "They're as useless to me as they are to the doctors who order them."

"What do you mean?"

"The polyclinic has quotas for tests, so they do tests. Or they just make the numbers up to fill the quotas, so their money and supplies don't get cut. The polyclinic's filled with these ghost patients and can't admit new ones."

"You have a growth in your brain the size of a lemon and they can't admit you?"

"They can't admit me *because* of the lemon. I'm not a viable patient."

"With your new face I can't tell when you're joking."

"Really, Smena, when was the last time you went out into the world?" Nika sighed, as if she were about to explain basic arithmetic. "The polyclinic doesn't want to exceed their death quota."

"Which I'm sure they've made up."

"Doesn't matter. The nurse said if they exceed the quota, they get investigated, and if they get investigated, it's worse for all of us."

"How nice of her to give you an explanation."

"It was," she said softly. "I gave her chocolates."

Smena looked at her neighbor. She was a shell of the woman who had first come to Smena's door two months ago, determined to get her way.

"At least you can make something useful out of the scans," said Nika. "Something beautiful."

Smena heaved herself to her feet. A vertiginous feeling overwhelmed her. She saw herself on the edge of a precipice, its bottom beckoning. She feared heights, perhaps because she also loved them—she always wondered what would happen if she jumped.

Smena swung open the cabinet above the fridge. She

retrieved the five albums she had made for Nika and spread them out on the table in chronological order. She pointed to the first, the Megadeth. "You won't like this one at first but it'll grow on you. Listen to it when you're alone, and imagine the sounds pouring from your own mouth." She pointed to the rest: "Pink Floyd, to relax to. Suzi Quatro and Julio Iglesias, to cheer up to." Nika studied the scans on the table, the ripening shadow at the base of the cranium.

Smena set the fifth, Coltrane, on the record player, and watched Nika see her skull spin into a milky blur as the needle sucked music from the grooves. The horn section came in, ecstatic, then melted away into the oily tones of solo sax. Nika closed her eyes, swayed lightly to the music. At the end of the song Smena lifted the needle from the record. She searched her friend's face for a twitch, a nudge, but was met with an unsettling blankness.

Nika opened her eyes. "Thank you."

Smena gathered up the bone albums. "Take them, they're yours."

"I said you were a good watermelon. Didn't even have to thump you to know it. Didn't I tell you?" Nika took the scans, placed them in her cloth sack with great care.

Smena wasn't sure what to say, or why she settled on "Cut me up and eat me."

"Don't think I won't."

"I'm all seed."

"I'm smiling, Smena. You just can't tell."

When Nika made to leave shortly afterward, Smena asked, "No more scans for me this week?"

Nika shook her head. "No more."

A few days later, Smena woke to hurried knocking on her door. On the other side of the peephole: Milena. Smena checked herself in the hallway mirror, discerned the blurry shape of her body through her thin cotton nightgown. She swung a fur coat over her shoulders before unhinging the locks.

"Heading out?" Milena asked when she stepped inside.

"Yes," Smena lied. "You'd better make this quick."

Milena locked the dead bolt behind her. "I got approached again," she said, her posture unusually straight. "Not by the same guy as last time, but this one was just as wormy. He gave me a record." From her long raincoat Milena produced a yellow vinyl sleeve, the same type Smena used for distribution. She slid out a bone album, set it on the record player. Smena recognized the perky melody. The Beach Boys. The quality of the copy was poor, mostly scratching and bubbling, as though the singers were being drowned.

After a few seconds, the music cut out.

A man's voice came on, in low and booming Russian. *Came for the latest tunes? You're done listening.* A slew of curses dipped in and out of the hisses and pops.

Smena let out a bark of nervous laughter. "Hardly the latest tune. That song is almost twenty years old."

"Smena Timofeevna." Milena hadn't used Smena's patronymic in years, and the sudden formality was more frightening than the cursing still blasting from the player. Milena slowed the record to a stop with her thumb. "We're fucked."

She looked at Smena, expecting instruction.

Smena picked up the X-ray record and did what she did with every new X-ray that fell into her hands: she hung it on her kitchen window. The morning light shone strong enough for her to make out a pair of lungs and a shadow of a heart. The center hole of the record had been burned through the aorta. With a sickening familiarity, she saw the tiny bulbous alveoli filled with mucus, laced around the bottom of the right lung. Pneumonia. Right where her own had been, a couple years ago. Since the corners of the film had been cut off, she couldn't check for the patient's name. Many people get pneumonia, she thought. This could be anyone's scan. Still, she couldn't shake the suspicion it was hers. It made her uneasy, to think of looking at her insides outside her own body, as though she were being dissected. She felt a peculiar wringing in her chest, a hand palpating her organs. She thought about the few people in her life who knew she'd been sick: her daughter. And, most recently, Nika.

Since Nika's first visit, Smena had known that she'd been caught. But she'd been foolish enough to believe the woman wouldn't follow through with her scheme. She'd allowed herself to forget: neighbors never visited each other.

She curled her fingers into fists, uncurled them, let her hands flop to her sides. "We'll need to warn Larissa."

"I just did. She almost seemed happy about it, our little martyr. Made me promise to teach her sparring techniques." Milena saw the pained look on Smena's face. "Don't worry about her. She comes from a model family with a squeaky-clean record. Worry about yourself."

Smena walked around the room, aimless. She took vinyl albums from the bookshelf at random, put them back. With Larissa's careful hands, each original sleeve and center label had been replaced with state-approved ones, from acts like Jolly Fellows, Good Guys, Contemporanul, Red Poppies. That Smena's music library presented as perfectly flavorless had always amused the three women, an inside joke. Perhaps she could keep just one or two albums? She briefly let herself entertain the possibility, then admonished herself. If back in the fifties keeping one album would have been as risky as keeping one hundred, why should things be different now? She turned to Milena, who was stationed by the balcony door, watching in silence. "We'll need to get rid of the equipment," Smena said. "And the music."

Milena gave a curt nod. "Leave it to me, Smena Timofeevna."

From her wardrobe Smena retrieved a linen sheet. She wrapped it around the record player and phonograph. "Wouldn't want them to get scratched." With utmost care she placed the cutting lathe and its metal arm into a pillowcase. She slipped the forbidden vinyls into another, trying not to think of the effort Larissa had put into procuring them. It would only take Milena two trips to her husband's beat-up Kombi, parked in the courtyard, to make the bone music studio disappear.

When Milena came up to get the second load, Smena asked, "What will you do with yourself now?"

"Leave town, get lost in the countryside. Something I've been saving up for anyway." Milena was trying to sound casual, but Smena thought she detected a tremor in her voice.

"Hard to imagine your husband in the country." The last time Smena had seen him two balconies over, polishing a loafer, she'd marveled at his delicate hands.

"Isn't it." Milena shot Smena a sly look, and for one moment Smena thought she intended to leave him behind.

Milena stalked down the hall with the rest of the equipment, her footsteps eerily quiet. Smena wondered if she would ever see her neighbor again. Then she imagined leaving her own apartment, sharing a sofa bed with her daughter again, and her daughter's husband, and her daughter's husband's family, and all those lovely, spirited grandchildren, and the knobby cats they brought home from the streets. She wept into the sleeve of her fur coat.

Smena was searching her apartment for tools or X-rays she might have overlooked when she heard the wail of a siren. She dropped to the floor. Her heart flapped against the linoleum, loose and arrhythmic. She wanted to shush it so the downstairs neighbors wouldn't hear. The siren grew louder, until it reached their building, then cut out. Hurried footsteps echoed from the depths of the building, but never reached her floor. Smena crawled to her bedroom window, peeked out. The source of the siren was not the police but an ambulance. After a few minutes, a pair of paramedics emerged from the building's entryway carrying a stretcher, and on the stretcher lay Nika. Sunlight glimmered on her cherry-red hair as the paramedics loaded her into the ambulance. Smena wanted to rush downstairs and—what? Strangle the woman? Embrace her? Both?

The vehicle lurched into motion, rounded the street corner, and disappeared.

Smena stood back from the window. She was still wearing the fur coat. The coat would have to do. The polyclinic was only four blocks away, but she thought she might be away for longer than the four blocks and so made preparations. She retrieved her reserve of cash from a jar hidden in the toilet tank, packed a few changes of clothing into a duffel bag. A dull ache set into her knees and hips from the earlier drop to the floor, from the crawling, but she quickened her movements, ignoring the pain.

Smena swung her door open, and stepped over the threshold. The exterior corridor was cold, dimly lit, smelled of stale tobacco. The damp climbed her calves and thighs, made her shiver in her coat. She wanted to turn around, banish the hostile world with a flick of the dead bolt. But her apartment had lost the protection it once held.

Taking the elevator was out of the question. Clutching the rickety metal banister, Smena descended one step at a time. She tried not to look at the cracks in the walls. A piece of candy perched on a stair and she reached for it before thinking, hungry, but the puffy wrapper was hollow inside, a child's trick. The entranceway at the ground floor greeted her with the stench of garbage and urine, a waft of boiled potatoes.

Smena stepped outside and, for the first time in more than a year, felt live air move across her face. Her windows and glassed-in balcony had been sealed against drafts—she'd forgotten that drafts could feel nice, like a gentle tickling. She parted her lips, let the warm autumn light fill the cavity of her mouth and throat.

"I'll be damned! She's alive," exclaimed one of the pensioners on the bench outside. The man had acquired a new sprinkling of moles and sun spots on his face since the last time she'd seen him. "How long's it been, Smena Timofeevna?"

"Too long, Palashkin," she answered.

She shuffled on, her feet unsteady on the cracked slabs of the sidewalk. The concrete ten-stories around her were identical to the one she had just exited, and Smena had the impression she was walking the same block over and over. She kept her eyes on the ground. She stepped on a curled dry leaf and its crunch underfoot delighted her. She stepped on another, then another, progressing leaf to leaf. Parts of the roads sagged. The edge of the town, where the sunflowers normally grew, was being closed in by cattails. Let it all sink, she thought. She imagined herself and the townspeople on the bottom of a great marsh, to be discovered centuries later, open-eyed, their skin blue, hair orange from the gases, preserved for eternity.

The next time she looked up, she stood in front of the building she thought might be the polyclinic. The gleaming white-tiled edifice in her memory cowered under the poplars, its walls matte with graffiti, many of the tiles missing.

Inside, wooden benches lined the walls of a small lobby. A nurse pushed a mop around the floor, transferring dirty water from one corner of the room to another. It didn't take long to find Nika, who lay on a wheeled bed in a corridor off the lobby. The two paramedics who had collected her were arguing with the receptionist. As Smena approached Nika, the expression on her neighbor's face transformed from happy surprise to terror. By the time Smena reached her bed, Nika had lifted the covers over her nose, as though expecting to be hit.

Smena stepped back. She'd been feared before, certainly—by Milena and Larissa, whenever she chastised them for an oversight—but not like this. It stung. "You can move your face again," she observed, attempting a level tone.

"Now it's my feet."

"Where's your son and the rest of them?"

"Work, the park, and the belly," said Nika. "But you came." It sounded like a question, Nika wondering aloud which version of Smena had come: the vengeful or the forgiving one. Smena still wasn't sure herself.

"So they're finally admitting you," said Smena.

Nika nodded at the men and receptionist yelling at each

other. "To be decided." She lowered the cover from her face. The skull with which Smena had become so well acquainted shone under Nika's pale, cracked skin, its outline disturbingly visible, now in three dimensions.

Nika gave a nervous laugh. "This is a bed, Smena. Look at it. It doesn't fold into anything. It's not a couch or a desk or a storage box. It's a bed and you don't feel bad lying in it. Try it."

"What?"

"This bed. You're going to try this bed." Nika pushed her head and shoulders into her pillow, wriggled the rest of her body toward the rail at the edge of the bed. Smena thought Nika was playing a joke until a pale leg poked out from under the sheets and draped itself over the rail.

"No, Nika—" She grabbed Nika's bony ankle. Nika swung a second leg over the rail, and now Smena held on to both ankles. "Keep down, will you?"

"You can't know till you're in it."

Nika's breaths were heavy, rasping, and Smena now saw the immense strength Nika's seemingly whimsical gesture had required. She heaved Nika's legs back onto the bed, rearranged the sheets.

"Tell you what," said Smena. "When you're well again and ready to go home, we'll get you a real bed. A big one. Have your son and his family move into my apartment. I don't need the space anymore. And as for me, if you want, I mean, only if the prospect doesn't sound too awful—"

"You'll move in with me." Nika's face softened. "It'll be like back in the dorms," she said. "But only the best parts. No exams. And you'll take the bed. I'll take the foldout."

"We'll get two beds. They'll take up the whole room."

"What if one of us takes a lover?"

"We'll work out a visitation schedule."

Nika looked up at the ceiling, spread her arms and legs out, letting herself float in the daydream. "If only we'd decided all this sooner."

"It's not too late." It felt so easy now, to play along, to plot their future together. Smena stroked her friend's hair. The roots were oily and she longed to grab them by the fistful, let the musky sheen settle between her fingers.

The nurse with the mop was eyeing them. Smena said, "I have to go." Where, she wasn't sure. It would be midday, the sun at its warmest. She could go to the bazaar, buy something to eat right from the stalls. Fried dumplings, filled with mushrooms or ground beef. Or sour cream, fatty yellow and runny, which she'd drink straight from the jar. And afterward? She could go anywhere, board any bus or train. The thought was terrifying and thrilling.

"Wait till I'm asleep," said Nika.

Smena didn't have to wait long.

MISS USSR

On Monday morning, the phone on Konstantyn Illych's desk rang. He reached for the receiver without taking his eyes off the budget sheets spread before him.

"You didn't alert us to the beauty pageant," said a woman on the other end of the line. She introduced herself as Irina Glebovna, the new Minister of Culture—his most superior superior. Never before had a Minister called the lowly Kirovka Cultural Club. He turned down the steady prattle of the radio, welcoming the interruption.

"My sincerest apologies," he offered. "Did you want to enroll?"

She ignored this. "Contestants lined up around the block. A victory parade. A marching band, Konstantyn Illych? With what funds?" She drew out her vowels but swallowed the word endings, exaggerating a posh Muscovite accent.

"People volunteered. Civic duty."

"I heard a recording of the winner's talent routine." She was referring to Orynko Bondar's singing of "The Glory and the Freedom of Ukraine Has Not Yet Perished," once the anthem of Ukraine, banned by Moscow since 1922. "The singing," Irina Glebovna remarked, "it wasn't very good."

Konstantyn did not disagree. He hoped this was all the Minister had to say on the subject.

"I can't help but think"—here her voice sharpened, a butter knife swapped for a boning knife—"that the girl, your Miss Kirovka, earned her title on political grounds."

Aesthetic grounds, Konstantyn wanted to argue. Orynko possessed an outlandish beauty: moonlit teeth, freakishly large amber eyes, long silvery hair that doused her back and shoulders like mercury. But Konstantyn, being what he was—a slouchy forty-seven-year-old male with an uncertain marital status—thought better than to extol a teenager's looks. He settled on "The judges chose her, not I."

"You must be pleased with yourself." The Minister's tone suggested the opposite. "Your counterpart in Kiev was so charmed by your contest, she was about to organize one at the national level—Miss Ukraine SSR."

"Whatever Kiev is planning, I have nothing to do with it." Yet Konstantyn couldn't help chuckling, proud his pageant idea had caught on.

"Kiev is no longer planning," the Minister corrected. "But next thing we know, it'll be Miss Estonia SSR. Miss Latvia SSR. Miss Georgia SSR. Miss Chechen-Ingush ASSR." Konstantyn knew that each of the countries she listed had been the site of recent mass demonstrations, calling for independence.

"And so? You can't stop them all." He regretted the words as soon as they tumbled from his mouth, knowing he'd gone too far.

After an awful pause, the Minister's words were soft, measured: "You'll make an announcement revoking the girl's title."

Konstantyn waited, hoping the Minister would break into laughter. This was the sort of thing the preceding Minister of

Culture was rumored to have done: pretend to bestow punishment, then tease his victim for being so easily duped.

"I understand it's a difficult time." The Minister's speech had regained its false drawl. "When was it your wife left you? Three months ago?"

Three months and six days; how did the Minister know? Konstantyn had come home from work to discover the Kombi gone, along with Milena's fencing gear and a few items of clothing. Milena's departure had left him spinning like a leaf blown from its branch; he stopped writing, relegated himself to mundane administrative tasks. Their marriage had never been passionate, but he'd envisioned her always being there, stoic and dependable, like a grandfather clock. Whenever he fell ill, she'd leave a pot of broth on the stove before work, and whatever it lacked in taste it made up for in nutrition. When he wrote a new poem, she was the first to hear him recite it, dutifully setting her book on her lap, even though her eyes might not have left its pages.

"At least, no children to split," the Minister kept on, in studied sympathy. "No need to prove yourself to anyone, Konstantyn Illych. I'll have a journalist give you a call. One small correction and you're done."

When the phone rang again an hour later—likely the journalist—Konstantyn did not pick up. He would wait this one out. Surely the press and the Minister had more important matters to attend to, and would soon forget about his dethroning statement, his backwater town.

Konstantyn had reverse-engineered the Miss Kirovka pageant from its American equivalent. He'd heard the broadcast of

Miss America 1989 on Radio Liberty that autumn, dubbed in Russian. It was the applause that caught his ear: the thunderous volume suggested an audience numbering hundreds, even thousands. All the while his Club's attendance had been dwindling for years, along with state funding. There was a time when the lectorium would fill for history talks and poetry readings; now the one meager draw of the Kirovka Cultural Club was Viktorina, an arcade game that tested a player's ability to identify traffic warning signs.

On a sheet of graph paper, Konstantyn had taken note of the Miss America pageant's key parts: the talent round, the bathing suit round, the gown round. He'd jotted down bits of contestants' speeches, observing how each sentence inflected upward, toward a bright future. Konstantyn had inferred, from the exclamations of the judges, the geometry of contestants' bathing suits. As he'd listened, he couldn't help imagining one of those Yankee county fairs he'd read about, with their livestock breed shows, but pushed this thought from his mind. He hadn't cared for the banter of the host, who seemed to forget that this was above all a competition, but such details could be tweaked. What was important was the applause. And the admission fee.

As it turned out, Konstantyn was among the many Kirovkavites who had tuned in to Miss America. What was American was countercultural, which made it trendy: Levi's and Coca-Cola had found their way into Soviet homes; the opening of a McDonald's in Moscow was less than a year away. So it was that Kirovkavites met the news of their very own pageant with a cautious, tight-lipped excitement. On the morning of the event, contestants of all ages—Konstantyn hadn't thought to specify an age range—formed a line in front of the Cultural Club, a line modest in length but not in coloration. One middle-aged contestant sported a tweed suit, as though about to deliver a lecture; another contestant, around eleven or twelve, wore her newly starched school pinafore; another shivered in a strapless sequin gown, her wide-eyed toddler chewing the hem. And of course, there was Orynko Bondar, who opted for full folk: embroidered blouse, sheepskin vest, poppy-red skirt and boots, a headdress of wheat stalks that stuck out like sunbeams. The contestants shot embarrassed glances at one another to determine which of them had misinterpreted the dress code.

When the contestants' friends and relatives began showing up—not just from Kirovka but from the surrounding towns and villages—Konstantyn had begun to feel hopeful. His event would be well attended, his Cultural Club once again the center of activity. A beauty pageant would hardly be the pinnacle of the Club's achievements, but Konstantyn had to be patient. Poetry camps don't organize or fund themselves overnight.

On the Wednesday morning after the Minister's call came a special All Union First Radio program announcement. The same nasal voice that intoned Party proceedings and member passings informed Citizens that in eight weeks, in celebration of the mighty Union, an unprecedented event would take place: a Miss USSR beauty competition. Young women from every republic—aged sixteen to eighteen, in good moral standing—were invited to Moscow to take part, and the legitimate winner would be crowned at the Yuon Palace of Culture.

In his office, Konstantyn listened in disbelief. A *legitimate* winner. An *unprecedented* event. Either Konstantyn and his town—his country, even—were being punished, or attendance numbers at Moscow's many Palaces of Culture had been lagging, too. He was incensed that Irina Glebovna was both crushing the legitimacy of his pageant and copying it. True, he had copied it himself, from the Americans, who had probably copied it from the Europeans, but he had elevated the pageant to a more palatable level by enlisting a philosopher, a painter, a novelist, and an astronomer as judges.

Normally he would have laughed off the injustice, feeling above the government's antics; over dinner he would have regaled Milena with his droning impression of the radio announcer. But without Milena, without an audience, to laugh now felt pathetic, akin to drinking alone.

Konstantyn turned off the radio. The Cultural Club grew silent save for the shuffling footsteps in the hallway outside his office, then the jingle of a fifteen-kopek coin being pumped into Viktorina. He didn't want to imagine what would happen if the arcade game broke.

The phone rang again.

This time, Konstantyn picked up. It was the journalist, a bored-sounding woman with a smoker's rasp, still looking for that statement about Olga Bondar.

"Orynko Bondar," he corrected.

"Sure," the journalist said, clearly unhappy to have been assigned a story about some yokel town with ethnically named residents.

Konstantyn loosened the scarf around his neck, feeling hot. "Not only will Miss Kirovka be keeping her title," he heard himself declare, "but she'll be competing in the Miss USSR pageant." A dizzying array of possibilities opened within him. Yes, Miss Kirovka would go to Moscow. She would not be silenced. Finally he and his town would take pride in something other than the canning combine or the rumored silo under the sunflower fields. "Watch out for Orynko Bondar, representing Ukraine," he proclaimed, voice rising. "She will win over an entire empire."

On Thursday morning, upon arriving at the Cultural Club, Konstantyn discovered a man sitting in Konstantyn's swivel armchair, behind Konstantyn's oak desk. The surface of the desk had been cleared, the usual piles of documents replaced by a potted African violet.

The intruder's magnified eyes swam behind thick glasses. "Do you have an appointment?"

Konstantyn stood at his office door, kept his hand on the cold metal knob. "Do you?"

"Ah, Konstantyn Illych." The man, irritatingly young, hair slick with pomade, gave a tight smile, apparently embarrassed for them both. "Haven't you received the directive?" When Konstantyn shook his head, the man turned to the telefax machine, flipped through the pages hanging from its mouth, plucked one out, and handed it to Konstantyn. The curt letter informed the Director of the Kirovka Cultural Club of his termination.

Konstantyn focused his anger on the potted violet on the desk. He wanted to shred its chubby leaves. Instead, he reached forward and grabbed the phone, clamped it between his ear and shoulder—a gesture of importance, of expert phone handling. "If you'll excuse me." He didn't know what he would say to the Minister, exactly. The damage had been done.

Konstantyn nodded at the door, but the stranger didn't move.

"I'm sorry, Konstantyn Illych."

For a moment the men stared at each other. Both wore navy industrial-made suits. Konstantyn planted himself in the metal wire chair across from the desk. He had never sat in it before. The chair was angular, possessed bones of its own that poked up to meet the occupants, hurry them out of the office. He must have the chair replaced, he thought, before realizing this would no longer be in his power. He reread the letter and this time its contents sank in. His words came slowly: "I've worked here for twenty years. I'm a respected poet. Ten years ago I was named People's Artist."

His replacement gave him a pitying smile. The man's hand swept around the office, calling attention to the peeling wallpaper, the cracked ceiling—everything that no longer mattered.

The phone nestled in Konstantyn's lap beeped impatiently. Dial or hang up. He hung up.

The new Director busied himself. He pinched a dead leaf off the violet, pocketed it. He slid a document from a drawer and held it in front of his face. Konstantyn pretended to read the words and numbers on the other side of the sheet, hoping the action would render him useful again. The man's wedding ring drew his gaze. Konstantyn hadn't stopped wearing his own; it gave a man, especially one along in his years, legitimacy. If a man could keep a companion, surely there was nothing too wrong with him.

"Whether or not I work here, Orynko will compete for Miss USSR," Konstantyn vowed. What could he lose?

"I'm afraid," the man's soft voice came from behind the sheet, "the girl is gone."

"Gone?"

"Recruited by the Thermometric Academy. All thanks to your pageant. The girl had mentioned her desire to pursue thermophysical study, no?"

Orynko had indeed mentioned this during her onstage

interview, halfheartedly, to please her parents, who cheered her on from the front row. "I've never heard of any such academy," said Konstantyn.

"Me neither." The man replaced the document in the wrong drawer and looked toward the exit, likely wondering why Konstantyn still hadn't used it. "But I can assure you there is such a place."

Konstantyn had never felt less assured, but he played along. "I'm sure Orynko can leave for one pageant weekend."

"I'm sure, yes." He paused. "In theory."

Konstantyn adjusted himself in the torturous chair, suddenly worried.

"If the town where she is studying were to have road access," the man added, "and if the sea route hadn't just frozen over for the next eleven months."

Konstantyn gawked at him. "Where is this place? Siberia?"

The man remained still as a wax figure, neither confirming nor denying.

"No." Konstantyn was breathing quickly. Had the air suddenly thinned? "You can't just ship people to Siberia," he blustered, "not anymore."

"Certainly not. I am but a humble Cultural Director. What can people like us do?"

Unemployment was not kind to Konstantyn. He spent his days moping around his stuffy apartment, full of books that had once brought him joy but now mocked him, reminding him that the paltry few he'd written had grown just as dusty, yellowed, soursmelling as the rest. He ate through his kitchen cabinets, went to bed early and woke late, but found little respite in sleep. His thoughts orbited Miss Kirovka, how it was his fault she was exiled, and that he hadn't a clue how to retrieve her. To make matters worse, while his provocation to the journalist had, predictably, been kept from the state media, his words had still somehow spread across town. Whenever he stepped outside for food or cigarettes—and only after counting and re-counting his cash savings—the benchers would accost him with questions. What would Orynko wear to the Miss USSR pageant, a squat bespectacled woman demanded to know. Was the girl taking singing lessons, a hook-nosed octogenarian inquired. Late one evening, when Konstantyn thought he was safe, a troupe of teenagers in neon windbreakers cheered at him from across the street. He tried to wave back but his hand grew limp, as if the tendons had been snipped. He couldn't bear to temper the townspeople's excitement, admit that they had, once again, nothing to hope for.

More and more, his wife's clothes haunted him. Blouses, trousers, sweaters spilled from drawers like shed skins. The nightgown he slept with exuded a smell he hadn't noticed before, spiced, herbal, as though he were a pest to repel.

Shirt by shirt, sock by sock, he began gathering his wife's effects into two cloth sacks. Somehow, wherever she was, she would surely feel him moving on, and the realization would hasten her return. He recalled when he was a boy, and he and his father would wait for his mother to come home from work, the dinner she'd made that morning reheated but cooling again. Only when they gave up and reached for their forks would she march in, as if she'd been at the door the entire time, testing their will. As Konstantyn folded away Milena's clothes, he couldn't help cocking his ear every few minutes, listening for the jangle of her keys. When he'd finished, he seated the cloth sacks on the sofa bed, unsure what to do with them. One never got rid of clothes—on the contrary, one spent every effort to acquire them in any size from near-empty shops, or saved them for gifts, or sewed them into different clothes, or, at the very least, repurposed them as rags. Banishing the clothes to his dacha wouldn't make enough of a statement, but he found he couldn't throw them away either, as this might anger Milena. Still, he was determined to go through the motions of closure. He would donate the clothes. The more obscure the cause, the more Milena would love him.

The car was borrowed, so Konstantyn took extra care as he drove along the muddy road. He wove over a hilly ridge, passed a rail yard, entered the forest. The orphanage hid deep inside it, 25 kilometers south of Kirovka.

It had rained the night before and the forest shone in the morning light. While it was a relief to briefly escape the town, to be anonymous again, Konstantyn felt a twinge of trepidation at what lay ahead. He had never visited Internat Number 12 before; the townspeople rarely spoke of it, as though fearful of invoking a ghost. But every time Konstantyn thought of turning back, the curtain of trees would part to reveal a breathtaking vista of hills and rivers; a squirrel would flash its golden tail in benediction; a butterfly would glint past in a streak of yellow and orange; and Konstantyn would remind himself that, after all, he was here to do good.

A cluster of cupolas peeked above the treetops. They appeared to have been skinned, with only the bulbous metal skeletons remaining. As he drove, the cupolas seemed to retreat into the distance, wary of the approaching stranger, but he soon caught up with them.

Internat Number 12, Konstantyn discovered, was an old monastery. The edifice sagged as if a great invisible hand were pressing on it from above. One of the towers had crumbled, its ruins laced with the roots of trees.

Konstantyn parked the rickety Zaporozhets alongside an iron fence. As he retrieved the first cloth sack from the trunk, he felt the weight of many eyes on the back of his neck. He gave a timid wave to the children watching him from arched windows. They kept still, as though painted onto the glass.

Finding the gates locked, Konstantyn turned to the small white box welded to a fence post, and pressed its red button. After a moment, a low staticky voice, a woman's, came on. "Yes?"

"I'd like to donate clothes." He said this loudly and clearly, as if his wife were hiding behind one of the pines, watching.

"You're from the Textile Union?"

"No."

"What's the organization?"

"Just a lone citizen."

After a pause, she asked, "What is it you want from us?"

He leaned in, thinking she had misheard. "I'm here to give clothing. To the children."

It was then he saw Orynko Bondar.

Or rather, a flash of Orynko Bondar, in another girl's face. One of the second-story windows was open, and a teenager rested her chin on the stone sill. Only her buzzed head was visible. Konstantyn thought she perfectly captured the vacant gaze of a fashion model. The orphan wasn't beautiful like Orynko, but there was something Orynko-ish in her—the dashes of the brows and lips, the jut of the jaw—as if an artist had tried to sketch the beauty queen in not-quite-sufficient light, using the nondominant hand.

"Leave the clothes by the gates," the woman instructed through the intercom. "I'll have someone pick them up."

Konstantyn set the sack down, but did not leave. He was still looking at the girl. Now he thought of the Greater Good. The Greater Good mattered most—wasn't that what he'd been taught his whole life? And so he could be forgiven a bit of deceit. He could slip the Orynko-ish girl into Orynko's place, to compete in the Miss USSR pageant. He would train her himself. In Moscow's vast Palace of Culture lectorium, each of the contestants would look no bigger than a pinkie finger onstage. Who could tell who was who, and who wasn't? As for the television broadcast: one could not overestimate the transformative effect of makeup, the distracting property of glitter. When Orynko had stepped onstage at the local pageant, her face powdered and painted, fake lashes flapping, she hadn't looked quite like Orynko either.

"I'd also like to foster a child," he announced, "for two months." He imagined the orphan's gratitude, and felt bolstered by it.

As the intercom rattled with instructions—forms to procure from the Ministry of Labor and Social Development, signatures to gather, and so on—Konstantyn gazed up, and thought he spotted the woman issuing them. At the fourth-floor window of the nearest tower, a broad-shouldered attendant in a white smock spoke into a phone.

"I'd like to proceed more quickly," he interrupted. "I'd be happy to leave the clothes here, but I'd also be happy to take them to another orphanage." He spoke to her as if she were his counterpart, without malice. They locked eyes in recognition, complicity. They both knew what it was to keep afloat an underfunded institution. Her tone softened. "You have a wife? It's not just you?"

"Not just me." The more he wanted it to be true, the less it felt like a lie.

"Your wife didn't come with you."

"She's preparing the extra room."

It seemed as if the attendant wanted this to be true, too. Her sigh crackled through the intercom. "Girl or boy?"

"How about—" Konstantyn feigned deliberation before pointing to the girl at the open window. "Her."

From her tower, the woman craned her neck out the window to look at the girl. The girl stared at nothing. For a terrible instant, Konstantyn thought she might be dead.

"I'll bring her right out," the attendant said quickly, her sudden enthusiasm unnerving. She retreated into the dark depths of the building.

A minute later the girl, too, was gone. The attendant appeared in her place, shut the window. Twenty minutes passed, thirty. Konstantyn considered ringing the intercom, but decided against it. Perhaps the girl was saying her goodbyes to the other children, who must be like brothers and sisters by this point. Perhaps she was tangled in their embraces, navigating the delicate terrain of their envy. Who was he to rush her? The longer he waited, the more he liked the girl.

At last the tall wooden doors of the monastery swung open. The attendant marched down the weedy brick path, pulling the orphan by the wrist. The girl struggled against the woman's grip, like a child who had just been woken. With her free hand she clutched a dusty pillowcase containing something bulky.

"No lice," the attendant promised, when the pair reached the iron gates. "You can see for yourself."

Up close, in full light, the teenager was not what he had envisioned. The arms and legs that stuck out of her baggy garment were very thin and pale, so pale they had a bluish glow. A thick white scar curdled her skin from nose to upper lip. This, combined with the buzzed head, the rough features, gave her a criminal look. And yet, once more Orynko flitted across the girl's face. This time the resemblance gave him a queasy feeling, recalled a shape-shifting octopus he had once seen on television, which survived its hostile habitat by mimicking anything from seaweed to a pile of poisonous snakes.

"Meet Zaya." The attendant pronounced the name like a challenge.

The girl regarded Konstantyn not with the timidity he expected of an orphan, but with a fierce intensity, as if she already knew Konstantyn and had decided long ago she disliked him.

Konstantyn felt his leg take a step back. He wanted to take another step, then another, until he reached the car and drove away. It took a momentous effort to twist his mouth into a smile. He leaned down to address the girl on the other side of the fence, but could not find anything to say. He had already forgotten her name.

The attendant unlocked the gates, ushered the orphan out, grabbed the sack of clothes Konstantyn had rested on the ground, clacked the gates shut. "Thank you for your kind donation. See you in two months."

When Konstantyn opened the trunk of the car, the girl drew back, as if he were about to throw her inside it. He gave a small high laugh. "It's for your things." He pointed at the remaining sack of his wife's clothes as an example (he had kept it back at the last moment for pageant needs). The girl gripped her bundle tighter to her chest. When he opened the passenger door, she made no move toward it. He rolled down the window, hoping this, too, would somehow prove the car's safety. He demonstrated getting in and out of the car while she watched, and thought he caught a cruel curl of her lip. He even suggested she walk beside the moving car as he held her hand—he feared she might run away—anticipating she would eventually tire and get in. But when he extended his hand, she struck it with the back of hers, hard. The orphan's strength alarmed him. When at last he threatened to drive away, leave her in that terrible place, she glowered at him, daring him to.

He sank behind the wheel but did not start the engine. With shaking, stinging fingers he tried to light a cigarette. On the fourth try he succeeded, and was about to take a grateful drag, when the cigarette left his lips.

The girl leaned in through the open passenger window. His cigarette hung from her mouth. She took a long, delicious pull before exhaling politely away from the car.

"I have more." He brandished the box, tapped the cartoon rocket shooting across its front. He hated himself for stooping so low.

At last the girl took the front seat. She sat her bundle on her lap.

During the drive, all conversation remained determinedly one-sided. Mostly, Konstantyn pointed at forest and meadow, saying, "See that big oak." "See that patch of daisies." "See those mushrooms, very poisonous." The girl kept her eyes on the muddy road.

He tried to ignore the smell of her, sweet and rank, like barley fermenting in urine. Keeping one hand on the wheel, he lit a second cigarette, inhaled. "Where'd you pick up the habit? From the older children?"

She shook her head.

"From the *sanitarki*?"

She nodded.

"You can talk to me. I don't bite."

She shot him a look: *I do.*

Konstantyn laughed; the girl did not. A rabbit dashed across the road. Her name came back to him. "What happened to your lip, Zaya?"

She said nothing.

"A bad fall," he guessed.

She shook her head.

"Thorny branch."

No.

"Fishhook."

No.

"Angry bird."

She took another pull. No.

"A three-headed dog you fought off valiantly."

No response.

"I thought so," said Konstantyn.

"An old *baba* sewed it up." The girl slurred her words. "She made leather boots."

Konstantyn winced. He didn't want to know more, but after a moment, he did. "This wasn't at the *internat*?"

She shook her head again. "I ran away, she took me in. Her hut burned down, she brought me back."

The forest receded. They drove between the sunflower fields

in silence. Soon Kirovka welcomed them with its bent metal sign framed by rusty braids of wheat. Konstantyn felt lighter. At least the girl could speak.

That night Konstantyn woke to a pinprick of orange light, felt nicotine breath on his face. He made out the girl's silhouette, bent over him. He jolted upright.

"Keep sleeping," she whispered.

He flicked on his reading lamp. No trace of Orynko in this girl's face. This stranger was wearing his wife's billowy dress shirt, which he'd lent her the evening before. She had brought no clothes of her own, had told him that her bundle contained only a saint, which had originally come with a hat before one of the other orphans stole it. A doll, not a saint, he assumed she'd meant.

"How long have you been sitting there?" he asked.

"Never seen a man sleep." She crossed one bare leg over the other, and stared at his mouth. "Odd, what lips are. Where you turn inside out."

Konstantyn tucked his lips between his teeth, protectively. The calm of her voice terrified him. She seemed capable of anything: she might break into dance or smash his skull with a skillet. He thought of the boot maker who had taken her in, could imagine the seed of the catastrophe: the girl gazing at a candle with the same cold fascination, wondering how the flame would look if it engulfed an entire house.

After that night he slept fitfully. He would wake up, listen for the girl's breathing, make sure that the breathing was at a suitable distance, that it came from the cot on the other side of the room, on the other side of the linen sheet he'd hung between them.

Of course, Konstantyn hadn't forgotten about the original Miss Kirovka. An encyclopedic search proved that the Thermometric Academy did indeed exist, in Norgorsk, deep within the Arctic Circle; the town was known for its smelting factory, which colored the snow pink, yellow, and black, and scented the air with chlorine and sulfur. In the early mornings, while the orphan slept, he wrote letters to Irina Glebovna and to the Chairman of Council of Ministers and his First Deputy Chairmen, State Committee Chairmen, and select members of the Presidium, calling for the beauty queen's repatriation. He'd received no response yet.

As for Miss Kirovka's double: before he could begin training her for the speech, the interview, the gown round, the bathing suit round—the radio announcement had not mentioned a talent round—the girl had to be caught up on the basics of civilized living. She never closed the bathroom door and he'd caught her squatting atop the toilet, feet on the seat. She balked at the idea of leg and armpit hair removal, saying that a buzzed head was enough to keep the lice away. She ate with agonizing slowness, inspecting each ingredient on her spoon with suspicion, yet she swallowed prune pits without a second thought. She feared the height of the balcony, and kept away from the windows. She slept with her dusty bundle at her side, refused to have it washed. She could recite the days of the week, but paid no heed to their order. If he thought he knew a subject, she probed him, out of curiosity or cruelty, until he reached the limits of his understanding. He could tell her about planets, how they were made of dirt or gas and moved in circles, but could not explain why they did so, only that gravity was involved. He couldn't tell her if time had a shape, or if the present and future could exist at once. She wanted to learn how a plane flies; he wanted her to learn to wash herself.

It took Konstantyn the first full month to broach the subject of the pageant. He led her to the park, where they sat on a pair of truck tires painted with polka dots. She no longer glared at strangers as if she wanted to maul them, which was no small improvement. The bundle lay at her side, appearing even dustier than usual in contrast to the pin-striped work shirt she was wearing (Konstantyn's). He divulged his plan: how she would be representing all of Ukraine as Miss Kirovka—more precisely, as Orynko Bondar, a girl who couldn't attend herself, although no one would know the difference. All Zaya had to do onstage, apart from twirl around in a pretty gown, was unfurl the sash emblazoned with MISS KIROVKA—he would make the sash himself, in whichever color she wanted—and wear Miss Kirovka's crown. An exact replica of the crown, rather. He told her about the judging panel of celebrated artists and Party members, about how every young woman dreamed of this kind of opportunity.

"I don't dream of it."

"Think of how pretty you'll be." He quickly added, "On top of how pretty you already are."

She watched a sparrow bathe in a murky puddle.

"You'll get to see Moscow. It's a hundred times bigger than Kirovka."

"This is why you came to the *internat*," she concluded. "Lucky me."

He swept his arm around the park, which was empty save for a few young mothers walking their strollers. "The country needs you."

The words had an effect on her, but not the one he'd intended. She stood up, and kicked the tire she'd been sitting on. "The *sanitarki* used to tell me, If you're so unhappy, send a letter to Brezhnev. And then it was Andropov, then Chernenko. They kept dying and we kept dying and I kept writing letters. Send a pair of stockings. Send iodine. I waited—not even a letter back. And now the country needs me." She pulled at the stiff collar of the work shirt, and set off in the direction of the apartment. He followed her, pleading. They were on the same side, he assured her, no one answered his letters either. But the girl marched on.

That night Konstantyn woke again. He listened for the girl's breathing, but heard only silence. He poked his head over the hanging sheet. Both the girl and the bundle were gone. They weren't in the kitchen or bathroom. He checked her cot again in the absurd hope he'd missed her the first time. He then stepped out onto the balcony, sick with panic. In the courtyard below, under the orange light of a streetlamp, he spotted the orphan squatting in an overgrown flower bed. She appeared to be digging. Her shoulder blades jutted out through her nightgown like the stumps of wings. The loyal bundle lay at her side. When he called her name, she froze for a second, then resumed digging with renewed vigor. He didn't want to approach her any more than he would a feral animal, but reminded himself that, regrettably, she was his charge. So he stuffed his feet into a pair of loafers, and raced down the concrete steps.

The girl didn't look up when Konstantyn reached her.

She had already dug an impressive hole using a flat stone. He demanded an explanation, but she gave none. When he begged her to come back inside, she ignored him. He took hold of her arm; she screamed. His hand jerked away as if scalded.

Several stories above, a window slammed shut.

For some time, Konstantyn watched her dig. If he were her father, he wondered whether he would know what to do. People with children always seemed to know.

A tuft of yellow hair poked out from the pillowcase. It looked remarkably real. Konstantyn sat on his haunches, pulled back the fabric. A face squinted up at him, brown and shriveled. Not a doll—human. Very dead. Oddly short. "What did you do?" he stammered at the girl, as though she had just murdered the thing, hacked half of it off, and was attempting to bury the evidence.

She grabbed a broken beer bottle by its neck, and brandished it at Konstantyn. He tipped backward.

"Use this," she explained. She was worn out, her breathing heavy.

It was then that Konstantyn felt something inside him melt. The bottle was not meant to be a threat—the girl was asking for help. For the first time, Konstantyn found he was not repulsed by her. He could sympathize with her as he was supposed to. Bolstered by his newfound virtue, he slowly reached for the broken bottle, the fragile offering. He began to dig alongside the orphan, averting his eyes from the mummified creature— "a saint," he remembered now. Not wishing to spoil the moment, he posed no further questions.

The night sky faded to a grayish green. When the girl stopped digging, so did he. With great care she lowered the bundle into the pit, which they then refilled with dirt. She pressed the fresh earth with her palms, and pulled dried weeds over it like a blanket.

They sat beside each other on the edge of the flower bed, silent. The girl's usual scowl had softened. She regarded the *novostroïki* enclosing the courtyard as though they had done something to disappoint her.

"Pageant or no pageant," she said in her slurring voice, "you want to take me back to the *internat*." There was no plea in her tone, only resigned observation. Konstantyn couldn't bring himself to lie. As he fumbled for the right words, she spoke again. "I'll go to Moscow."

This surprised him. He hadn't expected her to change her mind. "You'll run away."

"Already tried. I'll just end up back at the *internat*."

"Then why?"

She scraped dirt from under her nails. "Why not."

"We have three weeks. A lot of work ahead of us."

The orphan gave Konstantyn a searing smile. Her teeth were nightmarishly crooked, as though she had stuck them in herself as a toddler. "I'm your girl."

After that night, Zaya became surprisingly agreeable. She ate whatever Konstantyn cooked with a methodical determination: fatty cutlets, greasy stews, fried potatoes and pork rinds doused in sour cream. She plodded through tongue twisters to sharpen her diction. She attempted to straighten her teeth by pressing on them with the back of a spoon. She spent the crisp spring afternoons tanning her towel-wrapped self on the balcony—smoking dulled her fear of heights—and her bluish pallor gave way to a soft buttermilk. (Zaya still considered the issue of bodily hair moot, but Konstantyn made peace with this, not wanting to strain the fragile alliance.) To practice pivoting in heels, she wobbled around the apartment in a pair of velvet pumps Konstantyn found at the back of the closet—Milena's, surely, though he'd never seen her wear them. Konstantyn borrowed a silvery wig from a neighbor who had worn it during chemotherapy, and Zaya pulled it onto her shorn head and flicked the locks over her shoulders, like the actresses she observed on television. She rehearsed the speech he'd written for her: "My name is Orynko Bondar, from Kirovka, Ukraine," she would begin. Though Konstantyn felt strange hearing her use another's name, Zaya herself seemed unfazed, as though identity were nothing more than a hat she could slip on and off. "I love the sea and the smell of rain," she would chant at him. "I love animals, especially dogs." She would exclaim, "Beauty will save the world," almost as if she believed it.

For the gown round, Konstantyn unearthed a mustard-yellow dress with extra-wide bishop sleeves that gathered into elastic cuffs, gifted to Milena from his mother for their marriage registration.

Konstantyn fashioned the crown and sash replicas from the same materials he'd used for the originals: a three-liter tin can dipped in glitter, a polyester only-for-guests tablecloth. Zaya practiced the grand reveal. Upon reaching the end of the cat-walk (corridor), she slid the crown and sash from her sleeves, put them on, pretended to bask in the applause, and strutted back.

The bathing costume, also Milena's, was a thick wool tunic with knee-length bloomers, possibly procured from the Victorian era. Bloated with ruffles and pleats, the garment perplexed both Zaya and Konstantyn. "Even if I knew how to swim, I'd drown in this thing," she said the first time she donned it. Konstantyn, however, appreciated the full coverage. Though his own pageant had included a bathing suit round, he felt a moral discomfort about the impending one in Moscow. He did not like to imagine the leering eyes of the entire Union on the contestants, and on this contestant in particular, whose qualities could not be assessed by mere stage light.

The more Konstantyn occupied himself with training Zaya, the less he thought about his wife. One hour, two hours, would pass by without Milena flitting through his mind. When he woke in the morning, he no longer had to remind himself why she was not lying beside him.

"What's the one thing people don't know about you?"

Zaya stood atop a chair, her makeshift stage, holding a wooden spoon as a microphone. They hadn't rehearsed this interview question before. "What people?"

"Friends, family." He'd uttered the second word without thinking. She let him wallow in his own shame for a moment. "People at the *internat*," he amended.

"You can't take a squat there without an audience. Everyone knows everything about everyone."

"Some hidden talent," he ventured. "A secret wish."

Zaya peeled off her wig, rubbed her bristly scalp. The effect of the rich stews was beginning to show: no longer did shadows fill her cheeks, hang from her jutting collarbones. She resembled the teenage boys who roamed the neighborhood at night, scrawny but not skeletal.

"Sometimes I wish I'd never learned to talk," she told him. "What's the point?"

"We're talking now, aren't we?"

She nodded at the window. "But out there it's dead space. No use running your tongue because who listens? It's worse to know it." She turned back to him. "But I can't say that at the pageant."

If it were up to him, he wanted to assure her, she could. Instead, he said, "The judges want something hopeful."

"Hopeful." Zaya flashed a plastic smile. "How about a poem?" She lifted the microphone-spoon to her lips, launched into a recitation. "Belts bearings cab chassis / Decals duals dewy in the sun / Engine hitch . . ."

It took a moment for Konstantyn to recognize the poem as one of his own. What were meant to be free-flowing lines, carried by intuition and inspiration, were chopped up, forced into the metered lilt of a nursery rhyme. He'd been proud of that poem, how it concluded with the setting sun painting the metals red—a delicately hidden representation of rust, or societal decay. Now the words made him cringe.

"I read it in one of your books last night, while you were asleep," Zaya said. "But I already knew it. A *sanitarka* used it to teach us tractor parts."

"Tractor parts!" He found himself yelling. "It isn't *about* tractor parts."

Zaya descended from the chair and slumped down into it, arms hanging between thighs. Her expression was mean and satisfied; the insult had hit its mark.

"Sit up straight." He threw back his shoulders as an example, to no effect. "The *sanitarki* taught you tractor parts but not the order of the days of the week?"

"Want me to recite the one about gears?"

He put out a hand to stop her. He realized he preferred to think no one read his poetry anymore.

Makeup proved to be a challenge. Konstantyn hoped that, by virtue of being a girl, Zaya held some innate ability to apply it. From the depths of the bathroom cabinet he dug out a nub of lipstick, a tiny jar of flesh-colored paste, a tube of mascara—remnants from the rare times he and his wife had gone out. He placed the objects on the kitchen table, in front of Zaya. She uncapped the mascara, smelled the unsheathed brush. He realized she hadn't a clue what it was.

"To darken your eyelashes. Let me," he offered, taking the brush. He instructed her to look up at the ceiling, open her mouth.

"Why?"

He didn't know. It was how his wife had always arranged her face to apply mascara. "Just don't blink." But when he brought the brush to her eye, she threw her head back as though he held a weapon. He tried again, with the same result.

"Do it to yourself first," she ordered.

"It's not for me."

She crossed her arms. "You have eyelashes."

He sighed, and held up the compact mirror. He watched himself bring the brush to his right eye. The lashes were thin and straight and stuck downward. He'd never paid attention to them before. He applied the clumpy purplish black paste. A few times he missed, and grazed his eyelid. He tried to wipe the marks off but ended up smearing them further, giving himself a black eye.

"See? Nothing to it." He smiled meekly, holding up his hands to prove he was unarmed.

Zaya leaned in to study his work. Her brown irises were flecked with amber, like sparks about to ignite. He cast down his eyes to avoid them. To his relief, she took the brush, but instead of using it on herself she lifted it to his left eye. Now he was the one who wanted to squirm from the brush. He willed himself to keep still, to show that he trusted her even though he didn't, not quite.

As she worked, the heel of her hand rested on his cheek like a cool stone. He held his breath, immobilized by her touch. He tried to remember when he had last been in such proximity to another person, and his mind slid back in time, trying and failing to latch onto some distant memory.

"Your eyes are all wet," she remarked.

"Must be mascara in them."

"Sorry," she said. "It's leaking." She pressed the back of her hand against his cheek to catch it.

"How do I look?" he asked.

"Like Miss USSR." She handed over the brush. "Just don't take my eye out."

They proceeded this way, taking turns with the eye shadow—a metallic powder that clung to the mascara like mold—and the lipstick, which exuded a waxy fragrance, faintly petrochemical.

This left the foundation. He suspected he had mixed up the order of operations. He opened the jar of paste, which contained a circular sponge. When it was his turn, he dabbed it over Zaya's face haphazardly. The color was a shade pinker than her skin, but the effect wasn't bad—it made her face seem flushed, a tad more alive. When he passed over the thick scar below her nose, she flinched. He could see white specks where the boot maker's needle had pierced the skin; the strokes had been quick and indelicate. Since the woman had taken the time to sew up a child's face, he thought with a pang of anger, why not take a few extra minutes to do it well? If he had been there—

The thought went unfinished. He hadn't been there. He wouldn't have taken in the child, in the first place.

He and Zaya stood in front of the bathroom mirror, appraising the colors on their faces. Their shadowy eyes and smeared lips made them looked vaguely related.

The next day, Zaya and Konstantyn took a two-car *elektrichka* from Kirovka to Kiev, then an overnight train to Moscow. Zaya's distrust of cars did not seem to extend to other forms of transportation. In fact, it was Konstantyn who was nervous, breaking out in a sweat every time the conductor made rounds to check tickets. Once or twice, on previous trips, Konstantyn had seen men asked to provide a birth certificate for an accompanying child or teenager. Yet no one questioned him. Perhaps when the conductors saw the young woman sitting beside him, long silver locks spilling from her fur hood, heeled boot pumping impatiently, they assumed she was related to him, and not by blood. When they arrived in Moscow the next morning, the arched iron and glass roof of the Kievsky Terminal slid over them like a long net.

The Yuon Palace of Culture was a granite amalgamation of angles and planes, as if a committee of architects had failed to agree on a single design and so combined several. Konstantyn and Zaya edged along the Palace's jagged perimeter until they came to a back door. Locked, as expected. But within a few minutes a rotund middle-aged man rushed out clutching a broken stiletto, and the pair slipped inside.

Chaos greeted them in the narrow corridor. People were running about, barking commands at one another. A heavily made-up teenager in a white slip, undoubtedly one of the contestants, limped in circles, sobbing. Another girl, hair set in pink rollers, was dry-heaving over a dustbin. Konstantyn observed, with some satisfaction, that no one seemed to know what they were doing or where they should go. It was true that his pageant had been much smaller, but its lead-up had been incomparably calmer, better organized.

He kept an eye out for the Minister of Culture, for the wide-jawed, handsome face that occasionally graced television broadcasts and newspapers. Konstantyn suspected, and hoped, she wouldn't condescend to oversee the tedious backstage details.

As they pushed through the corridor, Konstantyn caught envious glances at Zaya's thinness. A tall blonde, who was slicking Vaseline onto the teeth of her daughter—a taller, blonder version of herself—asked Zaya which diet she kept. "The *internat* diet," Zaya answered. The mother turned away, as if the girl had uttered a curse word.

A small, quick-moving woman with a glossy folder clamped under her arm intercepted Zaya and Konstantyn.

"Changing room?" he tried.

The woman shot Zaya a disapproving glance. "All contestants are accounted for."

When Konstantyn asked if it wasn't possible to accommodate another, the administrator said of course it wasn't possible, these girls had been vetted in their respective republics before being sent here from all over the Union. Konstantyn probed his mind for useful people he knew, or could pretend he knew; it occurred to him that one of the judges was a composer who, according to the lore of the intelligentsia, coded his favorite granddaughter's name into his music. Konstantyn invoked that name now, in diminutive form, as if he personally knew her. Surely the granddaughter—and by extension, her famous grandfather, and by extension, the Minister of Culture—would be crushed if the girl's best friend was not allowed to compete? The administrator stared at Konstantyn with indignation. He knew the woman didn't believe him, but he also knew she wouldn't be willing to risk the chance his story was true. She pulled her folder out from under her arm and opened it. "You're in luck," she conceded, "we had a contestant pull out after she twisted her knee." She unclipped a pen from her shirt collar, and turned to Zaya. "Age?"

Zaya looked blank.

"Sixteen," Konstantyn intervened. This was Orynko's age.

"Engaged or married?"

Zaya shook her head.

"Children?"

"What about them?"

"Do you have any, or are you expecting."

"She's sixteen," Konstantyn repeated.

"If she bleeds between the legs it's possible."

"I don't bleed between the legs," said Zaya.

Both Konstantyn and the administrator turned to her in surprise. The subject had never come up, but Konstantyn had assumed it was because Zaya was tending to it on her own, stoically, the way women did.

The administrator ticked something on her page. Seeing the look on Konstantyn's face, she said, "I don't make the questions." At last she asked Zaya, "Name and provenance?"

"My name is Orynko Bondar, from Kirovka, Ukraine," the girl announced, in a stage voice Konstantyn wished she'd save for the stage. He tensed, the gravity of the moment settling on his shoulders like a lead coat. The original Orynko Bondar had been carted away hundreds of kilometers to prevent her from being here today, from uttering those simple words. Konstantyn was ready to pull out a small envelope of cash in case the administrator recognized Miss Kirovka's name and refused to add it, but it appeared that no such directive had trickled down to her. "How about a stage name? Something a tad more"—the woman paused, choosing her words—"urban."

Something a tad more Russian, he knew she'd meant. "We're keeping the name."

The administrator shrugged, recorded the name, and opened the dressing room door for the new contestant. Fumes of aerosols, eaux de toilette, and singed hair burst forth, as did the sounds of spraying, peeling, and other torturous acts. The administrator rushed down the corridor to tend to the girl with the hair rollers, who had begun retching again.

Zaya and Konstantyn stood at the doorway. He could accompany her no further. He was supposed to hand off the suitcase with the marriage-registration dress, bathing costume, makeup, crown, and sash, but found himself unable to do so. The dressing room threw a cold, cutting light on Zaya's skin. He had an urge to yank her away from it, reverse his horrid plan. He could no longer convince himself that, once the face of Miss Kirovka's double was broadcast around the Union, she would be safe. After all, he had not been able to predict Orynko's exile.

"You don't have to do this," he blurted. "We can turn around, go home."

With that last word, "home," the future rearranged itself in a splendid vision. His home would be hers, too. He'd sleep on a cot in the corridor, give her the entire room. Never would the girl suffer again. He'd enroll her in school, a good school, where she would be surrounded by knowledgeable people—much more knowledgeable than Konstantyn—who would teach her about the dynamics of flight, planetary orbits, anything she had ever wondered about.

"Kostya," she said softly, "I'm living out a girl's dream." Her face was closed to him, as though she were already gone. She took the suitcase, stepped into the dressing room.

The Palace of Culture lectorium dwarfed the one in Kirovka. Its four curved balconies hummed with spectators waiting for the show to begin. A red runner carpet—the catwalk—bisected the stage. To the right a television crew hustled around a nest of cables. To the left stood the judges' table, the six brass nameplates designating the seats waiting to be filled: MINISTER OF CULTURE, CHAIRMAN OF COUNCIL OF MINISTERS, STATE COMMITTEE CHAIRMAN, PROCURATOR GENERAL, PAINTER, COMPOSER. Snatches of melody rose from the narrow orchestra pit, where the musicians were warming up.

Konstantyn sat in the second row, main level. He was so close to the stage, he could smell its newly varnished floor. He tried to let himself sink into the cheerful chatter around him. He envied the other spectators their simple motive for being here—to enjoy themselves, watch a good show.

The lights dimmed. An oboist blew a piercing note, joined by the woodwinds, brass, strings, timpani. Konstantyn had heard an orchestra tune only a handful of times in his life and, despite his nervousness, the sound of the instruments joining in a single voice made him shiver with pleasure.

A small bearded man in a burgundy suit—an actor whose name Konstantyn couldn't remember—stepped onto the stage and the hall burst into applause. He welcomed everyone to the Miss USSR beauty competition, the first of its kind in the Union ("Second," Konstantyn muttered), and reminded the audience of the prizes to be claimed: a victory tour around the Union, a large-screen television, and a white dress. The orchestra played the city's anthem as the judges filed in and found their seats, solemn faces fit for a court proceeding. Irina Glebovna was the last to enter the stage. She wore a brown pantsuit with thick, armor-like shoulder pads, and her skin possessed the yellowish sheen of the embalmed. Before taking a seat, she installed herself in front of the announcer's microphone and gave a spirited speech about the importance of a Union glued together not only by a common economy and language, but also by a common culture—three components guaranteeing peace, to be enjoyed by many generations to come.

The pageant opened with the gown round. The thirty-five contestants waited at the far end of the stage, a row of silhouettes in the dim lighting. When called, each stepped into the spotlight, and strutted down the runway holding a white paper fan labeled with a number. Unlike the hodgepodge of contestants in Konstantyn's pageant, the young women here had a uniform look: pastel gowns, teased hairstyles, aggressive teeth-and-gums smiles.

Contestant Number 14, from Turkmenistan, bobbed a curtsy at the end of the runway.

Contestant Number 18, from Georgia, blew a kiss.

Finally the announcer called, "Orynko Bondar from Kirovka, Ukraine!"

The Minister of Culture straightened in her seat. She raised an index finger to the camera crew in warning: Be ready to cut.

Zaya marched in front of the Party members, the spotlight trailing her like a blazing eye. She wore makeup so thick it looked creamy, like something that needed refrigeration—an administrator's doing, he assumed. Zaya's puffy sleeves—decades out of style, Konstantyn saw now—bulged with the crown and sash. Did he still want her to put them on? He tried to catch her eye, but on she trooped, one high-heeled foot in front of the other. She appeared unshaken by the size of the audience, gazing straight ahead as if walking a tightrope. In one moment Konstantyn felt himself rising in his seat, ready to snatch her from the stage's deep maw; the next, he egged the girl on: show them, Miss Kirovka, show them that neither you, nor your townspeople, nor your country, will be silenced.

At last she reached the end of the runway. And—nothing happened. Instead of revealing the crown and sash, she simply turned on her heel and strode back upstage, as if this had been the plan all along.

Konstantyn felt dizzy with relief. He was grateful for her disobedience. Had the spectators recognized the name? Had they caught the significance of Miss Kirovka's presence?

Zaya rejoined the line of silhouettes. As the other contestants continued to file down the runway, domestic worries filled Konstantyn's mind, thrilling in their newness. He thought of the shoes and coat Zaya would need for the upcoming winter, the schoolbooks he would have to procure.

His attention was wrenched back to the stage at the word "Norgorsk." The twenty-first contestant stepped under the spotlight. Orchestral music swelled as she glided down the runway in an opal mermaid gown and a white fur shawl that glowed under the lights. Her silvery hair had been teased and crimped into a leonine mane. Konstantyn thought he had never seen someone so breathtaking, but as she approached, he realized he had.

It was Orynko Bondar. This time, the real Orynko Bondar.

Konstantyn watched in disbelief. The name the announcer had called couldn't have been hers—Konstantyn would have caught it. She had been given a stage name, he figured, something more *urban*. He searched Orynko's face for signs of trauma. She looked older, perhaps, her features settling into their adult state, but whatever trials she'd undergone during her exile seemed to have left no mark. She'd returned to her first home—the stage. She flapped her fan around her shoulders like a dove, to roaring applause. Charmingly bashful, she waved at the audience, as though she'd personally invited each one of them and couldn't believe they'd all come.

Konstantyn turned to look at Irina Glebovna. Was this her doing? Was she using Orynko, the seasoned contestant, for some nefarious end? But Irina Glebovna seemed just as surprised as Konstantyn by the original Miss Kirovka's reappearance. The Minister's expression wavered between wonder and anguish as she watched her grand pageant fade away. Later that evening, Konstantyn would learn the truth from Orynko herself: the remote Norgorsk also had a Cultural Club and its director had insisted, upon discovering her, that she represent the town. The smelting factory boasted its own private airport, and the rest had fallen into place.

Konstantyn sat on his hands, trying to contain his excitement. He couldn't imagine a happier ending to the evening.

The moment the pageant ended he would seek out Orynko and Zaya, and the three of them would return to Kirovka.

It was a pretty thought. Konstantyn held on to it even when, minutes later, between the twenty-fifth and twenty-sixth contestants, Zaya kicked off her pumps and broke from the line. She crossed the stage at a slow, deliberate pace, impervious to the unease passing through the other contestants. She stopped in front of the judges' table. As she considered the Party members one by one, they blinked back at her, shifted in their seats. The Procurator General, white-haired with opulent jowls, leaned toward the girl in the quaint yellow dress, ready to receive her message.

The audience fell silent then, ready for her message, too. The last chords of the orchestral piece hung in the air, and the conductor looked up from the pit to the announcer, unsure whether to continue. The twenty-sixth contestant, a tall Estonian in a gauzy dress, halted midstrut.

"If you could keep the runway circulation moving," the announcer told the Estonian.

Go back, Konstantyn mouthed to Zaya, his lips still curled in a frozen smile. Go back go back. She stood just a few meters away from where he sat—he could see the tip of her ear poke through her wig. If only she would turn to him.

Irina Glebovna sat very still.

Konstantyn could just make out Zaya's words. "You never answered my letters."

The wet lips of the Procurator General parted into a grin meant for a small child. He said something Konstantyn couldn't hear. Zaya flicked her chin up. The Procurator General jerked back, his mouth open. He touched his cheek.

It took Konstantyn a moment to realize that she had spat on him. The hall erupted in gasps, jeers.

Irina Glebovna made a slicing motion at the camera crew.

Now the State Committee Chairman twisted back, as if slapped.

As Zaya was sucking in her cheeks, drawing up saliva for a third attack, two men in uniform entered the lectorium from a side door. For a moment Zaya watched them approach, her face slack and her eyes deadened—the way they had been back at the *internat*, Konstantyn remembered. She seemed ready to accept whatever punishment these men threatened; it could be no worse than the one she had already been dealt.

Konstantyn sprang to his feet. He tore down the row of seats, treading on polished shoes and pedicured toes, and bounded up the steps to the stage as the guards closed in on Zaya. When her eyes met Konstantyn's, she jolted awake. Her lithe body slipped from the guards' hands, and she raced to the edge of the stage, toward the audience. Konstantyn glimpsed the pink underside of her foot as she launched herself into the air, leaping over the orchestra pit. For a moment he feared she wouldn't clear it, imagined the pit sucking her in. Her dress parachuted out as she landed—to Konstantyn's relief—in the carpeted space between the pit and the first row of petrified spectators. She took a second or two to steady herself, before she bolted up the aisle, heading for the exit.

"Konstantyn Illych?" Orynko shouted from the row of contestants.

Konstantyn reeled around. He could not let Orynko out of his sight now, lest she disappear again. He ran to her, grabbed her by the wrist, and set off after Zaya. The girl was already halfway across the lectorium, weaving between the spectators crowding into the aisle. A mustachioed man tried in vain to catch her. Konstantyn cursed the crowd, but was grateful for the added commotion, which sheltered him, and the contestant he had just whisked offstage, from the guards. By the time Konstantyn, still pulling Orynko in his wake, had waded to the exit, he'd lost track of Zaya. Outside, a bitter wind dashed between the tall stone buildings, slapped his and Orynko's faces. He thought he saw a streak of yellow, and ran after it. But one cavernous street opened up to another, unfolding endlessly.

"My feet hurt," Orynko protested, struggling to keep up in her stilettos. Passersby gawked at her, an apparition from another world. "Can't we go home?"

"One more street," Konstantyn promised. "Just one more."

As they searched, he thought of the moment Zaya had last looked at him, onstage. He conjured the expression on her face over and over, but each time her gaze changed. In one version, she was charmed but confused by the sight of Konstantyn racing toward her, calling her name as though she were the one who would save him; in another version, she struggled to remember who he was; in another, her face regained life and she found something to run for—Konstantyn, and their shared future. This was the version he held on to, in the years to come.

Orynko Bondar's homecoming was magnificent. The townspeople filled the platform of the Kirovka train station, and applauded as Orynko and Konstantyn descended the steep steps of the passenger car. Never before had Konstantyn seen such a crowd in his town. He hadn't slept the whole trip back. His eyes were red, heavy-lidded. Strangers slapped his back, shook his limp hand. He wished they would all go away.

Orynko's parents—short-haired, wearing practical foot-wear—wrapped themselves around the teenager, kissed her face. Konstantyn heard her father whisper in her ear, "But the Academy!" A small boy in a dress shirt thrust a bouquet of pink dahlias into Orynko's hands. A canister of home brew made the rounds.

Brave girl, foolish girl, the townspeople exclaimed. When had Miss Kirovka learned to spit with such aim, such force? From this, Konstantyn understood that the broadcast of the Moscow pageant had cut out right after Zaya spat on the judges. He found himself enraged at the townspeople. How could they have mistaken Zaya for Orynko, when she was so obviously Zaya? How could they have failed to recognize the real Orynko as the contestant from Norgorsk? Had the camera not zoomed in on the girls' faces, or had the townspeople simply wanted to believe the impossible? His convoluted plan had succeeded, and he hated himself for it.

Her name is Zaya, he wanted to shout, Zaya from Internat Number 12. An adept sprinter, a reciter of poems.

But now the townspeople pressed around Orynko and Konstantyn. They took Orynko's reticence for modesty, Konstantyn's red eyes for fatigue. As the pair stumbled out of the station, the crowd followed, boisterous as a victory parade.

PART
TWO

===

After
the
Fall

LUCKY TOSS

I'd been working as a guard at the saint's tomb for eighteen months before the trouble began. Konstantyn Illych paid me little but provided free lodging—an army cot and stove I could fold out in the corner of the tomb each night. The job consisted of telling pilgrims to keep hands out of pockets and lips off the display case. Sometimes children rapped the glass, bored by the saint's inactivity, and I would remind them that we were not a zoo.

The saint's display case, which Konstantyn Illych bought from a defunct delicatessen shop at quarter price, boasted a curved glass front and a steel ledge with tracks for plastic trays. Normally the saint basked under the fluorescent lamp like a glazed roast, but that particular day the bulb began to flicker, making the creature look as though it were twitching awake. At first the effect pleased Konstantyn Illych, who wanted the crowd of pilgrims to grow even thicker, but after the second pilgrim fainted he asked me to procure a replacement bulb—though not before we closed the tomb, at 18:30.

The tomb was a low-ceilinged concrete room in the crumbling building known as 1933 Ivansk. The room was bare as a bunker, containing only the display case, a narrow counter for the cash register, and a small bathroom (not for public use).

Before being a tomb it had been a hair salon and before that, a ground-level suite. The owner of the salon had knocked out the street-facing wall and replaced it with glass panes. When Konstantyn Illych bought the space, he knocked out the inner walls, too, to make room for the pilgrims. That the rest of 1933 Ivansk had not yet collapsed on us almost made me believe in the saint.

I'd approached Konstantyn Illych about the position after the Union fell and job prospects plummeted. He had already fired two guards for their substandard work ethic. Despite our unfortunate history—the letter of apology he never wrote or signed—we had reached a truce; I blamed him for ruining my career at the agency, and he blamed his failed marriage on the distress I'd caused, and so we were even. Even, but not equal, and Konstantyn Illych enjoyed reminding me of this fact: as my new boss he reveled in assigning me pointless tasks, such as dusting the insides of locks and buffing the stainless steel screws of the display case. I'd reached a similarly uneasy peace with Milena Markivna, who had returned to the building but not to Konstantyn Illych. For the past few months she'd been living on the ninth floor with a stylish young woman named Larissa and her two daughters, but Konstantyn Illych's repeated assertions that the women were merely roommates made me suspect they were more. Of course, I dared not ask Milena Markivna myself. The only time she and I had spoken since her return, she'd joked that I had finally realized my dream of becoming an Honor Guard. But I sensed my presence embarrassed her—I was a sticky residue from a past she longed to forget.

Most of the tomb's visitors were women and children. They laid portraits of men atop the display case. When the town's canning combine had closed, the men had taken to the sunflower fields, drinking cheap perfumes with flip-top caps, the brightly colored bottles shaped like grenades. Now, every evening, the men's portraits rustled like dead leaves as I swept them away.

We permitted photography inside the tomb. Konstantyn Illych believed it helped spread the word. Visitors loved snapping close-ups of the saint's teeth, a speckless set of ivories better preserved than any other saint's and certainly than any Kirovkavite's, dead or living. We townspeople all carried stomatological trauma, our mouths junk heaps of lead fillings, wire bridges, steel crowns, plastic prostheses. When the pilgrims peered into the saint's mouth—eternally thrown open, a model patient—they must have been transported to a happier time.

Most of the attention in the tomb centered on the saint, but on occasion I'd catch a pair of eyes on me. A glint of recognition, and perhaps contempt. Likely I imagined this. When the newspapers had begun publishing lists of names from declassified archives, I'd searched for mine but had not seen it. I did find an ex-colleague's name, from the agency. He must have found it, too—or worse, his family had. The next time his name appeared in the paper, it was to announce that he had hanged himself, "unable to bear the burden of his crimes." He had been much older than I, had operated in a different time. My tasks had been confined to the desk, and I'd never wielded anything larger than a pen.

Spotlights, striplights, pot lights, floodlights. There are myriad ways to illuminate a delicatessen display case, I learned at the hardware tent at the bazaar.

Most of the concrete storefronts sat empty, as they had before the Union's collapse, but the tents of the bazaar now sprawled ten blocks, selling anything from cow hooves to floppy disks. These tents sprouted and folded at an alarming speed; if one waited too long, it was impossible to find the same vendor twice. I hated this place, with its tantalizing colors and wafts at ever-inflating prices. I always came away feeling poorer, even if I hadn't spent a single *kupon*. The conundrum of former times—having money with nothing to spend it on—had been cruelly inverted.

"Are you displaying meat or fish?" the hardware sales boy yelled at me over the rattle of the electric generator by his feet. "Pastries? Greens?" He looked about fourteen and smelled of pomade. Behind him, a wall of shelves gleamed with a dizzying array of light fixtures. A few blinked and/or changed colors.

I didn't want to explain. "Meat."

"Fresh or cured?"

"Cured."

The sales boy warned against fluorescent bulbs, which made meat look blue; high-UV lights drained flesh to an unlively gray; incandescent bulbs promoted rotting. He insisted on halogen, which reacted with tungsten and brought out meat's natural blush. To demonstrate, he posed his face beside a bulb shaped like a tiny satellite dish. Indeed, a before-unseen pimple on his chin glowed a freshly squeezed red. "A halogen bulb sells your product for you," he assured.

A halogen bulb cost two hundred *kupony* and Konstantyn Illych had given me fifty.

"A regular bulb will do," I said.

The boy puckered his lips, now crimson, as if painted with lipstick. "A halogen bulb pays for itself," those lips promised.

When I showed the boy my lone bill, his enthusiasm wilted. Again I missed the years when one had fewer choices, fewer ways to disappoint.

—

The next day I woke at dawn. Konstantyn Illych had instructed me to change the bulb before the crowds of pilgrims arrived outside the tomb and gathered along the glass wall, so as not to detract from the mystique of the saint. I had several times suggested installing curtains to pull over the glass, but Konstantyn Illych said he did not have the money. I doubted this was true. All those coins, warm from pilgrim palms, must have amounted to a weighty sum. And I knew Konstantyn Illych was currently renovating his suite nine stories above. He had wedged an extra room into it, for his runaway foster child. She'd been gone for over a year, but Konstantyn Illych awaited the girl like the pilgrims awaited their savior. He'd even bought her a new wardrobe, in four different sizes, anguished that he couldn't know how much she had grown.

I unlocked the saint's display case, slid open its rear door. The smell of oil and dirt burst forth, as if something had been uprooted from the parched earth. I tried to unscrew the spent bulb, contorting my arms to avoid grazing the body, but the bulb had fused to its rusty socket. I could not work while the saint remained inside the case.

I paused and considered the wretched creature: legless, not much larger than a toddler, it screamed at me soundlessly, brown skin taut around its lipless mouth. Konstantyn Illych had told me that the saint belonged to his foster child, but not how she'd gained possession of it, and I had no desire to inquire further.

Things I'd have rather touched: a lamp full of dead insects, swamp scum, the raw cavern of an alley cat's ear, the slimy inside of a toilet plunger in a public bathroom that had run out of soap. I could have spent the morning bargaining against my fate, if only there had been someone to bargain with.

(I had watched the pilgrims trying to bargain with the saint all the time. They would bend over the glass, inspecting the saint's nostrils, eyes, ears, for bleeding. Rumors had circulated about the saint's powers—Tinnitus, soothed! Eczema, cleared! Drinking habit, broken!—but I did not believe them. To me the saint seemed wholly occupied by its century-long scream. Or yawn. I could never decide which.)

I averted my eyes from the mouth, and considered the saint's torso, hips, the bluish twist of robes where the legs would have been. I wondered if these limbs had broken off postmortem, when the catacombs were ravaged. If the saint had sensed the turbulence in its monastery above. If, in that particular monastery, the monks had been shot on the spot or if they'd had to dance through the town first. If those who'd refused to dance had had the soles of their feet singed with a branding iron, until at last it appeared as if they were dancing. Or had the monks been taken into the forest, away from the resisting townspeople, where only the pines witnessed their transformation: golden crosses torn from necks, rings wrenched off fingers, long hair and beards shaved to render them indistinguishable from the other bodies waiting in the pit graves. I did not want to know any of it, but the questions kept marching into my head until I seized the mummy, pulled it out of the case, and set it on the steel ledge. The body was surprisingly light, as though stuffed with straw. It gave off a sour dust that assailed the back of my throat like a long hairy tongue.

Coughing, sneezing, I attacked the old lightbulb. I pulled, pushed, wriggled, cursed until, at last, my arm shot back with the freed bulb.

I saw it then: the saint teetered on the ledge, tipped toward the floor. I dove to catch it—too late. For such a light object, the crash was momentous, as though the saint had resolutely hurled itself to the ground.

I stared in disbelief as this alleged producer of miracles, the rising star of saints of Ukraine, lay facedown on the floor.

The ledge had been wide enough for the saint—more than wide enough, or I would not have placed the bundle of bones upon it. My exertions with the bulb must have caused the entire counter to shake, and the saint to shimmy toward the edge.

Where the saint's face had made contact with the tiles lay its teeth. Nine of them, nacreous as pearls, roots curved like claws. Without question I would have to glue them back in. The teeth were integral to the saint's reputation, which was integral to me keeping my job.

Carefully, I stowed the saint back inside the display case, my palm beneath its head. The skin under the sparse hair felt leathery, like the rind of a baked ham.

Since I did not have glue, the teeth touch-up would have to wait until evening. Soon the pilgrims would start lining up, clutching coins for admission, and Konstantyn Illych's keys would scratch at the door's many locks. The austere tomb lacked a suitable hiding spot for the teeth—the saint's robes, perhaps, but I could not bring myself to rummage through them—so I slipped the teeth into my pants pocket for the day.

I noticed a few straw-yellow hairs clinging to my palm. I shook my hand, my arm, my entire body, until I was free of them.

Back when I asked Konstantyn Illych for the guard job, he'd inquired if I had experience managing crowds. I assured him

I did. During my time at the agency, I'd even worked with pilgrims. "You mean, worked against," presumed Konstantyn Illych, but neither of us were in the mood to quibble over semantics.

What I meant was that, at the agency, one of my tasks had been to regulate pedestrian traffic to Udobsklad, a fuel and artificial fertilizer storage facility that had once been a monastery. "Regulate" meant "stop"—a tedious task no one else at the agency wanted, so it was dumped on me, a novice at the time. Every spring, small groups of pilgrims would make an illegal procession of 25 kilometers, sneaking through Kirovka, through the forest, to the arched gates of Udobsklad. This they did in spite of the clearly marked signs warning of hazardous material. At the gates, the pilgrims would sing songs, as they had allegedly done for the past six hundred springs. They still considered the storage facility the holy site of some ancient, highly improbable event. The town council had tolerated the procession until we made an embarrassing discovery: among these fanatics figured respectable citizens—two factory directors and a senior lieutenant. Every spring henceforth I had to intercept groups traveling through Kirovka and fine them. One group tried to pass themselves off as a touring choir, another as a foreign delegation; most of the pilgrims, however, were candid about their purpose of travel, and their loyalty to their cause baffled me. At the end of the day I would trudge back to the office, my suit dusty and shoes scuffed, and my colleagues would make me recount all my dealings with the pilgrims while they laughed. Before long it occurred to me that my colleagues were laughing not at the pilgrims but at me, for having to chase after them.

When, after a few years, the Ministry of Labor and Social

Development converted the storage facility into a psychoneuro-logical *internat* and erected a tall iron fence around it, pilgrimage numbers did drop. But the hardiest pilgrims persisted. They set up at the iron gates and, worst of all, drew in orphans to sing with them.

If I issued too few fines, my superior questioned my vigilance; too many fines, and my superior scolded my stale thinking. And still the pilgrims crept back, year after year.

"Who said you could redecorate?" Konstantyn Illych stood at the doorway of the tomb, nodding at the linen sheet over the saint. Konstantyn Illych's hair was uncombed, still ruffled from sleep. The previous year it had turned white in one burst, like a dandelion gone to seed.

"Why not try it for a day?" I suggested. "Divinity needs a bit of mystery."

Konstantyn Illych closed the door behind him. The pilgrims lined up along the glass wall outside were eyeing the sheet, too. Like Konstantyn Illych, they did not look thrilled by its addition.

"Didn't Zaya keep the saint covered, in a pillowcase?" I reminded him. I'd never met the girl, or the pillowcase, but Konstantyn Illych had supplied me with plenty of details.

My superior's scowl softened. "I still have that pillowcase, starched and ironed for her return." His eyes darted about the tomb, as though the girl might materialize at any moment. I suspected that his ex-wife's new living arrangement added to his anguish. He'd once told me that women only turn to each other when there is a dearth of sensible men—"And am I not sensible?"—but I believed the core of his heartbreak lay elsewhere. While Milena had gained two children, who trailed around her in their school pinafores, braids bouncing—he had lost one. Surely he dreamed of walking Zaya to school, no matter her age, her hand clasped in his.

Konstantyn Illych unlocked the cash register and broke a roll of coins into it. He turned back to the shrouded mummy. "Nice not to have to look at that thing," he conceded.

"Or have it look at you," I muttered.

He placed a stack of laundered kerchiefs on his counter, available for rent to women who wished to cover their hair for worship but had forgotten to bring their own—a new addition to his business, following repeated requests.

"So long as the sheet doesn't affect attendance," Konstantyn Illych warned.

At the agency, we'd shared a courtyard with the Transport Workers' Union. One afternoon, on break, I'd overheard two railway engineers debate the best location for a new freight rail yard. The first potential spot sat north of Kirovka and would require the construction of a bridge. The second sat south of Kirovka, over Holinka Ridge, and would require the dynamiting of a tunnel. At the mention of Holinka Ridge, I put down my fish sandwich. The pilgrimage route I'd been monitoring passed over Holinka Ridge. Twenty rows of freight cars would lob off the procession, remove the need for policing any fence. I envisioned myself free from the tedium of chasing down pedestrians, promoted to more rewarding work.

Soon the engineers were yelling at each other, one waving her arms to make herself look larger, the other sitting with arms and legs crossed, unmovable in her granite-gray suit. At last they agreed to flip a coin. If a coin could break the tie between the Soviet Union and Italy in the 1968 European Football Championship, a coin could solve this much simpler matter.

A furious rummaging of pockets ensued.

But no coin!

The engineers turned to the table next to theirs, where I happened to be sitting. Their eyes flitted from my chin, still blotched from a not-unrecent adolescence, to my fish-flake-littered trousers, to the twiggy ankles that stuck out of them. The women's hard faces thawed with pity. I set my jaw. They must not have known who I was or where I worked.

I slid a copper coin from my pocket.

"If you wouldn't mind flipping it for us," said the engineer in the suit, arms still crossed. "We need a neutral arbiter."

"Oh, I couldn't." I was not being bashful—I had never flipped a coin.

A small audience of transport workers gathered around us. I waited for a volunteer to step forward, but none did. The unspoken rule: Your coin, your toss.

"Heads, we build south," said the engineer in the suit.

"Tails, north," deduced the other.

The transport workers cheered me on. Emboldened, I shook the coin between my palms like a die. Heads, heads, I chanted in my mind. I flung my hands out, imagining I were releasing a bird. The coin made a lazy arc over my head, bounced off my shoulder, and landed on the engineers' table, where it rolled on its side, slowly and pathetically, before falling between the wooden slats. A few spectators laughed. Neither of the engineers would deign to stoop for the coin. I did not want to stoop for it either, but soon I was on all fours, crawling under the table as the crowd goaded me on. Blood rushed to my face. The concrete grated my kneecaps. I hated the onlookers but hated myself even more, spineless as usual.

The result: tails.

I'd seen a one-kopek coin countless times before, of course, but now found myself peeved by the look of its squat elaborately serifed number, the folksy ears of wheat encircling it.

As I slowly rose from under the table, coin lodged in my fist, my eyes met the suited engineer's. My expression must have been apologetic: her shoulders dropped almost imperceptibly—she knew that she had lost.

I focused my gaze on a spot above the crowd, a blemish on the tiled wall behind them. The verdict came meekly, my tongue simply testing it out: "Heads."

"Heads," declared the suited engineer, voice hoarse.

"But neither of us saw it," the other engineer pleaded.

"Heads," shouted the crowd, over and over.

"Heads," I shouted with them.

The same hardware sales boy as yesterday intercepted me by the glue section of his tent. "Which type you looking for?"

Hundreds of tubes of all sizes and colors hung before me. I pretended to read their labels, wishing the boy would leave me alone.

He asked, "Permanent or semipermanent?"

He asked, "Food grade?"

He asked, "Medical grade?"

He asked, "Spray-on?"

"Just the standard," I conceded.

He asked, possibly rhetorically, "What *is* standard?" He unhooked a fat horseradish-colored tube, then a pink thimble-size one. "There's the standard glue for wood planks, and the standard glue for the heirloom teapot your wife doesn't know you broke."

"Closer to the latter."

The boy chuckled, conspiratorial, as if he himself had been married for years, had shattered many teapots. "Now," he said in a low voice, "are we talking vitreous porcelain, new Sèvres porcelain, or soft feldspathic porcelain?"

Too many minutes later, on my way back to the tomb, I stopped by a news kiosk for an issue of *Izvestia*. Recently the publication of archives had slowed. Readers were satiated. Back when they knew less, they'd felt safer.

I came upon an article about the rail yard that had been constructed south of Holinka Ridge. I'd almost missed it, wedged as it was between an advertisement for pantyhose and another for tax lawyers. During the rail yard's twelve-year operation, the article informed its readers, the pilgrims who had died crawling under trains in an attempt to reach the monastery numbered:

Men	6
Women	7
Children	2

I hadn't known the true numbers. Shortly after the construction of the rail yard had begun, my superior had declared the pilgrimage issue solved and taken me off the case. I'd ignored the rumors that there had been injuries, even deaths. Now I stared at the neat stack of numbers, reprinted from a railway report. I wondered, uselessly: Why were the children a separate, ungendered category? But as soon as I thought this, my mind conjured them—two girls, then two boys, then a girl and a boy, darting under the maze of freight cars, losing themselves in their game—and I clamped my eyes shut, as if I could unsee them.

If the rail yard had been built instead in the northern spot, zero pilgrims would have died. But the engineer who had vied for the southern rail yard had been the more charismatic, resolved one—surely she would have won, even without a coin toss, even without me skewing the result.

I waited until nightfall to mend the mummy. Inside the tomb, I kept the lights off to avoid attracting attention; a nearby streetlamp provided just enough illumination and, for the finer work, I was armed with a key chain flashlight. Glue at the ready, I reached into my pants pocket for the saint's teeth, but found only a small hole where before there had been none. I searched the other pants pocket, then all four pockets of my coat. My hand returned to the first pocket, to confirm the teeth were still missing.

If the hole had already been there, before the teeth, surely I would have caught it—the pants were my last remaining pair presentable enough for work, and I was vigilant about identifying and repairing any damage—and I would not have used a compromised pocket for valuables. For a moment I entertained the possibility that the teeth had chewed their way out. But no, I told myself, this was simply a case of bad luck, even if I did not believe in luck, bad or good.

I dreaded explaining the saint's disfigurement to Konstantyn Illych. I could not keep it hidden under the linen for much longer—Konstantyn Illych had asked to check on the saint the next morning, and I'd lied and said I'd temporarily misplaced the sole key to the case. If he saw that the teeth were missing, perhaps he'd think I gouged them out, and sold them on the black market. On occasion, relic hunters did visit the tomb. They were easy to spot. They'd kneel the lowest, pray the loudest, before offering money for a tuft of holy hair, a sliver of ear. From their corner-mouth whispers I had learned that five heads of St. John the Baptist were in circulation; thirteen palms, nineteen feet, and twenty-one skull fragments of Jezebel—whatever the dogs didn't eat; the foreskins of Christ and His footprints were particularly popular, as were the moans of David, the shivers of Jehovah.

Just then, between two floor tiles, an incisor twinkled in the lamplight.

I fell to my knees, ready almost to kiss this relic. This time I wrapped the tooth in one of the rental kerchiefs from the counter, and stowed it in my double-lined breast pocket.

Another tooth, longer, fanglike, winked at me by the exit. I collected it, stepped outside. One by one the saint's teeth appeared like stars in a darkening sky.

The third tooth glowed from a crack in the pavement.

The fourth and fifth teeth sat at the rusty foot of a seesaw.

They led me further and further from the tomb. I expected the teeth would retrace the route I'd taken earlier that day from the bazaar, but instead they led me in the opposite direction, toward an unlit park, as though someone had rearranged them as a sinister joke. It was imprudent to be out after sunset, when only thieves and thugs stalked the streets, but I kept on. I tried to imagine myself as a lover, following rose petals to a bed, but couldn't help feeling like a rodent, lured by crumbs to a trap.

The sixth tooth lounged on a tree root.

The seventh spilled from a half-eaten bag of chips.

The eighth bounced between a stray cat's paws.

I stopped there. I'd reached the perimeter of the park. Its patchy lawn sloped down to a copse of oaks and a well that had run dry. I needed that last tooth, but was afraid of where it might appear—at the bottom of the well? Under a sleeping pack of dogs? I inhaled the cool night air, tried to compose myself. These were only teeth, after all; I'd been living with a set of my own for forty years. I set off at a trot, down a paved path. When I spotted the ninth tooth roosting in an old flower bed under the oaks, lucent as its siblings, the tightness in my chest broke into laughter. Was this where the teeth had been leading me? To a patch of weeds? Carried by a senseless impulse to catch the tooth before it got away, I lunged forward. My foot caught a notch in the pavement. As I hurled to the ground, my screaming jaws bit into the concrete rim of the flower bed.

I do not know how long I lay in the dark, swallowing blood.

My heart climbed into my head and pounded at my eardrums, seeking escape. My jaws ground at the hinges. I spat out what I hoped was gravel. I clutched the saint's last tooth. Its claw sank into my palm.

By the time I stumbled back to the tomb, my entire body felt seared with pain. When I turned on the bathroom light, a bloated, scratched face stared at me from the mirror. A criminal's face. The lips oozed blood. I willed the mouth to open, but now my jaws were stuck shut. This was partly a relief—I did not want to see the damage my tongue had already rooted out. Rotten from a lifetime of avoiding stomatologists, my front teeth had given way easily. Their absence felt vertiginous. My tongue kept back, as though it, too, were in danger of tumbling out, and pressed itself against the molars. A few of these were fractured, their edges jutting sharply.

I opened the saint's display case, yanked off the linen sheet. Now the saint's crinkled eyes and thrown-open mouth seemed to be laughing. I knew then where the teeth had been leading me: not just to the flower bed, but also to the notch in the pavement.

I uncapped the tube of glue. Its cloying smell spiked my headache, brought on a wave of nausea. I reached into my breast pocket, unwrapped the kerchief. Inside, I found only a hole. With increasing horror, I discovered that the pocket, too, had a new hole. This time I could not chalk up the loss to bad luck: the teeth had gnawed through both layers of lining. And yet again they were at large, free to wreak havoc upon me.

When a locomotive begins to pull its train, the couplers between the cars tighten with a clack. The clack skips all the way down the train, head to tail, like the cracking of a spine.

When a locomotive begins to pull its train, and a person happens to be crawling under it, they hear the clacks pass over them. A warning: *get out, get out, get out.* Yet these pilgrims, these men, women, children, had crept on. In their final moments, did they regret what they were doing? Did they still believe that something better waited on the other side?

"Are you in trouble?" Konstantyn Illych asked me the following morning. "I don't want trouble in my tomb."

It was fifteen minutes before opening. I tried to ignore the many pairs of eyes trained on me through the glass wall. The swelling of my face and hands had grown overnight. A magenta bruise extended from the corners of my scabbed lips, giving me a clown's smile. My gums still leaked blood. Konstantyn Illych did not seem to believe a flower bed could do this much damage.

I couldn't bring myself to tell Konstantyn Illych the truth: yes, I was in trouble, just not the kind of trouble he meant. "I told you. I tripped," I mumbled. I still could not open my mouth more than a few millimeters.

A freckled teenage boy knocked on one of the glass panes, trying to catch my attention.

"If Zaya comes back and I'm not here, she'll see your face and run again," said Konstantyn Illych.

"I'll run after her."

"You haven't seen her run." He gazed at me as if we were separated by a great gulf; he had someone to love and I didn't.

"You never told me where Zaya got the saint." By now I had a hunch, and I dreaded the answer.

Konstantyn Illych scowled, pretending not to understand my muffled speech. I repeated the question, and he shrugged. "Her orphanage."

"You mean that former monastery?"

He glanced at the pilgrims. "Keep those pretty lips sealed. I hear the Church is trying to reappropriate what it can."

I began to shiver, and longed to run from the tomb, into the warm sunlight.

Konstantyn Illych slapped my shoulder affectionately. The muscles at the back of my neck locked in spasm. "You can take the day off, but I can't promise to pay you for it." He urged me to go see a stomatologist, but we both knew this was impossible. The last public clinic in town had closed, and few could afford the glittering private one.

I stayed in the tomb. We opened on time.

——

The duty of a guard is to be still, to be present with the world.
But over the next several days I could not keep still. Every cell in
my body howled. The bruising and swelling began to subside,
but the pain did not. Its hooks jerked at my gums, at the exposed
nerves of my shattered teeth. I subsisted on potato broth and
sour cream, and my stomach wrung itself with hunger.

When I wasn't thinking of my teeth, I thought of the saint's.
I feared their reappearance, their reassembly. I feared they
would punish me, as the noose had punished my ex-colleague.
The teeth would gnash me to bits. There were moments when,
as if on cue, a pilgrim would turn toward me and I'd catch an
opaline glint. In the evenings, I shook out my slippers, felt under
my pillow. I even peeked under the saint's shroud, hoping the
teeth had tired of their wanderings and resumed their post. But
the saint remained as gap-mouthed as a child.

Each shift stretched longer and longer. My fingers fidgeted
with the hole in my pants pocket, worrying it larger. I counted
and re-counted the pilgrims. Counting was not part of the job.
I did not like the crowd, and quantifying it made it seem even
larger, but I couldn't help myself. I counted the men in sixes. The
women in sevens. The children in twos. I imagined them crawling. Flat on the ground.

Thanks to the linen sheet, the relic hunter whispered in my ear,
no one would know if they were appealing to a saint or a pile
of sandbags. And wasn't that the power of prayer? The woman
brought her taper candle closer to her face, the light from its
flame stretching shadows across her features. She kept on: If a

saint, no, half a saint, brought this much hope, imagine what would happen if that saint were divided further, into many pieces, displayed in many glass boxes across many churches and homes. Didn't I want to maximize hope? She offered me a fine price. Would even throw in the sandbags.

It was a Sunday evening, which was when Konstantyn Illych habitually kept the tomb illuminated with sixty candles for sixty minutes. The weekly vigil coincided with the blackouts, which had started up again for the first time in years, but only in small towns like ours.

From her purse the relic hunter slid a yellowed portrait of a boy posing with a poodle. She positioned it among the other photographs on the display case. Likely she'd bought her prop at a flea market, to help her impersonate a pilgrim. The relationship was almost believable: the relic hunter and the boy in the photo shared pointed, elfish ears.

By the cash register, Konstantyn Illych's head craned over the crowd. His gaze landed on us. He shook his head at me in sympathy. They can be so *chatty*, he seemed to say. So *whiny*.

"That boy is someone's son," I whispered to the hunter.

"He was my sister's." Her dark eyes met mine, daring me to utter another rebuke. "Do we have a deal?"

For a second I considered; I desperately needed the money, and it would have pleased me to be rid of the mummy. But selling it to a butcher's block felt like a renewed violence. The duty of a guard is to guard, not to steal, and especially not from Konstantyn Illych. He had given me the job out of goodwill and I could not betray him. I shook my head.

—

I decided my pain was a test of will. To distract my thoughts from my mouth, and my stomach—I still couldn't chew solids—I instituted a Changing of the Guard. If we wanted to build a world-class tomb, I told Konstantyn Illych, we needed the pageantry.

Two minutes and forty-five seconds before the hour, every hour, I held the line. I marched out to the front of 1933 Ivansk, high-kicking Prussian style, upper body stiff while my lower body danced away the pressure that had accumulated during the past fifty-seven minutes and fifteen seconds. The old guard charged around the building. Precisely as the clock struck the hour, the new guard marched in from the opposite side. On occasion a child might call out, "But isn't that the same man as before?" and a snigger would ripple through the crowd. But I paid no heed. My choreography grew more and more elaborate: all taps, skips, and kicks, a wild whir of legs, as though the earth singed my feet.

Konstantyn Illych encouraged my displays; they were drawing larger crowds, which assembled at the top of the hour to cheer on my footwork. By the end of every shift I would exhaust myself, wanting nothing more than the sweet numbness of sleep. After two weeks, however, my hunger gave way to weakness. I lived with a sharp ringing in my skull, the air having condensed into two drills that bore into my ears. My uniform hung from my thinning limbs. I stumbled through the Changing of the Guard, then reduced its frequency, then gave it up. After that, I simply kept to my post, where the pain awaited me hotly, with pincers for arms and clamps for lips.

—

A knock on the glass wall startled me awake. The streetlamp illuminated the silhouette of a great hairy beast. It watched me for some time before peeling back the fur from its head. I recognized the naked ears that stuck out.

I heaved myself from my cot and waited out a spell of dizziness before shuffling to the door. I unlocked the dead bolt and cracked open the door, its chain still hinged.

The relic hunter's floor-length coat rippled in the orange lamplight. "Name your price."

I'd once heard a pensioner lament that to get your teeth fixed you had to give up a kidney. Without expecting an answer, I asked the hunter how much a kidney cost.

Without a blink she said, "Thirty-five thousand." She peered at my face. "Why, finally getting those teeth done? For thirty-five thousand, you'll be good as new." She thrust her hand through the door crack. "Final offer."

I cringed at the thought of the saint hacked to pieces. But the saint was already dead, as were the men, women, and children who crawled behind my eyes day and night. And here I was, living.

I gripped the relic hunter's hand. I wanted that hand, warm and moist, to pull me from the tomb, from my wrecked body.

Victims, the newspaper article had called the perished pilgrims. (The railway report itself had not called them anything, only quantified them.) When dredging up the past, the newspapers attempted to divide its players into victims and villains. My employment at the agency would mark me as the latter. But I had suffered, too. I'd grown up without parents. If a coin flip hadn't decided their fate, likely the tick of a pen had, or an act similarly arbitrary. After three generations, who were the victims, who the villains? We'd become a formidable alloy, bound by shame. The grand dream of equality realized.

I'd braced myself for the stomatological clinic of my childhood: a warehouse with many rows of barbershop chairs, in which a patient endured not only his or her own (unanesthetized) agony, but that of the other wailing patients.

But here, in the reception room of the new private clinic, a burbling fountain induced calm. Glossy posters attested to miraculous Before-and-Afters. Anything could be erased: nicotine and caffeine stains, calculus so thick it could be mined, maxillofacial birth defects, industrial accidents, head-on collisions.

After I laid out the stacks of bills on the counter, a rosy-cheeked stomatologist led me down a corridor. She lifted her chin and thrust back her broad shoulders with the bravado of an opera singer about to step onto the stage. Then she opened a door to a private sunlit room. A mint-green reclining chair greeted me, curved arms inviting, as though it had been waiting for me all along. The instruments of torture were nowhere in sight.

As she inspected my mouth, the stomatologist made small sounds of anguish. "Poor sir," she murmured, "poor sir." I lapped up the words; I hadn't realized how badly I needed them.

"For a case as severe as yours," the stomatologist pronounced, "only Western technology will do." She would extract my remaining teeth, which were past their prime anyway, drill holes directly into my jawbone, screw in implants with titanium rods. I recoiled at the idea, but already she had pressed a button, and the chair reclined until my head felt lower than my feet. My face had lost all color, she reported. She worried I would faint.

"The pain," I asked, "will it go away?"

The stomatologist waved away the question—it seemed beside the point. I would have the best smile in town, she assured me. She hooked a surgical mask over her ears.

It was not until she latched the anesthesia mask over my nose and instructed me to count down from ten that the instruments scurried from their hiding places. With a hydraulic wheeze, a metal tray rose from behind the chair, containing an assortment of pliers. Then came another tray, with two sparkling rows of drill heads. An oval lamp hovered over my face. I felt myself to be on the belly of a spider, each leg performing a task. The final metal dish slid into view, containing the implants. Panic seized me—I recognized their nacreous gleam.

The saint's teeth grinned at me from the dish, the full set, their roots now titanium.

I tried to warn the stomatologist about the cursed teeth, but my tongue refused to stir, my lips flapped uselessly. The room contracted around the stomatologist's blue eyes. They crinkled. Under her mask, she must have been smiling. My fear spiked, then burned away. All I could do was accept what was coming, like the clacks of a train pulled into motion. "You aren't count- ing, Mikhail Ivanovich. Start counting down."

ROACH BROOCH

Those who mourn quietest, mourn deepest.

When the grandson dies, the rest of the family squabbles over his estate, but the grandparents vow not to get involved. (Not all the grandparents—just the maternal set, Pyotr Palashkin and Lila Palashkina, the last of the family to live in glum little Kirovka, while the rest have escaped.) Considering the shedload of money the grandson earned abroad, doing who knows what, he must have written a will, as people abroad do. The grandparents think: The rest of the family will surely respect his wishes.

When the grandson's parents inherit his apartment and car, Pyotr and Lila don't grumble that these parents already own a two-room and don't drive.

When the grandson's girlfriend inherits the diamond ring he kept in his lockbox, it would be rude to remind her that he hadn't proposed yet, might've changed his mind.

The grandparents don't mention that they practically raised the grandson while his parents worked. He was the first grandchild, the only one they could help care for before the family dispersed. The child was born joyless, and they would try and try to cheer him up by pointing out small miracles: the first crocus bursting through snow; the newspaper photo of the crocodile who wears his turtle friend as a hat; the eerie curling of one's fingers when the inner wrist is pressed. If the grandparents couldn't make the boy happy, at least they kept him clean, fed—alive.

Everyone in the family is poor, but the grandparents are the poorest. When the Union fell and inflation spiked, their lifelong savings dissolved along with their peaceful retirement. Instead of lounging on his bench in front of 1933 Ivansk—the bench now swallowed by a sea of pilgrims—Pyotr sits with Lila on a pair of children's foldout chairs at the train station, selling bone albums to tourists on layover. They greet the tourists in a dim underpass that reeks of urine, the bone records spread over a checkered tablecloth on the concrete. Other elderly citizens sell Soviet army regalia, reprinted propaganda posters, painted wooden spoons. To procure the X-rays, the grandparents have to dig through the dumpsters behind the polyclinic, risking infection and grisly new diseases. Pyotr and Lila got into the business when a neighbor, Milena Markivna, posted an ad in the lobby offering her bone music equipment for a reasonable price. Included were a modified gramophone and sixteen vinyl records. The grandparents were overwhelmed with joy the first time they held the albums: Red Poppies! Jolly Fellows! Such ensembles used to perform on television all the time, with their smart suits or matching knit sweaters, bobbing in sync, abstaining from flashy dance. Pyotr and Lila couldn't hide their disappointment when Milena told them the vinyl sleeves and labels had been a disguise, that the *real* music only came through when you lowered the needle.

The record player turned out to be in poor condition, likely kept in the damp for years, and the volume knob broke at first touch. It's still stuck to one level: blaring. The grandparents have to live with Alice Cooper, KISS, Black Sabbath at full growl. It wouldn't be so bad if they couldn't understand the words, but Pyotr and Lila are retired English teachers.

"GO TO HELL," the music advises. "LIE DOWN AND DIE."

Also, "YOU SHOULD HAVE NEVER HAPPENED."

But, of small comfort: "I'LL MISS YOU WHEN YOU'RE GONE."

The family doesn't think the situation is so bad. After all, the grandparents get to listen to music all day, and make money doing it. Meanwhile the others have to drive trucks across the country, bend over microscopes at catheter assembly lines, check fares on packed trams, hawk bread out of moving trains. And those are just the day jobs.

"Grandfather has a tumor," Lila likes to remind the family over the phone, whenever they get smug. The tumor sits atop his bladder.

"Benign," they snap back.

"But growing, crowding out his organs," she tells them. "Even if very slowly, it will kill him."

"So get it removed!" The family has been pleading for this to happen for years.

But the situation isn't as simple as that. The grandparents can't get the tumor removed because as long as it exists, they're guaranteed a monthly pelvic X-ray. The shape of the spine and hips in the X-ray reminds the tourists of an electric guitar, and they snap that bone album up right away. The tumor is what feeds the grandparents.

"Why not just make copies of the same X-ray?" This, the snarky uncle.

"Don't think we haven't tried," Lila says. But no one in town will make copies. They've even asked the polyclinic receptionist for extras, and the woman in turn asked what they thought she was running, a medical facility or an X-ray press.

Finally the relatives sort out what the grandparents will inherit. Something the grandson must have treasured very much, they promise. They send one of the teenagers over to deliver it. A head taller than the last time the grandparents saw him, and newly handsome, the teenager carries a clear-lidded tin box repurposed from Belgian chocolates. With his stiff posture, bearing the gift in his arms, he looks like a suitor. He won't come inside, though, says he has to rush off to catch the next train back to his city, a train that doesn't stop here anymore, not fully—it only slows to a crawl along the platform because the town no longer deserves more than a minute of the train's time.

Since the major items have already been allotted, the grandparents aren't expecting an enormous or life-changing gift. They'd be happy with a keepsake, however small.

The tin box in the teenager's hands has a pinprick hole. Lila takes the box and peers into it, her mouth already set in a smile.

Inside the box is, well, the grandparents aren't sure what. A silver chain attached to an oblong pile of brown rocks, sitting on a piece of newspaper. It's roughly the size and shape of a stool. It looks much like the samples the grandson had to produce in his childhood, to be scooped into a matchbox—by the grandmother, who else?—then wrapped in newspaper, then a plastic bag, and submitted to the school nurse, who inspected it for worms. Each looming inspection would make the boy nervous, thus constipated—stage fright, Pyotr called it—and Lila would often have to produce the sample herself. The rest of the family liked to joke that the grandson would one day return the favor.

Is that what the so-called gift is about?

The most disgusting thing about the brown pile: two hairs sticking out of one end.

The grandparents look up from the box, but the teenager has already run off.

The pair of hairs twitches.

In shock, Lila almost drops the box. Now the entire pile lumbers from one side of the box to the other, toward its own reflection.

The grandparents draw their faces closer. The rocks, they realize, are glued to an insect. A giant wingless roach, by the looks of it. The hairs are its antennae.

Is it supposed to be a pet?

An art project?

Just the kind of thing the grandson would waste his money on.

The rest of the family may not know it yet, but Pyotr and Lila have stopped talking to them. If one of the relatives were to call, the grandparents wouldn't answer.

The grandparents keep up with the bone records. Keep ignoring the doctor's pleas to remove the tumor. The doctor brings props to the radiology room each month, to demonstrate the tumor's growth.

He holds up a pea. "Where we started."

He holds up a glossy chestnut. "Where we're at."

He holds up a lemon. "Where we'll be in a few short years."

Not the regular type of lemon, pale and pitted, Lila notes. This one is dark yellow, taut-bellied. Likely a Meyer, from a pricey store.

"Am I getting through?" the doctor asks. He's taut-bellied himself, with brown nicotine stains on his lips.

The grandparents nod along, but the gravity of the diagnosis has never quite sunk in. It just doesn't make sense, how a pea can metamorphose into a chestnut, then a lemon.

"Can we keep the lemon?" Pyotr asks.

At their sales stall, the grandparents keep a pair of flashlights. Tourists shine them through the X-ray records. Sometimes the reason for the X-ray is obvious: a broken limb, a spoon floating in a stomach. Other times, the X-ray shows a subtle swelling, a hairline fracture. The tourists enjoy the detective work.

For the layperson, Pyotr's tumor isn't easy to identify. Lila has to trace the faint orb above the bladder with her finger before the tourists say "Ah." She never attributes the tumor to her husband, sitting right beside her, so as not to dampen anyone's mood.

As with any growth or deformity, the tourists always want to know: "A victim of . . . ?" The tourists don't want to say the dirty word themselves, but are itching to hear it, pronounced authentically by this kerchiefed babushka.

Lila casts down her eyes, confirms: "Chernobyl."

She says this even though her husband never served in Chernobyl or had anything to do with it. The most he'd done was help hose off their apartment building, as per government recommendations, but the spray of the garden hose only reached the second floor, and they lived on the third, so who knew how much of the fallout they'd absorbed? The government had also recommended they drink wine to protect against the radiation, but the grandparents didn't have wine themselves and didn't know anyone so fancy. Pyotr's skin hadn't melted off like that poor woman's had, the one on the local news—she'd bathed in one of the rivers—but no one can prove that he *isn't* a victim. And the people who might take issue with the misuse of the term, the ones most territorial about it, tend to be dead.

Anyway, at the word "Chernobyl," the tourists have their wallets out.

The grandparents are eating nettle soup when they spot the roach sitting right above them, on the kitchen ceiling. Its silver chain swings back and forth as though to hypnotize them. Pyotr drops his spoon into his soup.

The lid of the tin box must have come open when Lila shoved it into the closet. But she doesn't want to be the one to put the roach back in the box.

Pyotr won't put it back either, even though pests are his domain, his only domain, while Lila cooks, cleans, and all the rest.

The roach stays on the ceiling, and the grandparents endure their meal.

They make sure not to leave any food out, hoping that the thing will leave the apartment on its own. But in the coming weeks, every time they think it's finally gone, it skulks out from under the stove or shoe rack, from between their clothes in the wardrobe, the chain dragging behind it.

—

What if something were to happen to the grandparents? Say they were to perish in a fire. Just last month, a sickeningly sweet smoke rose through the vents from one of the suites below, pouring into theirs, and Lila threw her best linens from the balcony to save them. Or the grandparents might succumb to gas poisoning. At this very moment, they could be two blue corpses splayed out on the floor—and the rest of the family wouldn't know it.

These past few weeks, no one has checked in.

Or maybe the family has tried to check in but the grandparents couldn't hear the phone ring over the roaring music.

"YOU'RE A TENDER LILY," the record player shrieks, "STUCK TO THE BOTTOM OF MY BOOT."

Maybe the family tried sending a letter, but the new mailman can't find the grandparents' building because some idiot chiseled the numbers out of the concrete beside the entrance all those years ago. Pyotr borrows a pink piece of chalk from the children hopscotching on the road, braves the crowd of pilgrims at the front of the building, and writes a large blocky "1933" above where the stenciled numbers used to be.

The family may even have tried to visit, but didn't knock loudly enough. Lila posts a note on the door: KNOCK LOUDLY. The grandmother's own grandmother had a sign like that on her gate in the village: KNOCK HARD OR THROW A ROCK AT THE DOG. At least she had a dog. All the grandparents have is this oversize roach.

And don't any of their children have a spare key? Maybe Lila should mail one of the daughters a spare key—just a key, no note or any other sign of life.

"Maybe we should just call everyone," Pyotr suggests. "Make sure they haven't been trying to check on us."

"Then what? They'll hear from us and won't need to check on us."

By having all these children, Pyotr and Lila thought they'd buffered themselves against isolation. Instead, the grandparents don't have friends because of all the time they put into the children. First came the sons, which Pyotr and Lila kept having until, finally, came the daughters. Daughters are supposed to stick around, help out. But now all the daughters live just as far away as the sons, in big cities with job prospects, busy caring for their own children, believing those children will stick around.

Maybe it's a law of physics. Once a baby is expelled, it will keep moving away at a constant speed unless acted upon.

Not that the grandparents will act first.

To repurpose the tin box, Lila yanks out the newspaper lining. Under the lining she discovers a glossy pamphlet featuring a photo of a fine-boned man in a plum blazer. Tethered to his lapel is a rock-laden insect just like the one the grandparents received. It emits a dull sheen, like a dusty brooch. Lila can't understand why anyone would wear a cockroach.

The Madagascar hissing cockroach, the manual explains. They breed under rotting jungle logs. The embellishments on their carapaces are among the rarest gems in the world: serendibite, in its uncut form.

"Serendibite," Lila repeats.

Rarer than diamonds, the manual insists. Infinitely more valuable. And on your pet, priceless.

—

When was the last time the grandparents saw the roach? Last week? Last month? They're ready to tear the whole apartment apart.

"The last piece of our grandson," Lila laments.

"His most beloved pet," says Pyotr. "And we lost it."

They find it two minutes later, drinking from a leaky valve under the kitchen sink. Lila plucks the roach off by the chain and it pirouettes in the air. In the strong midday light, its gems give off a bronze glint. The grandparents marvel at them.

When Lila lowers the insect into its tin box, Pyotr asks, "What now?"

"We care for it like we cared for our grandson," says Lila. Unpleasant as the grandson was as a child—with his mercurial stomach, his bulge-eyed tantrums—they never gave up.

The Madagascar hissing cockroach makes the easiest pet, the manual assures the grandparents. The Madagascar hissing cockroach is perfectly content with the simplest foods, like carrots! But it always loves a taste of home: guavas and papayas, lightly rotten.

The grandparents don't know what guavas and papayas look like, so assume they are expensive.

Provide plenty of water, to be replaced daily, the manual instructs. To mitigate the risk of drowning, place a sponge in the bowl, to be replaced weekly.

The grandparents don't use sponges themselves, only rags from old underwear.

The Madagascar hissing cockroach does not like direct sunlight, the manual warns. Wear the roach brooch only at night, otherwise your pet will burrow down your collar or into your hair.

Oh, and the Madagascar hissing cockroach is very clean, cleaner than people, but if kept under less-than-ideal conditions it is known to harbor up to fourteen species of mold, some of which are potent allergens. In the event of a mold outbreak, simply place the roach into a plastic bag with a half cup of extra-fine flour, gently shake the bag to dislodge the fungal roots—you may even have to rub the roach a little—transfer the roach to a sieve deep enough to prevent escape, and repeat as many times as needed to remove all the mold. Don't forget to vacuum the carpets, linen, and furniture to get any straggling spores, run an air purifier/dehumidifier, throw all your clothes into the laundry, and, finally, scrub your hair and skin. Reevaluate why you had the outbreak in the first place, and find ways to improve your cleanliness.

What the grandparents reevaluate: the grandson's wishes. What he truly wanted for them wasn't a pet cockroach, but a better life, a peaceful retirement. He would have wanted them to give up the bone record business, get that tumor removed. Turn that dreadful music off.

The pawnshop owner, a hulking man in a squeaky leather jacket, won't touch the roach brooch.

"Roach brooches are the rage in the highest fashion circles,"

Lila insists. She shows him the photograph of the model wearing a roach, but the pawnshop owner doesn't seem to know about these fashion circles.

"The gems are among the rarest in the world," says Pyotr. "Serendibite."

The pawnshop owner laughs, as if Pyotr has made up a word.

Later that week in the train station underpass, the grandparents try to sell the roach brooch to a French tourist, a rich-looking one. The woman has a mink fur coiled around her neck, the animal's tiny jaws clasped to its own rear. Lila tells the tourist that this is one of those mutant Chernobyl cockroaches, the ones there are rumors about.

"But why glue rocks onto it?" the French tourist asks.

"Serendibite," Pyotr shouts.

At last the grandparents find a jeweler two towns over, an ancient man whose skin hangs from his face and arms in doughy sheets. When he opens the box to appraise the contents, the roach gives a loud hiss, like an old bus when its brake is released, and scrambles up the jeweler's sleeve. The jeweler screams, slaps his arm, then elbow and shoulder, as though to put out a fire. He stops screaming only when he frees himself from his shirt and locks himself in the bathroom. It takes Pyotr and Lila half an hour to coax the roach from under the cabinet using crumbs and lint from their pockets.

"So long as the gems are touching that thing," the jeweler declares behind the bathroom door, "I'm not touching the gems."

———

Never attempt to remove the gems from the insect, the manual warns. Madagascar hissing cockroaches have a natural waxy covering, and the patented technology used to attach the gems took months to develop. They won't come off without harm to your pet.

Of course, the grandparents don't want to do harm.

Even in the labor camps, the guards would wait until a prisoner died before gouging out a golden tooth—or so Pyotr and Lila read. The rules of civility hold.

Roaches don't live very long anyway. In the past, whenever the apartment had an infestation of the lowly local ones, their corpses soon turned up everywhere.

The best thing about the Madagascar hissing cockroach, the manual proclaims: it can live up to five *years*!

If the grandparents stop putting carrot peels in the roach's box, or refilling the water, it isn't on purpose. They can be so forgetful, with their busy days, with the tumor, with the music that drowns out the tinny scratches coming from the box.

"I'LL BE THERE FOR YOU," the music promises, "WHEN THE FLAMES GET HIGHER."

The scratches may cease any day now.

Which family member will call first? One of the daughters, surely. But which?

Whichever daughter calls first will get a share of the money from the serendibite. Of course, this will be a surprise. Pyotr and Lila wouldn't want the money to be the main draw. They witnessed the greedy frenzy after the grandson died, and wouldn't want to repeat it.

Maybe nature isn't a circle of life, but a circle of abandonment.

It's true what they say about roaches surviving anything. Even without food or water, this one is looking as if it will survive both the grandparents.

The grandparents can't bring themselves to smash the roach with a frying pan. They can't fathom killing the last remnant of their grandson so violently, or risk damaging the jewels.

They can't bring themselves to drown it either. Or freeze it. Or suffocate it in a plastic bag.

The only sensible way to deal with it: treat the roach brooch like the insect that it is, and spray it with insecticide.

In a spray bottle, Lila mixes baking soda, chili pepper, soap-suds, and sunflower seed oil (this last one, to block breathing pores).

She turns to her husband. "I cooked, you serve."

Pyotr, solemn, sits the tin box on the kitchen table. He pops the lid with one hand, holds the spray bottle with the other. His finger on the trigger, he wishes the cockroach would try to run, display instinctual fear and distrust, like every other living thing. But the insect sits on its newspaper bed, wiggling its antennae. How could such a gentle creature possibly survive in the jungle?

In the corridor, the phone rings.

The grandparents look at each other in relief.

It must be one of their children. How silly the grandparents have been, to think themselves abandoned. How awful to imagine their beloved daughter (or granddaughter!) waiting at the other end of the line, worrying.

Pyotr stays with the roach while Lila hurries down the corridor. She cradles the phone against her cheek.

A deep male voice fills the line. A stranger's. "Have you taken the jewels off the roach yet?"

Lila's face contorts. She wants to slam the phone down, free the line for the children's calls.

The man introduces himself as an employee of the pawnshop the grandparents visited two weeks ago. Good thing his boss jotted down their phone number, the man says, if only to make them go away.

Lila finds her voice again. "We're just about to take the jewels off."

"Don't." Unlike his boss, this man knows about roach brooches, has seen the catalogs. He's willing to offer a fine price for it. He just needs her to check one tiny thing.

"I'll do anything," Lila says.

"On the roach's belly, between the front and middle sets of legs, should be a tiny RB. Like a logo plaque inside a Prada bag, proving authenticity."

From the corridor, Lila yells the instructions to her husband in the kitchen.

"I can't see its underside," her husband says.

"Lift it up and take a peek," she shouts.

"With my hands?"

"With your hands."

Pyotr holds his breath, hooks his fingers around the carapace. The bits that aren't encrusted with jewels feel slippery, like polished wood. The heft is surprising, and he wonders how much of the weight belongs to the living part of the brooch. The roach's legs swivel wildly as he turns it upside down. Its abdomen is composed of tawny segments that slide in and out of each other. He spots the small black head, bowed like a penitent's, the two matte bumps for eyes.

"I don't see any mark," says Pyotr, staring at the belly.

"My husband is still looking," Lila relays to the pawnbroker.

"It isn't here," says Pyotr.

"It got rubbed off," relays Lila.

"A genuine mark can't get rubbed off. It's branded onto the exoskeleton," the pawnbroker explains. "What you have there is counterfeit, the so-called jewels worthless as pebbles."

"But the insect—that part is real."

"Without the jewels," the pawnbroker says, "it's just a roach."

In the kitchen, Pyotr is still holding the insect. He's entranced by its rear end. There's something wrong with it. A wet white glob is squeezing out. The roach slips from between his fingers and falls onto Pyotr's stomach, where it clings to his woolly sweater. Its weight feels both repulsive and comforting. The white mass begins to separate into wiggling fingers, with tiny black dots at the tips. Eyes. The shimmering nymphs are attached to a string, like a crystal garland. Impossible to count them all as they unspool. Fifty, sixty?

Pyotr has never seen anything like it. His own children were born behind closed doors; he had to wait in a hospital corridor with the other expectant fathers, trying to distinguish his wife's howls from the chorus of other women.

In the light, the babies spring awake, detach themselves from their string. But they don't just scamper away. They crawl all over the mother, and she becomes furry with antennae. They eat the string that once bound them together. This is how they'll grow strong. Within an hour, their shells will harden to a caramel color.

At this very moment, the pawnbroker is imploring Lila to get rid of the knockoff as soon as possible. In the factories, the breeders don't bother to sort the males from the females; often the females are pregnant when sold.

But by the time the grandmother hangs up and reenters the kitchen, the grandfather's sweater is covered with babies. They eat the crumbs from his breakfast, hardly larger than crumbs themselves. Pyotr looks up at Lila and smiles, eyes shining. She can't help but smile with him when he says, "Aren't they beautiful?"

THE ERMINE COAT

On the way back from the bazaar, Aunt Milena points to the cracks under the balconies of our building. She warns me never to walk or stand under them, unlike those pilgrims lined up for the tomb. "Little by little," she says, "we're sinking into the soft earth."

Knowing what comes next, I lift my net sack to my chest, hide behind the leafy beet stalks. Over the past month Aunt Milena has used any excuse to remind me that our family's misfortune is my fault. Even the rat-size cockroach she was trapped with in the elevator last week—also, apparently, my doing. If it weren't for my misbehavior, my mother, sister, and I could have left this collapsing building, this collapsing country.

But Aunt Milena must be feeling generous today. Instead of scolding me, she sits on her haunches, studies her own boot print in the mud. "There used to be a village here," she says, and I imagine one no larger than her foot. She tells me the villagers spoke Ukrainian and picked cranberries for a living. Then the marshes were drained, sunflowers sown for oil, the villagers pried from their dung huts and stacked on top of each other. Many of them refused to move into the high-rises, never having lived so far from the earth. "The village was called Ivankiv," she says. "It lives on as our street name, but Russified." When she lived in the countryside, doing farmwork in exchange for a bed, the villagers would pass down secret lore.

Aunt Milena moved in with us two years ago, after Grandmother died. All she'd brought with her: the clothes on her back, a rapier, a record player and phonograph, and sixteen vinyl records for Mother to sell (but Mother refused, saying the records wouldn't be worth much these days anyway).

Some mornings I find Mother and Aunt Milena twisted around each other on the foldout, mouths agape, as though they escaped the same nightmare, just barely.

Like Mother, Aunt Milena is tall with a long pale face. She and Mother could be sisters. When they drop me and my sister off at school, no one asks, and we don't tell. The neighbors might whisper, but what can they do? Mother says we're living in an age of freedom. Aunt Milena says we're living in an age of fifteen brands of sausage, which is not the same thing as freedom. When I ask where are these fifteen brands of sausage, Mother says we need only visit Kiev to find them. Aunt Milena says no Kirovkavite can afford such an indulgence. But whatever the argument, Aunt Milena never wins, because when Mother takes Aunt Milena's face in her hands and beams her brightest smile, Aunt Milena breaks every time.

Last year, for a five-month stint, Mother and Aunt Milena sewed fur coats for the black market. Mother was already a master seamstress, and Aunt Milena caught on quickly. A large sweaty man whose face hung slack like a bulldog's would come for the coats on Mondays. Volkov never wore fur himself, only velvet tracksuits, usually maroon. After inspecting the coats, he'd toss stacks of *kupony* to Mother and Aunt Milena. Twenty, thirty stacks a week. The new currency looked like play money, with its picture of the Sofia Cathedral getting sucked into a flower-shaped black hole, and Aunt Milena told me it was worth about as much. Volkov would drop the next batch of pelts onto the kitchen table. Always the same slick black pelts, as if Volkov had ripped out the stitching from the week before and returned the pieces to be resewn, over and over. No one knew what type of animal they'd belonged to. Something long, caged. Its thick hairs snuck between our bedsheets, under our eyelids and tongues. I worried I'd start coughing up slimy ropes, as our neighbor's cat was known to do. We picked at our limbs, scratched our scalps. My schoolmates told the nurse I had lice, and if not lice, then definitely worms.

My little sister, five years old, thought everything sold on the black market had to be black. She liked to sit under the kitchen table, tracing the velvet humps of Volkov's calves until Mother yanked her hand away. I wanted his soft thick thighs, to bite through the fat and meat until my teeth hit bone. He'd been rounding out, a sign that his business was steady.

Now, because of me, Mother is back at her old job at a chemical plant two towns over, rumored to be shutting down anytime, and Aunt Milena cleans floors at a lamp factory. They get paid in perfumes and lamps, but the managers promise money soon. Lamps are bad for barter on account of the blackouts, but sometimes our right-side neighbor trades balcony-grown beans for the perfume. From his yowls and moans across the thin walls, we know he drinks it, but I like to think he's taken a lover and the perfume is for her.

As for the left-side neighbor, he gets paid in cosmetics, and Mother says his daughters whore around.

It was a Monday visit from Volkov, six months ago, that sealed our fate. He laid a bundle of parchment paper on the kitchen table, slowly unwrapped it. The furs inside glowed white, making everything else look tired and dirty. Each pelt began with two angry slits, the eyes, and ended with a black-tipped tail.

"Ermine," Volkov said. "Turns white in the winter, except for the tail."

"Why not the tail?" Mother asked.

"Must be how the animals find each other in the snow," Aunt Milena said. "Tiny flags."

"It's how hunters find them," he said.

My sister reached out to stroke a tail but Volkov shook his head, as though worried the furs would wake.

"Royal furs were made from ermine," he said. More impressive still: "Marilyn Monroe wore ermine."

We didn't know what to do with such narrow pieces. Aunt Milena nailed them to wooden boards for stretching, but they seized up, as though panicked. I dug my fingers into the smalls of their backs, the spot that makes the most skittish dog melt. Nothing worked. I understood: the thought of being sewn to rows and rows of other girls turned my skin stiff, too.

I suggested we sew a girl's coat, and Volkov loved the idea. One of his buyers, an Italian who lived in Canada ("double foreigner, double rich"), liked to spoil her daughter. As with every coat sold, we'd get a percentage of the profit. The ermine coat would earn a pretty sum. Volkov named a number high enough—in steady U.S. dollars, he assured us—to change a life, even ruin it. But the coat had to be perfect, he warned. The Italian who lived in Canada didn't just throw her money around. She bred miniature dogs, judged competitions. She could spot a blemish a continent away.

Volkov turned to me. "Her girl's about your age." His gray eyes sliced across the key points of my body: chest, waist, hips. Other men had begun looking at me this way on the streets. I'd become the sum of my chest, waist, hips—someone to be assembled. Soon I'd start wearing Aunt Milena's oversize frocks, wanting to be whole again.

That evening, when Mother pressed the tape measure to my skin, its cold metal lip made me think of Volkov. I conjured the buyer's daughter instead, soft in her ermine coat. She trudged across a snowy field, no trees or bushes around, not even a speck of dirt, nothing to mark movement except the slow crunch of her feet, and she'd better not slip and fall because no one would find her, despite her tiny flags.

Before the Union fell apart, the foreign films that made it into our country were dubbed by the same man. You could hear his dentures slap against his gums. No matter the character—man, woman, toddler—same droning voice. It flattened the characters' joy and sorrow, made us doubt their confessions. Did the heroine really love that man as much as she said? Vowing to die for him was going a bit far, wasn't it?

Sometimes the dubbing lagged so far behind, you had to guess who said what, guess how the film ended.

Volkov's buyers live around the world. Combined, they speak twenty-eight languages. I never met a single one of them, but somehow I knew they possessed that awful voice.

—

As Volkov said, the ermine coat had to be perfect: no visible seams or loose threads, the wooden claw clasps sanded by hand, lacquered without a single bubble. Normally a coat took four days to sew. This one ate up a week, two weeks. The closer Mother and Aunt Milena came to finishing the coat, the more undone they looked. Pins slipped from between their teeth. Their hands pecked at the same spot on the carpet over and over, until my sister or I found the pin for them. They seemed awake only at night, when they clattered around the kitchen chopping and frying whatever they could, mostly beets and onions. Aunt Milena would carry the ermine, a glowing bride in her arms, to the balcony, away from the smell.

How Mother and Aunt Milena met again, as told by Mother: Two years ago on her way home from work, her bus broke down near one of the villages. The next bus wasn't due for another hour, and she had to use the ladies' room. No such room was in sight, of course, only dirt fields and a few huts, their outhouses fenced off like prized bulls. Never had she relieved herself en plein air, like a brute, and she wasn't about to start now. She paced the road, every minute stretching longer and longer and her panic building, until finally she sank into a ditch, hitched up her dress, rolled down her tights, and let out a long moan. Only afterward did she realize she had nothing to wipe with. The panties she'd worn that day were more symbol than fabric, and she couldn't ruin the acorn-pattern tights she had crocheted herself, over five months, stealing time between work, chores, sleep. She would have reached for a leaf, but what was stinging nettle and what wasn't? She'd rather use the back of her own hand, then lick it clean. So she did. When she straightened up, a voice startled her from above: "Larissa?" A woman was peering into the ditch. Not just any woman, but our former neighbor—now a villager with a rake in hand and a grin so wide that Mother knew she'd witnessed all. Determined to keep a shred of dignity, Mother did what any neighbor, past or present, should do: she invited Aunt Milena over for tea.

If my mother had boarded a different bus? If she'd chosen a different ditch? She'd still be speeding by Aunt Milena's village.

The power cuts out every evening, but the moment of failure still catches me by surprise. Some secret flits between the lamps, refrigerator, television, the mixer in my mother's hand, and everything falls silent. The silence scares me more than the dark. Should we take cover, too? From what? From whom?

In our daily blind spells we've learned the geography of our apartment. The matches live two steps from the kitchen, in the bathroom cabinet, bottom shelf, but I'm not allowed to touch them anymore. The first candle: three steps down the corridor, to the left of the record player. The second candle: four steps to the right, on the windowsill by the onions sprouting from mayonnaise jars. To pass the time Aunt Milena sings folk songs she learned in the village. My sister and I belt along, garbling the Ukrainian words, understanding few of them. I had a favorite song, an especially cheery one, until Aunt Milena told me what it was about. Two Cossacks take a girl into the dark forest and tie her to a pine by her own braids and set the pine on fire— the pine burns, burns and won't go out, and the girl cries, cries and won't quiet down. After that, I want to cut off my braids but

Mother won't let me. She says I'll need them, although she won't say what for. I tuck them under my collar and never ask Aunt Milena what the words in the other songs mean.

When the coat was finished, I tried it on for the last time. The red silk lining—bought from one of Mother's old schoolmates, a urologist who also bred silkworms and therapeutic leeches—felt slippery and warm, as if the ermine had been freshly skinned. Volkov always said a good coat ought to feel like a second skin. This one became my own skin. To peel it off was painful. I'd briefly forgotten how cold the air felt, how sharp.

That evening, when my sister was safely asleep, Aunt Milena and Mother sat me down at the kitchen table, and spoke in stilted turns. They must have rehearsed who would say what. Aunt Milena: We'll use the money from the coat to get you, your sister, and your mother out of the country. Mother: They need chemists like me in the oil fields in Canada. Aunt Milena: It's so safe there, people leave their cars unlocked. (Mother, to Aunt Milena, voice low, off script: To provide pedestrians shelter from the polar bears.) (Aunt Milena, to Mother: Only in one town, up north.) Aunt Milena: Who knows, maybe one day you'll meet the girl in the ermine coat. Mother: You'll be wearing one just as lovely. Aunt Milena: Lovelier.

I asked why Aunt Milena wouldn't come with us.

"Canada will only take people who are related," Aunt Milena said, her voice suddenly hard, as if she herself had made the rules and the rules were perfectly sensible.

I waited to hear the rest of the plan.

Mother's teeth were clenched, her smile rigid.

Aunt Milena looked silently at a point above my head, maybe at an older, taller version of me, who might one day come back for a visit and thank her for letting us go, and say, "Yes, dear Aunt Milena, surely it was all for the best."

Back when we'd received our first batch of pelts, Aunt Milena had plucked a hair from one of them, held the hair over a lit match. It crackled, then burned back a few millimeters, into a neat nub.

"It smells just like burning human hair," she told me, "which smells like burning fat, only sweeter. Fake fur will stink like plastic and curl into little beads. That's how you can tell."

I remembered these words when, alone in the apartment the day after I was told about the plan, I let the flame eat away at the ermine coat. The angry fur sputtered in the bathtub, its many ermine backs arching and twisting until, all at once, with a last sigh, they gave in to the flame. Later that evening, when my mother slapped me raw, I lied and said I was only trying to see if the fur was real. It had smelled just like Aunt Milena promised.

Now and then, we still find slick black hairs on the sofa bed or on our clothes, and sometimes even a soft white hair. The hairs remind us of Volkov, the debt we owe him, as though he himself shed them for this purpose.

This is what I remember most: Before the blackouts. Before the ermine coat, before even the black coats. Aunt Milena's bag by the door, still unpacked. The four of us squeezed around the kitchen table. We had turned the lights off, lit the candles. Candlelit dinners were a luxury then. I'd learned a new song at school that day, and I taught it to my sister between forkfuls of fried cabbage. Mother got up, drew the curtains, and pulled Aunt Milena to her. As my sister and I sang, they clutched each other, tilting this way and that, as though to keep each other from falling. My sister turned to me, her face a question. "Silly," I said to her, "they're dancing."

HOMECOMING

Yet again, Zaya is returning to Internat Number 12.

Even as a nineteen-year-old, practically an adult, with a job, three changes of clothes, a new driver's license, and a rented room back in Moscow.

The *internat* closed a few years ago, its orphans released to the streets, yet here she is, hurtling toward it in a glossy black cargo van at 100 kilometers per hour. She's driving the van herself. Her own foot jerks the gas. The key to the iron gates rattles in the glove box. The key itself is iron, without a hint of rust.

The van belongs to a twenty-one-year-old heiress named Almaza Shprot. Almaza's father served as a Minister of Geology in the Soviet days, and now dabbles in the oil and gas business. Almaza owns more than three changes of clothes. In fact, if all her outfits formed a chain, cuff in cuff, and marched from her closet into the sea, the chain would never end.

Actually, Almaza's accountant would correct, the van doesn't belong to Almaza. It belongs to Almaza's company. You have to keep these things straight for tax purposes.

How the accountant classifies the company for tax purposes: TRAVEL AGENCY.

And it's true, the clients do need to travel to the company's many sites, around Russia, Latvia, and now Ukraine. But the tax forms don't have a category for the type of service the company renders once the clients arrive at their destination. Is it legal? Who knows? Certainly not a common accountant.

A better question: Is the service transformative?

Any millionaire can frolic with dolphins in Belize, catch a ballet in Paris, clear their complexion with a champagne bath, but how many can say they've feared for their lives? That they've been trampled on, reduced to nothingness, and from that nothingness been reborn? These days, in these circles—not many.

For instance, one of the company's trip packages re-creates *One Day in the Life of Ivan Denisovich*. Clients are carted out to the fringe of the Arctic Circle, to a defunct labor camp. Like the novel's protagonist, they must mop the guardhouse, lay brick walls with quick-dry mortar, fight over stone-hard bread—all this in freezing temperatures, in too-small boots, while a guard flogs them.

Almaza likes to experience the sites along with the clients. "Ivan Denisovich had one bad day, and got a whole memoir out of it," Almaza tells them. "Imagine the creative possibilities."

"I don't think it was just one day," an aluminum tycoon remarks, but nobody hears him through the burlap potato sack wrapped over his mouth and nose.

By the time the clients return to Moscow, dirty and bruised, they're ready to kiss the leather of their cars, kiss their drivers, even—grateful for any simple pleasure.

—

As an employee of the company, Zaya wears many hats. Depending on the trip package, she's the interrogator or torturer or prison guard, or some combination of the three.

Zaya has considered quitting. It's as demeaning for her to play the villain as it is for the clients to play victim—maybe more. But who else would hire Zaya, with that mean mangled lip? Her face screams knife fight. Gang affiliation. She'd have to go back to selling cigarette butts at the bazaar, where the company recruiter originally discovered her. And, loath as she is to admit it, she's good at this job. Better than her predecessors. She can distinguish between the shades of horror in her victims' faces, knows just how far to push until the victims reveal their most vulnerable spots, their deepest fears. When Zaya thinks back on it, wreaking terror has always been her specialty. As early as age six: one evening after she'd run away from the *internat* and the boot maker took her in, Zaya let a candle tip, watched the flames lap at the lace curtains. Zaya knew the boot maker wouldn't let her stay for long anyway, so why not let the flames climb, speed up the parting?

"What's the most intimate act between people?" Almaza once mused in Zaya's presence, leafing through a dog-eared porn magazine she'd found under a prison mattress. The throes of pleasure Zaya glimpsed inside resembled torment. "If not sex, then kissing?" asked Almaza.

Every time a client submits to Zaya, she wants to tell Almaza: "It's this."

"The child who is not embraced by the village will burn it down to feel its warmth." Almaza had been quoting her favorite African proverb while puttering at the Chernobyl site. She was chucking bits of concrete into a wheelbarrow, her paper hazmat suit crinkling.

The company hadn't been able to get clearance to use the real Chernobyl—and anyway, the real Chernobyl was looking too tidy these days, with the sarcophagus the French and Germans were erecting over it—so the site was a decommissioned reactor in Latvia. None of the clients seemed to mind.

Zaya urged on the cleanup crew as their faux radiation gauges beeped. They had to shovel sand over any debris they couldn't lift. One woman, a TV personality with cherry lipstick still caked in the corners of her mouth, fell to her knees in exhaustion. Zaya bent close to the woman's grimy face, considered her wide dark eyes. "Want pretty blue eyes instead?" she offered, her voice sickly sweet. "I'll reassign you to Reactor Four. The radiation inside is so high, I hear it does wonders." The woman stood up, knees shaking.

"My problem?" Almaza went on. "I was embraced too tightly as a child." Her parents had loved her in a simple, predictable way, giving her everything she wanted. As a result, she didn't have the capacity to do anything as poetic as burn down a village.

Almaza turned to Zaya, as though remembering that she had been a child once, too. "Where did you grow up?"

Zaya told her.

"How awful," Almaza whimpered. "Just dreadful." And then, gleeful: "I can't imagine a worse place."

Is this where Zaya went wrong? Is it because she evoked for Almaza the tall iron fence, the dark cavernous halls of the monastery, is this how she is being reeled back in now?

But maybe, even if she hadn't told Almaza about the *internat*, she'd be driving along this gravel road just the same, drawn in by some other conspiracy of circumstances. She can't escape the *internat*'s magnetic pull. It must be fated, like the lifelong slide toward death.

After hearing about Zaya's childhood, Almaza said: "What you need to do is harness all that authentic trauma into something great. A waste of trauma not to." She suggested Zaya could invent a raw new dance style. Immortalize her woes in a brutal tile mural. She could write a memoir.

"Just look at that other orphan, the one all over the news," Almaza reminded Zaya. The girl had grown up in an *internat* like Zaya's, and couldn't walk. Not that it stopped her from dreaming. She got herself adopted by a Finnish philanthropist, endured ten spinal surgeries, regained a bit of feeling in her right leg, and became a Paralympic gymnast. Inspired the whole country. She even posed for a beauty magazine, her long legs model thin.

Upon arrival at the *internat*, Zaya is disappointed to find the place intact. Even though she'd been absent for a short three years, she'd imagined coming upon a pile of bricks and plaster, impossible to reassemble. But the building stands; lush vines seal its cracks, cushion the iron fence. The vines shroud the mounds where the children were buried, and the unfilled pits, too—a relief, for Zaya. As a child, she had feared being mistaken for dead, waking up buried in one of these pits.

Now the grounds look charming, with the buttercups dotting the wild grass, the gates thrown open in welcome.

The clients—a venture capitalist, a socialite, a steel magnate, a lifestyle manager—are due to arrive the next morning. In preparation Zaya oils the gates' locks, mops the floors, stocks the canteen with food, straightens the rows of beds in the nave of the monastery. Cold, dim, with spider egg sacs suspended in the stone moldings, the hall still possesses an underground quality.

Zaya tries to remember which bed was hers. To pass the time as a child she'd stand on her bed, use a sharp rock to scratch open the tight-lipped mouths of the men frescoed on the walls. But it appears that other children took up the practice after her time: now every mouth within reach is agape, as if the painted figures are shocked to find themselves, after so many centuries, in the same stultifying place.

Roaming the chambers and corridors, Zaya feels a sudden absence on her hip, as though something has been carved from her side. She recalls she used to carry the mummified saint, in a pillowcase propped on her hip, not because she wanted its companionship day and night—the creature smelled like a stale dishrag—but to keep the other children from stealing it, yanking its hair.

In the back of the building, Zaya discovers a small cell-like room with bare plaster walls and an adult-size bed, likely for a *sanitarka*. She rolls out a sleeping bag. The thin straw mattress, ripping at the seams, is just as hard as the ones on the children's beds.

What about that other famous orphan, Almaza has reminded Zaya. When that girl's orphanage ran out of money, the *sanitarki* chopped off the children's braids and sold them to an Italian wig maker. Virgin hair, untouched by chemicals or curling irons. So what did this girl do when she got out? She started her own wig-making business, and partnered with a temple in India where the women cede their braids by choice, as an offering. Almaza herself owned one of these wigs back in Moscow. Finely woven, by three-strand bunches. It cost her fifteen thousand USD for one wig. Now the orphan drives a nice car, owns an apartment with French doors.

What does Zaya think of that? What's Zaya's excuse for her life?

The next day, a silver SUV deposits Almaza and the clients at the *internat*. Two men and two women, not including Almaza. The men are fleshy, grayish, the women tall and narrow with cinched, dehydrated looks. As instructed, everyone wears sensible shoes.

Zaya wears a white *sanitarka* dress—or rather, the company designer's interpretation of that uniform: a sculpted top half, double-breasted, vaguely military, with a long billowing skirt that drags in the wild grass, collecting spiny seeds.

After ushering the group into the courtyard and locking the gates behind them, Zaya orders everyone to make a line in front of her. Almaza, orphan-chic in her long black pigtails, distressed jeans, and threadbare cotton shirt, asks, "Make a line by height, net worth, or . . . ?"

"By age," Zaya improvises. "Oldest at the back."

But no one wants to admit their age, not even Almaza, who hardly looks older than Zaya. One of the clients, a leggy socialite whose tanned skin appears poreless, jokes with the group that she is ageless—her two pregnancies only made her look better, not worse. The clients shuffle on the spot until Zaya threatens to sort them herself, using the dates of birth on the IDs they submitted.

At last, everyone in a crooked formation, Zaya distributes to each client the single garment for their ten-day stay, as well as a garbage bag for their clothes, wallets, and other personal effects. They won't have access to their belongings until they leave, Zaya reminds them.

The clients take turns changing in the outdoor shower (out of service, they will soon discover). When the men and women reconvene in the courtyard, looking like a bridal party in their matching periwinkle frocks, they place their garbage bags at Zaya's feet.

"Phones, too," Zaya tells the impeccably postured lifestyle manager, who clutches a handset, the latest model. With a sigh the woman presses the phone against her hip to retract the telescopic antenna, then thrusts the bulky device into Zaya's outstretched hand.

The clients await further instruction.

Zaya hasn't thought of anything beyond this part. Usually Almaza supplies her with an itinerary of activities. But now, Almaza is regarding her with the same excited obedience as the others.

A nightingale sings from a nearby bush. A butterfly circles the steel magnate's parched knee.

Zaya struggles to remember how the *sanitarki* would entertain the children. Her mind leaps over long expanses of formless time. She slings the garbage bags over her shoulder and follows the brick path toward the arched entrance of the building, hoping for an idea along the way. The group trails her. She hears the steel magnate remark, "A shame this place closed down."

—

Apart from setting out food at mealtimes (a vat of rehydrated sea cabbage, with a tube of liver paste) and restocking the latrine with toilet paper (newspaper), Zaya keeps to her room. She lies in bed, blinking at the low vaulted ceiling. Like the clients, she came here expecting to feel something. Instead, she has found her senses dulled.

Maybe it's because she knows the escape hatch.

Or at least, the possibility of one.

She knows she could walk the 25 kilometers to Kirovka and stay with Konstantyn. Three months ago she saw a photo of him in a newspaper, standing in front of his apartment block, arms crossed. He'd bought up an additional suite, the article informed her, which he converted into a tomb for the saint.

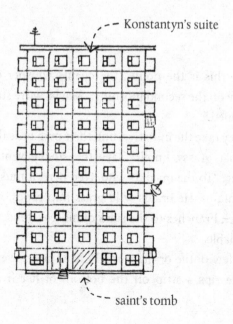

Konstantyn's suite

saint's tomb

"He's ruining the neighborhood," commented Lila Palashkina, 73, longtime tenant. "All these noisy fanatics, crowding in."

"The saint and I are not going anywhere," responded Konstantyn Illych Boyko, 50, business owner and poet, none of whose books remain in print.

White-haired with dark bulges under his eyes, he had looked tired in the photo, and much older than the last time Zaya had seen him. The building didn't look great either, blotchy, riddled with cracks. She wished for a photo of the saint as well, just to see it again; the article had mentioned a linen sheet covering the saint, and said that the tomb's guard refused to remove it.

If Konstantyn had taken Zaya in before, surely he wouldn't object to her presence now, for another day or two? Another expended bowl of pork stew, lusciously greasy? She could use him like he'd once used her. So long as she considered it a simple transaction, not a favor, she could let herself knock on his door.

"Maybe this is the point," the clients whisper outside Zaya's window on the second morning. "Maybe we're supposed to feel abandoned."

They take the initiative, find their own ordeals.

"That grassy knoll?" says the stocky venture capitalist, pointing. "To the invalids who lived here, it must have seemed a mountain." He braids wild grass into ropes, with which he ties thick branches to the sides of his legs, rendering his knees unbendable.

"A few of the orphans might have never even seen it." The socialite rips a strip off the bottom of her frock, blindfolds herself.

The steel magnate plugs his ears with poplar fluff.

Almaza fills her boots with gravel.

On the third morning, when setting out the latrine newspaper (one broadsheet per day), Zaya comes upon a second article about Konstantyn and the tomb, published a week ago.

The saint's tomb had caved in, the article reports. Sheets of vinyl flooring, rugs, furniture, appliances, hot-water radiators, framed photographs, toys, a porcelain dish set, jars of fermented tomatoes—all this piled into the tomb from the apartment above, along with a family of three, shocked but unharmed, their mouths, allegedly, still full of breakfast. Luckily, that morning the tomb was closed, its live-in guard having been fired for undisclosed reasons.

"Must be the shifting earth, the encroaching marshes," commented Konstantyn Illych Boyko, who had failed to insure his business and, the newspaper noted, had also failed in marriage.

"Must be those inner walls Konstantyn Illych knocked out," stated the former guard, who had been intercepted at the train station on his way to Kiev, where he would seek employment in customer service. The man, endowed with impeccably white teeth, wished to remain anonymous.

Zaya examines the accompanying photo. She wonders if the apartment block is wide enough for the rest of the structure to remain sound.

"You might want to clear out," Almaza tells Zaya from the doorway of the latrine. She has tied an off-center knot at the hem of her frock, for a fitted faux-slit look. "I slipped laxatives into the clients' breakfast. Dysentery day."

Konstantyn's suite

On the fourth evening at the *internat*, visitors start emerging from the forest, crowding the iron gates. Three at first, then five more follow. Most are around Zaya's age. Among the visitors is a teenage boy, orange-maned, laden with a tattered gym bag. His right eye is pressed deeper into his head than the left. He tells Zaya that he and the others had grown up at the *internat*, and heard it was reopening. They'd been living on the streets, and now they want back in. When Zaya tries to turn them away, the boy says, "But we walked all the way here." They'd started at sunrise, and now it was almost sundown. They'd been stalked by a wild boar, dive-bombed by crows. A bunch of them had turned back already. "But we made it," the boy insists.

Before this job, Zaya herself had been living on the streets, in Moscow's labyrinthine suburbs, huddling up to the warm aboveground pipes that fed wastewater from power plants to household radiators. "I'm sorry," Zaya says, but she isn't. She wants these visitors to go away. It's as if the *internat* is rebuilding itself, and soon the real *sanitarki* will return, a director will materialize.

A round-faced woman among the crowd at the gates smooths her dirty wrinkled blouse over her stomach, as if the blouse is the problem. She points toward Almaza and the clients, who are limping around the courtyard with their legs in splints, pebbles spilling from their shoes. "But you let *them* in."

"They paid to be here."

The group awaits an explanation.

After a pause, Zaya says, "I don't understand it either."

"Hey," says the woman in the wrinkled blouse, "I remember you."

On second look, Zaya remembers the woman, too, but she feigns ignorance. As a girl, this woman used to follow the *sanitarki* around, asking for the tips of their braids to make into hair dolls. Now the woman has a pair of thin braids of her own, wispy ends dusting her shoulders. Zaya, on the other hand, has kept her hair buzzed; any time it grows out, the strands feel like fingers on her nape, threatening to stretch around her neck.

"How'd you get to be a *sanitarka*?" asks a man with pink heart-shaped glasses too small for his face. Despite the bushy beard, Zaya recognizes him as well.

"I'm not a real one," Zaya says, more forcefully than she'd intended.

The clients are not yet asking for their money back, exactly, but would any of them recommend the place? Of all the other trips the company offers? Sure, the child-size beds are lumpy, the food lousy, the latrines reek, but no one has been properly traumatized. No one is falling apart or pulling themselves back together. And despite efforts to keep busy, the past four days have been downright dull.

It's also awkward for the clients to be forced to look at all those sad people loitering at the gates. More and more keep showing up. They sleep under sagging tarps. How many now, fifteen? Can't Zaya get rid of them? It doesn't help that Almaza barters with them through the gates. She trades slices of the liver paste for their coffee, fresh off their camping stove. She sighs at them in regret. "Honey," she tells the teenager with the pressed-in eye, "if only we could trade places."

On the fifth day, when Zaya sets out moldy bread and rancid margarine for breakfast, the clients don't show up. Zaya scopes out the building and the sunny meadow behind it, calling Almaza's name.

"Over here!" Almaza's hoarse voice reaches Zaya from the grassy knoll—seemingly, from deep inside it.

Zaya rounds the knoll to discover Almaza and all four clients crouching in a narrow, weed-strewn hole, looking small and scared. The hole is just deep enough to trap them. "What took you so long? We were calling for you all night," Almaza says, hugging her knees to her chest, her long black ponytail draped around her neck like a scarf. The venture capitalist and steel magnate have their arms wrapped around each other. The lifestyle manager picks at a crown of wilted dandelions atop the socialite's head.

"Is this one of the graves you told me about?" asks Almaza. "The to-be-filled ones?"

"They were never this deep," says Zaya.

"This one wasn't deep, at first, either." Almaza had stumbled into a shallow pit, everyone else had followed, and the ground beneath them caved in. "There are tunnels down here. We've been crawling around, trying to find a way out." Her face strains; she's on the verge of tears. "We could've been eaten by an animal. Or by a hundred spiders, whose venom would slowly predigest us. Something could've happened to you, and we'd be stuck here for days and days until our drivers found our hollowed corpses." As she lists all the ghastly scenarios, the clients nod along, gasping as one might do when presented with an exotic restaurant menu. Almaza delights in her performance, gesticulates wildly in the cramped space. She takes a dramatic pause. "We'd be like the orphans who died here, buried en masse."

Zaya glares at the clients, suddenly enraged.

She spots a rusty shovel leaning against the wall of the monastery, and uses it to fling a fist-size clod of dirt into the pit. It explodes against the socialite's knee. Almaza and the clients squeal in mock horror.

Next comes an entire shovelful. The venture capitalist receives the earth spilling over his bald head with rapture, as if it were holy water.

The lifestyle manager moans with pleasure. "I vow to quit my job, take up painting again."

The steel magnate shouts above them all, "I vow to get my wife and kids back."

The earth grows soft, welcoming Zaya's shovel. There's a rhythm to the slicing, the earth landing with a soft thud. She finds herself counting each stroke. Now the squeals of the clients are turning into screams, but she doesn't stop, doesn't break the rhythm. Her anger has ebbed, and is replaced by a logistical curiosity, cold and foreign: How many strokes to fill the pit? She stabs at a weedy ledge and the entire thing comes away, triggers a slide of earth and rocks. The clients try to scramble to their feet but are knocked back down. When the slide settles, they are buried to the chest. Zaya lifts the shovel again; her need to restart the rhythm, the pulse, is dire, desperate—as though her own heart has stopped. Five dirty tear-streaked faces tilt up in a childlike stupor. For a moment Zaya wonders whether they are looking not at her but at some wrathful deity behind her, capable only of destroying.

And yet Almaza says, "Oh, Zaya." Her voice is awed, naked, and she breaks into a smile. "Couldn't have planned it better myself."

"The adrenaline," whispers the steel magnate.

"We'll spruce up these graves," Almaza declares, slowly at first. "We'll make a maze of the tunnels, for more clients. We'll fix up your room, have you live here like you own the place." Almaza wrenches her arms from the dirt, shakes out her ponytail. "Technically you already own it. I bought the *internat* in your name."

Zaya feels dizzy, as though sun-stricken. "You did not."

"Did so. As a foreigner I'd have to pay an extra tax."

The shovel in Zaya's hands feels unbearably heavy. Does it, too, belong to her?

Apparently, wreaking terror is all Zaya is good for. Had she forgotten? She thinks of the boot maker again. After the hut had burned down and the woman had delivered Zaya back to the orphanage—this same woman who had found her on the forest floor, gasping for breath, with yellowed eyes and a slit lip that made Zaya look, the woman told her, like a fish dragged from the sea until the hook dislodged; this same woman who

had carried Zaya in her arms and nursed her back to health—
the abandonment hadn't hurt. Zaya had felt numb. She hadn't
let herself dream of living with the boot maker. Nor had Zaya,
many years later, imagined living with Konstantyn. When she'd
spat on the Party members at the pageant, she'd also spat on the
possibility (however slim) of a home back in Kirovka. The *internat* had taught her well: as soon as you want something, you lack
it; and if you do get it, it can easily be taken away. But this lesson
came at a cost—a dry unfeeling clump had formed in her chest,
had grown with age. She wonders now: If she slit her skin open,
would nothing but sawdust spill out?

Down in the pit, the clients are bickering.

The venture capitalist asks Almaza why she bought the
monastery instead of leasing it. Almaza tells him she doesn't
like leasing things. Does she lease the penthouse she sleeps in?
The jewelry she wears? The meals she eats?

Zaya considers. She can fill the pit, finish them all off. She
has no doubt now she is capable of this. Tantalized, she has
unlocked a secret chamber within herself, discovered its horrors.

She drops the shovel, backs away.

"Where do you think you're going?" Almaza calls from the
pit. "Get us out."

The soiled skirt of her white dress bunched under one arm,
Zaya crosses the grounds like a runaway bride. She heaves open
the iron gates, steps between the orphans sleeping on the dewy
grass, still waiting to be let in. She climbs into the black cargo
van and honks the horn, waking the campers.

"Get in," she calls from her rolled-down window. "We're
getting out of here, for good."

The campers squint at her sleepily. The orange-maned teenager props himself up on his elbows, nods toward the gates. "She left it open," he tells the others.

"Don't even try," Zaya warns. "Get in or I'm rolling over you."

"Where are you taking us?" asks the teenager.

Zaya thinks on it. "Wherever you were before."

No one moves.

"You get fired?" asks the woman with the wispy braids, adjusting her rucksack under her head.

"I'm trying to help you." Zaya is unsure, precisely, how. She slumps in her seat, suddenly exhausted.

"Does anyone else hear the screaming?" asks the man with heart-shaped glasses.

"I bet if you grow your hair out you'll get another job," the teenager says to Zaya, smiling shyly.

The others study Zaya's face, her botched lip, and keep silent.

Zaya backs the van onto the road in a swift arc, hoping to make plain her threat of leaving them behind. She begins to roll away, glancing in the rearview mirror, expecting the campers to jolt up, pile into the van with their tents and tarps and camping stoves. But they don't. One by one, they walk in the other direction, enter the gates.

The rest of the drive is a breathless full-throttle dash, Zaya narrowly making the curves in the road. This deep dread is what freedom feels like, she tells herself. She feels it every time she runs away.

She imagines what she'll tell Konstantyn. This stolen van is all she has to show for herself, unlike the superorphans Almaza is always raving about. Zaya hasn't remade her life into an inspiring lesson, hasn't grown rich or famous—and literally, she hasn't grown at all. Perhaps the fact that she remains small will also be a disappointment.

Kirovka looks more ratty than Zaya remembers it, its roads cratered, its lamp poles a drunken procession leaning in every direction. Only the banks and pharmacies appear new—almost every block has one or the other—their respective aprons of sidewalk freshly tiled. Zaya weaves along the town's streets, searching for Konstantyn's building. In the center of the tree-lined plaza, she spots a concrete pedestal, from the old Lenin statue. Only his feet remain now, big as bathtubs, rusty rebar curving from them like veins.

At last Zaya parks in front of 1933 Ivansk.

She beholds the sight, trying to make sense of it. Konstantyn's tenth-floor suite—she recognizes the red-and-white-checkered curtains—is the last left hanging intact between two pillars of rubble. She can see cornflower-blue sky through a gap in the center. The edifice seems, understandably, abandoned.

Still, Zaya calls his name.

A piece of debris flakes off Konstantyn's apartment, hurtles to the ground, and smashes into a fine dust.

Zaya doesn't know if it is hope, or the devastating absence of it, that makes her take a step toward the building.

Another step, tentative, as if she is approaching a sleeping bear.

Once inside, though, she bounds up the dusty staircase. An unsettling draft blows through the many cracks in the walls. A pair of roaches the size of her hand skitter down a dark corridor—no, surely just rats?—but still she climbs.

When she reaches Suite 76—its steel outer door freckled

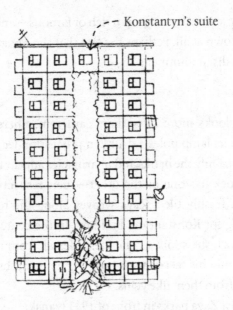

Konstantyn's suite

with rust—she lifts the heavy knocker and raps. After a moment she hears the click of the inner door's dead bolt. A familiar sound—yet under the circumstances, miraculous. She hears the inner door squeal open—its red faux-leather upholstery surfaces in her mind—then the ticking of more locks, like clockwork, followed by the gravelly melody of the chain sliding along its track, and dropping. At last the steel door swings open.

For a moment Konstantyn stands there, blinking, a dripping wooden spoon in hand.

He doesn't look at her with fear, as the clients did, but regards her with simple recognition. She feels herself shrinking, suddenly powerless, but also—with relief—less monstrous.

"Just in time for lunch," Konstantyn announces. His eyes flit over her billowy white dress but, mercifully, he doesn't ask questions. He steps aside to let her in, as if she's just returned from a stroll, as if he'd been expecting her.

The smell of the apartment greets her, unchanged. Old books, laurel leaves. A pot of soup bubbles on the stove, infusing the air with a sharp sweetness, like the underbelly of a rotting log. Zaya can't recall the last time she ate.

"Mushroom soup," he exclaims, as though nothing could make him happier. He gestures to a chair at the kitchen table.

The fact that the apartment hangs above an abyss becomes a distant worry.

The soup is salty but delicious, globs of oil shimmering over fungal caps and gills. She remembers not to scoop her spoon too deep, where the peppercorns hide. As she devours two bowlfuls with three slices of rye bread, uncertain if she'll be invited to stay for another meal, Konstantyn chatters away. The other tenants having evacuated, he's never lived in such quiet, he tells her. He thought he'd enjoy it, but at night he can hear his own pulse, like the drum of an approaching army. A few tenants moved to their dachas, others moved in with relatives many towns over. His ex-wife, whom he hopes Zaya might one day meet, left for Poland with her new family—he pauses at this last word, a seemingly difficult verdict.

"What happened to the saint?" Zaya asks. She wants to keep him talking as she reaches for more bread.

Observing how Konstantyn's face darkens, she senses that his chatter has been an effort to avoid the subject.

"I'm so sorry. The saint is gone," he says at last. "But at least it wasn't crushed under the rubble." A few days before the tomb caved in, Konstantyn discovered that the guard had sold the saint. When he demanded the saint's return, the guard told him it would be impossible, the saint could be anywhere. "Actually, *everywhere*," Konstantyn corrects himself. "It had been split into many pieces."

Zaya smiles at this thought, imagines the saint scattered all over the Earth, ever present. Satiated at last, she slips her half-eaten piece of bread into a pocket for later. "Why didn't you leave like the others?" she asks. "Go to your dacha?"

"I've been busy." His face erupts in a grin. "Home renovation. I've squeezed in a second room," he says. "Yours."

Konstantyn nods at a cherrywood door off the corridor. Zaya doesn't remember it being there before. He springs to his feet, beckons her over, opens it. They stand at the threshold.

In the years to come, Zaya will reminisce about this room. It's truly beautiful, everything she hadn't dared dream of as a child, and it will stretch larger and larger in her mind, hold more windows. She'll remember the telescope, the easel. The bronze gilded wallpaper and the painted sun shining from the ceiling, its rays twirling ribbons. The books, spines uncracked, take up an entire wall of shelves. Most of all she'll remember Konstantyn, beaming at her. "Welcome home."

She won't know, won't want to know, which of these remembered details are real.

She gets only a glimpse of her new room before its glossy hardwood floor gives out.

The furniture folds into the center of the room and vanishes, like a pop-up card closing.

One of the walls falls away, pulling a chunk of ceiling along with it. Zaya watches books flutter ten stories down, like a dole of doves.

For a second she thinks she could stay here until the entire apartment succumbs, but her body instinctively snaps into action. She grabs Konstantyn's hand and pulls him back through the corridor. Light floods in as the walls and the rest of the ceiling crumble behind them. They race down the staircase

two steps at a time, terrified of tripping, more terrified of slow-
ing down. At last they're outside, across the road.

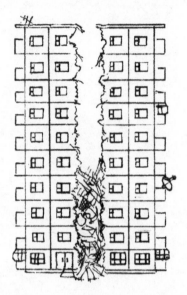

Konstantyn doubles over, panting. A deafening crack, and
the two halves of the building tumble into each other like lovers
reunited, then collapse. A great plume of dust envelops them.

With each passing year Zaya thinks, Perhaps just one more year? The place isn't so bad, after all. The Church has restored the cupolas, sealed the scratches in the frescoes and repainted them. Zaya keeps the *sanitarka* room, and Konstantyn sleeps in the sun-warmed attic. It was his idea to lease the monastery to the Church, after he and Zaya ate through the sea cabbage and squeezed flat the last tube of liver paste.

After 1933 Ivansk collapsed, Zaya had returned to the monastery with Konstantyn riding in the van's passenger seat. They found the place deserted, the orphans and clients gone. The orphans must have pulled the screaming clients out of the hole—not just a hole to the orphans, but a grave yawning open. The only things left behind were the papers attesting to Zaya's ownership of the property, thrown onto her bed. Zaya had imagined Almaza casting a last wary gaze over the lush grounds, their beauty having revealed a shameful secret.

Now Zaya wanders the meadows, watching the bustling monks as they hike up their robes to pull weeds. They try to fill in all the pits, but the property is large, and it isn't unusual to stumble upon yet another unfilled hole. They've torn down that old fence, and soon will build an even taller, sturdier one. For security. The forest is full of beasts, the monks say. We've got to keep them out.